BIRDS OF THE NILE

Vivid settings, crisp writing and a highly relevant story make *Birds of the Nile* a gripping read. Egypt's great inheritance and chaotic present are brought convincingly to life, and the politics behind the uprising deftly sketched. Against this background, a haunting love story develops to an unpredictable conclusion. I have always admired N.E.David's short fiction. His long-awaited first novel does not disappoint.

Pauline Kirk, Novelist and Editor of Fighting Cock Press

Birds of the Nile is a smartly written book. The elegant pace and rhythm capture the reader and the crisp tone of N.E.David's prose is both accomplished and poised. At every level, our sympathies are engaged by quality of voice, place and character. Ultimately absorbing.

Sandra Cain, Senior Lecturer in Creative Writing, Southampton Solent University

An evocative read, this takes you to Egypt and drops you into the middle of history. Along the way you meet Michael Blake who along the way meets himself. A book by N.E.David is a guaranteed trip out of your easy chair and with *Birds of the Nile*, you are given a trip to the Middle East. Highly recommended. I couldn't put it down.

Rose Drew, Performance poet and co-host of The Spoken Word

From the first page of *Birds of the Nile* the reader is hooked into the mystery and compassion of a narrative that spans Pharaonic antiquity and history in the making. N.E.David is a superb storyteller with a gift for evoking place.

Amina Alyal, Lecturer in English, Leeds Trinity University

This well-researched and insightful novel about an outsider who finds he has choices to make is a terrific read.

Pat Riley, Playwright and author of *Looking for Githa*

Birds of the Nile

An Egyptian Adventure

Birds of the Nile

An Egyptian Adventure

N.E. David

Winchester, UK
Washington, USA

First published by Roundfire Books, 2013
Roundfire Books is an imprint of John Hunt Publishing Ltd., Laurel House, Station Approach,
Alresford, Hants, SO24 9JH, UK
office1@jhpbooks.net
www.johnhuntpublishing.com
www.roundfire-books.com

For distributor details and how to order please visit the 'Ordering' section on our website.

Text copyright: N.E. David 2012

ISBN: 978 1 78279 158 4

A CIP catalogue record for this book is available from the British Library.

Design: Lee Morris

Printed in the USA by Edwards Brothers Malloy

We operate a distinctive and ethical publishing philosophy in all
areas of our business, from our global network of authors to
production and worldwide distribution.

Chapter One

There were times when he thought he could see the light – or at least sense it – a faint blur amidst the general darkness. He knew it was there, for each morning when he shuffled across the bare boards of his room and threw open the shutters to let in the day he remembered how it would come flooding in, great long shafts of it slicing into the space between the window and his bed, the covers turned back, the sheet still warm from whatever rest he had managed the night before. Then he would feel it too, the heat of it on his hands and feet, and for a minute or two he would bathe his face in it, slanting his chin upwards toward the sun which even at that hour still had the capacity to burn. It would strike him how pleasurable this was, and rather than go to the bathroom and take the risk of boiling a kettle and pouring scalding water into a sink, he would remain by the window and wash himself in a brightness he knew but could not see. And so another day would slowly but surely begin.

On this particular morning he had woken with a jolt. The dream which had continually afflicted his sleep had returned and was plaguing him once more. He had thought himself free of it, but it was back and with it the suspicion that it would never truly leave him.

And yet it always began so well. He would find himself running in the midst of a large crowd, almost like a herd of buffalo charging across an open plain. He was filled with a feeling of joy and light-headedness and he imagined he was carrying something in his hand (a flag perhaps?) which he seemed to hold aloft as if in triumph. Then he would become aware of the noise, the raised voices of the tumult surrounding him, the shouts and cries of the crowd and the deep rumble of stones landing on corrugated sheeting. And somewhere at the back of his throat he could taste the bitterness of gunsmoke.

Then the dreaded moment would arrive, preceded as if it were a herald's trumpet by the loud whinnying of a horse. The massive beast and its rider would suddenly appear out of the confusion and rear up before him. He would find himself staring at its hooves and a moment would pass in which he could hear nothing save a strange rattle as though a tin can were being kicked down the street. Then it would fall silent again for a second before everything erupted in a deafening roar and the searing pain would begin.

Here he would jerk himself awake and sit bolt upright in the bed, his upper body drenched in sweat and his breath coming in short, sharp gasps like those of a panting dog. He would stay there, his arms pushed back against the sheets behind him until he had calmed down and told himself it was only a dream. But after a while, as if hoping that all life since had been part of his imagination too, he would gradually prise his eyelids apart to test the reality. Yet still there would be nothing...

Eventually he would swing his legs over the edge of the bed and instead of trying to fall back to sleep and risk a repeat of the same painful journey, he would make his way across to the window where he would open the shutters once more.

It was as well that he'd already stopped working. Had he still been at the Embassy he could imagine what his colleagues would have said about it. Ever the butt of their humour, they would doubtless have joked at his expense.

What? A blind man who shutters his windows at night? That's a bit pointless isn't it? He must be crazy.

And they'd have been right – in a sense it was pointless. But they'd never understood him any more than they'd understood the country they worked in. To them Egypt was just another paragraph on their CV, Cairo another dot on the map that charted their progress to better things. Although there was probably some truth in their gripe – it was not the glamorous and sought-after posting it had once been. It no longer ranked with Paris, Washington or Rome, places where diplomacy was conducted in an atmosphere of wealth and style. These days, there was no comfort in Cairo, what with the heat and the dust and the flies.

The politics had moved on too. For many years Egypt had been a country of continuous change and excitement. After declaring itself a Republic there'd been Nasser, the Suez crisis, the patronage of the Russians and then their expulsion. Prior to his assassination Sadat had taken the country to war and although Arab-Israeli relations would always be an issue, under the prolonged regime of Mubarak things appeared to have quietened down. Beyond its boundaries no-one seemed to take much notice of Egypt anymore.

If you want to get on, I wouldn't get too settled if I were you, said Carpenter. Nothing much happens here these days.

How wrong they'd been! Even without the revolution Egypt was still a country whose history was to be treasured, a place where everything happened – all manner of human life was there. It was all on their doorstep if only they'd taken the trouble to look. Then they might have discovered the real Egypt, the Egypt that he knew rather than the stifling confines of the social round and the inevitable ex-pat's clubs. Yes, it was a crazy country and the Egyptians were a crazy people – but that was what made it so beautiful.

And so when the time came and his tour of duty was over, rather than seek the promotion and move on as he could so easily have done, he'd deliberately flunked his exams. He'd no desire to leave. Those with ambition deserted him, taking coveted posts elsewhere. Others elected to go back to 'the old country' but he'd stayed on and chosen to see out his service there, much to his colleagues' derision.

Michael Blake? He's a strange one. I think the heat must have got to him – the bugger's gone native, if you ask me.

But there'd really been nothing for him to go back for. He had no ties.

Over the years the shuttering of windows had become a habit. And now he'd grown older and sightless such habits were important. This simple daily ceremony was ingrained in his routine and for him it marked the moment that separated night from day, rest from consciousness. In his diminished condition how else was he to know the difference? How else could he keep track of time?

Sometimes he'd reach the openness of the balcony and find himself grasping at the solid metal rail as a means of reassurance. It was something he could cling to, something he could count on in the darkness. There was comfort in the touch of such objects. But he needed more than that and in the absence of sight he'd come to rely heavily on sound and smell to guide him through each day. And in truth, things would begin much earlier than his habitual trip to the window. At 6am the call to dawn prayers, delivered from a dozen different mosques around the city, would ring through the room. With their summons to remind him he'd no need of an alarm and yet he would still lie there, slowly coming round, before getting up out of bed.

Once the first buzz of traffic had subsided, the smell of fresh bread from Mr Sayeed's shop on the corner opposite and fuul, cooked at the kiosk outside, would excite his appetite and tell him it was time to take breakfast. He'd retreat into the room, carefully fold back his covers and slowly get dressed, then find his way into the small galley kitchen. There he'd find something to eat and return to the window where he'd measure out his waking hours with the cries of the street vendors and the honks of passing taxis.

As time progressed he learnt to distinguish every noise. He could tell the bark of a car from the growl of a truck or the roar of a lorry and soon he could identify each vehicle just by sound –

the laundry van, the baker's cart. In the concert of the street they each played their part.

You'll find that you'll develop your other senses to compensate, said Dr.Aziz. In time, they'll come to replace most of what you've lost.

What I've lost? So what are you saying? said Blake. Are you telling me I'm never going to see again?

I'm afraid so, Mr.Blake. The nerve endings are completely burnt away. There's no chance of recovery.

And it was true – there was so much you could discover through the use of your nose and your ears. If you paid enough attention they could tell you everything. For instance, he knew for a fact that the lady in the next apartment, Mrs Ibrahim, regularly went out to meet her lover at three o'clock in the afternoon. The sharp scent of her perfume and the throaty cough of the waiting car engine told him as much – he didn't need eyes to see that. All it wanted was focus and a little imagination.

He found himself particularly blessed in this way and he had an unerring ability to ascribe an action to a sound. He attributed this happy knack to his lifelong study of birds. He'd known them ever since he was a child. At first, in the garden of his parents' home there had been robins, blackbirds and dunnocks. Then, as he'd grown and roamed further afield, he'd discovered the birds of the countryside – pigeons, larks, crows and finches. Over the years he'd come to know them all – their size, their shape, their colours and most importantly, their call.

To define a bird by its song was to him the most satisfying of skills – and as he'd come to realise, the most efficient. He'd soon learnt it was far easier to come to judgement as to species by spending a few moments listening rather than thrashing around in the base of a thicket in the hopes of a sighting. So even if he'd caught no more than a glimpse of the bird, he'd still know he was right. By the age of eleven he could tell a hawk from a falcon purely on sound, never mind flight, and no longer needed to look.

But all that had been before the darkness had come and his sight had been taken, so now it was only the hearing. The tragedy was that, after a lifetime of freedom to explore the world and its avian life, with his movements restricted to the confines of his flat all that was left was the plaintive coo of Palm Doves and the incessant chirruping of sparrows.

In the street outside there was a lull in the traffic – it must be nearing ten. Soon, his visitor would arrive. He would know her coming by the creak of the street door and the scrape of an upturned crate as Abdu, the ancient doorkeeper, would rise from his makeshift seat and nod his greeting. Then he would hear their voices echo in the hollow of the stairwell.

Good morning.

Good morning, Abdu.

Blessings be upon you.

And upon you...

By way of preparation he'd have already cleared the small occasional table that stood between the two wicker chairs facing into the room. He always dressed for this appointment – a clean white shirt, a light linen jacket. With the addition of a tie, this had been his uniform at the Embassy. Then he'd take his place in the seat he'd defined as his own, its shape rounded to his form. This was his domain, the point from which he surveyed the world and all that lay within it. He'd no need of going out and facing all its dangers for as he'd already discovered, he'd only to open the shutters and he let all of Cairo in. And if that were not enough to occupy him and fill up his time, then there was always memory and the studied recollection of what he already knew.

Day by day, hour by hour, he relived his life, each moment treasured or reviled according to its worth. But this next hour, this coming hour, of all of them was now the most precious. This was what he lived for, this was what he valued most, for in this next hour he would revisit a world beyond anything he could find in his room, a world beyond the social round and the expat's clubs, a world beyond even Cairo. For in this next hour there would come to him a world he had once thought lost to him forever as, with the help of Lee Yong, he would once again see the fabulous birds of the Nile.

Chapter Two

She'd been coming to him for just over a month now. Her visits had been sporadic at first but as their relationship had gradually re-established itself, they'd become more regular. She'd only ever meant to call the once, just to say hello and to see if he had news, but she'd immediately taken pity on him and felt compelled to return. When it became clear that they shared a mutual interest, she would make the journey daily if there was something to report. Even if not, he knew that she'd not leave it long before boarding a cross-town bus and mounting the stairs to his flat to give that precious hour that meant so much to him.

Their first meeting was filled with emotion. She'd turned up entirely unannounced and that was a surprise in itself. Even before he'd left the Embassy he'd been unused to receiving visitors. True, Carpenter would occasionally drop by, lumbering up the stairway armed with his usual bottle of whisky ('the quinine of the desert' as he called it) and insist on a couple of drinks – but beyond the routine calls of the cleaner and the laundryman, he passed his days alone. Who wanted to spend time with him, now he'd so little offer? The fact that it was her of all people to break the mould only seemed to heighten his strength of feeling.

I never thought I'd see you again...

Strictly speaking, he couldn't, but what he meant was her presence, her touch, her feel. He could tell that she'd changed. She no longer wore jeans (he could hear the swish of her skirt as she came in at the door) and the clump of her Cuban heels had been replaced by the scuff of soft-soled shoes. Her voice had mellowed as if in the year since they'd last met, her youthful confidence had been squeezed out of her and the girl he remembered (she'd been no more than that at the time) had become a woman. Her hair would be different now and he imagined she'd let it grow long. Sometimes, all he wanted was to reach out and touch it...

His condition had come as a shock to her. She wasn't prepared for it and there had been tears, hot on her cheek and the back of his hand.

She'd brushed them off saying, "Sorry, I had no idea..."

"...that I was blind? Did no-one tell you?"

You'd have thought someone at the Embassy would have made her aware and explained it to her (why hadn't Carpenter done so for God's sake?) – but apparently not, so she'd been forced to find out for herself. To see him so reduced had brought out an overwhelming sense of compassion in her. So despite her intention to make just the one visit, when that first meeting ended and she began to take her leave, she'd accepted his invitation straight away.

"You will come back, won't you?" he'd said.

"Yes, yes, I will," she'd responded instead of a perfunctory *Of course.*

A few days later she'd returned and their newfound friendship began.

At first they'd filled their time with small talk. There'd been much to catch up on – his enforced retirement and loss of sight, her experiences in America and the reasons for her return – all had to be talked through. But he knew there'd come a point when these topics would be exhausted, there'd be a lull in the conversation and she'd ask the inevitable question. Although when she did, it was couched in the most general of terms.

"I don't suppose you've seen any of the others, since?"

He braced himself for her reaction, knowing he'd have to contend with her disappointment when he told her, no, she'd been the first. There'd been a protracted silence while she'd digested the news, then they'd resumed where they'd left off, politely, as if to cover over the point.

After two or three of these get-togethers she made a

suggestion. She'd clearly thought about it in advance as she introduced it carefully into the conversation. She must have felt that she wanted to be of service to him in some way and had realised how inappropriate it would be for her to offer to cook or clean or wash his shirts. Besides, these were matters that were already taken care of.

"Why don't you let me read to you?"

"I'd be pleased if you would," he'd replied.

As opposed to chores, this was a pleasure she could readily provide.

To begin with, she came armed with a newspaper and gave him snippets of the latest events. But he was already up to date with affairs, the small radio in the corner of the room tuned permanently to the BBC. He clearly wanted more than that and when she'd gone on to ask him his favourite author so she could bring a copy on her next visit, he'd immediately pushed himself up out of his wicker chair and tapped his way across to the bookcase on the other side of the room (he used a thin cane in the flat rather than the stout white stick he took outdoors). He reached up and took down a small volume before returning to his seat and handing it to her.

"Here, this will be fine."

She'd expected something classical, Dickens perhaps, or Austen – or in the case of poetry, Shelley or Keats, but she was presented with a complete surprise. The work he'd given her was a small reference book, filled with a mixture of text and coloured plates. On closer inspection she could see it was worn and well-thumbed, but even then she thought that in his blindness he'd made a mistake. She read out the title to confirm his choice.

"'A Photographic Guide to Birds of Egypt and the Middle East' by Cottridge and Porter. Is that really what you meant?"

"Exactly."

Then, still puzzled, but somewhat reassured, "So where should I start?"

"At the beginning..."

He didn't want to sound facetious, but neither did he want to miss a single word.

So she simply turned to the first page and began.

"'In terms of its birdlife, Egypt is one of the better-studied countries in the Middle East. A large number of species have been recorded, and the country list stands at over 470. Because of its strategic geographical position...'"

He took a long, slow breath as he heard the words he'd read himself so often before. She was not yet halfway through the opening paragraph and the memories were flooding back – and she'd not even got to the birds!

She paused, thinking there was something wrong.

"Are you alright?"

"Yes, absolutely fine. Please continue."

Now that he'd got her started, he'd no thought of stopping her.

At their next meeting, after she'd completed the preface and the introductory chapter, they moved on to the catalogue of species with its individual descriptions and coloured plates. It was divided into sections, beginning with ostriches and grebes, and at first he allowed her to read right through, letting each description illuminate the picture in his mind. It was when she reached herons, egrets and storks that he asked her to adopt a different approach, omitting the title at the top of each page so he could make a guess from her verbal depiction. In her desire to please him, she was happy to comply.

"'A plump heron, which is much smaller than Grey Heron, and in adult plumage is easily distinguished by its grey plumage with black crown and back. In flight the bird's appearance is largely grey...'"

It sat on the stern rail of an old felucca moored beneath the steps at the back of Elephantine Island. Stock still, it stared at him, its long white crest plumes fluttering in the breeze.

"Night Heron."

"Yes, well done."

She nodded and moved on.

"'A small, dark, coastal heron. The adult is identified by its black crown, bluish-grey upperparts, paler greyish neck and under-parts. At close range, note its rather marked facial pattern...'"

The boat had come to a halt next to a mangrove swamp. Crouched beneath the overhanging branches he'd seen the bird before it had suddenly taken fright and rushed for cover, extending its long yellow legs.

"Striated Heron."

She soon came to understand the depth of his knowledge and the reading of the book became like a game to them. She'd try to disguise the descriptions as much as she could, challenging him to reach his conclusions. From time to time she'd skip a section and move to something new and out of context with a view to catching him off guard.

"'A large waterbird, as big as a chicken, and easily told by its stout bright red bill, pinkish red legs and bluish-green plumage. Those occurring in Egypt are of the green-backed form...'"

Her attempt at deception had made him laugh.

"That's unfair! It's Purple Gallinule, by the way."

He could see it now just as clearly as he had then, a great fat bird, strutting through the reedbed, tugging at the vegetation.

After she'd failed repeatedly to catch him out, she asked the obvious question.

"You know these birds?"

"Yes, of course."

"You've seen them all?"

He nodded. He had – and so could she have done if she'd only taken the trouble to look but she'd had no interest in such things at the time. Her mind had been engaged elsewhere, as far from the study of birds as it was possible to be, and they'd had no meaning for her. They had no meaning for her now, but for him they were everything – they were the world in his head, the world beyond Cairo, the world he could no longer see. And besides, they served to remind him of the trip they'd taken in each other's company just over twelve months before...

Chapter Three

It had begun amidst the smog and sultry heat of a late November morning at the Embassy building in Cairo. The pile of papers which had been steadily accumulating on Blake's desk during the previous fortnight had finally started to annoy him. His in-tray was full to overflowing. God knew what was in there – memos from the First Secretary, the quarterly report of The Council, there might even be something on the Trade Exhibition he was organising in Alexandria. But whatever it was, there was far too much of it. Soon he'd have to have a blitz and get rid of it all – otherwise he wouldn't be able to function.

It amazed him how much paper there was for him to deal with. In this age of computers and electronic communication you'd have thought there'd have been less of it, but the reality was quite to the contrary. Computers meant protection, encryption and the constant need to avoid hacking – so in the end it was simpler just to send someone a piece of paper. There was something solid and dependable about paper, you could rely on it being in no more than one place at any one time – unlike an email, which once you'd committed it to cyberspace could simultaneously be anywhere and everywhere.

The Diplomatic Service was an empire built on paper, a position it was not going to give up lightly. Procedures, manuals, circulars – tome by mighty tome it was an edifice studiously erected over the years. Minions in Whitehall depended on it, minions the world over depended on it – you couldn't simply dismantle it at the touch of a keyboard. Like so much else in the organisation, paper was both a strength and a weakness.

The Service was full of contradictions. Blake felt it was like Marmite – you either loved it or you hated it. Yesterday, when he'd walked to work through the busy streets of Cairo and had entered the building, cool and elegant despite the heat, he'd loved it. Today, faced with a mound of meaningless paper he'd somehow have to plough through, he hated it. And yet, for the sake of his job he would manage it. As Oscar Wilde would have said – there was only one thing worse than being in the Diplomatic Service and that was being out of it. If you wanted to survive, you just couldn't have it both ways.

In the end he decided to delegate – Carpenter could be called on to assist. For the moment, his colleague had excused himself from the room and Blake took the opportunity to split the accumulated pile and pass half across to the other's tray. To solve the problem it would have to be shared – and in this respect, Carpenter was your man. Carpenter had a strange and enviable way of dealing with paperwork – a way which, given his own inherent sense of responsibility, Blake could not bring himself to employ. His in-tray was invariably empty and his desk perpetually clear, although he himself never seemed to do any work. Carpenter, it seemed, was not the working kind.

Large, shambolic and untidily dressed, it occurred to Blake that if Carpenter were an animal, by appearance he resembled a bear. But by nature he was quite the opposite and rather than grump and growl, he would amble cheerily about the building dispensing his particular brand of bonhomie. A constant optimist, he could be relied on to see the upside of any situation and was always supportive – but when it came to work, he was a sloth. Nevertheless, he had his advantages and dealing with paperwork was one of them.

Having relieved himself of half his load, there was no time for it to dwell on Blake's conscience as he'd hardly completed the move before Carpenter reappeared.

"I see the postman's been while I was away."

"Indeed he has," said Blake, unrepentant.

"No problem," said Carpenter, surveying the burgeoning contents of his in-tray on an otherwise empty desk. "I'll soon get rid of that. Oh, and by the way, the First Secretary wants a word."

"What, now?"

"Now, later, whenever you've got a moment."

Carpenter was typically vague – precision was not one of his strong points.

Blake opted for now. Audiences with the First Secretary were not often granted and it paid to respond straight away. And if it meant he could defer tackling the paper...

"Sit down." The First Secretary motioned toward the empty chair on the other side of his polished mahogany desk. "Take a seat."

There was something about the repeated invitation that suggested to Blake this was not going to be an ordinary conversation. What else did the man expect him to do, other than sit down? He was not so revered that you felt obliged to stand in his presence. Blake still thought it best to comply. To be truthful, he needed the rest.

The First Secretary shuffled his papers as he prepared himself for whatever was to come. It felt like a five-minute wait at the least and Blake noticed that he coughed twice during the course of it as if he were reluctant to start things off. Eventually Blake decided to help him with what was obviously a burden.

"I suppose this is to do with my note about the Brotherhood."

"Well, no, actually. But now you come to mention it, it did raise a few eyebrows." This was clearly a diversion, although the First Secretary seemed glad of the opportunity to expound. "I thought your comments were rather ill-judged, quite frankly."

A few years ago, Blake would have bristled. Now such responses were like water off a duck's back. Truth was a commodity in short supply in diplomatic circles – but if they didn't want to listen when it was on offer, so be it.

The First Secretary warmed to his theme.

"As I'm sure you're aware, the last thing HMG wants is for Egypt to become The People's Republic of Islam. It'll turn into another Iran and God knows where that will lead. There'll be state-sponsored terrorism and we can't afford for al-Qaeda to gain a stronghold in North Africa. The Americans will be horrified, the Israelis will see themselves surrounded and they'll think the West has abandoned them – then it won't be long before somebody presses a button."

Blake sighed with frustration. He could always rely on the First Secretary to peddle the official line, but it was still a disappointment. The situation as he saw it was somewhat different.

"It may interest you to know that in Egypt, the Brotherhood has nothing to do with al-Qaeda. I thought I'd made that absolutely clear."

"You may be right, but it isn't the sort of thing HMG wants to hear. Anyway, I don't know where you get this kind of nonsense."

The First Secretary waved his hand toward his pile of papers as if he were warding off a fly.

Blake took umbrage.

"I mix with people. I hear things. Something's been going on and it's coming to a head. What would you have me do? Leave it unreported?"

The First Secretary leant purposefully forward and put both arms on the polished mahogany desk. In Blake's experience this was usually a sign of irritation.

"Look, Blake, I don't care what you get up to in your spare time but while you're here as a member of the Trade Section, you shouldn't concern yourself with these political issues."

That old chestnut – the Trade Section, commerce and the grubby business of making money. For Blake it was as dry and as dusty as the desert beyond Giza. He'd left Cambridge with a degree in Ancient History yet he'd been reduced to organising trade missions in a back office in Cairo.

"You don't do yourself any credit with these constant excursions off message," the First Secretary continued. "You're seen as something of a sympathiser, you know."

And thereby a threat. That was the clear implication, although it came as no surprise to Blake – he'd heard it countless times before. It probably helped to explain his current position in the Trade Section.

"But that wasn't why I asked you here." The First Secretary deliberately cleared his throat. "I've been looking at your file. I see you've an important birthday coming up."

He gave a wry smile of expectation which to Blake looked distinctly like a smirk.

So that was it – that damned birthday! Blake had tried to deny its existence and had done his best to put it out of his mind. Secretly, he'd hoped they'd do the same and fail to notice so it would somehow slip by without comment. Apparently not.

"We'll be sorry to see you go, of course."

Somehow Blake doubted it – on the contrary, they couldn't get rid of him quick enough. It was frightening how easily such words could slip off a diplomat's tongue. Old habits died hard. Fortunately, Blake had already prepared a response in case of such eventualities.

"Actually, I was hoping for an extension. I thought perhaps I could stay on for a while – at least until the Alexandria project's been concluded. I'd like to see it through if I could."

"Impossible, I'm afraid." The First Secretary shook his head. "As you know, London's in a complete flap over these budget cuts. We daren't spend a penny more than we have to, and to be frank," (he looked around as if he were about to divulge some great national secret) "we're going to have to lose a few people. So as much as I'd like to keep you on... Anyway, Carpenter can take care of Alexandria – he's not got much on at the minute."

Carpenter never did have much on...

Blake digested the news.

"So that's it then?"

"I'm dreadfully sorry, but there's no choice. Rules are rules, I'm afraid."

Blake did not need reminding – a lifetime of drafting agreements and protocols was never going to convince him otherwise. Yes, rules were rules, but that was the thing about bureaucracies – decisions were made by people who didn't know what they were doing and carried out by people who didn't care. And there was no bigger bureaucracy than Her Majesty's Foreign and Commonwealth Office.

Having dropped his bombshell, the First Secretary was keen to move on.

"Done anything about your pension?"

"No, I thought I'd wait..."

Now Blake shook his head. Of course he hadn't. It would only have attracted attention and the last thing he wanted was to advertise the fact he was nearing retirement.

"Speak to the Management Section, they'll help you sort it out. I'll give them a ring and let them know you're coming."

The First Secretary's offer was followed by a protracted silence. The interview was over and all he wanted now was for Blake to take his leave. But Blake was not in the mood to comply so easily and sat with his arms folded, looking defiantly out of the window. Two or three storeys below them, at the end of the manicured lawn, the Nile flowed sluggishly by, brown and muddy, while the sails of the feluccas moored next to the Corniche shivered in a gust of winter wind.

Suddenly, the First Secretary was standing up. He cleared his throat once more and extended his hand.

"I'll see you before you go, naturally."

Naturally...

The First Secretary had achieved his objective and so tried being jolly – which, under the circumstances, was weak and always doomed to failure.

"Well, what do you plan to do with your retirement? You must be looking forward to it."

"I don't know," Blake mumbled in the direction of the lavishly carpeted floor. "I'll find something, I suppose."

Although in reality, he wasn't looking forward to it at all.

He went straight back to the office. Carpenter was sitting in his customary position, his hands clasped together behind his head, staring out at the same view Blake had been contemplating just a few moments before. While he'd been away, the in-tray on Carpenter's desk had been completely cleared and the wastepaper basket next to it was now full.

"God knows how anyone makes a living in this wretched country," said Carpenter, scathingly. "I've been watching those boat johnnies down on the quayside. I don't believe they've moved a muscle in the last twenty minutes. For the life of me I can't see how they get by."

Blake elected to let this blatant piece of hypocrisy pass without comment. To point it out now would have served no useful purpose.

"Anyway," said Carpenter, turning to face his visitor. "So how was the Old Man?"

"I wouldn't go there if I were you," said Blake, trying to warn him off. It was a touchy subject.

Carpenter ignored the message and remained curious.

"Oh, really? Why's that?"

"Well it seems that I'm the one who's old. I didn't tell you, but I'll be sixty in a couple of weeks."

He'd learnt not to trust Carpenter with all his secrets. He was old school tie and a 'good sort', but in his desire to be affable, prone to indiscretions.

"Good Lord! I'd never have guessed. You've kept that pretty quiet, old boy. This calls for a celebration."

He reached for the bottom drawer of his desk where he kept the bottle and two glasses he used for 'office emergencies'. Blake held up a restraining hand.

"I'd rather not, if you don't mind. There's really nothing to celebrate. They're making me retire early and it's something I'd hoped to avoid."

"Retire? You lucky dog! If they made me an offer like that I'd be off out of here like a shot, I don't mind telling you."

Carpenter had a wife and two children and the comfort of a fireside somewhere in England to go home to. Blake, on the other hand, did not.

"So what are you going to do with yourself, old boy, now that you'll have all this time on your hands?"

Exactly... What was he going to do with himself? It was the second time he'd been asked that question in the last half an hour and as yet, he still had no sensible answer.

He looked hopefully at the clock hanging above the row of filing cabinets. There were another forty-five minutes before he could reasonably take lunch and, unable to settle, he spent the time fidgeting at his desk, ruminating. Why was it, he asked himself, that whenever you reached the bottom of the cup, the dregs always tasted so bitter?

His birthday was actually in the second week of December. The natural thing would have been to work through to the Christmas break, but his request for this was denied and with its age-old propensity for being exact, the Civil Service insisted on his immediate departure. As a result he was obliged to forego access to the seasonal round of parties and receptions – a right which in previous years he would have scorned, but whose loss he now resented. But that was the point – when something you didn't value was taken away, it merely made things all the more galling.

On reflection, he would still not have attended – and it was not sour grapes that made him think so. The prospect of saying goodbye so many times over was unappealing and he had no intention of becoming the object of disdainful comment.

Well, well, look who's here. And I thought they'd given Blake the bullet...

So instead, he moped about his apartment for the best part of a month, feeling aggrieved at his enforced condition of idleness. Finally, almost in a fit of pique, he decided to book himself a holiday and found a place on a cruise ship going up the Nile.

It was a journey he'd been intending to take for some time. He'd already visited most of the other bird-watching sites in the country – Lake Qarun, Wadi El Rayan and even the Hurghada Archipelago. He'd been on an exploration of the Delta whilst on secondment to Alexandria but for some reason the upper reaches of the Nile had always eluded him. He'd told himself then that if he wanted to find more of the real Egypt and learn of the culture and origins of the Upper Kingdom, he'd have to go south to Aswan and experience its reportedly African feel – the birds that inhabited the First Cataract and its surroundings were supposed to be worth the trip alone.

The voyage was to begin at Luxor. It had once been the ancient city of Thebes, the capital of the New Kingdom, and was in itself a place of considerable historical and archaeological renown. Here were the Valley of the Kings and the Temple at Karnak, recognised sites of international importance. Then the tour would progress upriver, visiting temples and sites of interest en route until it eventually arrived in Aswan. As to exactly what birds he might discover, he couldn't be certain, but that was part of the excitement of the trip.

And so, with his telescope and its supporting tripod stashed in his luggage and feeling marginally better about his future, in the third week of January he found himself on an aeroplane, heading south.

Chapter Four

He had decided to fly from Cairo, an hour in all, rather than risk the long and laborious road journey. That would have taken him through territory where it was best for people of Western appearance not to be seen, even those of his extensive experience. Armed gangs were rumoured to roam the area between Assyut and Luxor, and there had been robberies, beatings and even deaths. Some said the gangs were simply bandits, others that they were terrorists – in either event they were to be avoided. Horrific though it might sound, it was probably better to be blown up in the air than be captured and shot on the ground.

Despite these concerns he arrived safely in the early evening, the lights of the airport lounge glowing gently in the dusk as he cleared the terminal and was guided to his shuttle bus. He clambered aboard, stowed his backpack and found himself a seat. Soon, they were speeding through the city of Luxor and after half an hour or so, the slab-white outline of a cruise ship appeared against the night sky.

The bus turned off into a car park adjacent to the mooring and the slow but necessary process of embarkation began. First, the luggage had to be off-loaded. Half a dozen local porters had been engaged for the purpose and were standing on the quayside, dressed in their long galabeyas and turbans. As if they'd been waiting for their cue, a squabble immediately broke out amongst them as to who had the right to begin. Blake descended from the bus and took the opportunity to stretch his legs. The driver had already got out and was loafing on the tarmac, smoking a cigarette. In Egypt, this kind of operation could take a while.

It was something the management had foreseen, and to amuse the passengers during their unavoidable wait they'd engaged a pair of whirling dervishes to perform. Beneath the street lights at the edge of the car park, their coloured costumes flared like a rainbow.

It was while he was studying their technique that he became conscious of a second altercation which had just broken out behind him. The luggage compartments of the bus had been swung open and various sets of suitcases had been pulled out onto the car park. Nearby, a middle-aged woman dressed in a cream-coloured top and matching slacks, a Westerner, was becoming agitated as two of the local porters began badgering her for money.

"Baksheesh! Baksheesh!" they were crying. They had doubtless provided some small service for her and were demanding what they thought was their due.

It would have been unfair to say she was dripping with jewellery, but there were at least two rings on each hand and it was evident she was not short of a few bob. But even if she'd been plain and unadorned, to Egyptians such as these the mere fact that she could afford to ride in a bus was proof enough that she was wealthy. Although just at the moment, she looked far from in control of affairs as her ringed hands fluttered about her head as if she were trying to shoo away a wasp.

"Go away! Imshi! Imshi!"

It sounded like the one word she'd made sure she'd learned from the phrasebook before setting off in order to protect herself – now she was being called upon to use it at the first time of asking. If she'd studied her guide a little more thoroughly, a better choice might have been 'la, shukran' (no, thank you) which, although meaningless in the current context, might have been a little more calming. Instead of allowing the porters to get on with their job, she'd made the mistake of becoming involved. Perhaps her luggage was not being treated with the care she thought it deserved – or perhaps she'd simply made some chance remark. Whatever the reason, she'd put herself under pressure and it had induced an inappropriate reaction. What she failed to realise was that she need only give her besiegers a few small coppers and the matter could easily be settled.

Blake fingered the coins in his own pocket, kept there for that very purpose. In Egypt someone invariably wanted tipping. There was always a door to be opened, a bag to be carried, a way to be pointed, some small service to be performed – it was part of the custom of the country. And to help the lady out, all he had to do…

But it was not in his nature to interfere and his hand stayed firmly in his pocket. He had long since convinced himself that he was not responsible for the problems of others – people should be left to resolve their own affairs. Such matters could take their course without him. It was not that he was a mean man, either with money or in spirit, but it was rather a question of belief. And like so much else in his life, it stemmed from his love of birds.

Birds were a part of nature – and nature was a force to be reckoned with. You altered nature at your peril and it seemed to Blake that every attempt to do so had met with disaster. The loss of rainforests, the melting of polar ice-caps, global warming – they were all the large-scale results of human tinkering. On a personal level, he took the view that birds were to be observed and enjoyed but most importantly, they should be left in peace to get on with their lives. However they'd arrived on earth, be it through the hand of God or through the natural process of evolution, they were not intended to be played with like toys. And as with birds, so with man – or in this case, woman.

As it happened, there was no need for him to become involved. The thought of assisting her had barely crossed his mind when a third party intervened and came to the lady's rescue. A small crowd of onlookers had gathered round the door of the bus. One of them, an Egyptian, heard the fracas and broke away, walking smartly across. He was a young man in his late twenties, clean-shaven and heavily built. He had a soft round face, and although he lacked the aquiline features that accompanied some form of nobility, his bearing suggested he was still of good family. Dressed in Western clothes, he wore a dark suit over his white shirt and tie – a sure sign he was part of 'the management'. He spoke in a dialect Blake did not understand, barked a few sharp words at the porters then, with a distinct motion of his head, signalled they should leave. They immediately backed off, a hand reached out and a small note was discreetly passed across. Their palms had been greased and all would be well. With this resolved, the young man could now turn to the lady and give her reassurance.

"You must excuse my countrymen. They do not always understand Western ways."

Nor she theirs, thought Blake.

But if the young man had the same idea, he was far too polite to express it.

"Your bags will be taken up to your cabin," he continued. "Everything has been clearly marked. It is all arranged." His English was perfectly phrased although delivered with an accent that marked him out as of Middle Eastern origin. "You have nothing to worry about, I assure you."

"But my jewellery box is missing," the woman protested. "I should never have let it out of my sight."

"It will be found, I'm certain. The loading of the bus has been most carefully supervised."

"Well I certainly hope you're right. It contains some valuable pieces."

"I'm sure of it. It will be delivered to you immediately. I will see to it personally. Now, what is the number of your cabin?"

"Wait a moment. Here…"

She fumbled in her shoulder bag for her travel documents and produced a booking confirmation which the young Egyptian inspected.

"Aha! Number 12. The upper deck. An excellent choice. I will have the box brought up to you straight away."

"Oh thank you, thank you so much." An emotion in the woman's voice presaged tears. In addition to the paperwork she had also fished out from her bag a small handkerchief and proceeded to dab at her nose. "My husband would never forgive me."

Her eyelids fluttered a little more quickly than the situation demanded and Blake noticed a distinct lack of moisture. To the practised observer, she was clearly more artful than upset.

But this feigned show of distress did not deter the young Egyptian from his duty.

"Please do not concern yourself. This will soon be resolved, I promise you. Now, if you would like to follow this gentleman..."

He guided her gently toward the gangplank onto the ship where a member of the crew stood waiting.

Blake struggled to suppress a wry smile at the lady's pantomime of concern. And as for the young Egyptian, you could not deny he had a certain adult charm, despite his boyish looks. As an exercise in mollification, he had to admit it had been expertly done.

The lady in cream was now halfway across the gangplank and casting an anxious glance over her shoulder. Back on the shore, the young Egyptian bowed his head and smiled politely. He waited until she had disappeared on board, then turned smartly on his heel and marched briskly over to the bus where he began to snap out his commands.

Blake's attention returned to the whirling dervishes. For the time being the incident was over and the steady, if prolonged, process of embarkation could be resumed.

Chapter Five

Blake's cabin was on the lower deck. It was not as prestigious as the one accorded to the lady in cream but that didn't concern him – he wasn't planning to spend a lot of time in it. There were twin beds (he'd asked not to have a double) and he chose one to sleep in and laid his birding gear out on the other – his telescope, tripod, binoculars and the illustrated guide he'd bought especially for the trip. Against the far wall was a small dressing table (somewhere to write up his notes, he thought) and in the corner by the plate-glass window, a chair faced out toward the river, a position from which he could view sunrise or sunset. Although personally, he'd have preferred to have been up on the sun-deck, out in the fresh air...

He'd hoped to get in an hour's birding before dinner. There were sandbanks close to the moorings and they should have provided a good selection of waders – godwits, sandpipers and stints etc. But it was gone half past six and the light was against him. The conditions would make viewing impossible and it meant he would have to wait until the morning for his first sighting.

He still had to unpack his bags so it was not until after seven that he was able to get changed and go down for the evening meal. Outside the dining room, a seating plan showed he had been placed at a table for eight in the far corner. As he approached, a familiar voice could be heard as the infamous lady in cream was holding forth in a loud and belligerent tone in stark contrast to the deferential manner she had employed earlier on.

"...but do you know, he was as good as his word because as soon as I got to the cabin, there it was on the dressing table. I couldn't believe it after all those goings-on with the bus. I was relieved, I don't mind telling you. It's nice to find someone in this damned country you can trust."

Her companion was an older man whom Blake took to be her

husband. Both his hair and his moustache were of the same silvery colour – as were his eyebrows which he was in the process of raising as if in protest.

"Look, dear, I'm sure it would have turned up eventually. I know these people, they're really not that bad."

"Don't you believe it, David. They had their eye on it from the moment we got off the plane. Mark my words, they're a shifty lot, if you ask me."

Blake pulled out one of the two remaining chairs and sat down. His arrival seemed to come as a welcome relief as the other two couples looked up and gave him a weak smile of welcome. Up until then they'd presumably been forced to sit and suffer in silence as the argument raged back and forth between the lady and her husband (whom he'd already christened Mr & Mrs White). But if the others had hoped that his incursion would put an end to the discussion they were disappointed. The conversation continued in the same vein for some while with Mrs White continually attacking their hosts and Mr White continually defending them.

"Look, dear, I was stationed here for eighteen months, remember. I do know what I'm talking about."

"Yes, but that was years ago – things have changed since then."

"I don't see that it's changed that much. It's still the same country – and it's still the same people."

"But it's different now. When you were here we were in charge – today we're just visitors and they think they can treat us how they like. Anyway, I don't care what you say, I still don't trust them."

It was a debate Blake had heard before, both within the Embassy and beyond it. Either diplomatically or on a personal basis, were the Egyptians to be trusted? Or anyone else from the Middle East for that matter. These apprehensions arose from a fear of the unknown – what you didn't understand, you treated with suspicion. The first barrier was the language – because if you couldn't understand the language, how could you understand the people that spoke it? Which was why, unlike so many of his colleagues, he'd taken such trouble over it himself. The British were notoriously bad at talking in other people's tongues and it was not just the Egyptians who were vilified, it was the world that existed beyond the English Channel. Johnny Foreigner was a rum lot and had to be treated as such.

His thoughts were confirmed when the lady seated immediately to Mrs White's right suddenly chimed in. She'd been anxious to break into the conversation for the last few minutes and had only managed to contain herself by continually fiddling with her napkin ring. Finally, as Mrs White's tirade against their hosts came to an end, she was able to interject. Blake had expected a British voice but it was an American who cut in. Its owner was older, although not elderly, and if the fleshy condition of her upper arms and shoulders were a clue, seriously overweight. Based on what he could see of her above the table Blake surmised that like an iceberg, there would be a lot more of her below it. Her mousy hair was kept short and she wore a shapeless green top which did nothing to counteract the impression she gave as to size. You could hardly say she was a victim of fashion since fashion had ignored her as if it did not consider her a suitable case for treatment. But despite her unprepossessing appearance, once she'd managed to break in all heads were turned in her direction and she held the floor and spoke without a shred of self-consciousness as though she naturally expected everyone to listen.

"You know what, honey? You're so right. It's the same the whole world over. The Italians are just as bad. Why, only last year, Ira and me – that's Ira, my husband." She indicated the man sitting at the end of the table. He was of roughly the same age but as thin as she was plump – to the extent that Blake wondered whether he suffered from some sort of consumptive disease. And whereas she gloried in the occupation of space, he seemed to apologise for using it and sat with his arms folded in front of him, either in an attempt to make himself appear smaller or as a means of defence. Had she not pointed him out, he might never have been noticed at all. "Ira and me," she continued, "we were in Rome. We'd gone there for our wedding anniversary. We usually go to my sister's in Oregon but this year we decided to go to Rome because it was a special anniversary. What anniversary was it, Ira?"

Ira's reaction was to tighten his grip on himself. And before he'd had chance to respond, his wife had answered her own question.

"Our 30th. That's right, I remember now, it was our 30th. It's pearl you see and my daughter gave me pearls and I don't wear them – but that's another story. Anyways, we'd gone to Rome and we were staying in a little hotel – where was that hotel, Ira?" She turned toward her husband again but just as soon as he'd opened his mouth to speak, she cut him short again. "Well I guess it doesn't matter where the hotel was, but I wanted to go to the Trevi Fountain. My sister went to Rome the year before and she said, 'Whatever you do, honey, make sure you go to the Trevi Fountain.' So Ira took me, didn't you, Ira?"

"Yup."

This time Ira managed an abbreviated reply.

"And when we got there, I went to throw a coin in – because that's what you do at the Trevi Fountain, you throw a coin in and make a wish. Anyways, I went to throw a coin in and I couldn't find my purse. I looked everywhere, on the side, on the floor, but I just didn't have it."

"Lost the darned thing," chirped Ira, this time without prompting.

"No, Ira, I didn't lose it. I left it at the hotel. I know I did, so don't you go saying different. It was on the clerk's desk before we set off and I must have walked out without it. So we went back..."

"Took a taxi. Cost me darned near twenty dollars."

"...we went back and they said they didn't have it. I said, 'You must have it because I left it right here on the desk' but they said no they didn't. Well I knew from the look on their faces they weren't telling the truth. And do you know what? Two days later it turned up in a downstairs trashcan, empty, not a thing left in it. They'd taken the lot."

"Yup," said Ira. "Clean as a whistle."

"Well, we went straight to the American Embassy. The guy we spoke to was awful nice but he said he couldn't do a thing about it."

"Nope. Not a darned thing. Said anybody could have taken it."

"But it wasn't anybody, Ira. It was them, I know it."

"Darned near spoiled our holiday."

Ira's final comment seemed to encapsulate the point of the tale so well that his wife was content to let him have the last word and she sat looking smugly round at the others as if to say *There! What do you think of that?*

Blake's heart sank. He was concerned that the conversation would develop into a competition to see who could tell the best 'I was hard done by a foreigner' story. It was not a happy prospect. All eyes now turned to the couple next to him as though they were expected to respond – but this was a game they had no intention of playing and they thankfully held their tongues. An embarrassed silence fell over the table.

Finally the man on Blake's right, a gentleman in his late sixties with a craggy face, succumbed to the pressure.

"Well, as we're obviously going to be spending some time together, I suppose we ought to introduce ourselves. I'm Keith and this is my wife Janet." Janet dutifully nodded. "We're from Coventry."

They went round the table in turn. Mr and Mrs White were

David and Joan from West Berkshire while the large American lady referred to herself simply as Mrs Biltmore.

"You've already met Ira."

They certainly had.

"We come from Baltimore," she explained. "We're the Biltmores from Baltimore! Ain't that a hoot? It sure makes it easy to remember – you won't forget us in a hurry!"

Blake had an inkling they would not be allowed to – although her joke was successful in that it provoked some welcome laughter.

He was the last to speak, and when his turn came he sensed the others looking at him with a degree of anticipation and he became self-conscious. He was not used to, and nor did he want, such attention and his inclination was to keep things short and simple.

"It's Blake, Michael Blake. I'm from Cairo."

With Mrs White's eyes fixed firmly on him, he would have given anything to add *And I'm also an Egyptian*. But he could not and the opportunity to counter her prejudice was lost.

"Cairo?" said Keith, raising a wispy eyebrow. "You'll know your way around then. You're British though, I take it?"

Blake nodded – there was no point in denying it.

"Will your wife be joining us?" Keith probed gently, glancing at the eighth and empty seat.

"I'm not married."

Blake's reply was short and to the point. He knew full well it did not answer the intended question, and given what had gone before it gave him some pleasure to see them confused. Why should he bother to enlighten them?

As to the other member of their party, he had no idea and neither, it seemed, did anyone else. Someone would eventually arrive, that was certain – a place had been laid, a napkin provided and there was a room card with a number on it such as they all had. But who it belonged to and when they might appear remained a mystery.

"In that case," said Keith. "I think we should all go and get something to eat."

He rose, and led the way across the dining room.

Once they'd queued, their selections provided them with an ideal topic for discussion. Keith, who'd already appointed himself as the elder statesman of the group, started them off.

"I've really been looking forward to the food on this trip. I've never eaten Middle Eastern cuisine and I quite fancy trying it."

"You'll need to watch out for the sheep's eyes," joked David.

"Sheep's eyes!" exclaimed Mrs Biltmore. "Oh my, I don't think I could cope with sheep's eyes."

"Just kidding," said David.

"Well I sure hope you are," said Mrs Biltmore, her hand at her throat. "Why, I feel quite ill just at the mention of sheep's eyes. I don't see how anyone could eat such a thing. We don't do that back home, do we, Ira?"

"Nope," said Ira, tucking into a second helping of fruit cocktail. "We sure don't."

Although whether he meant this for better or for worse wasn't clear and much to everyone's relief the subject of what they did eat at home, like anything else that resembled sheep's eyes, was left untouched.

But the ice had been broken and the conversation, which had previously been no more than a trickle, soon became a flood.

Later on, over coffee, a discussion arose as to practicalities.

"What are we doing tomorrow?" asked David. "Is there a plan?"

"Haven't you looked at the noticeboard?" said Keith.

"No, what noticeboard? I didn't see one."

"The one in the foyer. We're going to the Valley of the Kings. It's a six o'clock start apparently."

"You're joking!"

"That means I'll have to be up at five," interjected Joan. "I can't possibly go anywhere without washing my hair."

"Good God!" said David. "And I thought this was supposed to be a holiday..."

Blake inwardly smiled. For all their faults and prejudices, these were refreshingly ordinary people. Before long they would be showing each other photographs of their children and sharing family intimacies.

He knew them well. White, middle-class and British, their relatives staffed the Embassy and filled the ex-pats clubs. The Biltmores were of the same stock – they were only the Brits whose ancestors had escaped to the other side of the Atlantic. They could all sound crass and terribly bigoted, but when put to the test as a body they were ultimately reliable – even if they were a little dull. At one time the British had ruled the world. Twice in the previous century they'd saved it – and afterwards they'd immediately gone back home to tend their gardens. They had no interest in foreign affairs – and unless it impinged directly on them, the machinations of Middle Eastern politics and the struggle between the Israelis and the Arabs meant nothing to them. History, for the most part, left them cold. Predictable and solid, they would certainly not surprise him. Sometimes, he felt that all he had in common with his countrymen was a language...

He managed to suppress his smile, but could not stifle a yawn.

"You'll have to excuse me, I'm afraid. It's been a long day and I'm rather tired." He pulled back his chair and got up from the table. "I'll bid you goodnight and see you all in the morning."

He received a perfunctory farewell. His presence would not be missed, and for all that he had contributed to the evening, they could carry on easily without him.

The truth was, he wanted a breath of fresh air before turning in.

He returned to his cabin to find a pullover and pick up his binoculars. His infallible rule was that if he left them behind, there was bound to be something he'd want to look at – a silhouette perched on the ship's rail, or the outline of an owl in a distant tree. Experience had taught him to go prepared.

He climbed up to the open top deck and made his way between the tables and the sun-loungers toward the stern. It was a bright, starry night and although there was still some warmth in the air, the temperature would soon drop sharply and it would turn cold. Beneath him, the Nile glistened in the moonlight, its regular flow inducing an enduring sense of calm. All was at peace, and for a moment he could stop and listen to the sounds of the night.

From the mud-walled houses on the far bank came the anguished cry of a young child. Somewhere in a nearby village, a dog began barking in response, echoing across the water. He turned to look for it and became aware of an orange glow emanating from an adjacent field to his right. Someone had lit a fire. A group of men had gathered round it and, raising his binoculars, he saw amongst them the porters from the quayside, sitting cross-legged, warming their hands and passing their cigarettes one to another. Other, younger men had joined them and were engaged in earnest conversation. One of the faces looked familiar and he instantly recognised the young Egyptian from earlier in the evening. He'd exchanged the suit and tie of management for a galabeya and was now indistinguishable from his compatriots, talking and smoking with the others. It seemed quite a heated debate.

Blake's face broke into a knowing grin. For all the trivia at the dinner table it had been an interesting evening. Yes, you could count on the British not to surprise you – but you could always rely on the Egyptians to do exactly the opposite. And if he knew anything about them they would be there late into the night, arguing and talking politics. He laughed to himself, folded his binoculars away and went off to bed.

Earlier, he'd felt excluded, as if he were a visitor to a club of which he was not a member. The need for small talk had bored him, but now the life of the land he loved had reclaimed him. Who needed to travel the world, he thought, when you could live in Egypt and see it all?

Chapter Six

By 7am the following morning, Blake's feeling of smug self-satisfaction had turned to one of distinct frustration. He was an hour into the second day of his much-awaited trip and as he would have put it, he was not yet 'in amongst the birds'. As Keith had predicted, they'd set off at six and when the bus made a brief stop at the Colossi of Memnon, he'd admittedly discovered a pair of Spur-winged Plover in the cultivated fields (possibly three, there may have been another hidden in the vegetation). There had been Palm Doves too, perched on the telegraph wires and softly cooing, and probably Barn Swallows, glimpsed from the bus as it wound its way through the villages. But where in Egypt could you not find Palm Doves and Barn Swallows? So now, here he was, standing amongst the crowd on the vast concourse in front of the Temple of Queen Hatshepsut, his teeth chattering in the nithering wind.

He zipped his fleece up a little further and let out a yawn. Considering he was as yet unused to the bed, he'd slept well but it had indeed been an early start. Coffee and rolls had been taken in the dining room at half past five. The thought of conversation at that hour had been too daunting to contemplate and thankfully, the meal had been conducted in silence. The fact that the eighth place at the table was still unoccupied had consequently passed without comment.

An early morning breeze was wafting up from the Nile. It was cold, unexpectedly so for Egypt, and even Blake had underestimated the conditions. The rest of the party certainly had and for the last five minutes he had been listening to Joan bemoaning the fact, continually rubbing her bare upper arms until at last she had snatched the coat David had thought to bring for himself and flung it around her own shoulders. Mrs Biltmore on the other hand, who with the addition of a floppy white sun-hat was dressed in exactly the same unbecoming outfit as she had worn at dinner the previous evening, seemed utterly impervious to the weather, her inner body presumably insulated by her outer layers of flesh. Standing next to her and looking emaciated by comparison, Ira's coat remained buttoned up to his chin. They were supposed to be listening to the tour guide who, in his obvious enthusiasm for his subject, seemed equally as oblivious to the conditions as the American.

"...one of which also boasted myrrh trees which Hatshepsut personally acquired from the Land of Punt in a famous expedition that is depicted along one of the facing walls..."

Blake's attention drifted. The history of the region, both ancient and modern, was well known to him. The only point of interest lay in the fact that the tour guide was the self-same Egyptian from the night before. The young man whom he'd last seen in a peasant's smock next to a late night fire had now reverted to his more conventional dress. As he'd already had chance to observe, these people played many parts – and in a country where you did what you had to in order to survive, the boy was no exception.

On another occasion Blake might have dwelt on this but for the moment his thoughts were elsewhere. He was convinced that the rocky, arid landscape in which he found himself was inhabited by at least one species of bird, and to pass the time before they moved on he'd set himself the task of finding it. He was hoping for wheatear (preferably one of the pied variety, Mourning or Hooded, either of whose distinct black and white markings would make it easy to spot) and he'd just completed his second visual scan of the surrounding ground when he became attracted by a movement to his right. Yes! Here was a bird surely – although it did not have the black and white plumage he was expecting. Something more plain and grey-buff was strutting about amongst the stones. Probably a lark then – but was it Desert or Bar-tailed? He needed a closer view to decide and raised his binoculars to look.

He was inwardly debating the finer points of bill size and plumage when he became aware that he himself was being watched. Somewhere to his rear, a pair of eyes was focused intently on him and, like a carpenter's auger, he could feel them boring a hole in his back. They carried an angry message. *What are you doing? Why are you wasting your time fiddling around with birds when you should be listening to the history of mankind?* A feeling of acute embarrassment came over him, and gently lowering his glasses he turned his head slowly toward what he perceived was the source of the scrutiny.

Some three or four yards behind him stood a young woman (he was tempted to say 'girl', she was so slight) of South East Asian appearance. Her eyes and face were of a deep brown colour, and to judge from her Western style of dress, he would have said Philippino or possibly Malay. She had on jeans and a pair of Cuban heels, which she presumably wore to make herself look taller as she was barely above five feet in height. She'd wrapped herself in a heavy three-quarter length jacket, the collar of which was turned up against the wind while her neat black hair blew about in the breeze. A pair of large round silver earrings dangled down each side of her neck. She was undoubtedly pretty, if not beautiful, although at the moment her face was contorted into a disapproving stare.

Blake smiled weakly back by way of apology. He slowly let go of his binoculars and told himself to face forward toward the tour guide and pay more respect. There was something unnerving about the girl's presence he did not quite yet understand. She possessed an intensely serious appearance, a feature made all the more daunting by her obvious good looks, and this outward force of character made him feel as though he were an errant schoolboy and she a teacher scolding him, as if he'd been caught shirking his lessons.

Keeping his head as still as he could, he risked a glance at the stony patch to his right where the lark had been just a few moments earlier – but the place was now empty. The bird had literally flown and any chance of confirming its identity had gone with it. He frowned ruefully to himself. Hopefully there would be other occasions when he might not be put off so easily. His attention returned to the young Egyptian who had fortunately reached the end of his speech.

"And now, if you would like to follow me, we will make our way up to the Middle Terrace..."

Cursing his luck, and the young woman who had so distracted him, Blake fell into line. Soon, he thought, they would be able to get back on the bus and out of the chilling wind.

Much to his disappointment, the ruins of Queen Hatshepsut's Temple were entirely devoid of birds and after what seemed like an eternity, the bus moved further up to the Valley of the Kings.

Their tickets had been booked in advance and included entry to three of the tombs. The question was whether to stick with the programme or to pay extra and visit the sepulchre of Tutankhamun – but it was expensive and the tomb was allegedly empty. Keith didn't think it was worth it, but Joan took a different view.

"I didn't get up at five o'clock this morning and slog all the way up here just to be told I can't see it." She'd already given David his coat back and was standing in what was now warm sunshine, soaking up the heat like a reptile. "Frankly," she continued, glancing round at the arid surroundings, "it's probably the only thing up here worth looking at."

Mrs Biltmore, who had said relatively little all morning and was allegedly suffering in the heat, professed herself happy to go with the crowd. "Whatever you people decide, why that'll be just fine by me."

She stood in the shade of the bus, fanning herself with her floppy white hat. As for Ira, no-one thought to ask. And with Keith remaining adamant that he would prefer to walk to the head of the valley rather than waste his money, they split into two groups, David and Joan heading off toward the ticket office while the rest set off up the main path and into the interior.

It was, as Joan had suggested, a desolate and unforgiving landscape that confronted them. Above ground there was nothing but stones and shale and without a tree or any form of vegetation in sight, the only shade was afforded by the occasional tin-roofed shelter erected at the side of the path. Here and there were the entrances to tombs, pin-pricks in the rocky hillside, those that were open signed and lit with tunnels deep into the earth, those that were not, dark and barred off by iron grilles. It was a formidable place. If the intention of the ancient Kings of Egypt had been to hide themselves away in the middle of nowhere, then they had certainly chosen wisely. As to what birdlife it supported, Blake was doubtful.

By this time it was mid-morning and a fierce heat had begun to beat down on them. The coats they had relied on earlier were discarded and replaced by sun-cream and headgear. Blake donned a favourite Panama (it was rather battered after years of constant use) and to protect the back of his neck, he tied off a linen scarf he'd brought for the purpose. Janet and Keith put on bush hats while Mrs Biltmore jammed her white affair back on her head and was busy lathering her flabby arms with a protective gel. Her legs were already covered by a voluminous denim skirt that reached down to her ankles, from beneath which protruded a well-worn pair of trainers. Their scuffed and shabby exterior did nothing to enhance her appearance. They grouped together at the start of the path and set off with Keith in the lead.

It occurred to Blake that the American would suddenly surprise him and turn out to be athletic, bounding up the path with unlooked-for strength and purpose. Surely, he thought, there must be some virtue, however small, hidden within so large a frame. But if so, it was not of the physical kind and he was sadly mistaken. As her size and shape suggested, Mrs Biltmore struggled to progress through the harsh terrain, huffing and puffing at every step and for ever in need of a stop to catch her breath.

"Oh my!" she kept protesting, looking up toward the head of the valley. "Do we have to go all the way up there? Why, I don't believe I'll be able to make it. Why don't you folks just go on without me, I'll be fine right here." And every so often she would affect to sink down on a nearby boulder.

But she did make it, for despite her objections and constant protestations to the contrary, she seemed inwardly determined and any strength she possessed lay in her will rather than her physical ability.

Ira brought up the rear, his slight frame bounding from rock to rock like a jack rabbit, but without at any point straying in front of his wife.

As they progressed upwards through the valley, the sixth sense which had afflicted Blake earlier in the day cut in yet again. He'd stopped to lend Mrs Biltmore his arm for the umpteenth time *Why, thank you Mr Blake* when he turned to look behind him, and sure enough, following them at a discreet distance, there was the girl from the temple. She'd dispensed with her heavy jacket to reveal a white T-shirt promoting some rock band or another and she carried a black parasol above her head. As Blake halted, so did she, and a look was exchanged between them. Then, when he and his charge resumed their painful progress, he could hear the scrunch of her Cuban heels on the stones once more. It was as if she were stalking him.

Keith was striding out in front. His plan, he had announced, was to head up to the tomb of Seti I – 'the finest in the valley' according to his guide book – and then work his way back down at leisure.

It sounded like an admirable idea and Blake was sure it

would have worked well but for the fact that Mrs Biltmore was proving an unforeseen and frustrating drag on their headway. In addition to which, after a good twenty minutes hiking and having turned off up a narrow spur, they found the tomb they had targeted was closed for renovation. The entrance was barred off and a sign in red Arabic lettering had been posted to the side. There was an immediate feeling of disappointment and after starting out with such good intentions, this discovery seemed to dampen their spirits.

"Well now that's a great shame," said the large American, blowing with exertion. "After all that effort."

Her will to continue suddenly evaporated in the heat and she did at last sink down onto a nearby boulder, collapsing into the shade beneath the overhanging entrance and fanning herself once more with her hat. Ira took up a position next to her, watching her like a sharp-eyed hawk. And with their main charge stranded and immobile like a beached whale, the whole troupe came to a grinding halt and they stood about like a yacht luffed against the wind.

"What now?" said Blake, hands on hips.

"I suppose we'd better go back," said Keith.

Janet instantly nodded, grabbing at his sleeve. She'd shown little interest in entering the tomb and seemed reluctant to descend below ground under any circumstances. Blake pressed on with his questioning. "So do you mean to tell me we've come all the way up here for nothing and now we're simply going to turn round and go all the way back?"

"It looks that way." Keith was apologetic.

"Isn't there another tomb we can go in?"

With his wife tugging at his arm, Keith grew suddenly diffident.

"I'm not entirely sure…"

"Oh for goodness sake…" said Blake, for whom this was just another frustration.

As they were talking, their period of indecision had allowed Miss Malaysia to catch up (Blake was now confident of her country of origin). She had continued to follow them up the narrow spur right the way to the entrance to the tomb and was now standing at Blake's elbow. No doubt she had come to chide him again, he thought. Surely she was not still pursuing him after the incident at the temple?

But before they had chance to acknowledge her presence and ask as to her intentions, she butted in without any form of introduction.

"Is there a problem?"

"Yes there is," said Blake, determined to be assertive. "We've come all the way up here to see the tomb of..." (and just as he wanted to appear decisive, the name escaped him)

"...Seti I," said Keith, helping him out.

"Seti I," continued Blake, "and the damned thing's closed. On top of that, Mrs Biltmore here," he waved a hand at the prostrate form of the distraught American, "has conked out on us and can't take another step. Besides which we're all lathered with the heat and our leader here has lost his get up and go. So all in all, I should say we're in a state of complete limbo."

An edge had crept into his voice as if to betray his mounting sense of disquiet. What he dared not add to this list was that along with everything else, there were no birds to be seen and as they'd ascended the valley, he'd become progressively more and more agitated. Now, driven to the edge of despair, it had all boiled over at once. And to top it all off, here was that damned girl, come to annoy him again.

By contrast, Miss Malaysia appeared cool and calm and looked round the group, assessing what action to take. Her first move was to produce a water bottle from her small backpack and thrust it in the direction of Mrs Biltmore.

"You should drink. Here, take this."

While the American took in fluid, she turned to address the

rest of them.

"You want to see tombs? This one's no good – it's closed." She pointed at the nearby notice. "Come with me. I can show you some tombs."

Far from pursuing Blake, it seemed she had other intentions.

Blake caught Keith's enquiring look. Who was this girl? Blake shrugged his shoulders and smiled blithely back. Beyond the scene at the temple when she had so affected him, he had no more idea than Keith did. And yet because of what appeared to be her relentless pursuit of him, he'd become curious. Why was it that this young woman should suddenly seek to take command like this and offer to show them around? What possible motive could she have?

Well, whatever it was she was after, he decided he didn't much care. If she knew something they didn't, well good for her, he was happy to go along with it. Unfortunately, she didn't seem interested in birds.

"Lead away," he said. "I've no objection."

"Fine with me," said Keith who looked happy to relinquish his self-imposed responsibilities.

"We'll go in here," said Miss Malaysia, indicating an opening immediately to their right. "Ramses I. Follow me."

They began to move off – all except Mrs Biltmore who remained rooted to the spot and declined to rise from her seat. Now that she'd made herself comfortable, the determination she'd displayed in getting as far as she had seemed to have deserted her.

"I think I'll stay here," she declared, mopping her brow. "That all looks a mite too difficult for a body like mine. Ira'll tell me about it later, won't you, Ira?"

"Yup," said Ira. "Sure will."

For a brief moment Miss Malaysia stared at Mrs Biltmore with the same look of contempt she had visited on Blake earlier. Then, realising that the American was a lost cause and in no way

presently susceptible to a lesson in culture, she thrust her parasol
into her chubby hands.

"Take this. We'll be ten minutes. Wait here."

This last command seemed rather superfluous as, given her
current state of exhaustion, it was not as though Mrs Biltmore
was planning on going anywhere.

Blake took the opportunity to donate a bottle of water, Miss
Malaysia having recovered hers.

"And this – you might need it."

Remembering to remove his Panama, he ducked down into
the tomb.

The first thing to do was get used to the light. After the blinding
glare of the sun, the interior seemed dim and badly lit – but as
the outline of the corridor and the walls became clear, pictures
and paintings began to emerge from the gloom. Here were men
and women, gods and goddesses with strange-shaped heads,
chariots, horses, cattle and much to his delight, birds. He
instantly recognised them – herons, egrets, geese – the same
today as they had been three thousand years before. Since then
man had moved on, built engines, rockets and travelled to the
moon. The world had changed around them, but the birds had
remained constant. And when he looked at them now, they
somehow brought the past to life.

Further down in the burial chamber itself, Miss Malaysia was
making a speech regarding its contents. It was noticeable that her
attention to detail and manner were clearly an imitation of the
young Egyptian guide. Keith listened intently to every word.

"How fascinating…"

Janet was not so engaged and looked distinctly edgy in the
enclosed space while Ira scurried about, ensuring that he
examined every detail for inclusion in his report.

They were underground for the full ten minutes that Miss
Malaysia had promised. When they returned to the surface,

blinking in the bright light, Mrs Biltmore was exactly where they'd left her, crouched on her boulder and sheltering beneath the black parasol.

"So, what was it like?" she was keen to ask.

"Very good," said Blake. "You really should have joined us."

But from the distressed look on her face he knew that had never been possible.

The question then arose as to what they should do next. The obvious answer was to ask Miss Malaysia. She replied without hesitation. "We'll go and see Ramses IX."

Blake was still puzzled as to her motives. He wondered whether she was really trying to help or whether they were just guinea pigs on whom she'd chosen to try out some newly acquired knowledge. Whatever game she was playing, Blake was keen to find out. He had no doubt that the tomb of Ramses IX would be much the same as that of Ramses I but for him, its interest now lay in the performance of their self-appointed guide rather than any of its contents.

As Miss Malaysia turned to make her way back down the valley, it was a signal for Mrs Biltmore to haul herself up from her boulder and prepare for the return journey.

"Well, I guess we're off again..."

She handed back the parasol by way of Ira and fell into line.

Blake took the opportunity to seek out Keith and make an apology. The visit to the tomb had served to calm him down and he'd begun to feel contrite.

"Sorry about my little outburst back there. I was a bit out of order, I'm afraid."

"Think nothing of it," said Keith. "To tell you the truth, I'd forgotten all about it."

"She's very good, isn't she?" said Blake, nodding in the direction of the young Asian.

"Very," said Keith. "Any idea who she is?"

"Not a clue. Someone off the tour, I suppose."

And for the moment, that was as far as they could get.

Somewhere toward the rear, Mrs Biltmore plodded gallantly on, gathering strength on the downhill stretch.

If anything, the tomb of Ramses IX was more impressive than that of his ancestor. The entry corridor was sloped rather than steeply stepped – and it was much more extensive, so there were far more pictures and paintings to admire.

Miss Malaysia's performance was no less polished than before and in her desire to be thorough, she enumerated every detail. As a result, they were longer underground than they'd planned and so by the time they'd completed the slow upward climb to the surface and emerged into the daylight, squinting again, almost half an hour had elapsed.

Mrs Biltmore had once more been left to her own devices next to the entrance and was fanning herself furiously.

"Well there you are! Goodness me, I'd thought you'd gotten lost down there or somethin'. Ira, I don't know what you've been letting these folks get up to, but you need to pay a bit more attention, honey. Why, I thought you were never coming back."

Ira deemed it sensible to remain silent.

There followed another 'what shall we do next?' debate. By now their appetite for tombs had been sated and the general consensus was that as much as they had enjoyed their impromptu tour, they should make their way slowly back to the bus. Keith made a short speech of thanks to their temporary guide, then the group split up and began to drift slowly back down toward the entrance.

It was now mid-morning and the influx of visitors was reaching its peak. Groups of tourists, most of them Japanese, were clustering round the entrances to the tombs and the lower end of the path was thronged with people.

Miss Malaysia hurried on ahead. Blake watched as her black parasol bobbed up and down above the crowd, charting her progress. Where on earth was she off to now? he wondered. He was convinced she'd chased him up the valley in order to teach him a lesson for his wayward behaviour at Queen Hatshepsut's Temple. And in pursuit of her lifelong mission to constantly improve herself and those around her, she'd targeted some other group or individual in similar need of reform and was on her way to administer to their needs. God help them, he thought, they deserved his compassion.

His thoughts were confirmed when he reached the bus park to find Miss Malaysia had succeeded in buttonholing the young Egyptian tour guide. They were earnestly debating (or so Blake imagined) some of the finer points of tombs and antiquities. It was an animated discussion. At one point she began to gesticulate and furiously waved her hands. Why did she have to be so intense? he thought. And why all the rush? Did she not realise she had a whole lifetime ahead of her to pursue these passions?

Blake sighed at the thought. From the lofty standpoint of experience he was advising patience – but in reality he was envious of the young. What must it be like to be their age again, to have their passions, their desires? He'd once said the same thing about himself and birds. *Oh, there's plenty of time. You can do that later, perhaps when you retire.* And yet here he was, gone sixty, and there was still so much to do.

The idea that he'd somehow wasted his life began to gnaw at him, and on the journey back to the ship, rather than slump down in his seat and doze off like the others, he sat staring out of the window in the hope of some form of redemption.

But there was nothing, just the dusty road, the flat arable fields next to the river and the ubiquitous presence of sparrows, swallows and Palm Doves on the overhead wires. He was hungry, he'd had nothing to eat since half past five that morning and it was only the prospect of a decent lunch that sustained him through the journey.

Chapter Seven

That afternoon Blake fetched his binoculars and his telescope from his cabin and went up onto the sun deck. His intention was to make up for the 'lost' time of the morning and catch up on his birding. The visit to the Valley of the Kings had been important but there had been little to see in the way of birds. True, Spur-winged Plover and the lark (of whatever type – he never did discover) were not to be sniffed at but he'd had to cut short his appreciation of it for fear of provoking Miss Malaysia. Her presence had constrained him and it annoyed him to think he'd allowed her to influence him so. She'd stolen his morning and the whole episode had left him feeling resentful – the afternoon and an intense study of the sandbanks adjacent to the ship would provide the necessary recompense.

But even as he gathered his gear together in his cabin he realised he'd left it too late. The ship was already in motion and the brown waters of the Nile were gliding gently past his bedroom window. They must have set off during the course of lunch but amid the various comings and goings at the table the transition had been so smooth as to be imperceptible. Now, the sandbanks were receding steadily into the distance and the chance to observe whatever inhabited them had been lost. It was another setback – but he was determined to remain philosophical and settled for the idea of scanning the river and the nearby fields. This tactic was soon rewarded as Pied Kingfisher were almost constantly in view, hovering over the shallows and diving for prey.

It grew hot in the afternoon sun. It was only the third week in January but the heat was intense. He'd retained his Panama hat and neckerchief and buttoned down the cuffs of his long-sleeved shirt to prevent his arms from burning. And once he'd taken these precautions it was actually quite pleasant to be out on deck – what with the river, the fields, the blue of the sky, and here and there the splash of kingfisher plunging. This was surely what he'd come for, to be outdoors in the fresh air, luxuriating in the quiet contemplation of birds.

It might therefore have been enjoyable had he not been subjected to a constant stream of interruptions. His telescope and tripod, standing nearby, continually attracted attention and he was eventually forced to go back to his cabin and the small dressing table where he attempted to write up his notes. He'd been on board for the best part of twenty-four hours and as yet nothing had gone down on paper. With his illustrated guide beside him on the makeshift desk, he opened his diary and began the first bird list of the trip, noting down the cast in order of appearance – House Sparrow, Barn Swallow, Palm Dove. He wanted to create a lasting record of the trip and what he'd seen – but he couldn't concentrate. He'd got no further than the Colossi of Memnon and the recollection of Spur-winged Plover when he was suddenly overwhelmed by a bout of tiredness and felt compelled to slip off his shoes and lie down on the bed. Within a matter of moments he had dropped off and his bird list remained frustratingly incomplete.

He awoke slowly and found himself lying on his back, staring up at a blank ceiling. For a moment he panicked, wondering where he was and how he'd got there. But then it all came back to him – the boat, the Nile, the search for birds, the fact he was no longer employed...

Outside his cabin window it was dark and there was no indication of movement. He looked at his watch. Five to seven already. He panicked and pulling open the side drawer of the dressing table, took out the itinerary he'd put there the day before. In the entry for the day an item was highlighted in red.

6.30pm. Cocktail Reception in the Forward Lounge.

Well, he'd clearly missed that! Then,

7pm Gala Dinner.

And if he didn't get his skates on he'd miss that too. He cursed silently – there was barely time to change and get spruced up.

He arrived in the dining room ten minutes late and a little out of breath. He'd taken off his neckerchief and rearranged his shirt, leaving the top button undone in an attempt to appear casual. Then he'd pulled on his linen jacket and had selected a formal pair of shoes rather than the slip-ons he'd worn on deck. He still felt horribly under-dressed. Gala Dinner. It wouldn't have surprised him if Keith had come down sporting a dinner suit and bow tie.

Something new awaited him at the table. He had assumed he would return to the same place as the night before but it was already occupied – by Miss Malaysia. It seemed she'd solved the mystery they'd all been pondering by announcing herself as the eighth member of their party. Blake was horrified.

She'd changed and having dispensed with her jeans and Cuban heels, was now sporting a long silver evening dress. Set against the brown skin of her bare shoulders, it made her look even more attractive. And although she'd retained the same set of earrings she'd been wearing earlier, she'd taken the time to restyle her hair which added to her elegant appearance. In her lap, she clasped a small matching bag. The overall effect was stunning. If he'd not already known who she was, Blake might never have recognised her as the slight Asian girl who'd stared him down that morning.

In his absence she'd taken the opportunity to move up a place, presumably so as to be closer to the middle of the table. If her objective was to become the centre of attention, then along with her choice of apparel she could hardly have done any more, for even allowing for Mrs Biltmore's continual failure of fashion (she was still in the same dull green top), the rest of the table looked positively drab by comparison.

Blake felt relieved rather than concerned. She could have the limelight – he personally had no desire to shine. If pushed to the front, what would he have chosen to say? No-one wanted to hear him talk about birds.

He pulled out the one remaining chair and took his seat on the end.

"Sorry I'm late," he mumbled. "Unavoidably detained."

"No problem," said Keith. Rather than the dinner suit Blake had feared, he too had opted for something casual. "In fact, you've got here just in time. Lee Yong was on the point of telling us all about herself."

Lee Yong! So she *was* Malaysian after all. Blake pricked up his ears – this was something he wanted to hear.

"...intend to travel the world," she was saying. "For a year. Maybe two. It depends." Although on what, she did not immediately make clear. "Then, I want to go to America to study."

"America!" exclaimed Mrs Biltmore. "You know what, honey? I am so glad to hear you say that. Why, there isn't a finer place for learning in the whole wide world than the United States – you just can't beat it."

Blake found himself rankled by this assertion. There were other equally good alternatives he could think of but for the sake of maintaining peaceful relations he decided to keep his counsel.

"And we know just the spot, don't we, Ira?" continued the American.

"Yup," said her husband. "We sure do."

After his bout of unexpected freedom that morning, Ira had reverted to his normal monosyllabic self – although with his wife's bulky presence looming beside him, there was probably little else he could do but concur.

"You need to come to Johns Hopkins, honey," said Mrs Biltmore. "I guess it must be just about the best university in the country. We sent both our boys to Johns Hopkins and they turned out just fine. We wouldn't have sent them anywhere else, would we, Ira?"

"Nope," said Ira. "We wouldn't."

"But we do have a little secret." Mrs Biltmore lowered her voice to a conspiratorial whisper. "He's too kinda bashful to tell you himself, but Ira used to work at Johns Hopkins, didn't you, Ira?" And then, before he could respond, "How long were you at Johns Hopkins? Thirty-three years, was it, Ira?"

"Thirty-four," said Ira.

"Oh," said Mrs Biltmore, taken aback. "I thought we discussed this the other day and you told me it was thirty-three years."

"Nope." Ira nailed his colours bravely to the mast. "Thirty-four."

"Now are you sure about that? We've been married thirty-two and I swear you said you'd been there just the one year before."

Blake sensed that this was about to develop into a repeat of the previous evening and he felt his blood pressure starting to rise. With her continual dominance of the conversation the American had begun to annoy him. He'd spent too long living alone to learn how to tolerate the foibles of others. He no more cared how many years Ira had worked at Johns Hopkins than he did as to whether Mrs Biltmore's handbag had been lost or whether it had been stolen. What he wanted was to hear Miss Malaysia's story and he'd have been prepared to interrupt affairs in order to achieve it. Fortunately it did not prove necessary as things moved quickly on.

"Anyways," said Mrs Biltmore. "I guess it doesn't matter if it was thirty-three or thirty-four, it sure seemed like a lifetime to me. Good old Johns Hopkins! Well, that's what I'd do if I were you, honey. And as soon as you're ready, you just come right over to Baltimore and Ira'll put in a word for you, won't you, Ira?"

"Sure will," said Ira, reverting to type once more.

Blake wondered what position at the university he might have held. His lack of words hardly seemed to qualify him as a lecturer. So had he been principal – or janitor? No explanation had been given and as he did not wish to delay matters further, he declined to ask.

"That's very kind of you," Lee Yong resumed, after the long interruption. "I'll definitely consider it. But I've a lot of travelling to do first."

"Of course." Keith had been waiting patiently on the sidelines. "But what do you think you might study?"

"I don't know yet. That's why I have to travel to find out."

Her innocent and unintentional joke provoked a ripple of laughter round the table. Even Joan managed to conjure up a smile. Up until now her face had been permanently sour. Blake thought it was probably because she'd been upstaged in the dress department since her own offering, although eye-catching, was nowhere near as stylish as that of the young Malaysian.

"So where have you been so far?" Keith continued.

"I started off in India – then flew to South Africa..."

There was an enforced pause as the starter arrived.

"You weren't here so I ordered you a soup," said Keith in a whispered aside. "I hope that's alright."

"Fine," said Blake. Soup was as good as anything else.

India. Along with his beef consommé, Blake tasted a twinge of jealousy. It was a country he'd always wanted to visit – but like so much else, he'd never got round to it. And yet here was this young woman, this girl (she could hardly have been more than twenty-two or twenty-three) who had already done in a few short months what he had put off for years. He imagined her standing outside the Taj Mahal, her beautiful figure swathed in a sari, scattering flower petals onto a pond – although in reality, she was far more likely to be stomping around in her Cuban heels and jeans.

"...and worked my way up country."

The word 'worked' attracted Blake's attention. He was certain she'd used it to mean 'progressed' rather than engaged in any form of paid employment. Lee Yong did not look like the type who 'worked'. She was no backpacker – her adventure was prepaid with no expense spared. She no doubt came from a wealthy family. Her father was probably an entrepreneur or industrialist, one of those who had built their empires in the economic boom of the 1980s and early '90s – cars, steel, computers, it could be any one of a number of sectors. Those who had been clever (or lucky) enough to survive the downturn that followed were still fantastically rich and a by-product of their fortune was the fact that their offspring were now free to roam the world without restraint. And here was one of them doing just that, in style.

Her immediate plan, Lee Yong explained, was to move on to Jordan and visit the rock-cut city of Petra. (Blake felt relieved – this was one place he *had* been to). Afterwards, she would take in Jerusalem, and possibly Damascus, before beginning a tour of the capitals of Europe – Paris, London, and Rome. Having conquered the Old World, she then planned to take on the New, crossing the Atlantic to America where she would explore the country as a tourist before commencing her studies (whatever they might be). It was an ambitious programme – Africa, Egypt, the Middle East, Europe, the States – the itinerary looked like a journey through time, the history of the world compressed into the space of eighteen months. And as yet, she'd failed to mention Russia, the Baltic, Scandinavia and South America – no doubt she would simply fit these in 'en route'. Nothing, it seemed, was beyond her. The question was not whether Miss Malaysia was ready for the world – that was obvious – but whether the world was ready for Miss Malaysia.

With the main course served and Lee Yong's travel plans laid before them, the conversation turned to how she might make best use of her time. There were innumerable suggestions.

"I don't see how you can go to Italy and not visit Florence..."

"When you get to Paris, there's a wonderful little bistro in the Rue de Rivoli..."

"Didn't Ron and Margaret buy a place in Spain? I can get their number for you if you like…"

Sat quietly at the end of the table, Blake reserved judgement. Surely they were missing the point. Here they were, privileged visitors to an ancient civilisation, surrounded by its treasures, and all they could talk about was going somewhere else. This obvious oversight irked him, but it was not until they were halfway through dessert that he was able to bring the discussion back to what he considered was its rightful starting point.

"But what about Egypt? How are you finding it?"

By now Lee Yong should have been overwhelmed by the relentless questioning, but far from it. In fact, she seemed to revel in it.

"I like it very much," she responded. "Very much indeed." Then, in an aside meant only for him, as if she were divulging some secret. "You will discover, Mr Blake, that I have a passion for all things Egyptian."

This casual yet deliberate statement puzzled him. Was she trying to appease him after her performance that morning? Or was there more to it than that? There was something mischievous about her, but before he could get her to elaborate, their tête à tête was interrupted.

A hubbub was pervading the dining room. All at once there was a general downing of napkins, a pushing back of chairs and people were standing up and getting ready to leave. This overall movement provoked Keith to enquire as to the cause and very shortly the report came back.

"Apparently we've reached the lock at Esna."

Not wishing to miss whatever spectacle this entailed, they all broke off from their meal and went up on deck.

A dramatic sight awaited them as they emerged into the night air. It was already dark, the sun having set an hour or so before, and the sky was inky black with just a few stars twinkling here and there. In front of them, a massive pair of lock gates rose up out of the water, and to the left a concrete dam spanning the width of the river penned back the upper reaches of the Nile.

They were not by any means alone. Ahead and astern of them a dozen or more cruise ships were vying for position in the queue to pass through the lock, their deck and cabin lights shining out through the gloom, and the sound of calling voices echoed across the water.

Close behind Blake, the laboured puff of Mrs Biltmore's breathing preceded her onto the deck as she slowly hoisted herself up the set of steep steps, towing Ira in her wake. Further down toward the bow, Janet and Keith had already joined David and Joan and all four were relaxing against the ship's rail as they watched the show.

Blake retreated to the shadow of an overhanging sunshade and waited for events to play out. He found himself speculating as to what Lee Yong might make of it all – the boats, the lights, the hustle and bustle of the quayside. No doubt there were similar scenes in her own country, and if such things were commonplace to her he imagined she might chide her companions for their casual waste of time. If not, then perhaps this was part of the international culture she seemed so keen to experience. He searched amongst the crowd at the front of the sun-deck and round the swimming pool in the hopes of finding her but failed. He couldn't recall seeing her come up on deck with the others – perhaps she'd gone straight to her cabin rather than risk the cool night air.

Eventually he caught sight of her, leaning on the rail at the stern of the ship, her slight form unmistakable even in the darkness. His first thought was to join her – but then he held back. He had no idea what he might say and besides, someone else was already standing in the shadows next to her. From his bulky outline Blake recognised the Egyptian tour guide. He'd been right about the chill of the evening for as he watched, the young man removed his jacket and draped it round the Malaysian's shoulders. Surely they were not still debating the whys and wherefores of tombs and temples? Had they not had enough of that earlier in the day? It hardly seemed the time to be talking shop.

But whatever they were discussing, the heat had gone out of their argument. Their demeanour was much more relaxed and they must have reached some form of agreement. To Blake that meant only one thing – Lee Yong had emerged victorious. She was not the kind who would easily give up, even when pitted against a professional – the 'passion' she had mentioned at dinner would guarantee that.

Blake found himself sympathising with the Egyptian. He was not the only one who had been subjected to the force of her character and had been obliged to bow before it – they both now bore the scars. But his pity soon evaporated as a pang of jealousy tugged at him. Whether he had won or lost, the young man was fortunate to have the sole attention of this remarkable girl. She was young, bright and beautiful and seemed happy to be alive – and for all her forward manner and lack of inhibition, the confidence and innocence she'd shown were to be much admired. The mysteries of the world lay in front of her, she had yet to be tainted by it and that in itself was something to be treasured. How exciting her voyage of discovery would be Blake could only imagine, and at that moment there was nothing he would not have given to share it with her.

A cloud passed over his heart. When had he last stood next to such a woman and inhaled the heady scent of beauty bound to intellect? He struggled to recall. Once perhaps, many years ago... But it was too far in the past for him to want to remember and he grieved at its passing as if some part of him had died and had left him incomplete. Lee Yong had her 'passion' and he had his, but now it was only for birds of the feathered kind. Moments such as the one he was witnessing would never come his way again and it saddened him to think of it.

Toward the concrete dam, a quiet calm had settled over the waters of the Nile. The calling of the boat crews and those on the shore had abated and in a moment the others would come looking for him. But the sight of Lee Yong and the young Egyptian had already become too much for him to bear and before his companions could return and glimpse his sorrow, he decided to go below and take himself to bed.

Chapter Eight

The following morning Blake woke early and rather than go out on deck, he decided to head straight down to breakfast. The dining room was deserted and the cold buffet of fruit, ham and yoghurt lay as yet untouched in its covering of clingfilm. From somewhere in the adjacent kitchen came the strangled wail of a popular Egyptian song as blithely unaware of his presence, a member of staff sang happily while he worked.

This time Blake chose to sit by the window (or rather, porthole, as it was barely above the surface of the water) where he could watch the Nile glide peacefully by and reflect on yesterday's events. He'd brought his notebook and a pen with him with the firm intention of completing the bird list he'd begun the previous afternoon. He risked being disturbed, but preferred the openness of the dining room to the confines of his cabin and had determined that even if the others arrived, he would stick doggedly to his task.

He used the word 'others' as if there were already some form of relationship between them and to an extent he supposed it was true. Personally, he was not finding it unpleasant. In fact, it was a major point of interest – they all had characteristics he could readily observe and before long he found himself wondering that if they were to come back in another life as birds, just exactly what birds they would be. Soon, he found himself gazing dreamily out of the porthole and his mind began to drift as if mesmerised by the steadily flowing water.

Suddenly, he came to as the voice from the kitchen re-erupted. On the table in front of him his notebook lay open, his pen next to it. So far, he'd been there for a good ten minutes and had managed only the one additional entry. But instead of Spur–winged Plover, as he'd originally intended, two quite different words stared up at him as he realised he had written down the name of Lee Yong. Annoyed with himself and embarrassed at his mistake, he crossed it out and determined to start again. But try as he might, he could not bring himself to remember what other birds he had seen and he was forced to admit that it was the Malaysian girl rather than any avian life that had been on his mind.

They'd met only the day before and yet in that short space of time she'd all at once succeeded in frustrating, infuriating and intriguing him. At first he'd deferred to her looks, although he'd convinced himself it was with the intention of being polite. Then, at the tombs, her behaviour had interested him and he'd taken delight in observing her. But when they'd returned to the ship he'd found her trick of dramatically appearing at the dinner something of a cheap charade.

From that moment on she'd dominated his thoughts and now he was gripped by the last view he'd had of her, standing on the sun-deck, more beautiful than ever, her silver evening dress rippling in the moonlight. He was immediately plagued by a terrible and frightening thought. Was it possible that he'd fallen in love with her? Was that what this obsession was about? He sincerely hoped not – love was an inconvenient if not impossible emotion, and in this instance could only lead to disappointment – but somehow the conclusion was hard to resist. Perhaps, after all these years... He shuddered and tried to push the idea away but despite his best efforts, he could not deny that there remained some form of longing.

He attempted to clear his mind and sought to convince himself that any feelings he might have were purely for her situation rather than for Lee Yong herself. To him she represented what he was not – young, passionate and forward-looking. All he could count on was the cynicism of age and his memories, or more to the point, the lack of them. Whatever other emotions she might have aroused in him, he'd never felt more remorseful than he had the night before, watching her at the ship's rail. He'd envied her then and he envied her now, waking up this morning with the whole of her life in front of her. All he had to dream of was the past – such as it was.

A lump the size of a blackbird's egg was forming in his throat. He sensed the onset of a debilitating melancholic mood and before it could start to devour him, he determined to set his mind in another direction. His intention had been to finish his bird list – and for his own sake he decided he must do so now. He took a firm grip on his pen and forced himself to write.

Spur-winged Plover...

But he'd hardly set the words down on paper when he suffered his first interruption of the day.

"Morning, Michael."

"Morning..."

David had also decided on an early breakfast. He pulled out a chair and sat himself down opposite, then poured out a glass of orange juice.

"I'm surprised you're not up on deck."

"Things to do," muttered Blake. "Trying to catch up..."

"Well, you missed a wonderful sunrise. Here, have a look at this."

David offered up his mobile phone and showed Blake the photograph he'd taken on it. It depicted a huge red disk looming over a row of palm trees and across its centre, a line of birds in flight.

"Any idea what they are by the way?"

Blake inspected them closely.

"Hmm... From the shape of their bills, I'd say they were Glossy Ibis."

Regrettably, it was a species he'd not yet seen on the trip. For all that he'd achieved by sitting around and indulging in a bout of introspection, now he wished he'd gone up on deck.

The dining room was beginning to fill. The voice from the kitchen had already ceased its carefree song, drowned out by the tide of chatter that had started to flood amongst the tables. One by one, the remnants of their party drifted in and took their seats – Janet and Keith, Joan, Mrs Biltmore and Ira. But there was one predictable and notable exception as Lee Yong was once again conspicuous by her absence.

Blake began to wonder as to why she missed her meals. His mind automatically went back to the vision he'd kept of her from the night before. The last he'd seen of her, she'd been deep in conversation with the young Egyptian. A second, and more dreadful, idea now occurred to him. Perhaps, after he'd gone, the two of them had linked arms and wandered off to her cabin and rather than face the others over breakfast she had chosen to stay in bed, lying in the arms of a newly found lover.

The image tormented him and he found himself burning with a shameful glow of embarrassment. Why did he insist on thinking about these things? It could only cause damage and he cursed himself for being so weak-willed as to consider it. Two people had spoken to each other – so what? It didn't have to mean anything, it happened all the time for goodness sake.

He determined to dismiss it as fanciful imagination and he told himself he should return to his bird list. But with the river of noise in the dining room now in full spate he was unable to concentrate, and despite his earlier assertion that he would sit there and finish it no matter what happened, his record remained incomplete. He ate his breakfast in a sombre mood and went directly back to his cabin.

At 10am the passengers reassembled in the Forward Lounge for the introductory tour meeting. The room had been transformed overnight, any evidence of the cocktail reception had been cleared away and the tables were freshly laid out with cups and saucers and complimentary pots of coffee. On each side, the sets of heavy red curtains had been pulled back and in order to disperse any fug which might have accumulated, the windows had been flung wide open. Outside, the Nile was now visible in all its glory and on either shore banks of lush vegetation slid steadily by. Looking at them now, it seemed to Blake that if anything the ship had increased its speed, a fact he had noted through the porthole at breakfast.

The meeting was opened by the captain, a slim young man of unctuous appearance, who introduced himself as Mr Mohammed. He affected an oily charm, giving his passengers an effusive welcome and assuring them of the best attention of both himself and his crew at all times. He hoped everything was to their satisfaction but if there were any problems, be they ever so trivial, they were to inform him at once and he would attend to it, day or night. If their shower didn't work, he would send a plumber. If the food was not to their liking, he would speak to the cook. If a light bulb was broken, he would find an electrician. In short, there was nothing he wouldn't do to ensure their enjoyment – his mere existence depended on it.

But with his very next breath he was forced to make an apology. He regretted that it had taken so long for them to get everyone together, but with the visit to the Valley of the Kings and the pressing requirements of the gala dinner, this was the first opportunity that had presented itself. But as they could see (he gestured toward the recently opened windows) they were making good progress and he hoped to have them in Aswan by the following morning. Given the vagaries of the country and its people, Blake thought it an overconfident boast.

When the captain had finished his talk the passengers split up into their various groups for details. Blake and his companions gathered in a convenient corner and waited as Keith, ever the one to take the lead, began pouring coffee and handing out biscuits. A management team had supported Mr Mohammed and of the trio of tour guides, it was the young Egyptian who came across to supervise their particular party. With recent events fresh in his mind, Blake determined to pay particular attention.

Looking at him now, he still found it hard to believe how un-

Egyptian the young man appeared. His smooth rounded features, his boyish looks, his slightly bulky figure – he might have been Far Eastern himself. Perhaps this was why Lee Yong found him companionable. His manner of speech was gentle too, lacking the harsh consonants of the typical Arab. And yet he was as Egyptian as any – the incident at the quayside and his attendance at the late-night bonfire had proved that.

He began by telling them he was called Reda – a traditional Egyptian name. He was to be their leader, their guide and their mentor for the week that they would be together. And just like Mr Mohammed before him, his sole objective was their enjoyment and the fulfilment of their desires, and any problems they encountered were to be referred to him for resolution. (This gave rise to some confusion as to whom they should speak to in the event of any trouble, but the general feeling was that double cover was better than none).

He asked how they were finding the ship. Were their cabins satisfactory? Was there anything they required? He needed to make them aware that there were certain changes to the itinerary and asked if they'd brought along their copies of the schedule as requested. He and his fellow guides had conferred as to the best arrangements in terms of the timing of visits so as to avoid the crowds and he laid their revised suggestions before them. As to the occurrence of what he termed 'hassle' he assured them that the further south they went, the less of a problem this would become and they were not to assume that the practices of Cairo (or even Luxor) would be repeated in Aswan.

As to contact, he gave each of them a business card which contained his name and a mobile phone number where they could reach him at any time. He finished by hoping they would find the trip both pleasurable and educational and looked forward to showing them the delights of his country. If there were any questions, he would be pleased to deal with them and for that purpose he proposed to remain in the lounge until mid-afternoon.

It was a polished and professional performance. Allied to the speech he'd given at Queen Hatshepsut's Temple, it showed that the Egyptian both knew his material and how to present it.

Blake felt a surge of resentment. Here were gifts that were denied him but that were readily given to others. His knowledge was probably as great as the tour guide's but when it came to projecting it, he was a novice. And if he'd hoped to see his assumed rival falter, stumble over some phrase or fact in an ill-judged attempt to impress, he was disappointed as it contained no such imperfections and remained solid throughout. In the end, he was forced to grant the young man a grudging respect.

Meanwhile, there was still no sign of Miss Malaysia.

The talk around the lunch table was all about the enforced alter-ations to the itinerary. Up until then the balance of opinion had been weighted heavily against the management and their changes. No-one wanted to be forced into doing something they didn't like – it was a matter of principle. Keith pressed the point.

"But if I understand it correctly, we don't have to go on any of these excursions if we don't want to, do we?"

"No," said Joan. "But what else are we supposed to do? If you think I'm going to sit round on the ship all day doing nothing…"

On further examination the revised plan meant that rather than visit temples en route in the heat of the afternoon, they would push on to Aswan that night. This would give them another day 'at leisure' when they would be free to explore the city or take up one of the extra trips on offer. A further day in Aswan was universally welcomed – but there was disagreement about what to do with it, and as a consequence they all decided to go their separate ways. Mrs Biltmore elected to stay on the boat (her feet were blistered after the exhausting tramp to the tombs) while Joan persuaded David to take her shopping, an excursion without which it seemed no holiday of hers could possibly be complete.

Blake did not find either of these alternatives appealing. For him it was a straight choice between an outing to a Nubian Village or a boat trip round the islands. The first offered a look at local arts and crafts, but when he discovered the second was actually a nature tour taking in the indigenous flora and fauna, he decided he was definitely going – it meant there was birding on the agenda. So as soon as lunch was over and he had been back to his cabin to collect his wallet, he returned to the Forward Lounge to get signed up.

Chapter Nine

The atmosphere in the Forward Lounge had altered significantly since the meeting that morning. The room was effectively deserted and although the windows had been left open for air, the curtains had been redrawn to ward off the heat of the afternoon sun. It was dark inside and here and there a few of the table lamps had been turned on to provide a dim and eerie light. The general impression was that of a nightclub the morning after the night before.

Reda was in attendance as promised. He'd removed his jacket and tie, loosened his collar and was now sitting in one of the booths along the far wall. On the table in front of him lay a plate containing the remains of a hastily eaten lunch while next to it a cigarette smouldered in a glass ashtray. Smoking was a habit Blake deplored, but one to which Egypt was unfortunately addicted. After his striking performance that morning, he instinctively marked the young man down.

He was hunched over the illuminated screen of an open laptop and as Blake approached, he quickly shut the lid. In the half-light of an adjacent lamp, Blake caught a glimpse of a web page with pictures and a bold headline. He was left with the impression that Reda had been doing something he should not, or at least something he wanted to keep private. 'Inappropriate use of the internet' sprang to mind, but with his boyish looks and rotund frame, it was hard to imagine him as the type. Even so, he appeared embarrassed at being caught unawares, stubbing out his cigarette and standing to greet his visitor.

"Hello? Can I help you?"

"I hope so. I was thinking about going on one of the tours tomorrow."

"Aha! May I recommend the Nubian Village?" advised Reda. "It's a fascinating place."

"Really?"

"Oh yes. The Nubian Village is a living museum. You will see much of the culture of the region there. And Nubia forms an important part of the development of Upper Egypt. In fact, some of our greatest Pharaohs were Nubian. In particular, during the 12th dynasty..."

Blake cut him short. He'd heard enough history lessons the day before and was in no mood for another.

"Actually, I'm more interested in the boat trip. My understanding was that it's primarily a nature tour."

"And indeed it is – but the Nubian Village has other, interesting features..." Then, seeing that Blake was not to be persuaded, he assumed a resigned look and motioned to an adjacent chair. "Please take a seat."

Blake made himself comfortable while Reda sat back down and shuffled his papers.

"And you are?"

"Blake. Michael Blake. Room 23."

Reda stopped shuffling and glanced up. His expression of disappointment had changed and now there was an interested glint in his eye.

"Ah yes – the gentleman who looks at birds. Aren't you what they call a 'twitcher'?"

"No, actually, I'm not."

Blake's response was rather snappy. 'Twitcher' was a description he abhorred – he thought it placed him in the same nerdy category as 'train-spotter'. He would have preferred to have called himself an amateur ornithologist but that sounded overly pretentious. All the same, he left Reda in no doubt that he'd touched a raw nerve.

"I'm a bird-watcher – there's a big difference."

"Sorry, I meant no offence."

"None taken."

Although it was a sure way of getting off on the wrong foot. Where had that information come from? Someone must have told him, it wasn't on his file. Surely that wasn't what he and Lee Yong had been discussing? Didn't they have better things to do?

"You will enjoy this trip very much I think," resumed Reda. "There will be many birds – many, many birds."

The statement aroused Blake's curiosity – it seemed out of context.

"You're coming on it?" he asked.

"Oh, no no no!" Reda's hands waved back and forth in enthusiastic denial. "No, Mr Blake, you misunderstand me. I know nothing of such things. My interest and expertise lies purely in the history – I leave matters such as wildlife to others. There will be a guide, a very good guide, and he will look after you. But no, I am afraid I will not be joining you."

"Ah..."

The young Egyptian began preparing the necessary paperwork and rather than let the conversation lapse into silence, made a typically polite enquiry.

"You are English?"

"Yes, but I've lived in Cairo for many years."

This qualification was not strictly necessary, but Blake felt he wanted to differentiate himself from the 'others'. And it was not just in Reda's eyes that he desired to make the distinction – his purpose was universal. He was not – and never would be – 'English' in the conventional sense of the word. He'd been away too long for that.

"Really? Whereabouts?"

"Dokki."

It was a suburb on the west bank of the city, known primarily for its plush villas and private hospitals. It was also a place of mixed social class. Reda would probably assume he lived in the fashionable area near the sporting club, whereas in fact he'd chosen an apartment in the poorer market quarter to the southwest. It had felt more in keeping with his desire to be thought 'Egyptian'. The explanation as to why would involve more than he was presently prepared to give so he elected to turn the question around.

"And you? Where do you come from, Reda?"

"I too am from Cairo – the Old Town. My mother still lives there. She has a small flat just off the Sharia Salah Salem. You know it?"

"Yes, I do." Blake nodded. In fact, he knew it well – he'd once had a place there himself.

"Then you will know how crowded and hectic and dirty it is, Mr Blake. And in the summer, the heat is almost intolerable. I have tried to persuade her to move on more than one occasion, but she insists on staying there."

"A true Cairene then..."

"Precisely."

"As stubborn as the mule that passes by her window..."

It was an old Arabic saying. In one form or another, it was one Blake had heard many times and in many places. He risked the wrong interpretation, but it was intended to show empathy rather than give offence. He waited for a reaction.

Reda's eyes narrowed as he considered the line. For a moment it looked as if it had gone awry, but then he gave a smile of appreciation.

"Aha! I see you know something of us Egyptians, Mr Blake. We are a strange people, are we not? Full of – what do you English call them? Contradictions? We are a proud race but we have so much humility."

"Indeed."

Blake was well aware of the Egyptian character.

"So... You're English..." mused Reda. "I should very much like to visit your country some time."

Blake gave a sardonic grin. He didn't really think of it as his country anymore and besides, the cynic that lurked inside his head told him that this was what every tour guide said to their guests – it was a way of ingratiating themselves. How to win friends and influence people – pay them compliments. And the bigger the compliment you paid them, the bigger the tip you could expect.

His reaction made Reda quick to qualify his statement.

"No, really," he protested. "It's something I've always wanted to do. My father (may he rest in peace) dreamt that one day I would go to Oxford for my education. He said it was the greatest seat of learning in the world and that's where I should aim to be. Sadly, he is no longer with us, but one day I have every intention of honouring his memory and going there to study."

Blake paused before replying. Mention of Oxford had set him on edge – he himself was a Cambridge man. He'd already resisted entering into the same debate with Mrs Biltmore and did not want to be drawn into a discussion about the merits of 'the other place'. He decided on a safer response.

"I'm sorry to hear about your father."

"Thank you, Mr Blake. It was a great sadness – both to myself and to my mother. It broke her heart and she has not been the same woman since. But as my father himself would have said, it was the will of Allah and we could do nothing."

"Of course. What was his profession?"

"He taught at the university – in Cairo. He was a great believer in the power of learning – it was the idea that sustained him. He said that learning was what separated civilised people from the rest of humanity." Reda assumed a serious look. "You see, civilisation is not something you inherit, Mr Blake – it's something you have to teach yourself. We Egyptians should know that above all people. Look at our history and what we have inherited – and look at us today. His great ambition was to see Egypt re-educate itself – it was how the Egyptian nation would raise itself up from the depths to which it has fallen. We were once a great country, Mr Blake. But now..." He shook his head with dismay. "We are nothing more than the sand that surrounds us – ground into dust..."

He stopped short, as if he were afraid of giving too much away. That morning he had delivered his speech in a neutral tone from which Blake had gleaned nothing, but now there was a touch of bitterness in his voice. He paused as if to compose himself and then continued.

"But I shouldn't burden you with the troubles of my country, Mr Blake. I'm sure you're well aware of them already."

Blake certainly was – he'd experienced them at first hand. Not only that, he'd written several papers on the subject, both political and economic. But just like his recent memo to the First Secretary, most of them had been consigned to someone's pending tray, never more to see the light of day. Trying to convince the Diplomatic Service to see the world as it really was had always been an uphill struggle.

"Everyone has their problems – Egypt is no different."

He had his own views on the subject. One day he might want to share them with this earnest young man – but Reda was as yet an unknown quantity and he would do well to discover more about him before declaring himself. They had only just met and in the dimly lit lounge of a cruise ship drenched in the afternoon sun, it hardly seemed appropriate.

"That's true – and I shouldn't complain. But in this country, it's hard not to." Reda smiled and tried to lighten up. "Well, you haven't come here to listen to me talk philosophy, you've come here to enjoy yourself – and my job is to make sure you do."

He rummaged through his papers to ensure everything was in order, then handed Blake his tickets.

"Here you are. Your boat leaves the quayside next to the ship at 8am, give these to your guide. I hope you enjoy your trip – let's hope you find many interesting birds. And I'm sorry, but now I have to ask you for some money."

So it only remained for Blake to make payment and withdraw, but he still had questions that remained unanswered – and they were not the kind he could readily put into words. He'd been unable to shake off the image of the website which Reda had tried to conceal when he'd initially walked in. There was something familiar about it that was bothering him. He waited, pretending to have trouble pocketing his tickets and extracting his wallet, then took out a couple of high-value notes.

"Here, take these."

Reda inspected them and made a quick mental calculation.

"I don't think I can cover that – I'll need to go and find some change. Do you mind waiting for a moment?"

"Not at all."

The young man rose and made off in the direction of the purser's office.

"I won't be long."

Long enough thought Blake. He waited until the lounge door had closed behind the Egyptian and then looked round the room. It was now completely empty. If he moved quickly, he would just have time...

The laptop lay, lid down, on the coffee table in front of him. He checked around once more, then raised the lid and pressed the power-on button. The blank grey screen flashed into life and after a few agonising seconds the website reappeared. It was exactly as he'd suspected.

The webpage Reda had been perusing was one he'd been looking at it himself not a few months before. All the same, he'd wanted to make sure. Attached somewhere close by there would be an email account and a host of private messages. But there was no time to go into that and anyway, his intention was only to confirm what had already been revealed – he had no licence to pry further. He reclosed the lid and sat with his hands clasped together, breathing deeply.

He was too long in the tooth to register a sense of shock – it was more like disappointment. Ever since he'd first encountered Reda in the quayside car park concerning the matter of Joan's jewellery box, the young man had presented a practised and solid appearance. Now a shadow had been cast over him that seemed strangely out of place.

A noise in the corridor alerted him. He assumed a schoolboy air of innocence and affected a bored look, as if he'd grown tired of waiting.

Reda returned, one hand clutching a sheaf of notes.

"I'm sorry, Mr Blake, but this is the best I can do."

"That's fine."

Blake accepted the offering and packed his wallet. All he wanted to do now was retreat and give himself time to think.

"Well, enjoy your trip."

"I'll do my best."

Then, as if it were for his benefit alone – perhaps because Blake lived in the country and understood, or even as some kind of test – Reda made an addition in Arabic.

"*Allah go with you, Mr Blake.*"

"*And with you,*" was Blake's automatic reply.

He headed for the door and the light of the outside world. In the dim and artificial surroundings of the Forward Lounge, something had fundamentally changed and for the moment he wanted to be away from it. For all his poise and professional bearing, Reda was not all that he seemed and Blake could not see him in the same way again. But as he was continually fond of telling himself, Egypt was a land full of surprises.

Chapter Ten

Blake returned to his cabin and sat on the end of the bed. It was heading towards the middle of the afternoon and a quiet calm had descended over the ship. Those passengers who remained on deck were forced to seek the shade while the rest had already retreated to their rooms and the comfort of a peaceful nap. Unlike the previous afternoon, Blake was determined to stay awake, and rather than slump into the chair overlooking the mesmeric flow of the river and risk dozing off, he elected to perch somewhere deliberately less comfortable where he could take stock and give himself time to review the situation.

Despite his interest in the politics of Egypt and his years of extensive research, Blake was quick to acknowledge that he knew little of al-Wasat al-Jadid. Its founder, Abou Elela Mady, had once been a member of the Muslim Brotherhood but had thought their political convictions too narrow and in 1996 had broken away to form his own party. They professed to be moderates and had sought to create a tolerant Islamic movement but its attempts to register as an official party had been rejected a number of times. Under the current emergency laws, they were still a banned organisation and had been brought before a military court on the charge of setting up a party as an Islamist front. To be identified as a member would be to lay yourself open to the risk of imprisonment and possible torture. Why then was Reda so interested in their website, and how deep was his involvement?

In the six or so weeks since his departure from the Embassy, and more particularly in the few days since he had been away from his base in Cairo, Blake had begun to forget what it was like to be at work. The prolonged absence was steadily etching away his memory. What on earth had he found to do all day in that drab and dreary office? How had he managed to fill his working hours? More especially, how would he have reacted to the current situation and what would he have done about it? Had he been in

Chancery he would probably have filed a report, but from his distant position in the Trade Section his only option would have been yet another memo to the First Secretary. *Certain political elements are active in the area south of Luxor...* And after expending considerable time and effort in setting out his views, he would no doubt have received the usual perfunctory reply. *Thank you for this valuable information which I have now passed on to the relevant area.* Then he would have heard nothing. What good had it ever done? Although in the mundane atmosphere of the Embassy, it had always been enough to make life bearable.

But as he kept reminding himself, he was no longer a member of the Service so he could hardly write a memo now. And as he'd quickly discovered, it was a radically different proposition to be confronted with affairs in the field rather than viewing them from the safety of the Embassy. If he was to solve his conundrum over Reda, an alternative approach would be required. He needed more information, he needed to talk to someone, someone who knew what was going on, someone who had their finger on the pulse.

A name immediately sprang to mind and he decided to give Carpenter a call. Carpenter – steady, reliable, British to the core and whose sole purpose in life seemed to be to gaze out of a window and watch the world go by.

The ship's phone sat on the bedside table in front of him. Blake wondered whether it was purely internal or whether it would have an outside line – and even if it did, he preferred not to risk being overheard. He took his mobile out of the drawer and turned it on, praying for a signal. Fortunately he was able to find an immediate connection, and after the inevitable round of buzzing and clicking, Carpenter's languid tones came on the line.

"Hello? Trade Section? Can I help you?"

"Carpenter? Is that you? It's Blake."

Even after just a few days away, it was a relief to hear a

familiar voice and to know his old world was still there.

"Good Lord! Aren't you supposed to be on holiday somewhere? I thought you'd be halfway up the Nile by now."

"I am."

"Good for you! I trust you're having a good time, you lucky bugger. I have visions of you lounging on a sumptuous barge, propped up by acres of cushions and being fanned by a cohort of dusky maidens."

"Not quite – it's just an ordinary cruise ship."

"Ah well, one can always live in hope. Anyway, how's the bird-watching going? Seen any of those dickney whatsits you were telling me about?"

"You mean Senegal Thick-knee. No, I haven't – but the birding's fine, thank you." Actually it wasn't, but he decided not to elaborate. "Look, something's come up and I need to ask you a favour."

"Fire away, old boy. You know me, always happy to help."

Exactly, which was why Blake had decided to call.

"I can't go into the details right now, it's a complicated story, but I need some background information on someone. Do we still have access to the Egyptian Police computer records?"

"I think so – such as they are. Subject to the usual bribe, of course."

"Of course. But don't worry about that, I'll sort it out with you when I get back. So if I were to give you a name, do you think you could see what they've got?"

"I don't see why not. Anything for a friend."

"Thanks."

So far so good. Blake cleared his throat in preparation for what was to come next. He knew he was pushing it a bit but it was always worth a try.

"And you might as well have a look at our own files while you're about it."

"Hmm..."

Carpenter baulked a little. Egyptian Police records were one thing – British Embassy files were quite another.

"That's a bit more tricky – but I'll see what I can do. Do you want to give me the details?"

Blake extracted Reda's business card from his wallet and held it out beneath the light of the bedside lamp.

"Here you go. The name is Reda Eldasouky. I'll spell that for you." He slowly read out the letters. However helpful he might sound, Carpenter was not renowned for the accuracy of his work. "He's probably registered in the Cairo area so it shouldn't be too difficult."

"Ok, I've got it – Reda Eldasouky. Is it anyone I should recognise?"

"Not as far as I'm aware. That's the point – I need to find out."

"Alright. So what's the timescale on this?"

"Well, as soon as you can really."

Blake was anxious to come to a conclusion for a number of reasons, not least of which was the safety of the passengers and the crew. If Reda had 'history' of any kind, he would want to know about it as soon as he could.

"Right. Well, as you can imagine, there's not a lot going on here at the moment so I'll get cracking on it straight away. I tell you what – why don't you call me back at home this evening? You've got my number. Probably better than ringing the Embassy again."

"Thanks, I'd appreciate it. Anything else to report?"

"Well, now that you've asked..."

Carpenter launched into a long and protracted description of the latest game of cricket being played in Australia. If Blake's 'passion' was birding, then Carpenter's was definitely cricket. On match days he would bring his radio into the office and give a running commentary on the score. He seemed to get more calls on the subject than he did about work. Why he thought Blake would be interested was a mystery, but still. After two or three minutes he rounded off his talk and finished with an incidental piece of news just as though it were of no consequence at all.

"...but I'd much rather have the Ashes, thank you very much, and at least they're in the bag. Oh, and by the way, speaking of ashes, some silly sod set himself on fire in front of the Parliament building the other day."

"Yes, I saw that." It had been headline news a day or so before Blake had left for his trip but he'd yet to catch up with the details. "What was that all about?"

"God knows. The usual, I expect – dissent amongst the masses and so on. Nobody thinks it's going to come to anything anyway. Other than that it's been as dull as ditchwater, I'm afraid."

"Ok. Well, I'll call you back later on this evening then."

"Yes, do that. Meanwhile, I'll leave you to your band of dusky maidens."

"I wish..."

A picture came into Blake's mind, but it was not the lithe athletic figure of Lee Yong that lay next to him on his imaginary barge but the plump and shapeless form of Mrs Biltmore. He shuddered and moved quickly on.

"Thanks, Alan. I'll speak to you later. Bye..."

"Bye..."

He shut off his phone and returned it to the drawer of the bedside table.

Earlier on, in order to make himself heard, he'd turned off the noisy hum of the air-conditioning and the room had grown warm and drowsy. He let out a yawn and consulted his watch. Three o'clock. He wondered whether it was worthwhile going back on deck. There would be nothing to see in the way of birds – at this time of day they would all be resting out of the sun, just like the passengers. He decided he could afford to join them and lay back on the bed with his eyes closed.

Carpenter would take care of things now, Carpenter could be trusted. What harm could there be if he dropped off for an hour?

At least there was no gala dinner he had to look out for.

This time it was the need to visit the bathroom that roused him. He made himself comfortable, then returned to the bedside clock to find out the time. It was now ten to five and he'd been 'out of it' for an hour and a half. He'd hardly been away from home for more than a few days and he was already sleeping in the afternoons. Was it wasted time? Or simply that his old and weary body was trying to tell him something?

He went up on deck and realised he'd missed afternoon tea. The weather had changed too. The sun had dipped behind a rare bank of cloud and a light breeze had sprung up, ruffling the sculptured edges of the parasols on the sun-deck. Here and there, scattered on the tables, discarded plates lay empty and on the serving stand at the ship's rail, the tea urns had been all but cleared away. If he was lucky he might find a half-empty, lukewarm pot... One day, he thought, he would learn to get his timing right.

He wondered how long he should leave it before he called Carpenter back. Was it best after dinner or before? If he'd found something out, there was no point in waiting until after, it might as well be before. He would probably get home around six – give him half an hour to get changed and pour himself a whisky...

Blake resolved to go back to his cabin and write up his notes while he waited. He'd still not finished what he'd begun at the breakfast table that morning. Apart from the name of Lee Yong (which he had attempted to scratch through) his bird list consisted of a few commonplace entries plus the Spur-winged Plover he'd found at the Colossi of Memnon – but he could not for the life of him recall what had come next. With all the distractions, he'd failed to keep up to date and he was now thirty-six hours behind. How could he be expected to remember it all?

He forced himself to think. After the Colossi, they'd gone to Queen Hatshepsut's Temple. That's where he'd seen the unidentified lark – but he could hardly record that. Then it was the Valley of the Kings – but that had been a blank. And as for today, other than Pied Kingfisher, nothing, not even a sniff. Two days of his holiday gone already and hardly any birding done. What on earth had he been doing? Making a fool of himself over Lee Yong, worrying about Reda...

At twenty past six he washed and changed so as to be ready for dinner. Then, on the dot of half past, he turned on his mobile.

The phone seemed to ring for ages before Carpenter finally answered. He sounded out of breath and uncharacteristically under pressure. Perhaps things were different at home than they were in the office.

"Sorry, old boy, I've only just got in. Would you believe it but the blighters have had me working late for once. Can you hang on a minute."

"Of course..."

There was a dull thud at the other end of the line as the receiver went down and then the solid clunk of ice cubes falling into a glass. A minute or two later, Carpenter returned to the phone, evidently refreshed.

"Ah... That's better. Now where had we got to?"

Blake took a deep breath and attempted to remain patient. As yet, they hadn't got anywhere.

"Reda Eldasouky – you were going to have a look at the police records."

"So I was... Well, I hate to disappoint you but there's not an awful lot to tell. I don't know what you were expecting but he's hardly Jack the Lad, you know, your boy. Both the police and State Security have got a file but there's next to nothing on it – certainly no convictions, although they've pulled him in for questioning a couple of times. They suspect he's a member of this April 6th Youth thing, but that's about all."

Blake sniffed. He was sure Reda did have convictions – although it looked as though they were of the political rather than the criminal kind. As for the April 6th Youth Movement, that came as no surprise. Almost every young person in Egypt under the age of thirty was either in it, or suspected of being in it, especially if they showed any signs of an educated mind – but that in itself would hardly warrant a police record. So if they'd pulled him in for questioning, it must be for something else...

"So let me get this straight – he's on their radar, but we don't know why?"

"Ah!" Carpenter's interjection promised a glimmer of hope. "I think I may have the answer to that."

"Go on."

"Well, I managed to get a peek at our files as you suggested."

"Tell me." If there was a price to pay, another bribe, then Blake was only too willing if it meant he could get to the bottom of it. "So what did you find out?"

"As far as Reda is concerned, nothing, we don't have a file. But here's the thing – we do for his father."

"Really?"

"Oh yes. Apparently, Ahmed Eldasouky was a founder member of..."

Carpenter halted as he focused on pronouncing what was in front of him. At the risk of stealing his thunder, Blake beat him to it.

"Let me guess. Al-Wasat Al-Jadid."

"Spot on, old boy! How on earth did you know that?"

"Let's just say it was an educated guess."

"Well it obviously means something to you. Damned if it does to me. And I'm afraid I didn't have the time to look it up."

A little more information would have been helpful, but Blake already knew enough to put two and two together. If the son was anything like the father, no wonder the authorities wanted to keep an eye on Reda.

But Carpenter had more up his sleeve.

"There's something else. Ahmed Eldasouky was arrested in

January 2001 and imprisoned in Al-Fayoum. No trial, of course, and there were accusations of torture. He died there in 2006."

Blake whistled through his teeth. The infamous Al-Fayoum... A favourite of State Security Intelligence, it was a notorious place of confinement for dissidents and political detainees. The rumour was that once you went in, you never came out.

"That explains a lot."

"I thought it might. Well I don't know what you're up to old boy, but I wish you the best of luck with it. It sounds awfully James Bond to me. You're not in any sort of trouble, are you?"

"I hope not, Alan, I hope not." It wasn't often they used Christian names but on this occasion it somehow seemed appropriate. "Look, I'm eternally grateful. If it's alright with you, I'll sort the bribe out when I get back. How much was it, by the way?"

"Don't worry about it old boy, glad to be of assistance. Just save me one or two of those dusky maidens. Although on second thoughts, a couple of bottles of Scotch might be a better plan..."

Blake made a promise to provide them on his return. The information he'd gained from Carpenter had been worthwhile and if asked, he'd have been prepared to give more. They ended the call with a mutual agreement to keep in touch and to speak again soon.

Blake turned off his mobile phone and consulted the bedside clock. Having missed tea, his stomach was reminding him it was way past time he should eat. He stood up in front of the mirror, straightened his linen jacket and tugged at the cuffs of his shirt.

Down in the dining room the early entrants would be filing in and taking their places, filling the empty space with their vacuous chatter. Someone would say how hot it had been, someone else would say they'd felt cold. Someone would say that they'd finished their book, someone else would say that they'd not. On his own table, it would not be long before Mrs Biltmore set off on another inane story like that of the stolen handbag or the worth of Johns Hopkins and they would all be obliged to sit in respectful silence while she rambled on. And outside the narrow porthole, the Nile would flow relentlessly by, flat and brown and seemingly never-ending.

But meanwhile, somewhere deep in the bowels of the ship, hunched up in one of the cramped cabins that belonged to the crew, a young man was lying on his bunk, thinking of his country, his father and dreaming of revolution.

Blake took a last look at himself in the mirror and as his groaning stomach let out one more rumble of complaint, he set off for dinner in a pensive mood.

Later that night, after they'd finished their evening meal and it had grown dark, the curtains in the dining room were dramatically pulled back to reveal a spectacular sight. Across the river on the far bank, the luxurious vegetation had given way to desert and a huge hill of sand rose up before them. Eerily lit by banks of arc lights, this was the Tombs of the Nobles, the entrances to which could clearly be seen. Mr Mohammed, the boat captain, had come good on his promise and they had reached Aswan a day earlier than planned.

It was a fact which Blake was to find significant.

Chapter Eleven

Blake anxiously paced the quayside, deep in contemplation. It was almost 8am, his boat would soon be ready to leave and the eagerly awaited birding tour he'd signed up for the previous day would shortly begin.

He'd been awake since before dawn, going straight up to the top deck in time to watch the sunrise. A huge red ball, it had appeared in the sky to the east, floating effortlessly upwards like a balloon above the skyline of the city. It was a spectacle he'd missed the day before – together with the flock of Glossy Ibis that David had captured on his mobile phone – and he was determined not to lose out again. The sunrise was certain, but the Ibis were not and he realised he would have to wait for another occasion. Behind him, on the opposite bank, the sun struck the hill of sand full on, igniting the Tombs of the Nobles with a dull orange glow.

After scanning the surroundings, he went straight down to breakfast where he ate alone, finishing before anyone else arrived. Then, having returned to his cabin to gather his things, he'd gone directly out onto the quayside rather than wait in reception. As a result, he was the first to arrive at the appointed spot and now had fifteen minutes to himself in which he could indulge his thoughts.

Left alone and with time to kill outdoors, his normal practice would be to look for birds. Today there were gulls, wheeling and screeching over the end of the wharf, but other than a cursory glance to establish their species (common Black-headed, he decided) he took no further interest. Ever since the conversation with his former colleague the previous afternoon, he'd been unable to shake off his thoughts about Reda. Yesterday morning it had been Lee Yong who'd preoccupied him – today it was the young Egyptian.

I don't know what you're up to, old boy, but I wish you the best of luck with it.

Those had been Carpenter's precise words. And what exactly *was* he up to? He didn't know the answer to that himself, let alone be able to explain it to anyone else.

He had a naturally inquisitive nature (you couldn't watch birds if you didn't) which partly explained his curiosity regarding Reda – but there was far more to it than that. As respectable as the young man appeared, Blake had to admit he was concerned – for himself, for his fellow travellers and the more he thought about it, especially for Lee Yong. He wondered whether they were under threat. What if Reda was a terrorist? The possibility worried him. The boy was both a Muslim and a political activist – and according to popular Western belief, such people were supposed to preach jihad and the destruction of the Infidel. What better way was there to attack the symbols of Western materialism than to blow apart a cruise ship on the Nile? It wouldn't take much, just a few pounds of explosives left in a backpack in reception – it was a chilling thought.

He'd known for some while that something was stirring in the hearts of many North Africans. He'd sensed it amongst the people in the markets of Dokki, seen it for himself in Alexandria and then had come the uprising in Tunisia. Like a boil that had festered for too long beneath the surface of the skin, it had suddenly burst open and violently erupted. Had Reda been infected by it too?

But all this was unsubstantiated nonsense – he didn't have a shred of proof. Just because a young man took an interest in politics and was a member of a banned organisation, it didn't mean to say he practised violence. In fact, the public proclamations of the party he'd joined suggested precisely the opposite. Blake realised he was in danger of falling into the same trap as he'd accused his travelling companions of doing – they'd made unwarranted assumptions and he'd chided them for it. *You can't trust the Arabs, they're a dodgy lot.* To presume anything about the Egyptian people, or Muslims in general, invariable proved false. He'd said as much in his memo to the First Secretary.

You seem to think that the Brotherhood's aim is to establish an Islamic state by violent means. They've realised that won't work. The Egyptians don't want a religiously run Republic – they want freedom. And they know it will only come about through democracy and not violence.

That, at least, was the theory. It had looked all very well on paper, sitting in the sterile surroundings of a comfortable office. Now he was faced with the practice out in the field, he couldn't help thinking things were different.

His train of thought was interrupted by a disturbance further along the quay. A small group of passengers had gathered some twenty yards further up next to a gangplank. From the direction of the town, an Egyptian boatman appeared carrying a large can of petrol. Wearing a dirty white cap, he was middle-aged and portly and the swathe of grey stubble on his chin merely strengthened the impression that he had only recently got out of bed. His dishevelled look did not inspire confidence and his arrival provoked a babble of conversation amongst the would-be trippers.

Blake caught sight of Janet and Keith in the queue, but he was not in the mood for conversation. A movement on one of the mudflats across the river temporarily caught his eye and forcing a weak smile, he retreated behind the safety of his binoculars. Meanwhile, the slovenly boatman had opened up his can and began pouring petrol.

The boat in which they were due to depart lay at the foot of the gangplank. It was a motor launch about twenty feet in length, the hull painted white with red markings, and it had clearly been built for sightseeing as it was covered by a canopy stretching from bow to stern to shade the occupants. The sight of it confirmed what Blake had already thought – he was not going to take his telescope. The boat was not a steady enough platform and if the guide that Reda had promised him was worth his salt, he would surely bring one of his own.

Eventually, after what seemed like an age during which the boatman uncoiled and recoiled several strands of rope, removed his cap, scratched the back of his head and tried to start the motor several times, the engine coughed and spluttered into reluctant life, their guide joined them and their journey began.

In the years to come, Blake would often wonder what it was that had made that day so special. He'd watched birds from a boat before – but it had never been quite like this. Then, it had been at sea and his experience had been confined to being tossed up and down in a rough swell, barely able to hold himself steady – never mind his binoculars – but now he was standing solidly on a deck that hardly seemed to move as the hull of the boat skimmed lightly across the surface of the water.

It grew warm as the sun rose ever higher in the sky, but it was pleasant in the shade of the canvas awning and the cool breeze that came with their forward motion. Behind him, the quiet chatter of the passengers blended with the thrum of the engine and before long, he had even forgiven the boatman his unprepossessing appearance. This in itself might have been enough to make it enjoyable. But then there were the birds – the fabulous, fabulous birds…

The guide had not in fact brought a telescope – but he was blessed with exceptional eyesight and as they neared the mudflats, the birds had come in so close that even Blake had no need of his bins. And it soon became apparent that the young man's depth of knowledge was outstanding.

"The smallest birds are Little Stint, the next in size are Ruff. The largest are Godwit, Bar-tailed I would say by the shape of the bill."

Of course they were – and now he came to mention it, Blake

remembered the details from his handbook.

"And over here," continued the guide, indicating to his left, "we have Black-winged Stilt."

Black-winged Stilt! Blake's head swivelled round to look. This was a bird he'd never seen, but he soon found it parading about on a sandbank. It was easily distinguishable, its improbably long pink legs supporting a black and white body and head with thin black bill. Its features seemed rather extreme, and yet there was an elegance about its appearance you could not deny.

On the other side of the boat, Janet and Keith had contrived to look in a different direction and with no Miss Malaysia to monitor his every move, he could indulge himself with a schoolboy-like enthusiasm. Black-winged Stilt – a first, a lifer, and all within a few minutes of setting off! Suddenly, things were looking up – now he truly was 'in amongst the birds'.

There had been times when he thought he would never get there – the first few days had been slow and there'd been constant diversions. But he'd been patient, he'd waited and now he was being rewarded. Birds were appearing by the dozen and from that moment on, thanks to the intervention of the guide, there was simply no looking back. And with these delights to distract him, it was not long before he had forgotten all about Reda and Carpenter and the Embassy and the Brotherhood and was off in a world of his own.

They moved further on upriver. Here the character of the Nile changed dramatically. It ceased to be the wide and comforting expanse of water that had carried them up from Luxor and turned into a series of deep and fast-flowing channels, wending their way between the massive rocks and islands leading up to the First Cataract. This might have been of some concern had it not been for the skill of the boatman who, despite his dirty clothes and unkempt stubble, steered a steady course. And there was always the continual distraction of wildlife.

On the opposite bank, herds of camel and water buffalo

meandered along the sands. While they were busy watching, a cry went up of *Look out!* as a cream-crowned Marsh Harrier broke cover from a nearby tree and sailed directly over their heads, looking for prey. Beneath it, poking its head out from the bushes on the rocky shoreline, someone spotted a mongoose. But even then they were not quite done. When the boat turned northwards and headed back down the eastern channel and past the Old Cataract Hotel, they found the way guarded by an Osprey sitting on a pole. As they passed, it lifted lazily from its perch and flapped its way downriver, leading them home.

They arrived back at the ship feeling rather jaded. If anything, it had all been too much – the weather, the boat trip, the birds...

Blake went straight to his room and made himself a cup of coffee. But instead of staying inside, he gathered his notebook and pen and took his drink up onto the sun-deck. His party had been the first to return and with the others still out on their tours, he could look forward to an hour's peace and quiet to write up his notes.

After a while he found himself falling back into the same train of thought that had engaged him on the quayside before setting off that morning. And the more he dwelled on it, the more he began to worry. Where was Lee Yong? She had not been at breakfast – had she joined David and Joan on their shopping trip, or had she gone out somewhere else?

A casual enquiry at reception revealed that she had taken the coach outing to Kalabsha and would not be back until late that afternoon. And where was the young Egyptian? Had he gone to Kalabsha too?

Suddenly he panicked and felt overwhelmed with an irrational desire to know – but rather than go back to reception he decided to walk the ship to look for him. He took a twenty-minute tour, checking out the sun-deck, the Forward Lounge and all the public areas. But despite exploring every nook and cranny, all he could find was a recumbent Mrs Biltmore, sprawled out on a sun-lounger, the paperback she'd evidently been reading now covering her face as she snoozed. Nearby, Ira paced the deck like a restless teenage boy.

But there was no sign of Reda, and when he'd exhausted all the possibilities Blake began to feel foolish and ashamed. What did he think he was doing?

Rather than hang about waiting, he decided to take an early lunch and afterwards sloped back to his cabin and resorted to compiling his notebook before lying down on the bed for an hour's rest. After the excitement of that morning's adventures, there seemed little point in exerting himself. But unlike the previous two days, when he'd fallen asleep and had missed important occasions, he was determined to stay awake and deliberately lay listening to the sounds of the ship. Somewhere towards the stern, probably in the engine room, a metallic clanging reverberated repeatedly, and through what must have been an open porthole he could hear the shouts and laughter of the kitchen staff preparing dinner. The same voice that had filled the dining room before breakfast was easily recognisable – someone, at least, was happy in their work. He vaguely recalled the tune – was it a traditional Egyptian song? Or some Western dirge delivered in a Middle Eastern style? It was hard to tell but whichever it was, it was certainly soporific and soon he found himself drifting...

He was woken by a repeated knocking on his door. Thinking the worst, he hurried to open it, rubbing the sleep from his eyes.

Keith stood in the corridor, hands in pockets, looking relaxed.

"Sorry – did I disturb you?"

"Not really..."

"Have you done anything about tonight?"

"Tonight? What about tonight?"

Still half asleep, Blake felt rather fuddled. Had he missed

something?

"You know, the Egyptian Evening?"

With the events of the morning having taken precedence, Blake had forgotten all about it but he vaguely recalled seeing something in his itinerary.

"Ah yes..."

"Well we're supposed to be in fancy dress so we're going to need to get kitted up. We've organised a trip into town. Reda says he knows a place along the Corniche."

I'll bet he does, thought Blake.

"Anyway, you're welcome to join us. We're meeting in the foyer in ten minutes."

"Thanks..."

He repaired to the bathroom, splashed some cold water on his face and hurriedly got changed.

A few minutes later he found himself downstairs, waiting with the others.

He was relieved to see that Lee Yong was already there, standing by the doorway in her now familiar outfit of Cuban heels, jeans and rock-band T-shirt. She caught his eye and came across to speak.

"Ah, Mr Blake. So, how were your birds?"

"Very good, thank you. And how was your temple?"

Funny how he could always manage more for her than he could for Keith.

"Also good. When we have time, I will tell you about it – perhaps over dinner. But now..."

She looked around her, as if she were searching for someone. Behind her, in the foyer, the others had been steadily assembling and they shuffled out as a group onto the sun-drenched Corniche.

Reda himself had arrived and was busy negotiating with the gaudily dressed owner of a fleet of horse-drawn caleches. A row of carriages and their emaciated ponies were waiting. There was the usual flurry of guttural Arabic voices, then the flash of white teeth and a handshake.

"This way," announced the young Egyptian. "Special price..."

Suitably encouraged, they clambered into their assigned transport.

Much to his annoyance, there was a mix-up in the seating plans and Blake found himself sharing with Mrs Biltmore and Ira. His intention had been to find a place next to Lee Yong, but she had been summarily whisked away elsewhere. The caleche was designed for two passengers but presumably as part of his deal, Reda had arranged for a third. It was a tight squeeze – but Ira was not one to complain, and at present neither was Blake. As for Mrs Biltmore, he assumed that she'd no space to breathe as she remained curiously quiet.

Up in front, after a moment's wait the cabby clicked his tongue, slapped the horse's reins and they trit-trotted off in silence.

Chapter Twelve

Tonight at 8.30...

Blake studied the notice board closely and wrinkled his brow. Somewhere there should be some instructions... And if he was lucky, he'd find the excuse he was so desperately seeking to enable him to go back to his room and get changed.

He felt acutely self-conscious and had done so from the moment he'd left his cabin a few minutes earlier. Fancy dress was not his forte and the idea that he should put on a peculiar set of clothing and parade himself in front of the ship's company in a vain attempt to look like someone he was not was alien to his nature. He had enough trouble being himself, never mind anyone else.

It was not a disguise in which he could readily hide himself. On the contrary, it made him aware of his own existence to a highly unnatural degree – and it struck him that if he could see through it himself, then surely so must others. Even the requirement to wear dinner dress at Embassy functions had made him uncomfortable. He'd hated those false and pretentious affairs and had borne them out of necessity rather than any feeling of pride. But he'd realised that other than retreat to the sanctity of his own quarters and hide way, there was little he could do about it. And tonight, having scanned the board from top to bottom, he'd failed to find anything of help and had concluded there was no other option – if he was to survive the evening, he would have to grin and bear it.

He was beginning to wonder how he might cope when he was interrupted by a voice from behind.

"Very nice..."

"I beg your pardon?"

"Your costume – I said it's very nice."

He turned and found himself face to face with David – although for a split second he failed to recognise him as his head and the lower half of his face were obscured by the folds of a giant white turban.

"Oh, yes, thank you. I'm sorry. I was miles away. Looking at the notice board."

"The Egyptian Evening?"

"Yes."

"Half past eight in the Forward Lounge."

"So I see."

"You're going?"

"I think so…"

Of course he was going – why else would he have got all dressed up? Although, his outfit was far plainer than David's and he was starting to feel drab by comparison – perhaps he really could avoid detection.

Together with the others, he'd spent the afternoon in the shop along the Corniche, choosing what they were going to wear that evening. He'd never been one for gaudy clothes and had gone for a simple galabeya and a Nubian cap. 'Traditional', Reda had called it. When he'd tried it on and stood in front of the mirror, he'd felt more like a peasant than a Pharaoh. But it suited him nevertheless.

Conversely, David had really gone to town. As well as the turban he wore a silk shirt and baggy trousers, fastened at the calves and bound together at the waist with a broad sash into which was tucked the curve of a vicious-looking dagger. His feet sported a pair of pointed sandals of the type that curled up at the ends. His get-up was certainly impressive – although it was anything but Egyptian. In fact, you'd think he'd stepped straight out of *The Arabian Nights*.

"You're looking rather splendid."

Blake returned the compliment of earlier.

"One has to keep up appearances," said David. "Actually, it was the only outfit they had which covered up the hair and the moustache. Never seen an Egyptian with a silver moustache and

I was damned if I was going to shave it off. Anyway, if you think this is exotic," he pulled at the hem of his robe, "you should see what Joan's wearing."

"Really?"

"Oh yes, she's gone completely over the top. As far as Joan's concerned, there's only ever been one Egyptian woman and that's Cleopatra. So she's gone and got herself a full-length gown, Pharaonic headdress and jewellery to match. She's upstairs now, finishing off her make-up and nails. When she comes down, it wouldn't surprise me if she's found a couple of hand maidens to carry her train. I should have known better than to let her loose in that shop – it's cost me a bloody fortune. She wanted me to dress up as Julius Caesar but thankfully they didn't have any Roman costumes – not the done thing, apparently."

No, thought Blake, in Egypt it was probably not.

"Anyway, she'll be down any minute so I'd better cut along or I'll get it in the neck. See you up there."

He shot off toward the stairway.

Blake glanced at his watch. Twenty past eight. Still time to visit the gents and make himself comfortable. A thought crossed his mind and he slipped the watch off his wrist and dropped it into the small carry-case he was holding. Despite the paucity of his clothing, he might as well try and look as authentic as possible.

At 8.30pm he found himself standing in the queue in front of the Forward Lounge, waiting for the doors to open. There was a crush in the narrow corridor outside and he had inadvertently become wedged between a bare-chested Nubian slave and what appeared to be a High Altar Priest. With their extravagant costumes and make-up, they could have been auditioning for a West End musical. He no longer felt so out of place as now, everyone looked ridiculous.

The doors swung open and the crowd surged forward. Blake

followed unhurriedly behind, anxious to avoid any unseemly rush, although there were plenty of tables to be had and he soon found one in a good position overlooking the dance floor. A babble of conversation filled the room but when it had died down, he realised there was background music as a famous female Egyptian singer began trilling like a nightingale.

Looking around, the Forward Lounge had been changed yet again. The dance floor in the centre had been cleared and there was some coloured lighting of a sort. In one corner, next to the bar, a small band of musicians had assembled and after about ten minutes, as the voice of the famous singer faded, the band leader gave a nod and they struck up a lively and typically Middle Eastern tune.

At this point the doors at the far end were flung open and Joan made her grand entrance. Dressed in full royal regalia, the would-be Cleopatra appeared to the oddly rhythmic strains of the modest Egyptian four-piece, and although something altogether more grandiose such as the Arrival of the Queen of Sheba might have been more appropriate, the overall effect was dramatic enough. She strode imperiously into the room, ably supported by Keith who looked equally as impressive in a long dark-blue robe edged with gold trim, his height and craggy looks enabling him to carry off a suitably aristocratic bearing.

They were followed by two characters in white – David the desert sheikh and Janet, whose veiled headdress, bodice, bare midriff and long pantaloons made her look as if she were a member of his harem. Given the theatrical nature of all four's appearance, the crowd let out a prolonged "ooh!" and broke into a spontaneous round of applause.

The group approached Blake's table and sat down. Any pretence at grandeur was immediately undermined as David tore off his turban and threw it onto the couch in a fit of pique. Whatever intention he may have had of disguising his hair and moustache had obviously been abandoned.

"Thank God that's over – have you any idea how hot it is in this thing?"

"I wish you'd stop making a fuss," scolded Joan. "You've done nothing but complain ever since you put the damn thing on. I don't know why you bothered."

"Because you told me I had to, that's why. I seem to remember you saying that you were damned if you were going to the trouble of dressing up as the Queen of Egypt if I was going to saunter around in what looked like a set of 18th-century night clothes."

"Well you weren't making any effort, David."

"Effort? You're accusing me of not making any effort? May I remind you..."

But whatever David was going to remind her of had evidently eluded him as he threw up his hands in a gesture of mock despair.

"Oh, somebody get me a gin and tonic for Christ's sake before I explode."

The row which must have started in their cabin had followed them downstairs and into the public domain, and he'd clearly determined to put an end to it before it became too much of an embarrassment. But Joan was not in a forgiving mood.

"You're not allowed to drink," she retorted. "You're supposed to be a Muslim, remember? Muslim's don't drink – I told you that earlier."

"I hardly think you're in a position to tell me about the practices of Muslims. I'm the one that used to live in the country, if you recall. Anyway, you can't hold me to it – and if you so much as even try, I'm renouncing my religion," said David, trying to make a joke of it. "Bugger it, I'm parched."

Then, as if to add insult to injury, Joan came back at him again. "Mine's a white wine by the way, if anybody's buying."

"I'll get them." Blake decided to intercede. Their bickering had begun to annoy him and if his offer to buy drinks failed to stem it, then he could at least spend a few moments away from them at the bar. But their party was not yet complete and he hesitated. "Do you think I should wait for Mrs Biltmore and Ira?" he asked.

Keith shook his head.

"I wouldn't bother if I were you. I don't honestly know if they're coming. It's probably not their sort of thing."

Although the words were hardly out of his mouth when they appeared.

They were never going to upstage Joan but their entrance did not lack an element of drama. And if David and Janet, the sheikh and his paramour, were figures in an Arabian tableau then Mrs Biltmore was destined to play the part of the tent. Unable to find anything that would fit, she had been persuaded to wear a burka of voluminous proportions. The benefit was that it covered literally everything, and rather than stride in like Joan, she rolled along like a galleon in full sail, the folds of her outfit billowing about her like the sea itself. Somewhere in her wake, it was as much as Ira could do to prevent himself from drowning in the excess of fabric.

Blake took the orders and joined the queue at the bar. He returned with a tray of drinks to find that the advent of the new arrivals had not succeeded in putting a stop to the ongoing spat.

Joan was on the point of lighting a cigarette. David, who had slumped into a position of feigned exhaustion on the couch, interpreted this as a provocative act and immediately objected.

"If you're going to do that, then I shall have to go and sit somewhere else."

He roused himself and stomped off to the other end of the table, presumably in retaliation for the earlier remark about Muslims.

But Joan was not to be put off that easily.

"Oh for God's sake, David, don't be so stupid. You're just like a child sometimes."

And she continued to light up, exhaling smoke in what looked like a deliberately exaggerated manner.

Blake set down his tray and handed out the drinks. There was an embarrassed silence around the table and not even the incongruous sight of Queen Cleopatra with a cigarette dangling from her lips could detract from the tension.

Fortunately, it didn't last long. After a few frosty moments the band came to a halt and everyone's attention was drawn to the stage as the boat captain, Mr Mohammed, stepped forward.

"Good evening, ladies and gentlemen, and welcome to our traditional Egyptian event. We have much entertainment for you this evening. But before we begin, let me introduce you to our band." He indicated the group of musicians in the corner, then named them one by one. "And now for our floor show…"

He was about to announce the first act of the night when the band burst back into life somewhat earlier than expected. Unable to compete, Mr Mohammed smiled unctuously and retreated to one side. His moment of glory had passed.

The lights dimmed as two shadowy figures crept onto the dance floor, but then went up again to reveal – another pair of whirling dervishes. Blake tried to compare their act to the one he had seen on the night of their arrival, but could detect no difference. For all he knew, they might be the same artistes.

Keith seemed impressed and cried out, "Bravo!"

"Shh!" scolded Janet, mildly embarrassed at his outburst.

The act ended to enthusiastic applause and Blake expected Mr Mohammed to reappear but the following turn introduced itself. Or rather, herself, as no sooner had the whirling dervishes departed than a woman dressed as a belly-dancer ran in from the wings and out onto the centre of the dance floor. Her costume consisted of the traditional skirt and decorated top but she had added a set of finger cymbals and a veil to enhance her sense of mystique. She would have liked to have called herself young, but unfortunately she was not and the years had added an extra layer of flesh to the areas that mattered most. It was a feature which David clearly found attractive as he immediately sat up and began to take notice.

The band set off with a different rhythm and the dancer followed suit, jerking her hips to the music and undulating her ample belly. Excess folds of flesh wobbled enticingly. Sweat began to glisten.

"Now that's what I call a woman," said David, downing the last of his gin and tonic as if trying to cool himself off.

Joan, who was appreciably slimmer by comparison, had finished her smoke and now resumed her role as queen by huffing and turning away.

The dancer responded with ever more violent gyrations. Her finger cymbals clanged, demanding attention. Soon, she would come looking for a partner…

Blake retreated behind the safety of the table and pressed himself into the shadows – he had no intention of being selected. Although David, sitting just a few paces away, seemed a more than willing candidate.

The dancer soon left the stage and began a tour of the room, twirling around in front of each group, her long skirt flaring. Occasionally she stopped to wind a flimsy scarf around the neck of an unsuspecting tourist and blow provocatively in his ear. As she approached their table, David stood up and leaned forward to volunteer, stretching out a hand – but the dancer effortlessly evaded his grasp and he fell awkwardly forward while she twirled on to the next group. Some of the crowd burst out laughing.

"Stupid old fool," muttered Joan, delving into her handbag for her packet of cigarettes.

Meanwhile, the dancer had found herself a partner at the next table but one. Reaching into the shadows, she pulled someone to their feet and led them out into the light. To Blake's surprise, it was Reda.

Later, Blake was to ask himself whether it had been a deliberate choice and rather than risk the antics of some unsuspecting tourist, it had been decided to use the talents of a member of the management. Reda had certainly identified himself as such. Instead of fancy dress, he was smartly attired in suit, shirt and tie and the peasant clothing he'd worn late on that first night had been left in his room.

And he certainly had talent – perhaps a little too much of it, as it transpired. Emerging onto the dance floor, he slid comfortably across it, and with an ease of movement that belied his bulky figure, he readily supported his partner. When she jerked her hips, he jerked his. When she rotated her torso, he responded. Circle left, circle right – he knew the steps. And it wasn't something he'd been taught, it was something he'd inherited, he was a natural.

His performance delighted the crowd, and before long they were clapping encouragement. The tempo of the music increased and, whipped up by the band, the pair danced ever faster, the belly dancer's finger cymbals clashing furiously while Reda kept pace. Blake began to wonder where it all might end – and he'd no sooner asked himself the question than it was answered in no uncertain fashion.

Lee Yong and Reda must have been sitting together at the same table from which he'd been pulled out earlier. Blake had either walked past them on the way in or they'd slipped in afterwards, unnoticed. But now she too had come out into the light and was walking determinedly toward the dance floor. It was the first time he'd seen her that evening.

Her appearance took his breath away. She was dressed in much the same outfit as Janet, i.e. as a woman of the harem, but rather than plain white her costume was of a deep blue with a gold waistband hung about with trinkets. Her head and face were covered but her midriff was bare, and whereas Janet's figure was somewhat matronly, Lee Yong's was lithe and supple.

She looked stunning. Seated just a few feet away, Joan stiffened. She had elected to deck herself out as a queen – but Lee Yong was truly a princess.

It was not just her looks that caused Blake to take notice – it was also her manner. Her walk was determined and resolute – this was no casual stroll to join Reda, this was a mission to rescue him. The young Egyptian was in danger of falling into the clutches of a seductive Siren and needed to be recovered. To the audience that watched it, the scene must have appeared scripted and they might have thought it part of the act.

She arrived on the dance floor to another "ooh!" from the crowd and at once began a dance of her own. The band, thrown into confusion by her appearance, abruptly stopped playing. Reda and the belly-dancer stopped too, and for a moment Lee Yong continued alone.

Her dance came from much further east than that of her rival and was altogether more subtle, the wild gyration of hips replaced by graceful twists and turns. Abhorrent of a vacuum, the band soon picked up her rhythm and began a wistful tune of the kind that would charm a snake. The crowd hushed, and in the space of a few seconds the atmosphere had completely changed.

Reda stood transfixed. In this strange ménage à trios, he literally did not know which way to turn. The belly-dancer, deprived of both her music and the attention of her partner, stood to one side with her hands on her flabby hips and looked distinctly put out. Seemingly unperturbed, Lee Yong danced serenely on.

Two's company – three's a crowd, thought Blake, and was wondering how this might resolve itself when there was a movement to his left. Suddenly David was up from his seat and halfway across the dance floor. Swaying gently under the influence of his third gin and tonic, he stumbled forward, confronted the belly-dancer and began to contort himself to the music, inviting her to join him. The crowd welcomed him with a great "Hooray!" and although his action had been entirely selfish, it freed Reda from his predicament and allowed him to dance with Lee Yong.

This seemed like the ideal solution – but it did not satisfy everyone. Now there was a movement to Blake's right and it was Joan's turn to be up and halfway across the dance floor. Incensed by David's performance and with a face like thunder, she marched straight toward her husband who, unaware of her impending arrival, continued making a fool of himself. The crowd burst out laughing once more and the situation was on the verge of descending into farce.

Then a strange thing happened – Blake felt compelled to intervene and without a second thought, he sprang up and followed after the queen. His immediate intention was to persuade her to dance with him. The delicate balance that David had created was about to be destroyed and a voice deep within him said he did not want that to happen.

But whatever his reasons, he was soon overtaken by events. Janet and Keith were right behind him and in a matter of moments they were all on the dance floor together – a queen, an emperor, a sheikh, a belly-dancer, two ladies of the harem and himself dressed as an Egyptian peasant. If there was any one of the party who looked out of place, it was Reda.

The crowd took their intervention as the general signal to join in. Soon the scene was one of utter chaos as they all flooded forward and in the melee that followed, Blake found himself in the one position he did not want, i.e. face to face with the belly-dancer. Relieved that she had finally found a reliable partner, she resumed her act and he was forced to submit to the indignity of mimicking her movements. He'd set out that evening with the intention of remaining unnoticed, but he could hardly have felt more exposed.

He soldiered on, acutely aware of himself and the spectacle he was creating. In the morning he could expect a few ribald comments – *I saw you last night, you sly old devil. You seemed to be doing alright for yourself* – but he was not finding it enjoyable. The task he was undertaking was a duty rather than a pleasure and he would seek to relieve himself of it at the first available opportunity.

Whatever his original intentions, his intervention had an effect. David and Joan were reunited, albeit reluctantly, Janet and Keith were next to each other and from time to time, Ira's slender form would appear from behind Mrs Biltmore's swirling garments. And buried in the crowd just a few feet away, Reda and Lee Yong were dancing together, seemingly without a care in the world.

Blake began to relax. Soon his dancing partner would tire of him and withdraw to the comfort of her dressing room where she could reflect on what had been an eventful evening. If there were no more alarms, he would shortly follow suit and take himself off to bed. Tomorrow was another early start and he needed his sleep.

Chapter Thirteen

He woke, as usual, some time in the hour before dawn. But rather than go out on deck to greet the new day, he chose to lie in bed and think about the events of the previous evening. It had sounded innocuous at the time, but the music which had filled the Forward Lounge was running insistently through his head like a dripping tap he couldn't turn off and for the moment, any idea of going out to watch birds had been banished. His boat trip the day before had sated his desire and even the prospect of Glossy Ibis and their early morning flight across the rising sun (a sight he was still yet to witness) was not enough to move him.

Something had 'happened' at the Egyptian Evening but he couldn't quite put his finger on it and yet he was convinced it was important. Contrary to his principles, he had contrived to interfere in something that was none of his business. The outcome was that he'd succeeded in ending up in the arms of an overweight middle-aged belly-dancer and he wanted to understand why. He tried to reconstruct the chain of events which had led up to it, but it had all happened so quickly that it was difficult to piece it together. Had he been trying to save them all from embarrassment? He doubted it – he was far more used to letting people struggle on alone. All he could think of was that he'd done it for the sake of Lee Yong, but in the chaos that had followed David's charge he'd missed her. Had he gone out there to claim her? Or to save her? He was confused as to his motives and he needed time to think. He turned over to face the wall and away from the distractions of the window.

Down in the kitchen below, the breakfast chef had started singing again. This time it was a slow, doleful tune of the kind intended to lull you to sleep and he soon found himself drifting back.

Then his reverie was broken by the jagged call of his alarm, jerking him into to the present. The bedside clock showed 6.30

am. If he didn't get his skates on, he was going to miss the bus.

For once he was the last down to breakfast. After the frenetic action of the night before, it was a subdued atmosphere that greeted him at the table. As expected, Lee Yong was absent while the others were quietly going about their business – all except David who had his elbows on the table, his head in his hands and was moaning softly to himself.

"Morning."

"Morning..."

David's response was barely more than a grunt and for a change it was Janet who started the conversation off.

"Didn't we all have a good time yesterday evening?"

"Yes, I think we did actually." Despite his personal misgivings, Blake had to concur. "Although David looks as though he's suffering a bit today."

"Don't remind me."

David's reply seemed to emanate from somewhere in the region of the tablecloth.

"Oh dear." Blake smirked, rather self-righteously. "A bit too much alcohol last night?"

"You could say that," groaned the distant voice.

"It's his own fault," said Joan. "I've told him not to mix his drinks but he doesn't take a blind bit of notice. Two large glasses of wine with his dinner, followed by a string of gin and tonics. What do you expect? He's only got himself to blame."

"Thanks for the sympathy!"

"Well, you don't deserve any. You never listen to a word I'm saying. Perhaps if you'd paid more attention to me than chasing after that... Anyway, I don't know why you don't stay in the cabin this morning and sleep it off. You'd feel an awful lot better for it."

"We discussed that. We're going to Philae. I can't miss it."

(Philae boasted a temple which was the object of their morning's visit.)

He clipped his words, as if the act of speaking were painful in itself.

"Well maybe you should have thought of that last night before you decided to get tanked up. Give yourself a break, David, for God's sake – it's only another pile of stones."

"It's not just another pile of stones," David protested. "It's important. You don't understand the history. Just get me another cup of coffee. I'll be fine."

Keith hailed a passing waiter and guided him in David's direction.

They took the opportunity for a refill and after the waiter had gone, Blake pointed casually at the inevitably empty place.

"Any sign of Lee Yong?"

It was a question he soon wished he hadn't asked.

"No, I don't think anyone's seen her this morning," reported Keith.

"She seemed to be enjoying herself last night though," added Janet.

"Did you see her outfit?" said Joan, raising an eyebrow.

"I certainly did," said Keith. "I don't see how you could miss it – absolutely stunning. I was impressed, I don't mind telling you."

"So was Reda by the look of him," said Joan.

It was this chance remark that caused Blake to become concerned.

"What do you mean?" he asked.

"You can't tell me you didn't notice!"

"I didn't notice what?"

"Are you kidding?" Joan gave him a knowing look. "The way they were cosying up to each other on the dance floor, that's what. If you ask me, I think they're an item. And all I can say is, if you can't see it you must be blind."

"Who?"

"Reda and Lee Yong."

"Do you know, I thought that too," agreed Keith. "They certainly seemed to spend a lot of time together. You don't suppose there's something going on there do you?"

This last comment prompted Janet to interject.

"Keith! I'm surprised at you! That's an entirely inappropriate thing to say. You shouldn't be speaking about people like that."

Joan, on the other hand, had no such scruples.

"Well, it wouldn't surprise me..."

This form of random speculation filled Blake with horror. How could they be so casual about something so personal? What business was it of theirs! For that matter, what business was it of his and why should he feel so precious about it? And yet, in the girl's case, he was filled with a protective desire...

Suddenly, he found himself blurting out without thinking: "Well, I for one don't believe we should be talking about them behind their backs."

Joan instantly took offence.

"Sorry, I'm sure..." And as if to cover up her embarrassment, she changed the focus of the conversation by deliberately consulting her watch. "Good God, look at the time. We've got to go. Come on, David, get yourself together."

"I'm coming, I'm coming," moaned the dislocated voice and the head to which it belonged gradually raised itself up and grimaced.

David forced himself to his feet, a hand held over his eyes. They all rose to leave, and as Blake folded his napkin, Janet whispered an aside.

"You're quite right, it's none of our business what these young people get up to. I'll have a word with Keith about it – he shouldn't be talking like that."

Something in her voice suggested a sensible and motherly instinct was at work. Given the right subject perhaps Janet wasn't always the mouse that she seemed. Blake breathed a sigh of relief. At least there was someone on his side and with Janet's help, the speculation might be kept under control. Left solely in Joan's hands, there was no telling where it might lead.

So the suggestion was that Lee Yong and Reda were in a relationship. Blake walked slowly back to his cabin, turning the proposition over carefully in his mind. It was not how he wanted to see things. Perhaps he was in a state of denial but if it were true, it would explain a lot – the meeting in the coach-park at the Valley of the Kings, the scene on the ship's rail, all culminating with the goings-on at the Egyptian Evening. And he'd thought they'd been discussing antiquities and the history of Egypt – so much for his powers of observation! He'd spent a lifetime looking at wildlife and prided himself on being able to detect the signals – the alarm call of a thrush, the angle at which an otter raised its head – they all had meaning. And just as he might watch birds, so he thought he might watch people.

How ironic that the skill he'd acquired through the study of animal behaviour was not one shared by the others! Earlier in the trip he'd castigated them for failing to understand the Egyptian character – they couldn't possibly understand the country the way that he did. Now, in the space of a few short moments, they'd exposed his own shortcomings and it filled him with apprehension. How could he have missed something so obvious? Or was it that he'd simply refused to face up to it?

Another, more damning, thought occurred to him. What if their relationship encompassed more than something personal? Malaysia was a Muslim country and Lee Yong an active and forthright person. What if she and Reda were in collusion?

The implications of this possibility multiplied within him. But the evidence to hand was purely circumstantial, and beyond his own observations and the offhand chatter at the breakfast table there was a lack of any hard facts. This in itself proved nothing and it wanted something concrete to put the matter beyond doubt.

Blake became determined to find it. As much as he was driven by curiosity, there was also a lingering sense of duty – he was not long out of 'uniform'. And besides, he needed to restore his sense of credibility. A spoor had been pointed out to him and like the tracks of an animal walking on wet sand, he needed to follow it to its conclusion. Yesterday, Reda had been a worry to him – the day before it had been Lee Yong who'd engaged him. Then, whoever they were and whatever they might be doing had been no more than a passing interest – today it was about to become an obsession and for the moment he could think of little else.

Relying purely on habit, he stumbled through his morning routine – but when he came to packing up his telescope he hesitated. To take it or not to take it? That was the question. A few days earlier and it wouldn't have been an issue. Up until then it had accompanied him everywhere and it was as natural for him to include it as it was to put on shoes or a shirt. But what was the point of it now? He wasn't going to be watching birds. In the end, he settled for just his binoculars and left his room feeling slightly underdressed.

He arrived on the quayside out of breath but with his backpack and bins at the ready. With its door open and engine running, the bus was already waiting. His bout of indecision meant he was the last aboard and rather than cause further delay, he slumped into a seat right at the front.

"You've cut it a bit fine," someone called from the rear.

"Sorry…"

"Good morning, Mr Blake," came a familiar voice from his left.

In his struggle to cope with his seatbelt he had failed to notice he had sat immediately next to Reda. The young Egyptian looked at him and smiled, but said nothing more as the bus moved off into the bright morning light.

The trip to Philae Temple and the island of Aglika had now taken on an entirely different complexion. Joan had described the place as just another pile of stones, but David had deemed it historically significant. But this was not what had interested Blake, and for him it had always been all about the colony of White Storks. These large and distinctive birds were not known to breed in Egypt and were normally only seen on migration. He'd come across them before, in Greece and southern Spain, but this was an opportunity to view them in their wintering habitat before they flew north up the Nile Valley to their breeding grounds on the other side of the Mediterranean. Normally he'd have taken out his bird guide on the bus and swotted up, but today it remained in his backpack. Today he was intent on observing another species – and one that was sitting not a million miles away. Even the fact that he'd been forced to take an aisle seat did not perturb him. What would he have seen if he'd been able to look out of a window? Only the usual suspects – sparrows, swallows and the inevitable Palm Doves. Inside the coach, things were potentially much more interesting...

Although, as it happened, nothing of consequence took place. Nor could it, for with Reda sandwiched between Blake and the window, and Lee Yong presumably ensconced somewhere toward the back, there was no chance of contact. It was the same on the boat and it made Blake wonder as to the reason. Had they fallen out after the events of the night before? Was Lee Yong sulking? Or had they come to some agreement about how to behave during business hours? Perhaps Reda had put his foot down. *Not while I'm working.* Whatever the cause, for the time being they simply weren't speaking and Blake realised he would have to be patient. Still, as a practised birder he was used to that.

Things didn't change once they were on the island. The pair kept their distance and Blake could not help thinking that in the context of their group, she and Reda could hardly be further apart. Even during Reda's introductory speech, Lee Yong remained curiously aloof – perhaps it was a question of respect.

Finally, after what seemed like an age, Reda's talk came to an end. He finished with an announcement. There was to be an hour's free time to explore the island, after which could they all please meet at the stone benches in the southeast corner where a local guide would be on hand to answer questions. But if Blake imagined this was some arrangement which would enable the young Egyptian and Miss Malaysia to sneak off somewhere together, he was soon disillusioned. Reda went straight back to the boat while Lee Yong remained steadfastly with the group. Under the circumstances he thought he might as well excuse himself and go and look for his Storks.

He found them on the northern shore, a flock of twenty or so, standing about on the scree and the rocks above the waterline. It was a strange place to see them – but that was what it was all about, bird-watching out of season. They were as big as he remembered them, black and white and easy to locate. This was just as well as without the assistance of his telescope, it might have been difficult as they stayed eerily silent. Later in the breeding season they would pair off and throw their heads back, clacking their bills together in a weird courtship display. But for the moment, like Reda and Lee Yong, they weren't speaking – and in the absence of their calls it all felt rather anticlimactic.

Later, back at the stone benches, he sat through the local guide's replies, but there was nothing in them to excite. All in all, it had been a disappointing morning and his search had proved fruitless.

Hot, and a little bothered, he returned to the launch feeling sadly deflated.

Chapter Fourteen

It wasn't that he doubted himself – and if anything, the events of that morning had strengthened his suspicions. He had convinced himself that Reda and Lee Yong's decision not to communicate was just as deliberate as their sitting together in private at the Egyptian evening had been the night before – they were anxious to conceal their relationship and not to arouse suspicion. Were things otherwise, they surely would have spoken to each other.

His theory was all very well, but it still wanted proof. And having failed to obtain it in tangible form that morning, he determined to get it at lunchtime – although the possibility that Lee Yong might not come down to their table caused him to alter his plans. He dropped his stuff off in his cabin and rather than go straight to the dining room, took a deliberate detour past her room in the hopes of determining her whereabouts.

Her cabin door stood open, and in the corridor outside a pile of dirty linen lay next to a janitor's trolley. From somewhere within came the steady thrum of a hoover.

Inside, a young girl was cleaning, but on Blake's entry she turned her machine off to deal with his enquiry.

Was the lady in?

The girl shook her head.

Had she seen the lady?

Yes, she'd returned a few minutes ago but had gone straight out again.

Did she know where she'd gone?

No, she did not.

Was the lady alone?

No, a gentleman had been with her.

What kind of gentleman?

An Egyptian.

And what had he looked like, this Egyptian?

The one with the face of a boy.

So he had been right after all...

Blake thanked her and pressed a small note into the palm of her hand. In this country, it was wise to pay for such services – you never knew when you might need them again. He returned to the corridor as the door closed and the hoover resumed its rumbling.

It was obvious then – having denied themselves any form of contact that morning, with the afternoon 'at leisure' they had decided to take advantage and go out somewhere together. That much was clear, but to be on the safe side Blake hurried downstairs to check.

In the dining room, the customary haze of chatter floated amongst the part-filled tables. No, it was just as he'd surmised, they weren't there, and his instinct told him that they must have left the ship. On an impulse, he elected to forego his midday meal and took an apple and a banana from the buffet bar and crammed them into the pockets of his linen jacket. From his table in the corner, Keith cast a glance in his direction and raised an enquiring eyebrow. Blake chose to ignore it, and affecting an enforced sense of urgency, set off back toward the foyer. Wherever they were, he would find them and discover their secret.

But first, he would return to his cabin and collect his trusty telescope and binoculars.

In the ten minutes or so that had elapsed since they'd left her room, Lee Yong and Reda could not have gone far. It was unlikely they would have rushed – it was hot and with the time having just turned half past twelve, the sun was at its highest. The best they could manage was probably a steady stroll – but in which direction? Blake gathered himself together on the quayside and considered the possibilities. They were three in number.

Directly in front of him lay the town of Aswan. The immediate prospect was of a large open square leading up to the

Governorate building. Perhaps they had crossed the Corniche and walked up toward the railway station – in which case they might now be sitting outside one of the cafés at the top. A quick scan with his binoculars revealed that they were not, and besides, having been so circumspect that morning, Blake thought it unlikely that they would choose somewhere so public for the afternoon.

It was just as unlikely that they'd gone south along the Corniche toward the Old Cataract Hotel. Here there were equally as many tourist attractions – the Coptic Cathedral and the Nubian Museum drew many visitors. If they were seeking privacy, this would also be a poor choice.

So unless they'd taken the ferry across to the Tombs of the Nobles (yet another public place), the most plausible solution was that they'd gone north. In that direction there was nothing but the pathway which petered out into open fields along the riverbank. Quiet and secluded, it seemed the perfect location for a secret assignation. Blake set up his telescope and pointed it up the path. There, in the far distance and wobbling in the heat haze, two figures were walking side by side.

He folded his telescope away and prepared to go after them. And if anyone should think it odd that he was wandering along the riverbank in the full heat of the day, equipped as he was, he was quite ready to play the part of the eccentric Englishman – mad dogs and all that. Young lovers too, by the look of it...

It reminded him of the only time he'd ever really 'twitched'. Some four or five years before, it had been the last working day of the week and he'd been sitting at his desk at the Embassy after lunch, the window flung wide open. The metal overhead fan had been turned on full blast to moderate the stifling heat and a light breeze was riffling through his papers. A trade mission was due from the UK at the end of the month and there were arrangements to be made. It had not been the most engaging of tasks and with the prospect of two days off yawning before him, he was on the point of packing up and going home when Carpenter had reached across in that nonchalant way of his and dropped something casually in front of him.

I thought you might be interested in this, old boy.

It was a cutting from the English-speaking paper bought by the ex-pats. The headline read *Rare bird turns up in desert*. It was not the first time he'd been 'alerted' – there were any number of rarities you could go and gawp at – but he prided himself on being a more sophisticated class of bird-watcher. He did not normally react, but the news had found him at a particularly low point. An unfulfilling weekend pottering through the hot, sticky markets of Cairo and a return to his desk on Monday was not exactly enthralling. He thought about it for barely a second, then picked up the phone – and first thing the following morning found himself in an old ex-US army jeep with a native driver bounding down the rocky road to Wadi El Natrun in search of a Spectacled Warbler. He'd never been to El Natrun and he'd never seen a Spectacled Warbler. Sometimes you needed an injection of excitement into what was an otherwise uneventful life.

Out in the desert, the wind had pushed sand into their faces. The jeep bounced like a bucking bronco and with one hand hanging on for dear life, he'd been forced to use the other to cover his mouth and nose with a scarf. He'd felt like Lawrence of Arabia, charging toward some violent military encounter.

The reality was far more mundane. They found the bird flitting about in the low scrub, but in winter plumage it was hard to distinguish from Common Whitethroat. Although that was not the point – the day had been about the effort and the chase and if the end result was disappointing, so be it. Now it was different. He expected to find something sensational and he was not going to give up until he'd got it.

He shouldered his telescope and walked northwards along the

pathway at a steady pace – but it was still a full fifteen minutes before he reached the open fields and the point at which he'd seen the two distant figures. The high sun seared at his skin, but with his straw hat, neckerchief and the long sleeves of his linen jacket covering his arms, he felt quite well-protected. Soon, he thought, his quarry would need to find shade.

Blake took out his handkerchief and mopped his brow. It was hot and enervating work. To his right, the parched fields wilted in the sun while to his left, the cool waters of the Nile slid languorously by. What he wouldn't give to bathe in their refreshing stream right now.

Somewhere in front of him were Reda and Lee Yong – but just exactly where? He raised his binoculars to find them – and for a moment panic set in as he realised that the two figures he'd seen were no longer on the pathway.

They must have wandered off into one of the fields and he began to scan the landscape in front of him. In his mind's eye he had constructed a vision of what he expected to see – heads propped on hands and elbows, they would be lying on their sides facing each other. Spread between them would be the contents of an open backpack, a napkin from the dining room, some pieces of fruit (Blake's own apple and banana still languished in the pocket of his linen jacket – he'd not even given them a thought). They might even share a pot of yoghurt, although at this distance it would be difficult to tell. Then, with their impromptu picnic done, they would talk, their mouths moving silently in his eyeglass, spilling out their words...

He wouldn't be able to hear them. In truth, he didn't need to – he knew in his heart what they would be saying. It was part of an age-old process. They would be sharing themselves, their thoughts, their hopes, their dreams, intimate details, secrets of the soul, all would be poured out and consumed with their picnic. Then they'd return to the ship and digest what they'd heard.

Blake felt a pang of envy. Even now he still hankered after that elusive liaison – whispered words late at night, the holding of hands in a restaurant – but above all, he missed the ability to exchange his inner self with another. Within the stifled confines of the Embassy and the boundaries of ex-pat life, all that had passed him by. Other friends he knew had taken lovers, but that wasn't what he'd wanted – it was more than that. His chance had never come and he'd been left staring at life from a distance through his binoculars. And as much as he both liked and enjoyed them, you couldn't talk to birds...

This was what he imagined, but for the moment his way was blocked. A hundred yards or so further on, an old boundary wall of crumbling brick topped by a tangled mass of thorns bordered the edge of the path, cutting off his view. He'd already decided to move on up to its corner when a slight movement above it caught his eye. His instant reaction was naturally *bird* but he quickly realised it was not as it resolved itself into a thin wisp of smoke. Had they lit a fire? he wondered. If so, what on earth for? His curiosity ever more aroused, he hurried on to the end of the old wall and carefully peered around it.

At first he could see nothing but a broad expanse of dry scrub dotted about with patches of twisted briar. He looked again for the smoke and soon found it on the far right, curling up from the vicinity of a clump of trees. Focusing in, he saw not one, not two, but in excess of a dozen people gathered beneath the broad outstretched leaves of a grove of date palms. To one side, a small iron tripod had been erected, a fire lit and tea was being brewed. This was no lovers' tryst – something else was going on, and what looked like a business meeting was in progress.

He needed a better view and ducked back behind the crumbling brick and quickly began assembling his scope. There was no need for stealth as given the distance and the cover afforded by the wall and intervening scrub, he was sure he could not be seen. Even so, he still fumbled nervously with the toggles.

But soon he was ready and zoomed in again on the scene.

As far as he could tell, the group consisted entirely of men – Lee Yong was not amongst them. But Reda was there, dressed once more in his peasant's clothes, and were it not for the fact that it was broad daylight instead of under the cover of darkness, Blake might have been looking at the self-same gathering as he had at Luxor on the night of his arrival, the Egyptian working class, at leisure after a day's toil. Following the debacle with Joan's luggage, it had amused him and he'd thought nothing more of it. Now he was puzzled – the day was barely half over and it was not yet time to relax. Why the assembly?

He looked again more carefully, searching for a clue. They were a close-knit band, tightly huddled. But it was not the same company as at Luxor and there were a number of different faces. And instead of being at ease, the language of their bodies spoke of tension, each one sat forward rather than back as they conversed. Reda seemed to be doing most of the talking and from time to time he would emphasize his point by slapping one hand hard against the palm of the other. Someone would respond, stabbing the air with his finger and what looked like heated discussion would ensue. Was it a dispute about pay perhaps? Or a political debate? If so, this sort of thing could go on for hours.

Blake gave a sigh of irritation. This was not what he'd come for, to watch some local council thrash out the minutiae of their lives in the searing glare of the midday sun. Another disappointment. Egypt had surprised him yet again – but this time for the worse. His shoulders slumped as if he were a burst balloon and he lowered his glass. What was he doing, for goodness sake? He'd missed his target and now here he was, a good mile or so up the riverbank, labouring in the heat to no good purpose.

He turned to leave and his attention was caught by a dark shape fluttering above the riverbank some hundred yards or so further down. A bird was hovering over the marshy fringes of the river. Its distant presence brightened him a little – this at least was a legitimate target. He reassembled his telescope onto its tripod and trained it on the object. A medium-sized raptor came into view, predominantly grey but with prominent black patches on its wings. *Black-shouldered Kite.* At any moment it might swoop down to seize its prey. This was a good 'spot' by any standards – a first for the trip – and now he could go back with some feeling of justification for his afternoon's exertions.

But there was something wrong. The image that was presented was not as it should be – birds should have two wings, not four. The picture was blurred and it appeared as if everything were double. He looked again and attempted to refocus. It made no difference and now he could see that the background was blurred too. There must be something amiss with his equipment – perhaps the eyepiece had come loose or there was some other problem. He stepped back to check and located the bird with his naked eye to establish a reference point. Still blurred – and whichever way he looked, it was the same. Across the river the tawny wastes of the Western Desert wavered in the heat – but it was not the haze that had made the sand-dunes double in number. So it clearly wasn't his telescope at all...

The discovery frightened him. His eyes were his world – he couldn't lose them. He stood beside his tripod, clasped his hands firmly together and pressed his eyelids tightly shut. Breathing deeply he counted to ten. If he focused hard, perhaps he could make the problem go away – or better still, he could convince himself that it was all part of a dream and had never really happened. But when he opened them again, his eyes were the same – nothing had substantially changed.

He told himself not to panic. It was probably a strain brought on by tiredness and excessive use of the scope and the binoculars. At least he could still see, albeit strangely. He convinced himself that what he should do was get back to the ship where he could lie down in his cabin and rest for a couple of hours until the tiredness had gone – then it would be alright. He packed up his telescope, slung it over his shoulder and headed back down the path toward the town.

He was facing south now, straight into the sun, and he pulled at the brim of his hat to give himself relief from the glare. He never wore, or carried, any sunglasses. His theory was that they got in the way when you were birding – he couldn't be doing with forever taking them on and off when trying to use the scope. It was a habit he now regretted. Somehow he needed to cut back the light – perhaps it would be better if he looked down.

But that was even worse and the sight of his two feet doubled made him feel queasy. Rather than endure that, he chose to remain facing forward with eyes half-closed and his free hand over his brow. He stumbled on, trusting himself to the narrow pathway and hurried toward the ship. It had taken him a quarter of an hour to reach the boundary wall on the way out – at this speed it must surely take less to return.

Halfway home, he became aware of the pain in his head. A nagging discomfort at first, it grew steadily in intensity with each passing step. Soon it was pounding at him like a jackhammer – until by the time he reached the gangplank it was as if someone had clamped his eyeballs in a vice and was gradually turning the screw. He blundered into reception, fearing the axe that was trying to split open his skull.

Someone (was it Keith?) called out.

"Michael?"

But he ignored it and marched directly on. There was only one thought thumping through his mind. *Get to bed.*

The few seconds that it took him to find his room key and apply it to the lock left him in agony. As soon as he'd got inside and shut the door, he let go, dropping tripod, scope and backpack onto the floor in a heap, then climbed straight between the sheets. He didn't even stop to take off his shoes – it was much too painful to bend.

Once beneath the covers his problems simplified. He didn't need to worry about Lee Yong or Reda or birding anymore. Gone was the harshness of daylight and the double vision – all that was left for him to deal with was survival and the war inside his head. He tried desperately to think of nothing at all in the hope that by emptying his mind, he could also cleanse it of pain. Something impure had got hold of him and he needed to get rid of it.

The day before, after lunch, he'd lain in exactly the same position. Then he'd taken comfort from the chatter of the crew and the metallic sounds of the engine room. Now they were a torture to him, each spoken word a jabbing prick into the silence, each clang like a pair of cymbals clashed between his ears. The pain was relentless.

Blake buried his head deep beneath the pillows. His journey into darkness had begun.

Chapter Fifteen

He slept for in excess of twelve hours – but when he awoke, he was still hiding beneath the covers, not daring to open his eyes. His headache had mercifully abated and when he did finally expose himself to the morning light, so had the blurring. The memory, however, equally as painful, still remained.

It was not the first time he'd experienced such symptoms – blurred vision, headaches – he'd had them before. There had been other 'episodes' such as the one on the riverbank, moments of extreme pain when some inherent weakness would flare up and attack him. He'd always put them down to the over-zealous use of his telescope and binoculars – there must come a point at which continually staring at birds had a deleterious effect.

When it had developed into full-blown migraine, he'd usually attributed the cause to dehydration. For example, on the day in question, despite having the presence of mind to furnish himself with two pieces of fruit (neither of which he'd eaten) he'd neglected to take any water. It was a mistake for which he'd paid a heavy price.

But he didn't ascribe this particular incident purely to his failure to drink fluids. He was riddled with a sense of guilt and he believed it was more likely karma rather than the effects of the sun that had reduced him to his present condition. Consciously or not, he had set out along the riverbank with the intention of intruding into the lives of others. This had been unacceptable and in a form of retributive justice he was being made to pay for it. He tried to redeem himself with the idea that he'd never wanted to intrude and that what he'd discovered was there for all to see. As with Reda's laptop, he'd never meant to spy, all he'd wanted was confirmation.

But it was of no help. He shuddered and the desire to observe Reda and Lee Yong evaporated like an early morning mist in the heat. He could admit to being vicarious – but in no way was he voyeuristic. This foolish pursuit would have to stop. Anyway, hadn't he already proved his point? How much more 'evidence' did he need? He resolved to put an end to these adventures and from now on he would restrict himself to the ship where he could potter about the sun-deck with his binoculars and his illustrated guide, watching birds.

After an hour of immobile contemplation, he forced himself to get up and went down to breakfast, only to find his table empty of companions and the dining room virtually deserted. He returned to reception. The itinerary for the day advised him it had been another early start and that they'd all gone out on an excursion. While he'd lain stricken in his cabin, buses had been laid on to take them to Edfu. Here was another regret. Of all the buildings to be visited on the trip, Edfu Temple was the best preserved and the one he would most like to have seen. Because of his imprudent behaviour, that was being denied him too.

He contrived to make breakfast last until ten, then went to the Forward Lounge to drink coffee. Another time he would gladly have fetched his scope and binoculars and gone up on the sun-deck, but for the moment his appetite for birding had left him.

He hung around the empty ship, poking about in the gift shops although he had no intention of buying anything, waiting for the others to return. With nothing else in prospect, after a solitary lunch he went back to his cabin and feeling rather sorry for himself, lay down to rest.

Around half past four he became aware of voices on the quayside and he guessed it was the coach party returning. Joan's strident tones were unmistakable.

"David? Did I leave my bag on the bus?"

As if this were a signal for action, he swung his legs off the bed and went down to reception to greet them, his hands nervously jangling the keys in his pocket.

He no longer wanted to be alone and was desperate for the society of others. He'd spent the best part of his lifetime comfortable in his own company, but suddenly he was not. He somehow felt vulnerable as though the events of the previous day had sapped his self-confidence. He'd always despised the idle chatter of everyday life, but now he wanted to immerse himself in it as if by doing so it might enable him to recover. Even the mere presence of another human being might be enough to reassure him.

Keith was the first to spot him and came straight across.

"Hello, Michael. So where were you this morning? We waited for you at breakfast but you didn't show."

"I had a bit of a lie in. To tell the truth, I didn't feel too well."

"Let me guess – tummy trouble. There's a lot of it about this morning. Janet was up in the night, poor thing. We think it may have been the shellfish yesterday evening."

Keith had either forgotten or had failed to notice that he hadn't been at dinner the night before. Blake decided not to correct him and settled for the obvious.

"So, how was the temple?"

"Excellent – best I've seen yet. D'you know, it's almost complete. I never realised how much of it's still standing." Keith looked pointedly over his shoulder, then whispered an aside. "Between you and me, I've seen that many temples in the last few days, I'm beginning to lose count. Janet thinks I'm going senile. We were talking last night about some bas reliefs or another and I couldn't for the life of me recall where I'd seen them. The ones where the god had the head of a dog – or was it a hawk? And it was clutching a sheaf of corn. I don't suppose you remember?"

Blake shook his head. His days of studying such things were long gone.

"Hmm, pity... There's so much to take in – and we haven't been to Karnak yet."

"No..."

With their conversation faltering, Keith provided a change of subject.

"So what have you been up to while we've been away? Manage to get in a spot of bird-watching, did you?"

"Well, actually..."

Blake was about to tell his story but then thought the better of it and cut himself off. Keith took this as a 'yes' and soldiered on regardless.

"Good, good. See anything interesting?"

"Sort of..."

He had, but it was not for public consumption. It was another vague response but it seemed to satisfy his companion's feigned interest. Keith was already looking around, presumably trying to spot Janet.

"Well, must dash or my wife will have my guts for garters."

"Indeed..."

He headed back toward reception.

The other members of the party had gathered in the foyer behind. Blake wondered as to the whereabouts of Lee Yong and Reda but told himself to stick to his recent resolution and tried not to look too hard.

David arrived back, having gone to retrieve Joan's bag from the bus. He was sporting a brand new pair of sunglasses – a fact given away by the price tag still dangling from one of the hinged corners. With deep black lenses they made his character seem almost impenetrable. Blake immediately took notice.

"Have you just bought those?"

"Absolutely. Couldn't find mine this morning and I wasn't going off without any. I've spent the whole day in the blazing sunshine and my head's killing me."

Headache. The mere thought sent a shiver down Blake's spine.

"Where did you get them, as a matter of interest?"

"You know the gift shop on the first-floor landing? Bumped

into the guy that runs it in the corridor and persuaded him to open up and sell me a pair. He wasn't keen at first, then I waved a ten pound note under his nose – that did the trick. Bloody lifesaver if you ask me."

"Do you think it's still open?"

"You can always try, you might be lucky…"

Blake set off in the direction of the stairway, then called back over his shoulder.

"Don't start tea without me."

"We won't…"

He'd never worn, never mind bought, a pair of sunglasses since arriving in the country. It was not just the effect they had on birding that prevented him – it was also the culture. Native Egyptians didn't wear them (they probably couldn't afford to) and if he wanted to live amongst them and not be marked out, why should he? So he'd made himself do without them. Eventually he'd grown used to the light, coming to love its hues, its patterns, its coming in the morning, its going at night. Now, in the aftermath of the riverbank, he feared it.

The shop was still open. It was one he'd walked straight past that morning, but the thought hadn't entered his head. Contrary to David's assertion, the owner proved more than willing, and five minutes later Blake emerged wearing a pair of his own.

It was a different world he could see through them, looking out of the window in reception – darker, indistinct, the colours muted. On the roadside opposite, passers-by melted in and out of shadows, almost unnoticed. Above the buildings, the birds were still the same, swallows, sparrows, Palm Doves – the usual suspects – but now he was forced to pick them out by shape rather than by plumage. That would be enough to challenge him for a while, but eventually he would yearn for the colours again. Had he known he would one day lose them completely, he might not have been so willing to compromise.

Afternoon tea had been delayed by an hour pending the arrivals from Edfu. It was now almost five. The intense heat of the day had eased and everyone was on the sun-deck, waiting.

David had already secured a table and Blake duly joined him. Joan soon arrived, hauling herself wearily up the steps and collapsing into her chair, seemingly exhausted. She didn't wait to be asked about her day.

"Well, I wouldn't want to go through that again."

"Why ever not?" asked Blake. "Was it that bad? Although I must say you look pretty shattered."

"Are you kidding? I feel as though I've been on that bloody bus all day. My neck is killing me."

She rubbed the back of her shoulder blade.

"It must have been worth it though," Blake continued. "I mean, Edfu is pretty special, isn't it?" There was a trace of envy in his voice.

"I suppose so. But you get to the point where when you've seen one temple, you've seen them all. You know what I mean? Rocks, carvings, statues – they're all much of a muchness."

It was the same sentiment as Keith had expressed earlier.

"Well, at least I can say I've been..." She waved a jewelled hand in the air as if to dismiss the matter – but soon started on another. "I tell you what though, it was bloody hot over there. Come midday, I thought I was going to get cooked. Which reminds me," she said, looking round. "I'm gagging for a cup of tea. Are you going to sit there all day, David, or are you going to make yourself useful?"

David rose silently from his chair and headed off toward the tea counter. Fearful of being saddled with his wife, Blake followed suit.

Two tables away, Lee Yong was sitting with Ira and Mrs Biltmore. Heads together, they were deep in conversation and oblivious to the rest of the party. When Blake returned with his tea, he made a casual enquiry.

"What's going on there?" He nodded in their direction.

"God knows," said Joan between sips. "They've been as thick as thieves all day. I can't say I mind though – it keeps that loud-mouthed American quiet."

"That's a bit cruel," said David.

"Well, she gets on my nerves, always on about this and that and the other."

"Lee Yong doesn't seem to mind," observed Blake.

Joan shrugged and took another bite at her marble cake. It was left up to David to explain.

"I think Mrs Biltmore's rather taken her under her wing. They were together yesterday afternoon too."

It explained something that had been puzzling him. As Lee Yong hadn't been on the riverbank, Blake had wondered where she'd got to. Rather than join him, he assumed that she and Reda must have agreed to go their separate ways. The two figures he'd seen had admittedly appeared hazy but he was certain one of them had been Reda. If it was not Lee Yong, the identity of the other was a mystery. His curiosity aroused, he looked round for the young Egyptian.

Reda had already taken his tea and was doing his rounds rather like a house doctor, stopping at each table in turn. Blake asked whether he'd gone to Edfu with the rest of the party. Yes, David assured him, he'd travelled with them and had been their guide.

Hmm... Blake mused. No clandestine meeting today then.

Shortly, the young Egyptian was standing at his shoulder.

"So, how was your day?" Reda looked round the group.

Blake passed up his chance to respond. He had no desire to discuss his troubles – and besides, they paled by comparison to Joan's trials and tribulations, a subject on which she began to expound at length.

"...and that shopping trip you sent us on was a complete disaster. I just couldn't be doing with all that hassle. If I want to buy something, trust me, I'll buy it – I don't need somebody breathing down my neck all the time."

Reda listened with the same dutiful sympathy as he had done concerning her luggage.

"I'm sorry to hear that. Normally we don't have any trouble here. We must do something about it at once. Why not let me take you? Why don't we all go? Tonight. After dinner." He extended his arms to include the others. "Let's pay a visit to the souk. And if we get any trouble, we can link arms and walk as a family. It will be fine – I promise you."

Joan shrugged for the second time. "Well, I suppose that's alright with me."

And with whatever motive in mind, Reda left his offer on the table and went on to the next group of guests.

Chapter Sixteen

Reda was as good as his word and after they'd finished their evening meal, he arrived in reception to find them waiting.

"Aha!" He rubbed his hands together in anticipation. "Is my team ready for this?"

He seemed in an ebullient mood and his enthusiasm must have infected them as they all chorused a *Yes!* Although Joan, in whose honour the expedition had been mounted, remained distinctly unimpressed.

Lee Yong appeared. She'd been at dinner but had arrived late. Blake noticed that she retained her daytime outfit of boots, jeans and T-shirt rather than change into more formal evening wear. He felt a twinge of disappointment and for a brief moment he thought she might not be joining them.

"You are coming with us, I take it?"

He tried to sound as casual as he could.

"Of course I am. You don't suppose I was going to miss this, did you, Mr Blake?" she responded, tongue in cheek.

They formed up into a line on the quayside and prepared to cross the Corniche. On the other side, the wide open space of the central square stretched up toward the railway station. Night-lights sparkled and beckoned from a distance, inviting them forward. It was already dark and the traffic on the Corniche was busy. Most had headlamps on, but some did not and with self-preservation in mind, they took Reda's suggestion and truly did link arms.

Blake found himself next to Lee Yong and as she slipped her hand into his, he could feel the smooth warmth of her skin. For a second his thoughts became scrambled as an old thrill rang through him and he took his eye off the traffic. But Reda was already leading the charge and he was quickly forced to refocus. Rushing across the road they landed safely in a heap on the opposite pavement and burst out laughing with relief. It was a party atmosphere.

"Come on!" said Reda, and began to lead the way up toward the railway station.

The others fell in behind. They had dropped hands now and although there was no need, Blake held on for as long as he could.

At the top of the square, Reda brought them to a halt and pointed down a well-lit side street.

"This is Sharia Al-Souk – the way to the market. Look, you can see." A little further down, a row of shops began. "This is good, you will be fine from now on. I have some business to attend to, but if you need me I will be here, in the House of Umm Kulthum." He indicated a café on the corner to his right.

"I thought you said you were coming with us," Joan chided him.

"Don't look so scared!" Reda responded. "Stay together as a group and everything will be alright, I promise you. Enjoy."

He turned and headed off in the other direction.

Sharia Al-Souk was a narrow thoroughfare, full of bright lights and packed with people. Eager for business, the local population was out in force for the evening and apart from the tourists, the crowd was predominantly men, mostly of African appearance. A long row of shops lined the way on either side, their contents spilling out onto the street. Intentionally or not, rails of dresses, shirts and garish tops barred the route. Here and there, outside the vegetable markets, hessian sacks bulged with assorted grains. Piled on top, both dried and fresh fruits were in abundance, and on every corner there was the musty tang of spices.

In the dimly lit backstreets Blake was aware that there were other, less-common goods on offer – gold, silver, ivory, the skins of rare animals and much to his disgust, even the feathers of exotic birds. But that was the way of it in this part of the world – men had been buying and selling their wares here for thousands of years. More likely than not, you could source whatever you wanted, and if you had the right money you could probably find someone who'd sell you a camel.

Keith resumed his position as leader and with Janet clutching one arm, used the other to ward off the constant attentions of the vendors. Close behind, Ira clung to Mrs Biltmore like a limpet sticking to a rock. This time Lee Yong hung well back – it was not the kind of place where women went out in front. Following after David and Joan, as if he were the tail guard of an army patrol, Blake brought up the rear.

Every so often, Sharia Al-Souk was bisected by a side street and at each crossing a gust of warm air wafted up from the Nile. Blake instinctively counted every intersection – in these places it was crucial to know where you were.

After they'd gone past three, the street closed down even further and with the thick crowd surrounding them, Blake began to feel hemmed in.

Joan had asked for a spice shop and they had started to look round when there was a sudden commotion in the street. A panic had set in amongst the traders and racks of goods were rapidly being removed from the pavements. A cry went up, swiftly followed by the blare of car horns from behind them as a cavalcade of vehicles approached down the narrow thoroughfare. Preceded by a pair of motorcycles, three white unmarked cars rumbled forward. In the back seats, men in brown uniforms peered out in disapproval at the crowd. The police were doing their nightly round.

This unlooked-for intervention caught everyone by surprise. Confused by the general hubbub, the group split up to let the cars pass. Janet, Keith, Mrs Biltmore and Ira took to one side with Blake while David, Joan and Lee Yong went over to the other. The cavalcade came to a halt beside them, horns still blaring. Further on, some unfortunate beggar had blocked their path and was hurriedly removed. Pandemonium ensued. There were several blasts on a whistle, then the road cleared leaving Keith and his party alone. Across the street, there was no sign of the other group.

In a moment of panic, Blake took control. On their immediate right was a spice shop, probably the one they'd been searching for. It looked like a suitable refuge. He pointed toward it.

"You go in there – I'll go and find the others. If all else fails, I'll see you back at the ship."

Keith nodded and led his charges inside.

Blake turned and set off in the direction from which they'd arrived.

The police cars had moved on, their tail-lights blinking in the dark. The atmosphere was calmer now and there was a sense that things were returning to normal. He soon found David and Joan happily poking about amongst the recently restored rails of dresses and cotton shirts. Had they seen Lee Yong? No, they had not. This disconcerting news left him in a quandary and he wondered whether he should retrace his steps to the spice shop or continue his search. Lee Yong was self-reliant, but an overwhelming sense of responsibility was weighing down on him. If anything should happen, he would never forgive himself.

Then a thought occurred, and with some sense of purpose he headed back toward the House of Umm Kulthum.

The café of Umm Kulthum was not one of Egypt's best. It presented a rather rundown appearance and standing on the corner overlooking the well-kept square, it looked distinctly out of place. It had no frontage to speak of but gave out directly onto the street, the neon-lit Coke sign above its open entrance in need of repair and flashing intermittently. Inside, there was just enough light to make out a row of pinball machines at the back. Punctuated by their continual pinging, the piped music of Umm Kulthum herself floated out into the warm evening air. It was the same mellifluous voice that Blake had heard at the Egyptian evening.

As he'd suspected, Reda and Lee Yong were sitting at an outside table. After his efforts the previous day when he'd struggled to find them within a hundred yards of each other, here they were together at last, in plain view. They seemed casual enough, and if they were 'an item' then they'd either decided not to make a secret of it, or they were oblivious to all concerned.

Reda was smoking a water-pipe, and every so often took a puff, blowing out the sweet smell of applewood. On the table in front of him stood a glass of karkaday he occasionally sipped at. He'd obviously failed to persuade Lee Yong to try something as traditional as she'd opted for the more familiar taste of latte.

She seemed relaxed in Reda's company. When she'd become detached from the group perhaps she'd simply headed for the rendezvous Reda had nominated – although it struck Blake that their meeting was no accident and that after the incident in the souk she'd taken the first opportunity to seek him out.

He approached their table.

"Do you mind if I join you?"

"Please do." It was Reda who responded. "Take a seat, Mr Blake. Have you had enough of shopping already?"

Blake shrugged. It had never been his intention to go shopping – he'd merely gone along for the ride. He pulled out a chair and sat down.

"I hope I'm not interrupting anything."

"Not at all. We were just talking about America."

Blake wondered whether he meant geographically, politically, or as a tourist destination. He searched their faces for clues but came up with a blank.

"But I'm forgetting my manners," continued Reda. "May I get you something to drink?" He hailed a passing waiter.

"Mint tea will be fine. And why don't you call me Michael?"

Being continually addressed as 'Mr Blake' was beginning to

wear a bit thin.

Just at that moment the piped music flared up again and his comment was lost beneath the wailing words of Umm Kulthum.

"You were saying," he resumed, "about America?"

"I was just telling Reda…" Lee Yong broke in.

"…about your plans to study?"

"Exactly."

Blake had heard them before, but he was keen to encourage Lee Yong to talk. Reda didn't eat at the same table and all this might be news to him. She leant forward and stirred aimlessly at her latte.

"Although I'm not sure I've been able to convince him of the benefits of it. He thinks it's – what do you British call it? Pie in the sky? Anyway, he says I'm fooling myself. But I'm absolutely determined, Mr Blake. I will do it."

Given what he'd seen up to now, Blake had no doubt of it.

"I've been trying to persuade him, but he won't have it. Perhaps you can make him see sense."

It was no surprise to Blake to discover that they disagreed on the matter. Reda would have his views and he already knew Lee Yong to be strong-willed. He doubted that she needed an ally, but if so he was only too willing.

"After what you told me the other day, Reda, I'm at a loss to understand. I'd have thought you'd have jumped at the chance of becoming an educated man."

There was a hint of irony – he was an educated man himself but he'd never thought of it as doing him any good.

"As I told you the other day, Mr Blake, my father wanted me to go to Oxford. But America? That is a totally different matter. He would be horrified."

"Why? What's wrong with America? Don't you like Americans?"

"I don't trust them, Mr Blake. Nobody in the Middle East trusts the Americans."

"What? Not even the Israelis?"

"Especially the Israelis, they above all people. At least we Arabs know where we stand. Whatever the Americans may say, they will always let us down – they never have been on our side and they never will be. But they give the Israelis hope, Mr Blake, and that is a very dangerous thing. If it wasn't for that, perhaps we wouldn't have half the trouble that we do."

There was an element of bias in what he said, but it was still a serious point. Reda was a serious young man. He'd previously talked of philosophy, today it was international relations. Strictly speaking, this was Blake's territory and yet it was he who was being given the lesson. Although Reda was absolutely right – and in the murky pool of Middle Eastern relations it often took the youngest eyes to see the most clearly. Had he thought this out for himself? Or was it something he'd gleaned from his illicit website?

"Oh, and where did you come across that piece of ideology?"

"Don't worry, Mr Blake." Reda drew deeply on his water-pipe. "I'm not one of your fundamentalists. I've been taught, not indoctrinated. I may have my views but they're very much my own – and whatever I believe in, I do so out of my own free will."

This admission came as a relief to Blake – the danger of brain-washed extremism had been a worry. He glanced across at Lee Yong to gauge her reaction.

So far she had taken little part in the conversation and seemed disinterested, her cup of latte remaining untouched on the table in front of her. He began to wonder how much she knew and whether Reda's political activities were as much news to her as her plans to study were to Reda. She looked up and caught his eye.

"Oh, don't look at me, Mr Blake – politics doesn't interest me in the slightest. I have no desire to change the world – merely to explore it. It's Reda who has other ideas."

Blake looked back at the young Egyptian.

"You see, I've already been to college," said Reda.

"Oh, where?"

"In Cairo."

"Really? And what did you study?"

"Politics, History and Economics. Everything you need to become a tour guide."

"But don't you wish for something more than that?"

"Yes, perhaps." Reda shrugged his shoulders. "But where I come from we have a saying." Here, he turned to face Lee Yong as if his remark was addressed to her. "'Happy is the traveller who knows where to stop'. Do you not say something similar in your country?"

Blake shook his head – if they did, he was not aware of it.

"You see," continued Reda, "I count myself a lucky man, Mr Blake. I am exempt from National Service, and unlike those poor fellows who escorted the bus to Edfu today or sit in watchtowers twelve hours a day guarding pieces of empty desert, I get to do something I actually enjoy. The history of my country is a precious thing, Mr Blake, and I would much prefer to guard that."

"You're exempt? How so?"

The requirements for Egyptian National Service were stringent. If Reda had escaped them, then he was indeed a lucky man.

"When my father died, I registered myself to look after my mother. She is not in the best of health and she needs my support. I do what I can, although I don't earn a great salary. I had started to save, but…" He shrugged his shoulders again. "That is the will of Allah and I must obey it."

Blake was surprised to hear him express such fatalistic views. For all his modern thinking, the young Egyptian was still bound to his roots. He looked back across at Lee Yong. She was still not speaking and had even turned her head away and was staring out into space. Had he touched a raw nerve?

"As for myself," Reda continued, "I prefer this part of the world." He extended an outstretched arm in the direction of the square. "It's much more peaceful and relaxing, don't you think?"

He drew on his sheesha again and let out another waft of the apple-scented smoke. From a loudspeaker poised above his head, the voice of Umm Kulthum warbled her approval.

Despite the recent press of the souk, Blake felt inclined to agree – there was definitely something laid-back about the place. Compared to Cairo it was relatively calm and its provincial feel and open space gave it a certain seductive quality. Over the way stood the great mass of Elephantine Island while in between, the white-sailed feluccas plied gently back and forth with their cargoes. On the far bank, the tawny wastes of the Western Desert stretched endlessly into the distance…

He turned to Lee Yong.

"What about you? Do you like it here?"

She must surely have a view but for the moment, a grudging "It's alright…" was as much as he could wring out of her.

He was forced to continue his conversation with Reda alone and they carried on for another ten minutes or so, dissecting the politics of the Middle East. Eventually the situation was relieved by the arrival of the others who came wandering back from the souk.

"So this is where you've been hiding," said Keith. "We wondered where on earth you'd got to."

With a screech of scraping metal, he dragged over another table and they each pulled up a chair and sat down.

"And how was the spice shop?" Blake decided to show interest.

Joan had already started to unload her shopping bag and they crowded round to inspect the contents.

"Just look at these – aren't they wonderful?"

To her credit, Lee Yong immediately roused herself from her reverie and took an interest in Joan's purchases, thrusting her nose amongst the packages.

"They smell nice…"

After they'd settled down, a waiter appeared and they ordered themselves something to drink. Blake had long since finished his glass of mint tea and decided to ask for a second.

The group soon split into two – the women still discussing Joan's purchases while amongst the men, the talk got round to the future.

"So what are the plans for tomorrow?" Keith was anxious to know.

"Haven't a clue," said David. "But I'll take a bet it involves another early start."

They turned to the young Egyptian for an answer.

But Reda had taken the opportunity to distance himself and was sitting to one side. He'd left off his water-pipe and had taken his mobile phone from his pocket and was checking his messages. A distinct look of concern crossed his face and he immediately began tapping out a response.

Chapter Seventeen

It took ten minutes or so for the drinks to arrive. While he was waiting Blake gradually became aware of the beginnings of a disturbance. Initially masked by the singing of Umm Kulthum, raised voices were making themselves heard somewhere nearby. He lifted his eyes from the dregs at the base of his glass and looked round to discover the source of the noise.

Before him lay the wide expanse of Midan Al-Mahatta. On the other side of the square, a crowd was gathering outside the imposing frontage of the Governorate building. During the course of his conversation with Reda, and latterly with the others, a steady stream of passers-by had been making their way towards it. At first he'd thought them a mixture of tourists, late-night shoppers returning from the souk, or workers on their way home. But now he could see that they'd all been heading to the same spot and what had started as a small, inconspicuous grouping had steadily swelled into a large and vociferous throng. And all the while, more and more were joining them from the various approaches to the square.

He turned toward Reda with the intention of asking for some explanation, but the young Egyptian's head remained lowered as he continued to attend to his texts.

Blake consulted his watch. It was precisely ten o'clock and as if timed with some predetermined signal, a fuzzy voice suddenly blared out through a megaphone, drowning out the unfortunate Umm Kulthum.

"What on earth was that?"

Keith was startled from his seat and within a few seconds the whole party were craning their necks in the direction of the noise. Too late and too strident to be confused with the wailing of evening prayers, it had succeeded in taking them all by surprise.

The Governorate was an elegant building. Dressed in a coating of shiny white marble, it looked down on those who confronted it with disdain. But the crowd gathered in front of it was clearly not to be put off and had grown to a few hundred strong. One of their number, a young man in a leather jacket and jeans, clambered up the steps leading to the entrance and began addressing them through a loud-hailer, urging them to join him in achieving greater things. A loud cry went up in response, then another, and within a matter of moments the whole crowd had broken into a chant.

Mubarak out! Mubarak out! Mubarak out!

Small groups of people started jumping up and down in time with the slogan and here and there the Egyptian flag was being waved.

Keith got to his feet to get a better view.

"What are they saying?" asked David, still seated.

With the voice of Umm Kulthum warbling in the background and the fuzzy blare of the loud-hailer, Blake struggled to make it out – but he could easily hazard a guess.

"They want rid of Mubarak."

"What, Hosni Mubarak, the president?"

"Yes, the very same..."

"Why would they want to do that? I thought he was well-respected."

Blake shrugged. It wasn't for him to speak on behalf of another nation, even if it was one he might consider his own. He pointed in the direction of Reda.

"If you want the answer to that, you'd better ask an Egyptian."

Reda was only too happy to enlighten them. He looked up from his phone to respond.

"He might be respected in the West, but in his own country he is despised. You only know what you read in your newspapers and see on your televisions. You think he does a good job because he keeps us Muslims under control and you never think of Egypt as a threat. But all the while he keeps us pressed beneath his thumb, we suffer for it. He's kept us down for almost forty years – but the Egyptian people have had enough. Now they want their freedom and they're prepared to stand up and fight for it."

"Good Lord." Keith was genuinely shocked. "I had no idea..."

Blake shook his head in dismay. In the realm of international affairs, his countrymen could be disarmingly naive. But as he'd said before, this was Egypt – a place where things were not always what they seemed.

The clamour from across the square had increased in volume. The young man at the top of the steps was joined by some of his friends and now four or five of them were passing the megaphone from one to another and making impassioned speeches. On the Corniche away to the left, traffic had slowed to a crawl and a number of cars had pulled off the highway and onto the sidewalk to watch. Their drivers leant permanently on their horns, adding to the dreadful din. The overall effect was deafening and if the general aim was to attract attention, it could hardly have been more successful – the whole of Aswan must have heard it.

Blake wondered as to the protestors' final objective. The building itself was empty. There were no lights on, the employees and officials having left work some hours before. Was it the intention to storm the place in their absence? If so, it would not be long before someone heaved a brick through a window.

And where were the police? They'd already made an appearance earlier that evening, prowling round the souk, looking for trouble – they surely couldn't ignore this. It occurred to Blake that perhaps the demonstrators had deliberately waited until their nightly patrol was over before showing their hand. The action appeared chaotic, but Blake's suspicion was that events had been carefully planned. And here was Reda, casually checking his watch and texting on his mobile phone...

For a while, no-one spoke – even if they had it would have been difficult to make themselves heard above the din. Distracted by the blasts of the car horns and the constant chanting, they were all engaged in watching the action that was unfolding on the other side of the square. Like spectators at an open-air performance that had been laid on for them to witness, seated in comfort at the House of Umm Kulthum and for the price of a cup of coffee, they could view their entertainment from a safe distance.

But that was about to change and any thought that they could remain isolated from events soon evaporated. Umm Kulthum was suddenly cut off in her prime and the rickety neon lights of the café behind them flickered for the last time before they were shut off. The few customers who had lingered on inside through fear of venturing out soon emerged, quickly followed by the patron who smartly pulled down the rollered steel-shutter before locking it and disappearing into the night.

"I hope this isn't going to get out of hand." Keith watched him go with apprehension.

"Calm yourselves my friends." The childlike enthusiasm Reda had shown earlier in the evening had abated. "These affairs are not intended to be violent. Stay here with me and all will be well, I promise you."

Despite his attempt to hearten them, a sense of unease settled on the group. Keith remained standing and started fiddling with the loose change in his pockets. Behind him, Janet vowed she was not going to be moved by anyone or anything and clung to her chair with a vice-like grip. Mrs Biltmore, unable to sit steadily on her seat, wobbled like a jelly on a plate and rather than haranguing the others, resorted to talking to herself and mumbled under her breath. Next to her, Ira sat bolt upright and said nothing. And in order to calm her nerves, Joan had already delved into her cream-coloured bag for her cigarettes and had lit up, blowing a trail of acrid smoke across the table. Of the six of them, it was only David who remained completely impassive. As an old soldier, he'd probably seen it all before.

Blake didn't feel comfortable himself. Now that the patron had fled and the shutters were locked the option of retreating back inside the café was denied them, and there seemed little alternative but to stay where they were and sit things out. The direct route back to the ship was cut off – nobody would have wanted to walk across Midan Al-Mahatta at present – and the idea that they could slip away down some side street seemed risky. They'd have Reda to guide them of course, although he was preoccupied with his mobile phone and didn't appear minded to suggest it. They were completely in his hands and yet he was doing nothing. Someone needed to formulate a plan so if push ever came to shove, they were prepared.

Blake looked to his left and Lee Yong. She'd come to their rescue at the Valley of the Kings, taking control and guiding them through the tombs. They'd willingly given themselves up to her then and had allowed her to carry them along in her wake, awed by the force of her character. But this was different – this was no casual jaunt through history – and Blake wondered whether she could be relied on to repeat the performance. As things stood, he doubted it – she was equally as absorbed in the action as the others.

She'd said little all evening. Since his arrival at the café, Blake's conversation had been primarily with Reda. Lee Yong had seemed subdued and distant, and he'd formed the impression that some coolness had grown up between her and the young Egyptian. A lovers' tiff perhaps? Or had she too discovered his involvement and disapproved? Perhaps that was why she now looked away. Whatever her reason, Blake could tell she was not in the mood to be positive.

Across the square, the protest rumbled on. The crowd outside the Governorate had continued to grow and like a gathering storm whose clouds were about to burst, the feeling was that at any moment it might all spill over.

They'd been watching from the café for a while (ten or fifteen minutes perhaps – unlike Reda, Blake hadn't been keeping track of time) when the blare of car horns on the Corniche was augmented by the howl of sirens. Of the drivers who had pulled onto the sidewalk, one or two made off – they were presumably known to the law and had no desire to be recognised – but most stayed on to jeer the police when they arrived.

It was the same three cars which had been on duty at the souk earlier that evening that sped into view. The honking doubled like a flock of raucous geese – but the police had no intention of waiting to enjoy their greeting and simply mounted the kerb and drove straight toward the disturbance. The crowd turned to face them and for the moment ignored the rantings of their leaders on the steps. At the sight of the three cars they immediately changed their chant, abandoning their cries of *Mubarak out!* for the shout of *Down with the police!*

Blake doubted it was a wise move. At this stage the crowd far outnumbered the law and other than bolster their confidence, it served no practical purpose as the police were bound to resent it and prepare themselves to retaliate. It was as if someone the size of Mrs Biltmore (Blake couldn't help but make the comparison) was being bothered by a wasp and rather than ignore it had chosen to swipe at it with a rolled-up newspaper – an act which could only enrage it further. Later, it would doubtless return to implant its sting.

But the police were aware they were too few to respond and settled for drawing their cars up in a line across the centre of the square facing the demonstration. Beyond announcing their presence, this too was a pointless move as the square was so large that the crowd could easily have dispersed around them. But with neither side inclined to back down, a stand-off was bound to ensue, and what with the blaring of car horns, the wailing of sirens, the abusive chanting of the crowd and the amplified exhortations of its leaders, it was hard to hear yourself think.

"Now what?" bellowed Keith.

With the arrival of the police they should have felt less vulnerable – but if anything it had the opposite effect and heightened the tension.

"Be patient," replied Reda.

"Well I'm not so sure we shouldn't be making a move."

"No, there's nothing we can do, we wait."

And weather the coming storm, thought Blake. He was struggling to come up with options – but there were none he could think of. They were completely in the hands of the young Egyptian. Hopefully, he had good reasons for his advice.

Keith resumed his seat. He'd spoken for them all but to no avail. They were powerless and continued to sit, immobile in their chairs, tight-lipped and anxious.

There was a predictability about these events that Blake found depressing. The police would call for reinforcements, confrontation would ensue and the inevitable battle would take place. No-one would want to give way. He'd seen it many times before – random acts of violence played out in the backstreets of Cairo. Anywhere injustice was felt, the seeds of rebellion were stamped on and weeded out before they had a chance to take root. Egypt had been a battleground for years. The suppression of popular dissent was commonplace and brutal (look what had happened to Khaled Saeed in Alexandria). Yet it was so easily explained away – *We're keeping the Islamists under control* – that no-one took any notice, least of all the West. And here was another example, thrust right under his nose.

It irritated Blake intensely that he should get caught up in it all. Wasn't he supposed to be on a birding holiday? He'd meant to leave politics behind at the Embassy – but with the exception of the boat trip two days before, precious little birding had been done. There was no chance of that now. He was sorely tempted to do what Keith had suggested, stand up and walk out – and were it not for Lee Yong, he undoubtedly would have done so. Without her, he'd have slipped away and headed down a side street, trusting his luck, but the grip she had on him held him back. He was anxious and his first priority was to protect her. His natural instinct was to grab hold of her and get her out of there, even if it meant taking a risk. The others would all follow Keith. They'd said nothing themselves and it had been left up to him to give voice to their feelings. Reda seemed to have his own reasons for staying on the scene and had told against him. Why were they so beholden to the young Egyptian? They hung on his every word – didn't they have minds of their own? Why did they have to wait?

Meanwhile, the police were being patient. Of the three cars drawn up in the square, only one of the occupants had thought to get out and he stood, hands on hips, surveying the scene. No more than fifty yards away the crowd roared in defiance, but he retained his pose without flinching and dared to raise his chin at his abusers. He was either mad, brave or supremely arrogant, thought Blake, and there was something about him that clearly suggested the latter.

A flabby paunch hung over the belt of his trousers – these policemen lived well. But unlike Mrs Biltmore (who was large for no discernible reason) he carried his weight with purpose as though he might at any moment use it to impose himself on others – big in character as well as in body, he dominated space rather than simply occupying it.

He shortly reached through the rear window of his vehicle and brought out a loud-hailer of his own. *Coals to Newcastle*, thought Blake. And he was right, for whatever message the policeman sought to convey was hopelessly lost amidst the general cacophony of noise. The crowd were unimpressed and carried on chanting and if they understood a word of what he'd said they gave no sign. The policeman nonetheless insisted on finishing his address before climbing back into his car where he began shouting his commands into the mouthpiece of a two-way radio.

Twenty minutes elapsed before the reinforcements he'd called for arrived. Blake guessed they were part-time volunteers and it would have taken them some time to assemble and equip themselves with the helmets, shields and batons with which they finally appeared. The police station (as he later discovered) was located half a mile away down Sharia Abtal, a turning off the square to their left, and the makeshift force had probably run all the way as they emerged into view at the trot. They formed up in the space between the cars and awaited their instructions.

The fat policeman got out to welcome them. He'd swapped his megaphone for a swagger stick which he brandished like a fly swat, pointing firstly at his troops and then at the opposition. His thick lips worked furiously and Blake imagined the savage words of exhortation – had he been standing close enough he might have felt the spittle landing.

The police chief gave a final flourish of his stick, then stepped aside and urged his men forward. They shuffled together to form a phalanx in front of the parked cars and on the command of their officer in charge they made their move. At neither a run nor a walk, but using the same steady trot with which they'd entered the square, they advanced toward the protestors in determined fashion.

Their intention was probably to drive a wedge through the crowd, split it in two and gain access to the ringleaders on the steps of the Governorate. If so then it was doomed to failure – there were simply not enough of them to achieve their objective and their initial charge was met with stiff resistance and immediately petered out. The cry of *Down with the police!* rose up once again and the crowd began pushing back. Now it was the police who were under attack and they responded by raising their batons and raining down blows on those in front of them. The officer in charge soon became lost in the crush and without his orders, what had begun as an orderly advance deteriorated into a melee. Scuffles broke out as groups of police tried to bring the protestors under control. Sticks were wielded like baseball bats, striking at what they could find. Yielding under the pressure, sections of the crowd began to break off and rushed for the exits. On the steps of the Governorate, the protest's leadership realised the game was up and abandoned their position, melting into the throng. At its edges the gathering was losing cohesion and like an old garment frayed at the hem, the protest was slowly unravelling.

Trapped outside the shuttered frontage of the café, Blake and his party continued to fret. With the scene before them descending into chaos, it was now impossible to escape without becoming embroiled. Reda had still not signalled they should take action, although the calm that had earlier pervaded his face had turned to a worried frown. If things did not improve soon, thought Blake, the young Egyptian would have a lot to answer for.

Out in the square, the gathering had finally fractured beneath the weight of the police reprisal. The general chanting had ceased, although here and there odd pockets of resistance carried on with their cries. Most were fleeing as best they could, running like mad to escape, then stopping occasionally to look back as if waiting for a friend before hurrying on.

Figures rushed by on either side. Immediately to their right, two young men sprinted toward a side street. Suddenly one stumbled, his sandal stubbed against the kerb, and he sprawled across the pavement. His companion close behind fell straight on top of him and before they could scramble to their feet, the policeman pursuing them was upon them. Standing astride the pair lying prone beneath him, he raised his heavy baton and brought it crashing down. The figure on top lifted an arm to protect himself but the policeman smashed it aside and continued his beating. Like a butterfly emerging from its chrysalis, the figure below succeeded in dragging himself clear and continued his flight into the darkness.

In front of the café there was a sharp intake of breath.

"Good Lord," said Keith, stiffening in his seat.

"Oh my!" said Mrs Biltmore, speaking for the first time since the episode had begun.

On the far side, Joan sucked hard on her latest cigarette while behind her, Janet finally let go of the frame of her chair – but only so that her hand could fly up to her face and cover her mouth. It was as well that she stifled her cry – no-one wanted to attract attention.

There was a movement to Blake's left. Lee Yong had instinctively grabbed hold of the sleeve of his linen jacket. She continued to stare straight ahead and with all her fortitude, it seemed that even she was not immune.

While they were registering their shock, the fallen protestor managed to escape his assailant and staggered off into the night clutching his shattered arm. Elsewhere the action continued and they'd barely recovered their breath when a second and more telling incident demanded their attention.

Another man was running from right to left in front of them. Older and smaller, he wore a dirty white galabeya and a traditional wound turban. He too tripped and fell, but before his pursuer could begin the inevitable beating, he rose to his knees and looked up, pressing his hands together in supplication. The officer stood over him, ready to strike, but the old man was saying something that stopped him, his mouth working furiously against the clamour. He began to look around in desperation, then his eyes alighted on the café and he turned toward it, pointing, *There!*

A shiver of recognition descended Blake's spine. The face that now looked in their direction was unmistakable. Old, wizened and with a straggly beard and blackened teeth, he remembered it from the meeting in the field the day before. Common amongst the rural poor, it was not the kind of face you could forget. Here too was the hazy figure he'd seen with Reda on the riverbank. Ancient Egypt was still alive and had come to betray them.

Reda had remained seated calmly on Blake's right. He pushed back his chair and slowly got to his feet. For a moment Blake thought he might run like the others, but he soon dismissed the idea. Whatever the crowd might do, that had never been part of Reda's plan. Even if he'd been so minded, it would have done him little good – with his stout frame he was not the athletic type and he'd soon have been caught. Rather than surrender his dignity in some ungainly chase, the young Egyptian had elected to give up his person more quietly. He carefully removed his wallet from his pocket and together with his mobile phone placed it gently on the glass table top in front of him.

"It would appear that the police would like to ask me a few questions. My apologies for any inconvenience this may cause you my friends, but please do not concern yourselves on my account, I beg you. Look after each other," (he looked briefly in the direction of Keith) "and when this dies down, as it will, go back to the ship. I will join you there later."

He then walked slowly out into the square to address the officer confronting him.

"It's me that you want. These people are tourists." He indicated the group behind him. "They have nothing to do with this."

The officer responded in a thick Arabic accent which Blake could barely understand. Beneath his feet, the old man still cowered on the ground, his ancient eyes flicking anxiously back and forth as he nervously awaited his fate. After a brief exchange, the officer swung a boot in his direction and he took a heavy blow to the backside before struggling upright and hobbling off toward the souk.

Blake was on his feet now, as were the others. They'd all got up, either to get a better view or, as was more likely, to be ready to make a swift escape. Lee Yong still had hold of his sleeve and as the officer laid hands on Reda, her grip on him tightened still further. Her face had become pale and drawn, and in the artificial light of the street lamps it looked as if she'd lost her natural colour. And yet, despite her pallor, she still seemed as beautiful as ever.

"*No!*"

She let the word out under her breath, then finally relinquished his sleeve and started forward. Blake instinctively extended his arm to hold her back.

"Wait – that will only make things worse. Trust me, we'll have to be patient."

Even in the heat of a moment such as this, his old tendency not to interfere still guided him.

Lee Yong took heed of his words as she continued to press against his outstretched arm but did not attempt to push past.

The others remained static – they had no desire to get involved – and they watched and waited as Reda was taken away. Encouraged by the regular prod of the policeman's baton, he walked stoically toward the line of the white police cars. One of the rear doors was flung open and head bowed, he was bundled into a back seat. The officer who had taken him leaned in, no doubt to make some fatuous comment – *This one's no trouble, he didn't put up much of a fight* – then slammed the door shut.

No sooner had Reda been closed in than the car roared away, siren blaring, and to the accompaniment of honking horns and the jeers, shouts and waving of fists from the drivers pulled up on the sidewalk, it set off at high speed along the Corniche.

Chapter Eighteen

Reda's departure was met with a stunned silence. In the square the crowd had all but dispersed. The police had succeeded in clearing the front of the Governorate building and had moved on to the process of mopping up. Any 'action' had been transferred to the side streets where small groups of protestors, pursued by the law and hemmed in amongst the narrow walkways, turned to face their attackers. Apart from these occasional eruptions, things had quietened down and for the first time since the conflict had begun it was possible to hear yourself think. They'd been struck dumb by the proceedings but suddenly they all had something to say and everyone started talking at once.

"What on earth was that all about?" Keith turned to face the others. "You speak the lingo, Blake – what was going on with Reda?"

"He's been asked to assist the police with their enquiries."

"You mean he's been arrested."

"If you must put it that way – yes."

It was a word Blake had wanted to avoid. Lee Yong might find it distressing and he regretted the fact that Keith had used it. Better to soften the blow.

Keith, however, persisted.

"What exactly does that mean?"

"Probably a night in the cells, at least."

"And then?"

"Who knows…"

Blake shrugged. This was Egypt. Anything was possible. The long-standing emergency law and its enforcement was an arbitrary affair. Its introduction had given the police unlimited powers. People could be 'arrested' for no good reason and held without trial for an indefinite period. Their release depended upon a complicated system of paperwork and usually the payment of a bribe and the intervention of some high official.

Sometimes, in the absence of either, they remained in prison and eventually disappeared without trace. Conversely, known criminals who were prepared to pay for the privilege were allowed to roam the streets. And all the time, it was the police who grew fat and arrogant on the proceeds.

"Did someone say Reda's been arrested?"

David had picked up on it and much to Blake's annoyance, it was now public knowledge.

"That poor boy," said Janet. "Whatever did he do wrong?"

"If you ask me," said David, "I think he had something to do with the riot."

Unlike Janet, who was quite prepared to give Reda the benefit of the doubt, Joan was scathing in her view.

"Typical! I might have known he couldn't be trusted." Her comment harked back to the conversation they'd had at the dinner table on their first night together. She'd either forgotten the service Reda had performed for her regarding her jewellery box, or she'd dismissed it as a one-off occurrence. This latest act of apparent treachery played to her agenda. "Well, he's left us in a fine mess I must say," she added, and hurriedly lit another cigarette.

"Anyway, it wasn't a riot" said Keith. "At least, it wasn't until the police arrived."

"Did you see how that young man got beaten up?" said Janet. "Right in front of our eyes. It was appalling – I couldn't bear watching, I had to look away."

"Well, I'm sorry but he won't get any sympathy from me." Joan remained hard-hearted. "If you come on this sort of thing you've got to expect trouble."

Apart from Blake, Mrs Biltmore was for once the quietest of the group. Her posture was still causing discomfort and as she'd presumably never been arrested or involved in a riot, she'd no cause to make comment. This, combined with her evident shock, reduced her to repeating the single phrase "Oh my…" over and over. Even Ira had more to say on the subject.

"Darnedest thing I ever saw..."

Lee Yong slumped back onto her chair as if her body had collapsed like a deflated balloon. Her complexion had not improved and was, if anything, worse and it seemed it was as much as she could do to prevent herself from bursting into tears. Blake's hand found her shoulder as he tried to give her comfort.

"Don't worry – it'll be alright."

Although if pressed, he didn't quite see how.

They all fell back into a contemplative silence which lasted until Joan stubbed out her latest cigarette.

"So what do we do now?" she asked.

The question had been at the back of everyone's mind, although the answer was obvious – their first priority was to get back to the safety of the ship.

They elected to take the direct route and go back the way they'd come. While the demonstration was in full swing, Blake had considered the alternative of slipping off down a side street and finding his way through the back alleys – but that was now the more dangerous option. The situation had significantly changed. The last of the police cars had moved off elsewhere as the wail of sirens could be heard across the city, but the square itself was relatively peaceful. It had been cleared of protestors and was empty save for a small gathering of police who had regrouped in the centre. Some of them had removed their helmets and were sitting smoking.

Around them lay the scattered remains of the conflict – a shoe lost in flight, a coat torn off and not returned for, pieces of rubble uprooted from the kerbs and pavements for use as weapons. On one of the flowerbeds, an Egyptian flag lay with its pole snapped in two.

Keith led them gingerly round the perimeter, not wanting to venture out into the open for fear of attracting attention. Mrs

Biltmore, relieved that she could at last abandon the discomfort of her chair, still had to be supported, although this time it was neither the terrain nor the heat that afflicted her, but rather the shock which had weakened her legs.

Even Lee Yong was in need of help. At first she was reluctant to leave the café and sat staring straight ahead. Any inner strength she might have possessed seemed to have crumbled beneath the burden of events. Blake offered her an arm.

"Come on. Whatever else has happened, you can't stay here."

With his encouragement she raised herself slowly to her feet but continued to cling to him as if he were her only hope.

Behind them, Joan insisted on loading David up with the pile of shopping bags she'd accumulated earlier that evening.

"I've spent good money on these – if you think I'm leaving them behind just because a few Egyptians decide to sound off, you're mistaken."

Weighed down with his cargo, he grudgingly brought up the rear.

Halfway down the square on their left, they passed the entrance to Sharia Abtal, the street from which the police had emerged. Here there were signs of a struggle, pieces of assorted debris lying amongst the broken shards of a glass bottle. Propped against a wall lay the body of a man, his legs splayed out while blood oozed gently from a temporary bandage wound around his temple. A few feet away, his two companions debated loudly as to what to do next.

At the main road, the cars which had pulled off onto the sidewalk had moved on and had reverted to racing up and down the boulevard, horns blaring. Packed to capacity, their occupants leant out of the open windows, shouting and waving their flags.

The party waited for a lull so they could safely cross. Once on the other side of the Corniche they left the street lights behind and although it was dark, they somehow felt safer.

"Thank God for that," said Keith, as they finally sighted the ship.

With their feet planted firmly on the gangplank, they could all breathe a collective sigh of relief and for the moment their ordeal was over.

It was now approaching midnight. Having set off just after dinner they'd been away for almost three hours although it felt like a lifetime since they'd last enjoyed the comfort and safety of the ship. And yet as soon as they set foot on board, they realised things were not as they should be. At this late hour they would normally have tip-toed across the foyer so as not to disturb anyone, but tonight there was no need as the rest of their fellow passengers were already out of bed and gathered in reception. Some were still in their street clothes, some were in their bathrobes and slippers, but the foyer was packed and filled with their animated chatter. The ship was in turmoil.

In the far corner, a group of Germans from the dinner table next to Blake's were besieging the manager's desk. Behind it stood the captain himself, Mr Mohammed, his oily skin glistening as sweat dribbled from his temple. While one hand clasped a telephone receiver to his ear, the other was held outstretched, palm forward, as if to fend off his attackers.

"Bear with me, please. A moment, I beg you."

He pleaded with the crowd, then returned to jabbering into the telephone at high speed in Arabic.

Mrs Biltmore, oblivious to all that was going on around her, sank onto the sofa immediately next to the doorway and lay awaiting rescue. Ira had the presence of mind to fetch a magazine from a nearby coffee table and began to fan her with it, but her only response was to repeat the phrase she'd used earlier.

"Oh my…"

"I think she needs help," said Janet and went over to offer assistance.

Meanwhile, Keith had made a discovery.

"Here, I think you'd better come and have a look at this."

He led Blake to the other side of the foyer where a TV monitor hung high up on the wall. The picture it showed was of another square, brightly lit, and of another demonstration, far larger than the one that they'd witnessed. Blake instantly recognised the location. With the tall edifice of the Nile Hilton rising behind it, it was unmistakable.

"Good God! That's Tahrir!"

"Tahrir?"

"Midan Tahrir. Tahrir Square – Cairo."

"I thought it must be somewhere important. So what's going on?"

"I don't know…"

And yet he had an inkling – the gas beneath the pot he'd watched simmering on the stove had been turned up and it had suddenly boiled over.

Back at reception, Mr Mohammed had at last finished his telephone call and had both hands free to restrain his audience. Even so, he still had a job to persuade them to quieten down.

"A moment please. If you don't mind. If you would just let me speak."

The babble subsided and he began to talk quickly – but it was mostly in German with the occasional phrase in Arabic.

"What's he saying?" Keith strained an ear.

"Shush," said Blake. "Let me listen." He began to interpret. "He says there's been an uprising of some kind. The centre of Cairo has been occupied by demonstrators and the situation appears confused. Much more than that he can't tell us, although he claims the Government is still in control. He urges us to stay calm and not to worry. He says we're perfectly safe here and suggests we all go back to bed and get some sleep. He'll try to find out more and let us know as soon as he can. In the meantime he's called a meeting for ten o'clock in the morning in the Forward Lounge."

As the captain's announcement ended, David returned from taking up Joan's shopping.

"Just a minute – weren't we supposed to have an early start for a trip out tomorrow?"

"Yes, I believe you're right. Let's go and have a look."

They went back to consult the notice board beneath the TV monitor which was still showing pictures of Tahrir. The itinerary for the next day had been posted and then crossed through with the word 'cancelled'.

"Hmm... I'll bet that's what's upset the Germans," said Keith. David nodded.

"Very likely – although I can't say I'm all that disappointed. I never did like those early starts."

"Well, I for one agree with Mr Mohammed. I think we should all go to bed and sleep on it. I can't see there's anything to be gained by staying here." Keith indicated the crush in the foyer. "I don't know about you, but I'm shattered and I know Janet's the same."

"Joan's already gone up."

A wry smile crossed Blake's lips – it would take more than a revolution to come between Joan and her beauty sleep.

They made their way over to the sofa. Mrs Biltmore had recovered sufficiently to be able to get to her feet and with Ira in close attendance, she painfully ascended the stairs.

Lee Yong had been sitting beside her along with Janet. She'd still not made any comment and other than her muted outburst at Reda's arrest, she'd remained strangely silent. She looked as if she were in a state of shock and even the presence of those she might call her friends couldn't shake her out of it. As the others departed, Blake volunteered to see her back to her room, but she was in no mood to talk and as soon as he'd bid her goodnight he went straight to his cabin.

The television in his room had not been plugged in, never mind used, since his arrival on board. He got it working and soon the same images as he'd seen in the lobby flashed up onto the screen. The set was tuned to Nile TV, a station run by the state, so it was known to be biased and provided only limited coverage. The pictures showed the occupation of Tahrir Square but focused on the police. They were designed to give the impression they were in control and depicted the rioters in retreat. He retuned to Al Jazeera which presented a different perspective.

There, it became apparent that the scenes they'd looked at in Cairo and those they'd witnessed for themselves in Aswan had been repeated in varying degrees throughout the country. In the northern cities of Alexandria and Mansoura there had been mass demonstrations and tens of thousands had taken to the streets. In Suez there had been violent clashes with the police and there were reports of casualties. In Tanta, Beni Suef and elsewhere it was the same. Even Abu Simbel, far to the south, had seen protests. The whole of Egypt was in uproar.

Blake lay on the bed and watched as the news unfolded. Some reports seemed to conflict with one another, but bit by bit it became clear as to what had happened. After years of subjugation and suffering the Egyptian people had finally decided to act, and through a massive feat of organisation and with great determination they had risen up as one. Despite the confusion, they had only one purpose – to get rid of their leader. The man they called the lapdog of the West, he who had licked the hands of the Israelis and barked at the so-called extremists – he was the one they wanted rid of. To judge by the extent of the protests, it looked as if Mubarak was finished. The question was whether the army was prepared to intervene. If they did, there would likely be bloodshed, but if not then the will of the people would prevail. After Tunisia, it had only been a matter of time...

Blake closed his eyes and let the sounds wash over him. What more could he have done? He'd given his warning as best he could. Anyone who'd looked at his memo to the First Secretary and read between the lines could see that. *The day approaches my brothers* – those were the words he'd heard used. It was as though they were expecting a second coming. He'd feared some violent terrorist act – even another 9/11 – and yet, what they'd actually been planning was a peaceful revolution.

He wondered whether he should feel triumphant. If he could only see the First Secretary now he would have every right to be as he'd been proved correct. He ought to have felt some sense of vindication but he did not. The nation was too precious for that and he was worried for its future. A wind of change was blowing through the Middle East and North Africa and stirring up the desert sands. Egypt, the county he'd adopted, the country he'd loved and lived in, the country he'd planned to grow old in, was about to be transformed. Where would it all lead?

An hour later, a chill in the room forced him awake and he found himself lying on his back, fully clothed, the remote control in his hand and the bedside lamp still on. He yawned and looked at his watch. It was a quarter to two. In the far corner, the noise from the TV had abated and the screen had reverted to a fuzzy blank. He turned it off and got undressed, then slid into bed and turned out the light.

Chapter Nineteen

Then it was morning and the first glimmer of daylight was creeping into the room. Propped in the corner next to the doorway he could discern the shadowy shape of his telescope and tripod, and as the light grew stronger it grew more and more distinct. This was usually the signal for him to get up and go out on deck to continue his exploration of the world of birds. There would be a sunrise to watch (he'd still not seen the flight of Glossy Ibis) and the sandbanks would be teeming with life – godwits, sandpipers, stints, all scuttling across the mud. But today the call was weak and for the moment he'd lost interest. How could he think of watching birds when the world was in such a state? He could hardly go out on deck and pretend that nothing had happened.

The events of the previous evening seemed surreal. Perhaps he'd imagined them, perhaps it had all been a dream, and to convince himself of their existence he got out of bed and went to turn the TV back on. But he was no more than halfway across the room when he realised he'd no need – he already had a reminder right in front of his eyes.

Reda's mobile phone and wallet lay on the desk where he'd left them the night before. They proved the point and confirmed the reality of things but their unlooked-for presence bothered him. Why were these foreign objects in his room? What was he supposed to do with them? They didn't belong to him, he had such things of his own. And yet he'd invited them into his life.

He wondered what had induced him to pick them up. He'd no need of further proof regarding Reda's involvement – the quick look he'd taken at the young Egyptian's computer had been enough. Nor did he want to pry further into his affairs and the thought of opening them up and perusing their contents was not an option. But he recalled that as soon as Reda had set them down, he'd lifted them from the table and hidden them in his pocket. The young man had deliberately placed them in front of him – it was as good as him saying *I trust you, Mr Blake. I want you to look after these for me.* And, like a fool, he'd taken the bait. Now he'd assumed a responsibility he was not at all sure he wanted. He got back into bed and lay there until it was time to get ready for breakfast.

After he'd washed and dressed, he slipped the wallet and phone into his pocket and took them with him as if he'd convinced himself that by removing them from the room it might somehow lessen the burden. If left, they were bound to be there on his return – away from his cabin, there was a chance they might be got rid of.

He thought he'd gone down early but he found the dining room full and in a state of chaos. Only half the normal breakfast was on offer – there were no fresh rolls and no hot buffet, although someone had hard-boiled some eggs. A rumour was circulating amongst the guests that most of the kitchen staff had absconded during the night and gone back home to be with their families. If true, although inconvenient, it was quite understandable.

Other than Joan, whose purpose in life was to complain, the rest of Blake's table had adopted an attitude of stoic resilience. A wartime spirit prevailed and with it, the thought that they could overcome any obstacle. *We'll manage. We're used to this sort of thing. We're British.*

Rather unsurprisingly, Lee Yong had not come down to join them.

They reconvened at 10am in the Forward Lounge to hear the captain's news. Their first meeting had been good-natured and relaxed but this one was accompanied by an air of tension. The curtains had been drawn back as before and the place was packed with almost every passenger attending. All the seats were taken and those who arrived last were obliged to stand at the back. The babble of conversation exceeded that in the dining room and here and there, heated debates broke out amongst those of a more Latin temperament. In front of the plate-glass windows, a middle-aged man clasped his wife to his chest as she burst into tears. Her mournful lament could be heard by all.

"I knew we should never have come on this holiday. Now look what's happened. We'll all be murdered in our beds!"

Outside, the Nile flowed peacefully by, seemingly unperturbed.

Mr Mohammed appeared, more than ten minutes late and looking rather flustered. The same sweat which had affected him the night before beaded on his damp forehead. Flanked on one side by the chef and on the other by the chief engineer (both no doubt pressed into giving moral support) he hurried to the front clutching a piece of paper and prepared to make an announcement. After a few shushes to quieten the crowd, he cleared his throat and began to speak.

He started by apologising for keeping them waiting but the information he'd been seeking had been late in coming through as the internet wasn't working. He'd attempted to speak to his superiors in Cairo by telephone but the lines were busy and he'd been unable to get a connection. For the moment he could tell them little more than what they already knew, but as soon as things improved he would update them. All he could confirm was that Mubarak was still president and that rumours of a military coup were inaccurate.

This assurance of stability was welcome but his general lack of news was anticlimactic and greeted with a groan from the passengers. After such a hyped build-up they'd expected something more concrete. A flurry of questions ensued, starting in one corner and running round the room.

"The television says the Government is still in control. How do we know that's the truth?"

Mr Mohammed shrugged his shoulders. He didn't know. Nile

TV was controlled by the state and they could say what they liked.

"I've heard there's been looting and some of the protestors have been fired on. What's the situation in Aswan?"

Mr Mohammed nodded. He'd heard that too. In Aswan, the police were out on the streets (Blake could vouch for that) and this morning everything seemed peaceful. Besides, they were safe on board his ship where he and his crew could protect them.

"But hasn't half the crew gone missing? There was hardly anyone at breakfast and the boat looks deserted of staff."

Mr Mohammed tugged nervously at the collar of his shirt. Yes, it was true, some of the crew had indeed gone home. But as they all could see (he indicated the chef and the chief engineer) he was being ably supported by his colleagues and would soon have the situation under control.

"So what exactly are you planning to do?"

Palpably relieved, Mr Mohammed took a deep breath. A plan of action had been prepared and he could give a positive answer. He'd sent out into the town to recover what crew he could and to take on fuel and provisions. As soon as he was ready he planned to sail back to Luxor as per the original programme. He was well aware they had flights to catch and connections to make and he was anxious to get them back safely. Most of the crew came from Luxor and they were keen to go home too. All being well, he planned to leave the following morning.

This last revelation was met by a nodding of heads and general approbation. That they were going to get home in one piece was the first thing they wanted to hear. But it did not satisfy everyone and it was left to one of the more mercenary amongst the passengers to put the query the rest had been pondering.

"What about our trips out? Some of us have paid a good deal of money. What's going to happen about that?"

Mr Mohammed shrugged his shoulders again. The question of trips out was the least of his worries. For all he knew, some might be running, some might not. It was a confused picture. He suggested they speak to their tour guide.

Blake pursed his lips – in their case, that was easier said than done.

A few more queries followed, but these were of a minor nature and the questioning soon subsided. Mr Mohammed took out a handkerchief and mopped his brow. At their first meeting he'd pledged himself to their wellbeing – he would fix their plumbing, he would change their light bulbs, he would do this, he would do that, he'd promised them the earth. But when it had come to the crunch, he'd fallen at the first hurdle. He hadn't banked on having a revolution to deal with and he couldn't fix that. As to his sympathies in the matter, he'd given no indication of his feelings. It left Blake wondering which side his bread was buttered.

The meeting broke up and everyone drifted down to the foyer where they gathered in their various groups to compare notes. Blake found himself surrounded in front of the notice board while above his head, the TV continued to show pictures of Tahrir Square, still occupied by protestors. He was soon joined by David and Keith, both of whom wore serious expressions.

The events of the previous day had been a shock to them. They'd come expecting a holiday, a break from the drudge of everyday life, and had not been prepared for a crisis. Yesterday their heads had been full of tombs and temples and pyramids – today they were filled with guns and tear gas and screaming people and the deeply unpleasant idea that they might be in some kind of trouble. But now they'd had a night to sleep on it, any sense of panic had subsided and replaced by sober thought and consideration of how they might get out of their predicament.

"What do you think's going to happen?" asked David.

"It's too early to tell." Despite his diplomatic background,

Blake was unsure. "It'll depend on the army. They're the ones who pull the strings and they've not shown their hand as yet."

"Hmm..." David looked pensive. Mention of an army gave rise to thoughts of bloodshed and violence. As an old soldier, he wasn't too keen about the idea. "What are our chances of getting back home?"

"From Luxor? Pretty good I would have thought." Keith sounded optimistic. "It's a small regional airport. It might be different if we were trying to get out of Cairo."

Blake nodded – it would be. His problem was getting back into it.

"How's Janet taking it?"

"Pretty much as you'd expect. Right now she's had enough of Egypt. She just wants to get back home in one piece. Last night put the wind up her a bit. Put the wind up all of us, actually." Keith turned to David. "What about Joan?"

"As you can imagine, her reaction's been completely over the top. She's planning a lawsuit against the travel company for ruination of her holiday."

"You're joking!"

"No, I'm perfectly serious."

"That's ridiculous!"

"I know – but you try telling her that. She had me up half the night reading through our travel insurance."

"That's a thought. Find anything?"

"Not really." David shook his head. "I think 'revolution' comes under the heading of General Exclusions. I tried phoning them this morning to check but the captain's right – you can't get a phone line for love nor money." He paused while this registered with Keith. Then, "Shame about Reda."

"Yes, I wondered about that, you know."

"What?"

"Whether he'd been set up. That old Egyptian feller seemed to get off scot free."

"Yes, it did look rather odd. I don't suppose there's anything we can do?"

Blake absent-mindedly fingered the contents of his pocket where Reda's mobile phone and wallet lay next to each other. Caught unawares in Keith and David's interchange, he suddenly realised the remark was directed at him.

"Are you asking me?" He raised his hand to his chest, then pushed the suggestion away. "I shouldn't think so…"

It wasn't his problem.

Keith consulted his watch.

"It's half past ten. I'm going back to the room. I want to make sure Janet's alright and I'm going to give the phone lines a try. With a bit of luck I might get through to the airport."

"Good idea," agreed David. "If there's any news, let me know. Shall we meet for lunch as usual?"

"If there is any… Mind you, if push comes to shove, we can always sort ourselves out."

"I'm sure we can."

They spoke as if it were something they might relish and moved off in the direction of the stairway, leaving Blake to ruminate alone.

Over at the reception desk, Mr Mohammed had returned to his duties. Faced with a large and disorderly crowd, he'd begun perspiring again.

On the other side of the foyer, Mrs Biltmore had reclaimed her seat on the sofa by the doorway. Ira was with her and so too was Lee Yong. It was the first time Blake had seen her since escorting her to her room the night before. Then, she'd been contemplative and silent and he wondered whether she had recovered some of her former spirit. She'd not been at breakfast, nor had he noticed her at the meeting. Seeing the three of them together, he assumed they'd been among the latecomers crammed in at the back of the Lounge and had only just made their way down to talk things over. She shortly caught his eye and having given Mrs Biltmore a gentle pat on the shoulder, excused herself and made her way across the foyer towards him.

She'd reverted to wearing her Cuban heels and jeans, although the T-shirt she'd chosen for the day was a little less extravagant than the one she'd had on at the Valley of the Kings. It seemed to suit her mood because as she approached he could tell she was still subdued. For all the time she'd had available to rest (it was now approaching eleven) she looked tired, and when she drew close he could see that her eyes were red. She'd either had no sleep or she'd been crying. Possibly both, he thought.

"Mr Blake?"

"Why don't you call me Michael?"

Why couldn't she address him by his Christian name? Was it that she might blush at the idea?

"Michael… There's something I want to ask you."

"Fire away."

"When Reda was taken away, you said you didn't know what would happen to him. Was that actually true?"

"Well, no – not exactly…"

Now it was his turn to blush.

"Then why did you lie to us, Mr Blake?" She'd very soon dropped the 'Michael' – calling him 'Mr Blake' enabled her to retain a degree of distance.

"I was trying to protect you, I suppose."

"Protect me from what? Finding out the truth?"

"Yes, from that. I didn't want to see you hurt."

He declined to look her in the eye and inspected the stitching of his slip-on shoes instead. So far, he'd been truthful in confessing his sin – to be consistent, he must also be truthful in confessing the reason.

Lee Yong accepted his statement and went on with her line of questioning.

"Mrs Biltmore says she thinks he'll be tortured. She says she's read that the police in Egypt do things, horrible things, and that's how they carry on here."

"Mrs Biltmore has a vivid imagination."

"That's not to say she isn't right."

"Maybe..."

"You don't deny it then?"

He'd tried to divert her but she'd soon seen through his ploy. Unless he was to lie again, it left him no option.

"No, I don't deny it, it's quite possible." She'd eventually force it from him anyway so it was best to be straight with her now. "Well, to be frank, it's likely."

His openness failed to shock her. It was the answer she'd been expecting and she was prepared for it.

"I can't let that happen, Mr Blake. We have to do something about it."

We? Where had that come from all of a sudden? Why did she assume that he was involved in all this? Her presumption caused him to bristle.

"So what do you suggest?"

"I don't know." She shrugged. "That's why I've come to you. You know the country. There must be something we can do. What about the British Embassy?"

He'd wondered how long it would be before someone raised that subject. Somewhere along the line he must have let it slip out – but even if he'd still been employed, it would have been of no use to them now.

"That's no good. Reda's an Egyptian national. If he were a British subject it might be a different story and we could press for his release. But as he's not and we've no grounds for an appeal, it wouldn't work."

"What then?" A look of desperation crossed her face. "You have to help me, Mr Blake."

As reluctant as he was, when she looked at him in that heart-rending way, he knew he could not deny her. Like a notice on the adjacent board, she had him pinned to the wall and he could not escape without some form of commitment. He didn't want to admit it but he'd committed himself the moment he'd picked up Reda's mobile phone and wallet. As much as he'd deny it, he could never have disposed of them as easily as he liked to imagine – all he'd been waiting for was the right moment to act. Was that the real reason he'd put them in his pocket and brought them with him? A few minutes ago he'd stood in exactly the same spot and told David and Keith there was nothing he could do. And yet for Lee Yong, it was different...

"There might be a way… It would cost money of course."

He regretted sounding so mercenary. He didn't want her to think it was he who needed rewarding. Although the remark did not seem to concern her – on the contrary, it gave her hope.

"That's not an issue, Mr Blake. I'm prepared to pay."

"How much have you got available?"

"Whatever it takes."

He didn't doubt it. Back home in Malaysia, the wheels of a whole industry were turning to provide her with whatever funding she required. But that was of little practical use – he would need it here and now.

"No, I meant here, in cash."

"There's ten thousand US dollars in the purser's safe. It was meant to be my spending money for the trip."

That was more than enough for Blake's purpose. What he'd had in mind was more like ten thousand Egyptian pounds.

"Hopefully we won't need that much."

"So you'll help me?"

Once again, she'd seen straight through him. There was the straw she'd been looking for and she'd grasped it with both hands.

"I'll do what I can – I can't promise anything."

"Thank you, Mr Blake, I'm very grateful."

Even now he'd relented, she could still not bring herself to call him Michael. What had he expected? He attempted to cover the moment by raising a practical issue.

"You don't happen to know the whereabouts of Reda's computer, I suppose?"

If that fell into the wrong hands, it could be disastrous.

"I've already taken it, Mr Blake – it's in my room."

In that case…

"How much did he tell you?"

"About what?"

There was a sense they were testing each other out, probing at the edges.

"The Brotherhood, Al-Wasat Al-Jadid, that sort of thing."

"Everything."

"I see…" So there were no secrets between them – and yet she'd seemed so shocked at his arrest. "You'll need to give me some time."

"Take as long as you need – I can wait."

"I don't mean now – I'll have to go and work on it. I'll come and find you when I'm ready. In the meantime, you'd better go and talk to the purser."

"Very well…"

She nodded, then opened the small shoulder bag she was carrying and began fiddling with the contents. For one precious moment Blake thought it might be the prelude to some moment of intimacy – but it was not, and she snapped the bag shut and confined herself to a small wave of the hand before starting out across the foyer.

Reda's mobile phone and wallet were still in his pocket. He'd considered giving them to her to go along with the computer – but had then thought the better of it. After their conversation he'd begun to feel more comfortable with them. Reda was something they shared, a bond that held them together, and he did not want to see it broken.

Above his head, the TV continued to pump out its message of

defiance and, despite the attentions of the police, the protestors in Tahrir Square maintained their vigil over the nation. Their persistent presence said one thing – *We will not be beaten.* In a similarly determined mood, Blake turned toward the stairway and set off in the direction of his cabin.

Chapter Twenty

David was right about the telephone lines – there were few to be had, and even less that were working properly. Luckily, Blake had remembered to charge his mobile overnight and for once it gave better access. Besides, this was another call he wanted to keep private and he didn't trust the ship's system.

Eventually he got through, but the switchboard at the Embassy was permanently engaged. No surprise there, he thought. Every mother in the UK with a loved one in Egypt would be worried.

After half a dozen unsuccessful attempts he resorted to using the direct line into the Trade Section. It bypassed the switchboard and was for use strictly in emergencies – but if this wasn't an emergency, thought Blake, then what on earth was? And anyway, it wasn't as if they could sack him for using it now.

Carpenter must have been sitting on top of the phone as it answered after just two rings.

"Hello? Who's this?"

"It's Blake. I'm calling from the ship."

"Good Lord. I wondered who on earth it could be on this line."

"I couldn't get through via the switchboard."

"No, you won't do, old boy. We're totally overrun."

In the background he could hear the sound of voices, movement and the scuff of heavy furniture being dragged across the floor.

"What on earth is all that noise?" asked Blake.

"We're packing up ready to leave. We're on Code Red, you know."

Carpenter had to bellow into the mouthpiece to make himself heard.

"Why, are you under attack?"

"Everything but. We're just making sure we're prepared. You

know what the Old Man's like – he doesn't want to be seen taking chances. They're talking about boarding up the ground-floor windows. Wouldn't surprise me if one got smashed any minute."

"Really? So what's it like up there?"

"Absolute bloody chaos. Here, listen to this."

Blake heard the sound of a catch being freed, a window being opened, then the familiar noise of chanting and the continual wailing of sirens.

"It's been going on all day," said Carpenter. "And most of last night – barely got a wink of sleep." The window closed, dulling down the clamour. "It's a warzone out there. Burnt-out cars, rubble all over the streets. There's an overturned bus on Talat Harb and they've been using it as a barricade. I took my life in my hands getting into work this morning, I can tell you."

"How did you manage?"

"Well, hardly any buses are running and it's pointless using the Metro and trying to come through Tahrir. The exit at Sadat is blocked so I got off at Gezira and walked across the bridge. That was an experience I wouldn't want to repeat. The police are everywhere, running about like chickens with their heads cut off. They're all a bag of nerves. I thought one of them was going to take a pot-shot at me. God knows how I'll get back home tonight. I may have to doss down here if it gets any worse. Fortunately, I've plenty of supplies in."

In addition to the bottle of Scotch in the bottom drawer of his desk, Carpenter kept a strategic reserve in one of the filing cabinets.

"So how's the First Secretary coping with it all?"

"Totally demented, as you'd expect. He's spent the whole morning charging round like a bull in a china shop. I'll give him credit though, at least he's made the effort to get in. There's a lot that haven't. Anyway, how are things with you?"

"Fine. We're all safe aboard the boat. Although half the crew's done a bunk and we're stranded here for twenty-four hours until the captain gets things sorted out."

"So where exactly are you?"

"Aswan."

"Any signs of trouble?"

"Are you kidding? It all went off with a bang here last night."

"Really?"

"Yes, and it looks as though it was our boy who lit the blue touch paper."

"You mean Mr Eldasouky?"

"Indeed."

"Well, well. It seems you had him pegged. I take my hat off to you, Blake. You certainly saw it coming. It's been a shock to the rest of us, I have to say."

Clearly it had. And yet, he'd given them as much warning as he could although that was of no consolation now.

"Alan…" Unlike Lee Yong, Blake reverted to Christian names as soon as he needed support. "I need to ask another favour."

"Ha!" Carpenter gave a derisive snort. "You're pushing your luck, old boy, under the circumstances. They've cut the internet and we can't get a peep out of the computers."

"I know that and I'm grateful for what you've done already. But Mr Eldasouky, God bless him, managed to get himself arrested and I need to bail him out."

"Bail him out? What on earth for?" Carpenter sounded shocked. "I can only assume he owes you money. Although there must be a better reason than that – but I don't suppose for one moment you're going to tell me."

"Let's just say it's for a friend."

"A friend?" It was said with an element of scorn but Blake could understand his surprise. As far as Carpenter was aware, he didn't have any friends. "I haven't a clue what's going on down there, Michael – I just hope you know what you're doing."

"To be honest, Alan, I'm not sure what I'm doing." It was true – he was confused. He'd gone away on a birding trip but he'd met

Lee Yong, there'd been a revolution and somehow things had all got tangled up – and it was too late to go back on it now. "But I'm going to go ahead and do it anyway. Do we still have our contact in the police force?"

"Yes we do. He's the one I got the information from in the first place. Although he's probably out and about at the moment rounding up protestors – but I can always try. You realise we can't help you with this – it's entirely unofficial. You're on your own, you know."

"I'm aware of that. But if you could get me a name and a number for someone in Aswan, someone who'd be prepared to do business, I'll take it from there."

"And is that it?"

"That's it."

Another filing cabinet scraped across the floor. He heard Carpenter giving instructions – *Careful with that* – and then he was back on the line.

"Alright. Give me ten minutes and I'll see what I can do. It might be easier if I rang you back."

"No, don't do that. I'll hang on if that's alright. It's hell's own job getting through and I don't want to lose the connection."

A dull thud told him that the receiver had gone down on Carpenter's desk, then he sensed his colleague lumbering off toward the office doorway. In the background, somewhere between the rustle of paper and the occasional graunch of metal, he could still make out the chants and sirens reverberating beyond the closed window. He focused on them for a moment, knowing that at any second the tenuous line that bound him to them might be cut. It was a slender thread that linked him to this piece of hope, this vague wild idea that he could somehow help to gain a young man's freedom – and even save his life if it came to that.

And then there was Carpenter – it frightened Blake to think how much they depended on him now. Soon, like a soppy

Labrador sent to run after a stick, he would come lolloping back to the phone, bearing whatever information he could find – although it wouldn't surprise Blake to find that while he'd been away, he'd stopped to sniff out the latest cricket score...

He took the full ten minutes he'd suggested and finally returned, unhurried and without even affecting to be out of breath.

"Blake? Are you there?"

"Yes."

Indeed he was, ready and waiting.

"Well, that wasn't easy. Have you got a pen and paper?"

"Wait a moment." Blake scrabbled on the desk top and located his notebook and pencil. "Go ahead."

"The man you want is Hossein Rasheed. He's the one who runs things in that part of the world. Very much feared by the locals apparently. Our contact knew him straight away."

"Is he venal?"

"Aren't they all, old boy? And I'm sure he will be. Must be a nice little number, Aswan, tucked out of the way in the sticks. He'll be looking to make a few bob out of it that's for certain. You'll need his number by the way."

Blake took it down next to the name.

"Alan, I'm eternally grateful. How many bottles is it I owe you now?"

"Four, at the last count. I tell you what – why don't you make it a round half dozen and put yourself in credit?"

"I'll have a serious think about that."

Although in the foreseeable future, he hoped he wouldn't need any more help.

"Well, whatever you're up to, I wish you the best of luck with it. Let me know how you get on. I'd use my home number from now on if I were you. Can't guarantee being here much longer."

The muted wail of sirens and the continuous scraping of furniture lent his suggestion audible support.

"I will do," said Blake. "And thanks."

He shut down his mobile phone and sat back on the bed – then crossed his fingers and prepared himself to make another call.

Chapter Twenty-one

The role of hero did not come easily to Blake. In fact he was uncomfortable with it and rather than exciting him, he felt it was a burden, a weight bearing down on his shoulders he was anxious to remove. He was not, by nature, a brave man and throughout his life he'd sought to avoid confrontation. Unlike most of his contemporaries, he'd never challenged his parents at home, or 'the system' at college, or his superiors at work, but had always preferred to stand aside and watch rather than act. What had there ever been to be brave about anyway? Nothing of consequence had ever crossed his path – and in the absence of external influences he'd not really challenged himself. Bird-watching was not exactly the most daring of pastimes.

The truth was that if it hadn't been for Lee Yong, Reda would have been allowed to rot in jail and Blake would have been left to contemplate the vicissitudes of life and the inherent cruelty of human nature – it would never have occurred to him to interfere. But where he was callous and indifferent she was resolute, and although she'd initially been stunned by Reda's detention, her night of anguish seemed to have strengthened her determination rather than weakened it. On the other hand, his first instinct that morning had been to dispose of the young man's mobile phone and wallet as if they were no more than an inconvenience. If ever proof were wanted he was cowardly, then surely that was it.

This realisation made him feel ashamed. He was weak in such matters and he hated it. He told himself he should know better – here he was at sixty with a lifetime of 'experience' behind him, and yet all he had to offer was the cynicism of age. How much he could learn from Lee Yong, if only he'd allow himself to? Why had he not paid more attention to life when he was her age instead of burying his head in books and chasing after birds?

Talking to Carpenter had been easy – but in its own way, dangerous. Their cosy camaraderie had instilled in him a false sense of bravado. It had made him feel he was doing something special and for a while he might bask in the sense of his own puffed-up glory. But as soon as he'd shut down his phone, his feeling of wellbeing had evaporated and he'd been left alone with his fears. The brave part was still to come.

Hossein Rasheed was a formidable man – his reputation preceded him – and talking to him was a different proposition than chatting to the likes of Alan Carpenter. He'd therefore approached his call to him with trepidation – but he'd screwed up his courage and done it. This achievement alone should have imbued in him some feeling of pride – and the fact that his negotiations had been successful might have allowed for a sense of elation. But he felt neither of these things and it was still the underlying want of fortitude that governed his thoughts. And so, as he went off to seek out Lee Yong and give her the news, he did so apologetically rather than in triumph.

After searching the foyer and the Forward Lounge (she was rarely found on the sun-deck), he located her corridor and knocked quietly on the door of her room. She was slow to answer and eventually appeared barefoot and sleepy-eyed, the soft glow of the bedside lamp behind her falling across the rumpled covers where she'd been resting. Next to her pillow, a half-read paperback lay upside down, abandoned as she caught up on her sleep.

"I'm sorry – I didn't mean to disturb you."

"That's alright, I was just having a nap. Won't you come in?"

She held the door open and he slipped past her into the room.

The layout was the same as his own and he immediately looked for the chair in front of the dressing table as somewhere to sit. A pair of tights had been hurriedly draped over the back of it, and she quickly retrieved them and pushed them into a drawer. In the centre of the table lay a laptop computer which Blake recognised as Reda's, while around it the space was littered with a collection of bottles and sprays and other assorted items of makeup. On the floor beneath, the contents of a rucksack had been tipped out into a heap.

The disorderly state of her room disappointed him. Given the trouble she took over her appearance each day, he'd expected her to be neat and tidy – perhaps it was the pressure of events that had disrupted her.

He took the chair and sat forward with his elbows on the armrests and his hands held together. Lee Yong perched uncomfortably on the edge of the bed. It all seemed rather awkward and before she had time to settle, he blurted out his news with no preamble whatsoever.

"I've spoken to the chief of police – it's all arranged."

"Thank you…"

She seemed genuinely grateful but her expression remained solemn. Just as in the foyer, he'd hoped for some sign of warmth but yet again she'd denied him. Perhaps it was foolish of him to expect it, and her muted response caused him to lose what little confidence he'd arrived with.

"Well, I think it is anyway. We've to go down to the police station later on."

"Must I go? I was hoping not to have to."

Rather than look at him, she stared down at her hands. He noticed that her nails had been painted a deep crimson colour.

"I think you should. There'll probably be forms to sign…" He waited for a response, but none was forthcoming. "Did you manage to speak to the purser?"

"Yes, it's on the dressing table."

She indicated a flimsy brown envelope hidden amongst the bottles and sprays on the desk. It was stuffed with cash. She must have withdrawn every penny, he thought.

"I don't suppose we'll need all of that. I've agreed ten thousand Egyptian pounds. I hope that's alright. Although if I were you, I'd take a little more than that, just to be on the safe side."

She didn't seem worried as to the amount. He supposed it didn't matter to her whether it was ten or a hundred thousand, she could afford it however much it was. But he'd wanted to get it right if only for his own sake – negotiating bribes wasn't his speciality.

Lee Yong was more concerned with confidentiality.

"Have you told any of the others about this?"

"Of course not."

"I'd prefer it to keep it that way if you don't mind."

He was certainly no gossip and after all the effort he'd made, Blake felt put out that she should think he could be so indiscreet.

"Fine. I had no intention…"

"I'm sorry," She interrupted him. "I didn't mean to imply anything… Oh God!" Her hands flew up to her forehead, partly obscuring her face. "I'm really not thinking straight at the moment. Perhaps we could talk about this later."

"Ok…" He leant back in the chair so as not to crowd her. "But we don't have a lot of time. Do you think you'll be coming down to dinner?"

"I don't know. I'll try. It depends on how I feel…"

Despite her extra rest she remained tearful. Her eyes were still red and next to the bed, the waste bin was half-full of wet tissues. He desperately wanted to go over and sit with her and fold her into his arms and tell her everything would be alright. But at present that was not possible and as much as it hurt him, he knew he would have to leave her to find comfort from within herself. He'd seen glimpses of her inner strength – now she would have to draw on it. For the moment, and until such time as she recovered, he felt powerless to help and all he could do was look to the future.

"Well, if you can't make it, I'll meet you in the foyer after the meal – say, nine o'clock?"

She nodded but said nothing. She'd lowered her hands to

uncover her face and seemed a little calmer now – although what state she might revert to after he'd gone was open to question. Blake thought it safe enough to take his leave.

"I'll see you later then…"

Outside in the corridor he stopped to reflect on their interview. He was in two minds and dithering as to what to do. His first instinct had been to stay and comfort her – but he did not want her to think that he was forward and it had not seemed appropriate. But now her door was closed behind him he regretted leaving – how heartless it was of him to walk away when she most needed help! Then he remembered that he'd neglected to pick up the envelope full of money – although whether she'd intended him to take it or not, he wasn't entirely sure. Nevertheless, it was an excuse to return and he raised his fist to knock for the second time – but then lowered it again as caution got the better of him and he walked off, berating himself under his breath for his lack of conviction.

Chapter Twenty-two

She was ten minutes late but Lee Yong did come down to dinner that evening. Perhaps she'd not been affected as much as Blake thought, as her appearance was immaculate and she arrived without a hair out of place. How long she'd spent in the company of her bottles and sprays to achieve the effect he'd no idea, but on closer inspection, all that remained of her earlier distress was a hint of tiredness around the eyes – and that in itself was barely perceptible and certainly not seen by the others.

She'd changed into a fresh top, although she'd not 'dressed' for dinner and had kept her jeans and Cuban heels – a move which Blake took to signal she was ready to go out. As she approached the table he stood up and pulled out her chair then handed her into it, giving her fingers a gentle squeeze of encouragement. After his failure to console her that afternoon, it was really the least he could do.

The meal itself was a makeshift affair. Word had got round that the chef had re-engaged two of the staff and between them they'd cooked up a simple stew and some mashed potato. For pudding there was ice cream and a selection of fruit. Given the circumstances, even Joan had no cause for complaint.

The talk at the table was of nothing but the revolution and how it might affect their trip. Some of the tours they'd booked had actually been running that day – whether free or under the yoke, the working Egyptian still had mouths to feed and expenses to pay – but most had elected to stay in their rooms and watch things as they unfolded. In the Forward Lounge the captain had set up a widescreen TV, and to placate the passengers he'd laid on free tea and coffee for the day. After the events of the previous evening, no-one had wanted or dared to leave the ship.

In Cairo, the protestors continued to occupy Tahrir Square. Other than the removal of Mubarak, they'd vowed that nothing would persuade them to move. As a counter measure, and to deny them their means of communication, the Government had cut off the internet – which explained why those who'd spent the day on their computers trying to email home had been unsuccessful. As Blake had discovered, some of the phone lines were working and this had allowed David to solve the mystery of the travel insurance. Both rebellion and revolution were excluded, he informed them (there was a groan of disbelief at the news) but as he went on to point out, no-one had as yet suffered any quantifiable loss. That would arise if they missed their flight connections and had to stay over.

This prompted them all to look at Keith. He'd been deputed to contact the airport and he advised there was nothing abnormal to report and everything was running as it should. All in all, rather than the wholesale upheaval they had feared, things seemed to have gone off like a damp squib.

Blake found it significant that no-one thought to mention Reda. With their minds focused on their own problems, he seemed to have slipped off their radar. It was a helpful development as it was a topic that neither he nor Lee Yong wanted to see raised.

The others had grown used to his early nights so it aroused no comment when he excused himself from the table and with a pointed glance at Lee Yong, slipped out to the foyer. Having collected her shoulder bag, she joined him a few moments later. The reception desk was unattended, their only company the television above the notice board, but he still felt it prudent to whisper.

"Are you alright?"

"Yes."

"You brought the money I take it?"

She nodded and fetched the brown envelope out of her bag and handed it over to him.

"To be honest, Mr Blake, I think it would be a good idea if you took it."

He saw her point – in countries such as Egypt, it was better for a man to be seen to be doing the business.

Blake counted out what was needed and stowed the rest in his back pocket. It was best not left in the bag – if they were accosted for any reason, it was too obvious a target.

They left the ship as discreetly as they could and headed toward the Corniche. The sky was again pitch black but the town was lit by the glow of street lights and the torch-like beams of car headlamps cutting through the night. Ahead of them the square, which had been the scene of such disruption barely twenty-four hours earlier, stood empty save for the same discarded evidence which had littered it the night before. Doomed to be forever parted from its mate, the lost shoe still lay unclaimed amongst the wreckage.

Once across the road, Blake began looking for a turning to the right.

"I'm told it's down here somewhere..."

Sharia Abtal was the same street in which they'd seen the young man with his head bandaged – but he was long gone and so too at least was the broken glass, cleared away by some responsible shopkeeper. All the same, other traces of the conflict remained.

The police station was half a mile down on the left hand side. Unlike the Governorate building which was new and of modern design, it was old and single-storied. Of rather decrepit appearance, it was painted in a sandy brown colour that matched the shade of the surrounding desert. It reminded Blake of the jailhouse in a cowboy western and on entering, he half expected to see John Wayne with boots and stetson sauntering across the set. Instead of which they were greeted by a dimly lit interior and the stale warmth of humanity, the scent of sweat tinged with a whiff of urine. Above their heads, a solitary ceiling fan whirred disconsolately, shifting the foul and humid air from one side of the room to the other. Lee Yong immediately covered her nose and mouth with her hand to prevent herself from gagging.

Behind the counter a clerk sat at a desk, shuffling paper. He was evidently Nubian – dark-skinned, short and of slight build – and had found his way into the uniform of a sergeant that was far too big for him. He looked like a child who'd discovered his father's wardrobe was unlocked and had tried on his clothes, his hands barely extending beyond the ends of his sleeves. Round his neck, his buttoned collar hung as if suspended on a stick. He slowly got up and came to the counter, but rather than make any effort to speak, he enquired by jerking his head sullenly in their direction.

Blake doubted he'd understand English and so spoke in Arabic.

"We've come about Reda Eldasouky."

The clerk didn't flinch. The name obviously meant nothing to him.

"Have you filled in a form?"

"No."

The clerk pushed a pen and a grubby sheet of paper across the counter towards him.

"We don't need to fill in a form," said Blake. "We're British."

In remote parts of the world it was always worth a try. Had he still been employed by the Embassy, he'd have considered invoking diplomatic immunity.

The clerk shrugged, totally unimpressed.

"Everyone fills in a form."

Blake pushed the pen and paper to one side and tried a different tack.

"We're here to see Mr Rasheed."

This time there was a flicker of interest.

"The chief? You'll be lucky – there's a queue…"

Behind them, a row of plastic chairs was set against the wall. A young black, barefoot and in combats and a sweat-stained top lay slumped in the far corner, asleep. Halfway along, beneath an iron-grilled window, an unshaven Egyptian dressed in shorts, singlet and open-toed sandals sat forward, elbows on knees, his leg jiggling uncontrollably. They were an unprepossessing pair. If this was the queue and the clerk expected backsheesh to jump it, he was out of luck – they were paying enough already.

"We're expected," said Blake.

The clerk shrugged again. *So?*

"Passport?" he asked.

Blake fished in an inside pocket and placed it on the counter. The clerk flicked carelessly through it to the back page, glanced at the photograph, glanced at Blake, then snapped it shut.

"Wait here," he commanded and taking the passport with him, meandered slowly off down the corridor, whistling loudly.

High above their heads, the ceiling fan groaned at its thankless task while beneath the row of plastic chairs, a cockroach scurried towards its hole.

With her hand still covering her face, Lee Yong shuddered.

"Can't we just collect him and go?"

"Unfortunately not," said Blake. "There's a protocol to go through. We'll just have to grin and bear it."

In Egypt, jail was not a hotel you chose to stay in.

The clerk returned, but at no greater pace. And to pay Blake out for the incident regarding the form, he waited until he'd recovered his position behind the counter before pointing back in the direction from which he'd just arrived and giving another economical jerk of his head.

"Oh, for God's sake!" Blake steered Lee Yong away by the elbow. "Come on, let's get it over with."

At the far end of the corridor, a door stood open, inviting them forward.

Hossein Rasheed was indeed the fat policeman. During his discussions Blake had thought as much and now his suspicions were confirmed. Even when seated close at hand he was every bit as big as he appeared from a distance. It was not a position that flattered him, as with the need to stand upright removed, everything about him seemed to sag. The bags which hung beneath his eyes gave him a debauched look and his chin fell all too easily into the folds of his neck. The paunch – a feature Blake had previously admired – no longer stood out but slid below the edge of his desk like the aftermath of an avalanche. All in all, like so many of Egypt's monuments, he resembled an old and collapsed building. His desk was completely clear except for Blake's passport which lay neatly aligned in the centre. Behind it, Rasheed sat waiting, his hands clasped together across his ample belly.

He eyed each of them in turn and then barked out, "Sit!"

Blake stiffened. He was used to receiving instruction by invitation rather than command, and although the First Secretary had used the same word he'd been far more polite. The effect was still the same – in circumstances like these, you did as you were told. They took their seats.

There followed a protracted silence during which the fat policeman appeared to be weighing them up. Rather than come to any conclusion, he eventually decided to ask.

"Well?"

"We've come about Reda Eldasouky," said Blake. There was no preamble and he'd not prepared a speech – the talking had already been done over the telephone.

"I know very well why you're here." Rasheed's English was perfect and suggested a foreign and expensive education. "Give me a reason as to why I should let you have him."

"We have an agreement," said Blake.

"We have no agreement," snapped Rasheed, "and I do not wish to hear you speak of one. If I so decide, he will be released, you will sign for him and there will be the normal administrative fee to pay. If not, then he will stay where he is. Let me make myself clear – there is no agreement."

A play with words, thought Blake. *He's covering himself.*

"What puzzles me," continued Rasheed, "is why the British Embassy should take an interest in such a man. You're a long way from Cairo, Mr Blake. He must be one of your better spies."

Reda? A spy? Is that what they thought? Blake was astounded. If the young man were not in such danger, the whole idea would be laughable. Where had that suggestion come from? Unless of course it was Carpenter's contact who had passed the information on to Aswan. That would have been worth a decent backhander at the very least.

"That's ridiculous. This has nothing to do with the British Embassy."

"It has everything to do with the British Embassy. You work for them, don't you, Mr Blake? You cannot deny it."

"I used to, it's true." There was no point in hiding it. "But I left their employment a month ago. I'm here on a birding holiday."

Although it wasn't turning out to be much of one...

"Hah!" Rasheed guffawed with disbelief. "A likely story! You don't seriously expect me to believe that, do you?"

"I can assure you it's the truth. And anyway," Blake went on, "this is a private matter."

The fat policeman inclined his head and nodded in the direction of Lee Yong as if to ask, *Who's she?* So far she'd sat in silence, her hands held respectfully in her lap and looking as demure as possible. Blake took this as his cue to introduce her.

"This is Miss Yong." He'd meant to say she was purely a friend – and whether it was the pressure of the situation or an attack of nerves or the thought that he needed a better explanation of their presence, but he suddenly lost control of his tongue and before he could stop himself, he'd blurted out a story which had been running fancifully through his head but which they'd neither agreed nor rehearsed. "Miss Yong is Mr Eldasouky's fiancée. She's travelled all the way from Malaysia for the wedding in a couple of weeks' time. His arrest has come as a great shock to her and she's asked me to place a sum of money at your disposal which she hopes will secure his release."

The point was that it sounded believable – and for all Blake knew, it could be the truth. And if Lee Yong was embarrassed by the deception, she failed to show it and remained calm and collected.

Blake took the envelope out of his pocket and placed it carefully on the desk opposite his passport, then folded his arms and sat back to wait.

Rasheed eyed the envelope, then Blake and then Lee Yong. That he was tempted to take it clearly showed but an inner doubt appeared to hold him back. Perhaps it was conscience that battled with his greed. Although that was unlikely, thought Blake – it was probably some other form of self-interest that was driving him. Was it best to take the money? Or was the information he might extract from his prisoner worth more? It was a neat calculation. It was certainly not Blake's story that had moved him. Although it had been delivered with conviction, Rasheed didn't look like the kind of man whose range of emotions included an understanding of love. To prove it, a sneer of contempt crossed his lips.

"Why should I believe this fairy tale?"

Now it was Blake's turn to shrug. *Because we're paying you to.*

A podgy hand reached out for the envelope and riffled casually through the notes. Blake wondered whether it was it enough – but apparently it was. Greed had triumphed and the fat policeman opened the side drawer of his desk, swept the envelope into it and slid it shut, then pushed Blake's passport towards him.

"You can have your precious Mr Eldasouky." His decision came barbed with scorn. "He's a worthless son of a bitch! Why keep these minnows when there are bigger fish to catch. I tell you straight, I'm only too happy to throw this one back. It's not worth the price of keeping him. I know the type, he'll tell us nothing. He's had his lesson!"

There was an element of sour grapes in his tirade. He'd reached a decision he didn't much like and felt the need to justify it to himself. And even if he believed Blake's story, there was no attempt to spare Lee Yong's feelings. Blake glanced toward her, hoping she'd stay quiet. With the battle won, the last thing he wanted was for her to give a feisty response and upset the deal.

"So, you know who the ringleaders are then?"

It sounded as though he was fishing, but his hope was to move the discussion elsewhere.

"Don't you worry, Mr Blake – we know what's going on. These Islamists think they're going to take over the country, but we know better than that. We'll soon sort them out – then you and your American friends can sleep easily in your beds."

He evidently believed his own propaganda.

Throughout the policeman's provocation, Lee Yong had remained thankfully silent, but Blake could not resist rising to the bait, just as he'd done with the First Secretary.

"But this has nothing to do with Islam. It's a popular uprising. In Cairo…"

"But we're not in Cairo," Rasheed cut in. "We run things differently here." He gave another sneer. "The authorities in Cairo are weak. They should never have allowed that protest to take root. They ought to come to Aswan – we could show them a thing or two. It's still like the old days here. We kicked the British out of Suez in '56. We kicked the Israelis out of Sinai in '73. You don't suppose we're going to let a little upset like this worry us?"

The scenes Blake had witnessed had been horrific. If they were anything to go by, he could well believe it – there'd been an element of ruthlessness about them he'd found chilling.

While Rasheed had been speaking, Blake realised he was in danger of falling into the same trap that had been laid for Lee Yong. He decided to concede the point.

"I'm sure you're right."

"Certainly I'm right, Mr Blake." Rasheed wagged a bloated finger. "And when we've cleared out this little nest of sedition, make no mistake, you will thank us for it. You must think—"

But whatever it was that Blake was supposed to think, he never did find out as the phone jangled on the edge of the desk and cut the fat policeman off in full flow. Rasheed took the call, then turned his back on them and began a fast and furious conversation, becoming ever more agitated until finally he was shouting into the mouthpiece just as he'd barked into his megaphone the night before. He spoke angrily in Arabic, but in a form that Blake could not fully understand.

Blake exchanged glances with Lee Yong and raised his eyebrows as a means of enquiry as to her wellbeing. There was no response. With her hands still firmly in her lap, she seemed calm enough.

Rasheed slammed the phone down and turned back to face them.

"These renegades are like flies. They buzz about everywhere and make much noise. They're harmless and they carry no sting – but it annoys me that they keep me so busy. Now I have work to do and it's late. You'll have to excuse me. Your Mr Eldasouky will be waiting…"

He dismissed them with a wave of his podgy hand and went back to his telephone.

Blake retrieved his passport and as soon as they were outside in the corridor they could hear his angry voice start up again. Blake ignored it. His first priority was to apologise.

"I'm sorry about that little story I concocted in there. But after that business about Reda being a spy, I felt I had to offer some other explanation. I hope you don't mind."

"No, not at all." Lee Yong shook her head. "Anything…"

So even though they were now alone, she still didn't bother to deny it…

They headed back down the corridor toward the front office.

Reda was already sitting on one of the plastic chairs, in much the same position as his neighbour, the jiggling Egyptian. He'd spent just the one night in jail and yet Blake expected him to look somehow different, as if the experience had fundamentally altered him. But he did not and he was easily recognisable, still as rotund as ever, and his face carried the same chubby weight of flesh as it had the day before. His clothes were soiled and he appeared a little dishevelled, but there was nothing to suggest he'd done anything more than have a bad night out on the town. It was not until he saw them approach and stood up that they noticed any change.

He hobbled to his feet and visibly winced as he leant to one side, trying not to clutch at the small of his back which was evidently the source of his pain. Movement of any kind was clearly difficult.

Blake had imagined that Lee Yong might rush forward and fling herself round Reda's neck, but she hung back – although whether this was because he'd mistaken their relationship, or because she didn't wish to add to the young man's discomfort, he wasn't sure. Instead, she stayed firmly by his side.

"Are you alright?" she asked.

Reda gave a weak smile and tried unsuccessfully to straighten up.

"A light beating, that's all. It's nothing to worry about, I assure you."

He held up a hand as if to say, *I'm fine* but then sank back down onto the chair.

"He can't walk back to the ship like that," said Blake. "We'll have to get him a taxi."

Fortunately, along with his passport and Lee Yong's money, he'd remembered to bring his mobile phone. A tattered poster pinned to the wall near the entrance doorway gave him a clue as to a number. Overhead, the ceiling fan whirred uselessly on like an old clockwork toy, and with the phone clamped to one ear, Blake covered the other with his hand to hear himself speak.

"Yes, yes, the police station – as soon as you can…"

In front of the row of black plastic chairs, Lee Yong was trying to set Reda upright.

"Here, let me help you with that."

Blake pocketed his mobile and went to her assistance. Between them they managed to haul the young Egyptian into a standing position and with an arm round each of their shoulders, he hopped awkwardly toward the doorway.

They were about to pass through the opening when their progress was halted by an imploring cry from behind.

"Hey! You forgot to sign!"

On the other side of the counter, the desk clerk was waving a pen and tapping at his grubby sheet, his oversize tunic hanging off him as if he were a scarecrow.

Blake gave a sigh of irritation. In his desire to get his charges back to the ship the matter of paperwork had slipped his mind. As always, it would have to be dealt with.

He looked outwardly displeased, but at heart he understood the desk clerk's need. He'd once been a bureaucrat himself. In fact, he'd once been part of the greatest bureaucracy the world had ever seen, Her Majesty's Foreign Office with all its memos, manuals and forms, and yet somehow he'd survived. Now he was free and rid of it all, but it was not beyond him to recognise when a fellow worker needed help. He untangled himself and having propped Reda's hand against the door jamb, returned to the counter where he took the proffered pen and signed off the sheet with a flourish.

The desk clerk beamed his thanks. His duty was done and he could go home that night with a clear conscience. For a few precious moments, Blake had made his impoverished life bearable, and he was happy. The chief would be pleased –

although whether he would remain so was open to question. It would depend, thought Blake, on how long it would take him to discover that his most important prisoner had just been released into the custody of a certain Mickey Mouse.

High above their heads, the ceiling fan reached a vibrating crescendo and shuddered at the prospect.

Chapter Twenty-three

Getting Reda into the back of the taxi proved difficult. His body didn't want to bend in the required places, or at least, not without pain. They finally settled for putting him in the front where they could push the seat back and allow his legs to remain straight. Lee Yong took up a place in the rear. Blake gave directions, then joined her and at the end of Sharia Abtal they turned down onto the Corniche and sped along the carriageway.

Framed against her side window, Blake watched as the light of each street lamp flickered across Lee Yong's face. She still had a dour, almost sullen look as if every care in the world had been heaped on her, and whatever relief Reda's release may have brought had not yet turned to joy. She'd said little since they'd left the ship and had remained mercifully quiet during the meeting with Rasheed, content to let Blake take the lead. He'd thought it a ploy designed to draw sympathy from the fat policeman, but she'd maintained her silence and he'd come to think of it as her normal state as if she became introverted when under pressure. Beneath that calm exterior, her mind was probably in turmoil and she was bursting with questions. She shortly turned towards him, and thinking she was about to speak he put his finger to his lips and gave a little shake of his head. They were not yet alone, and for their driver, the price of having a poster on display in the police station was almost certainly the provision of information.

They might keep their thoughts to themselves but they could not disguise their destination. On the quayside next to the Corniche, the cruise ship loomed large and was ablaze with lights. With a good deal of help they prized Reda out of the front seat and sat him on a bollard at the top of the steps leading down to the gangplank.

"Wait here," said Blake. "I'll go and see what's happening on board. We need to be as discreet as we possibly can."

They'd succeeded in setting Reda free but that was not enough – his whereabouts needed to be kept secret and the ship was full of prying eyes and wagging tongues. Blake crossed the gangplank and slipped unnoticed into reception.

He returned five minutes later and found Lee Yong pacing anxiously up and down. Reda, unable to move, had to content himself with subtle changes in posture to remain comfortable.

"We're in luck," said Blake. "Everyone's in the Forward Lounge watching television. The captain's found a video copy of *Casablanca* and he's put it on to keep them occupied. They daren't go out for a run ashore in case there's a repeat of last night. It looks as though half the crew's there as well, so if we make a move now we might just get away with it."

He turned to Reda who was beginning to get fidgety. "Here, put these on."

He'd taken the opportunity to visit his cabin and had fetched a lightweight green gilet, his battered Panama and the pair of dark glasses he'd bought a day earlier.

"It's better than nothing and there's a chance you won't be recognised. Oh, and I found this too." In the crook of his arm hung a wooden walking stick. "I've no idea who it belongs to, but they really should take better care of it. When we've finished I'll put it back where I found it, but in the meanwhile it'll come in useful. Now come on, let's get you ready."

Reda struggled to his feet. He was in no position to resist and allowed himself to be dressed. Much to Blake's satisfaction, the resultant disguise was quite effective and in a matter of moments the young Egyptian was transformed into an elderly gentleman with a bad back and a limp. Crouched forward and heavily reliant on the stick, Reda had no need to act the part. It came all too naturally and it was painful to watch as he hobbled gingerly down the steps, across the gangplank and into the foyer. Fortunately, the reception desk was unmanned and the lobby empty.

That was the easy bit, thought Blake. *Now we have to get him upstairs.*

But Reda had other ideas and began by heading down toward his old quarters below decks. Blake held him back.

"No, I think not. If you don't mind me saying so, I don't think that's wise. That's the first place someone's going to look – you'd be better off elsewhere. You see, it doesn't end here. I know these people – they'll come after you, trust me."

Reda was in agreement.

"Unfortunately I think you're right, Mr Blake."

He turned to come back, planting his stick firmly on the stairway. But if he could see the logic of it, then for the moment Lee Yong could not.

"I thought we'd paid their ransom – doesn't that count?"

"You have a point, and that's fine for Aswan," said Blake. "But it won't matter a damn where we're going. Things will be different in Luxor."

"So he's not exactly free?"

"I'm afraid not."

"So what do you suggest?"

"Well, I'd be happy for Reda to share with me," said Blake. "I've a twin-bedded room and he won't inconvenience me in the least. He may feel differently of course."

"No," said Lee Yong firmly. "That's far too obvious. I'll make space."

She was quick to make the proposal, although it was no more than Blake had expected. Reda, he noticed, did not object.

The stairs were as troublesome as Blake had imagined, and it was some while before Reda was ensconced in Lee Yong's room. Despite what she'd said earlier she made no pretence about 'clearing a space' and they lowered the young Egyptian straight onto the bed where he lay propped up by pillows. He expressed his thanks between grimaces.

"I'm very grateful, Mr Blake."

"It's not me you should be thanking," said Blake. "It's Lee Yong. I'll let her explain. Well, I think I'm going to cut along and leave you both to it." He'd already decided not to hang around – his continued presence was superfluous and a potential embarrassment. "I'm in Room 23 by the way. Call me if you need me. But don't use the internal phone – you're better off using a mobile. Here's my number." He found a scrap of paper on the desk and jotted it down. "I'll leave it turned on just in case." He took a last look round. "Well, goodnight."

"Goodnight, Mr Blake – and thank you."

Lee Yong showed him to the door. They were as safe as he could possibly make them, but her face still carried that careworn look.

"You needn't be so worried – it'll be alright."

She did not appear convinced.

He found himself alone in the corridor for the second time that day. Before departing, he'd recovered his belongings from Lee Yong's room. Draped over one arm was the green lightweight gilet while one hand held the dark glasses and the other the Panama hat. He put them on and affecting a pronounced limp, headed towards the stairway. To all intents and purposes, an elderly gentleman with a stick had gone into Lee Yong's cabin and one had come out. If anyone should ask, he'd decided to say he'd sprained his ankle coming up the gangplank.

It wasn't until he got back to his cabin that he remembered he still had over eight thousand US dollars of Lee Yong's money in his back pocket.

Chapter Twenty-four

He awoke as normal, at first light and with the image of his telescope and tripod materialising in the corner. The association was so strong that he wondered whether there really had been a day before. Perhaps he'd simply fallen back to sleep and dreamt it all – the scene in Lee Yong's cabin, the visit to the police station, it might all have been imagined in some semi-conscious vision. As if to confirm his delusion, Reda's mobile phone and wallet still lay untouched on his dressing table.

But this was not *Groundhog Day* – something had definitely changed and it was not until he'd got up to visit the bathroom that he discovered what it was. A slight vibration was affecting the ship through the thrust of its propellers and as soon as he'd made himself comfortable, he went to the window and drew back the net curtain. The view he'd enjoyed for the past few days, the hill of sand and the Tombs of the Nobles, that had all disappeared and been replaced by the banks of the Nile gliding slowly by. Just as Mr Mohammed had promised, the ship had set sail and was now heading north towards Luxor.

The news inspired him to get dressed and go up on deck. After all that had happened, he wanted to check the rest of the world was still there. While they'd been bottled up in Aswan, there'd been a revolution, Reda had been arrested, then freed. He wondered what else might have changed and he was anxious to find out.

The sights that greeted him were both disappointing and yet refreshingly familiar. He'd missed the sunrise (once again), so the chance of viewing his skein of Glossy Ibis receded still further into the distance. Neither was he the first on deck, and he soon discovered that the same social norms applied as people nodded their good mornings. The sky was still blue, the sun (now up) was still a bright yellow and the Nile, forever brown and muddied, slipped unhurriedly by. And yet, just as he'd expected Reda to have moved on after his one night in jail, he'd thought it might all be different.

Although in a way, it was. What had changed was not so much the physical nature of things but rather his perception of them. At times like these, the defining moments in life, you became much more aware of your surroundings. Today the sky was bluer, the sun brighter and the Nile more full of life than he could ever have imagined before. Merely to exist in this wonderful place they called the world was a thrill that ran through him, and he was suddenly overwhelmed by the desire to see it all before some accident, some unlooked-for freak event, snatched it all away. Tomorrow, it might not be there...

A return to birding was in order and he searched around, desperate for something to fix on. To his left, a pair of Little Egrets lifted from their roost and flew across the bows. Further downstream a sandbank approached, splitting the course of the river. Here would be the waders he'd spurned the previous day and he hurried toward the forward rail where he could set up his scope and tripod. With luck, if the ship kept its course, he could catch his prey in the full light of the sun.

The spit drew closer and he scanned the foreshore for stints and plovers – but there were none. Higher up the bank, tufts of saw-grass sprouted where the water couldn't reach and just above them, he detected a series of white blobs. His pulse quickened. These were the bodies of Spoonbills, surely, and focusing in he discovered a group of a dozen or so, taking refuge on the sandy island. Shaped like a flamingo, they possessed the same long necks and stilt-like legs, but instead of the upturned base of a hockey stick, their beaks were more like the blade of a cricket bat. Common on the Delta, they were rarer in the Nile Valley and were probably on migration, heading for the lakes and estuaries of Southern Europe where they could settle down and breed.

Spoonbills were a favourite of Blake's. As a young man he'd known them over-winter, like Avocets, close to his boyhood home, and on coming back each Christmas or New Year to visit parents he'd made a point of going out to find them. To him, they were the most beautiful of birds. And yet they were so inherently ugly. Perhaps that was why he loved them so much, and like an elephant and the wrinkled skin of its trunk, they defined the point at which ugliness became its own form of beauty. Their bills were quite preposterous, and yet they carried them with such dignity and grace that it was impossible to think of them without affection. And here they were, a dozen of them, waiting to be viewed...

He homed in to study them. Some were asleep, their long bills tucked beneath their wings, some awake and preening while others sifted through the shallows. They hadn't changed. Just like the sky, the sun, and the Nile, they remained blissfully unaware of Egypt and its troubles – their lives were as yet untouched by upheaval. It gladdened his heart to see it. These were birds whose painted image had graced the tombs of the Pharaohs – they had survived another 3000 years – they could surely hold on a little longer.

The birds might last, but the moment did not and the sandbank and its occupants slipped by. The experience had been transitory, but with his heightened perception of his surroundings it had given him a few minutes of unexpected pleasure. His foray on deck had been rewarded and before the memory of it could be tainted by some disappointment, he decided to pack away his scope and go back down below. For the first time in a while he was excited by his discovery – not just of the birds themselves, but more of his old love of them – and he wanted to mark it in some way.

He returned to his cabin, laid down his things then sat at the dressing table and opened his notebook. His intention was to add the word 'Spoonbills' to his bird list, probably with a star by it to indicate a particularly good view.

But if the point of such entries was to record what he'd been doing, then his recent jottings told a very different story. They showed it had begun with Spur-winged Plover, although that had been some days ago now. Then he'd absent-mindedly followed it with the name of Lee Yong. Further down the page, after what appeared to be a random space, were the words 'Hossein Rasheed, 10000 Egyptian pounds' and what he assumed was the telephone number of the police station in Aswan. It didn't seem right to follow that with 'Spoonbills'. The logical thing was to add 'Reda' or 'Mrs Biltmore' or even some of the others to his list. He was fighting a losing battle and he would have to start over. But it was too late for that now and with a feeling of resignation, he put down his pen and went down to breakfast.

It was an opportunity to catch up on what the group had discussed after he'd left the dinner table the night before – although there'd been little, if any, progress. The internet was still shut down, so there were no emails in or out. Phone lines remained difficult, but those with mobiles had at least been able to send texts, and most had succeeded in contacting and reassuring their loved ones as to their safety.

Other than that there'd been little else to do and rather than sit and speculate, they'd welcomed the captain's initiative and spent the evening watching *Casablanca*. It had been shown in English with Arabic sub-titles, and according to David the main point of interest had been the reaction of the party of Germans. They'd either failed to understand it, or had understood it only too well as they'd taken themselves off to their rooms where they'd spent their time playing cards. Everyone else had enjoyed it.

What had changed, though, was the general atmosphere. The day before had been filled with tension and with no-one sure of how much danger they were in or how they were going to get out of it, there'd been an air of uncertainty. But now the ship had set sail and they were on the move, they felt they were heading towards a solution and with the prospect of returning home, things had become more relaxed. Contrary to hysterical opinion, they had not been murdered in their beds. Nor were they in, or going to Cairo, Alexandria or Suez or any of the other major trouble spots. True, there'd been a 'minor disturbance' in Aswan, but that was behind them now and as yet there were no reports of problems in Luxor. Cocooned on the boat, they were floating free, and with the wide expanse of the Nile acting as insulation, to all intents and purposes they were in a world of their own.

"I was looking at the original schedule this morning," said Keith, pouring a round of coffee. "If we make Luxor tonight, which all being well we should do, I don't think we'll have missed out on very much you know."

"Oh, and how do you work that out?" David was busy tucking into a plate of scrambled egg. The breakfast offering had substantially improved and now there was a cooked option available, although it had not quite returned to the standard they'd first enjoyed.

"So today's Thursday, right?" continued Keith. "Given that we lost a day yesterday, I shouldn't think we'll be stopping at Kom Ombo or Edfu on the way back."

"Well that wouldn't be a disaster," said David. "We've already been to Edfu and I can't say I'd be sorry about missing Kom Ombo. That's supposedly a ruin with a tiny museum containing two stuffed crocodiles and not much else."

"Ugh!" Janet shuddered. "Well, I for one don't mind giving that a miss. I hate crocodiles. They give me the creeps."

"You and me both, honey," said Mrs Biltmore. "Why, I can't stand the darned things. The reason I won't go to Florida's because of the alligators. Isn't that right, Ira?"

"Yup," said Ira. "Sure is."

"You see," said Mrs Biltmore, "when we were on safari in

South Africa..."

With his fork poised in mid-air, David assumed an apologetic look as if he knew he was going to regret ever mentioning the word 'crocodile', while round the rest of the table there was a struck-dumb silence as they waited to for Mrs Biltmore to finish her story.

But she sensed their apprehension and cut short, contenting herself with an excuse. "Well, I guess it doesn't matter now what we did on safari..." as she too recognised that things had changed.

Keith resumed his analysis.

"As I was saying... If we get to Luxor tonight, that gives us all day tomorrow to look round Karnak. Then we can catch our scheduled flights home on Saturday, just as originally planned."

"You're assuming everything will be running as usual," said David. "There's no guarantee of that."

"You've got to make some sort of assumption. What else can you do?"

They looked in the direction of Blake in the hope he could provide an answer. He raised his eyebrows and shrugged. *Don't ask me.* This was Egypt. Even if everything ran as usual, there was still no guarantee, anything could happen. They'd already had a revolution for goodness sake – what more did they want?

As he'd anticipated, Lee Yong did not come down to breakfast. Today she had the burden of looking after Reda and besides, she was not known for her attendances at table.

More surprisingly, neither had Joan. Polite enquiries as to her whereabouts revealed that she was suffering from a bad case of sunburn which had manifested itself overnight and she'd decided to confine herself to her room until the effects wore off. Feeling it was unsafe to leave the ship, she'd apparently spent the previous afternoon stretched out on a sun-bed on the upper deck to improve her tan – *I can't be doing with sitting in the room all day* –

and had fallen asleep in the full glare of the sun. She'd also been wearing eye patches, and while the rest of her face was the colour of burnt sienna, her eye sockets had remained a deathly white. According to David, in her own words she looked 'hideous'.

"It's as though I've been visited by someone from the Rocky Horror Show," he explained. "Only for God's sake don't tell her I said so. Anyway, she asked me to fetch her something to eat, so if you'll excuse me…"

He left the table and made his way over to the cold buffet where he took a plate and covered it with a selection of bread, cheese, sliced ham, fruit and a pot of yoghurt. It struck Blake that he might do the same and take it up to Lee Yong's room. If she didn't eat it herself, he was sure that Reda would – there was no way the young Egyptian was going to come down to the dining room.

"That's a good idea," he muttered under his breath and having folded his napkin, he too got up and followed David to the buffet.

He found himself preceded in the queue by Mrs Biltmore. She was apparently on a similar mission, although her plate was piled far higher than David's and with greater variety. She and Blake exchanged polite smiles. He would not embarrass her with comment, but he'd often wondered how she managed to maintain her bulk when she appeared to eat so little. Of the two of them, it was Ira who over-indulged (he regularly ate three sweets at dinner) and yet he remained as thin as a rake while she picked at her food and grew large. Here then was the answer. Ashamed of doing so in public, Mrs Biltmore ate in private and was preparing a picnic to consume in her room. *Each to their own,* thought Blake. He took a plate and heaped it likewise.

His intention was to take it straight to Lee Yong's cabin – not that he needed an excuse to visit, but it would nevertheless serve as one. He was halfway up the stairs when he remembered Reda's mobile phone and wallet were still on his dressing table and he decided to double back and fetch them.

Once back in his room he took the opportunity to use the bathroom and clean his teeth, so it was fully ten minutes before he presented himself at Lee Yong's door. With a fully loaded plate in one hand, Reda's phone and wallet in the other and feeling like a contestant on a children's game show, he managed to fumble a knock. He was quite taken aback when Mrs Biltmore answered it.

At first he thought he'd made a mistake, and in his confusion had taken a wrong turning or come back up the wrong flight of stairs.

"I'm dreadfully sorry. I didn't mean to disturb you..." He instinctively checked the room number and when he saw it was right, "I was looking for Lee Yong..."

"Why, she's right here, Mr Blake." Mrs Biltmore shuffled to one side to let him in. "Lee, honey," She called across to the other side of the room. "Here's Mr Blake come to see us now." She turned back to him. "We've been expecting you. She kept asking me where you'd got to and I said you were right there in the dining room and I was sure you'd be along just any minute."

Blake stepped forward to allow Mrs Biltmore to close the door behind him.

Lee Yong was standing next to the dressing table in front of the net-curtained window. The floor around the desk had been cleared of its debris and the chair turned to face into the room. In it, Reda sat dozing. He was dressed in a clean set of clothes – but his feet were still bare which had allowed an ice-pack to be strapped to his troublesome ankle. Blake had fully expected he'd still be in bed, but while he'd been out watching Spoonbills, someone had been nursing the invalid since the early hours. He urgently motioned Lee Yong to come across to him and while Mrs Biltmore reverted to tending the patient, he drew her into a corner and out of earshot.

"Are you alright?" Blake's first concern was for the Malaysian – anything else, Reda's state of health included, was a secondary consideration.

"Yes, I'm fine."

The careworn look which had inhabited her face for the past two days had softened, but not to the extent that it allowed her to smile and she remained a picture of seriousness.

"What on earth's going on here?"

He nodded in the direction of the large American.

"You mean Mrs Biltmore?"

"Yes. It gave me quite a turn when she opened the door."

"I can imagine. She and I have been talking."

"Oh, really?"

There was a cynical tone to his voice – of the two of them, he could guess who'd been doing most of it.

"Yes. It was when we came back to the ship after the riot." (Blake recalled seeing them together on the sofa.) "She was quite upset – I think we all were. She said it reminded her of things she'd seen in Vietnam."

"Vietnam?"

"Yes. She told me that when she was young, she was a trained nurse in the US army."

"Mrs Biltmore? In the army?"

Blake was astounded. Looking at her now it didn't seem credible.

"Yes," Lee Yong insisted. "So I thought it wouldn't do any harm for her to have a look at Reda."

"Well, I hope you know what you're doing. I thought you said you didn't want anyone else to find out. You know what she's like. If word gets out that he's holed up in here, there'll be hell to pay."

"I trust her, Mr Blake. He needs medical attention – and we were never going to take him to hospital."

"Well, that's true." Blake was forced to relent a little. "Although at the moment it doesn't look as if he needs it."

"That's all been Mrs Biltmore's doing. The ice-pack was her

idea. She got him up this morning while I went down to his room and fetched his clothes. I was going to ask you to do it..."

But you were out birding...

"Ah..."

And for the first time in the proceedings he felt guilty.

Then he suddenly remembered his hands were still full of plated food and Reda's belongings and he tried to redeem himself by handing them over as if they were some sort of gift.

"Oh, and I brought these."

"Thank you. I'll put it with the other one."

Lee Yong relieved him of the plate and laid it on the bedside table next to a similar offering, which on closer inspection looked remarkably like the one that Mrs Biltmore had assembled.

Well, whatever else, at least they weren't going to go hungry...

Mrs Biltmore came back over to join them. If Lee Yong could not raise a smile then she certainly could. She appeared pleased with herself.

"You've been busy," said Blake. For the moment, it was as close as he could get to saying thank you.

"I do what I can," said the American. "Why, I'm just happy to help Lee here. Ain't that so, honey?"

Lee Yong nodded. To see them together, you'd think they were lifelong friends.

"We're very grateful, I'm sure."

Despite her obvious skills, Blake resented Mrs Biltmore's intrusion. Reda was something he and Lee Yong shared, and shared alone, and it was what had sustained him over the last twenty-four hours. He'd arranged to bribe a high-ranking policeman, he'd put himself in danger to secure the young Egyptian's release – and now his potential reward, the society and approbation of the young Malaysian, was being diluted. Not to mention that Mrs Biltmore might prove indiscreet and scupper everything. Lee Yong's friend or not, she would have to be warned.

"You realise that you mustn't breathe a word of this to anyone. It's important that we keep it to ourselves. This has to stay within these four walls – you do understand that, don't you?"

"Now, don't you go worrying on my account," Mrs Biltmore tried blithely to reassure him. "I'm not going to say a thing. It'll just be between the three of us. I've had to tell Ira of course. We've been together thirty years – we don't have any secrets! But if there's one thing you can be sure of, Mr Blake – he isn't going to talk, you can rest assured on that."

Blake believed it – but it wasn't Ira he was concerned about.

Meanwhile, there was Reda to consider.

"Anyway, how's the patient?" he asked.

"Why, he looks just fine to you and me," said Mrs Biltmore. "But under that T-shirt he's a mass of bruises. I don't know what they did to him in there, but they sure must have worked him over. Don't you wonder about this world sometimes, Mr Blake? Some people are just like animals. Why, it's a miracle they didn't break a bone in his body."

"They didn't?"

"Nope. Not one."

"What about his ankle?"

"It's just a bad swelling. If we keep that ice-pack on him overnight, in twenty-four hours he'll be as right as rain."

"Well, that's good."

Twenty-four hours… By which time they'd be in Luxor and preparing to leave the ship. Then what were they going to do with him?

Getting Reda on board had been easy – getting him off again would be much more difficult. They could hardly rely on the same flimsy disguise as the previous evening, it was much too dangerous. It was a complication Blake still had to consider and as yet he'd given no time to it. He began to regret his early morning bout of birding – the hour he'd spent with Spoonbills would have been far better employed in planning. And now there was the problem of Mrs Biltmore to contend with...

Not for the first time, he went back to his room feeling distinctly apprehensive.

And not for the first time he realised that despite his good intentions, he'd yet again forgotten something. He'd finally succeeded in disposing of Reda's mobile phone and wallet – but as a result of these mental distractions, he'd neglected to bring Lee Yong's money. And just as he'd returned the night before with his back pocket full of it, so it now remained in his cabin. It was as though he were haunted and however hard he tried, he could simply not shake these things off.

He resolved to go back again directly after lunch.

Chapter Twenty-five

The scene in Lee Yong's cabin had changed noticeably since his visit that morning. Mrs Biltmore had gone, although Blake was sure she would be back later in the day to check on her patient. Any tension that may have prevailed had gone with her and had been replaced by an aura of domestic calm. Reda was still sitting in his chair, the ice-pack clamped firmly to his leg, but now he was wide awake and avidly watching the television, soaking up the pictures from Tahrir Square and the commentary that went with them. He barely acknowledged Blake's entry but focused studiously on the news.

Their roles reversed, it was now Lee Yong's turn to lie on the bed propped up by pillows as she resumed reading the cheesy novel Blake had seen abandoned the day before. The plates of food assembled on their behalf had barely been touched and on the bedside table, two half-empty cups of mint tea stood next to each other. There was an air of homely normality about it that at other times might be found quite restful. Blake was loath to disturb them.

He wondered as to the young Egyptian's motivation. His voluntary surrender during the riot had been an act of bravado and he'd shown no fear of the police. But he was not, Blake had concluded, a terrorist and there was no possibility he would strap himself with explosive and blow them all apart. Was he seeking martyrdom of another kind? Perhaps he'd determined to sacrifice himself for the betterment of his country – but if so, it was a selfish thought for in doing so he endangered not only himself but also those who supported him. They'd put themselves in peril to help him – Lee Yong, himself and now Mrs Biltmore – but was he mindful of the risks they were taking? Somehow Blake doubted it, and although he might profess his thanks, the young man seemed tuned to his own agenda and oblivious to their safety.

Reda began stirring in his chair. Blake tip-toed across to speak to him and as he approached, the young Egyptian hauled himself up to sit straighter. Under the circumstances, he looked remarkably cheerful.

"Now then," said Blake. "And how are you feeling this afternoon?"

He sat down on the edge of the bed opposite. It was barely a day since Lee Yong had sat in the same position and he had been in the chair.

"Much better, thank you, Mr Blake," said Reda. "As you can see, I am in good hands." He nodded in the direction of his carer.

"Yes, you're a lucky man to have such attention." There was a touch of jealousy in Blake's comment. "Mrs Biltmore tells me you took a bit of a pasting the other evening."

Although there was clearly no jealousy in that.

"As I said to you last night, Mr Blake, it was a light beating, nothing more. In fact I consider myself fortunate. Many of my colleagues have suffered far worse than I. Some have died already. And I don't doubt that many more will do so before this work is finished."

"You take all this quite seriously, don't you?"

Blake didn't mean to sound flippant, but at his university, protest had often been a matter of style rather than conviction.

"Of course we take it seriously!" Reda was indignant. "You don't imagine we enter into this lightly, do you? It's not a game, Mr Blake."

"I'm sorry, I didn't mean to belittle..." He paused and attempted to recover himself. "But what about the police? Doesn't their attitude bother you?"

"Pah!" Reda scoffed. "The police? They're nothing more than Mubarak's Gestapo. We don't let them intimidate us with their presence. They've always been there and they always will. But now it's time to move on. They think that they can hurt us with their bullets and their batons, but they can never take away our dignity."

"Is that what this is all about – dignity?"

"That, and justice and freedom. Those are the watchwords of our revolution, Mr Blake. It's our response to how humiliated and how hopeless we've been made to feel over the last four decades. You see, we've been bullied into thinking that nothing can change – but we know that's not true, and now we'll show the world that it can."

As a historian, Blake had studied revolution in many forms. The subject fascinated him – and here he was, right at the heart of one.

"Oh, and how do you intend to do that?"

"There is only one way, Mr Blake. We have to get rid of Mubarak. Only when he's gone will things be different. Mohamed Bovaziz in Tunisia gave us the strength to get started when he set himself alight. Now it's time for us to put a torch to Mubarak. He's the one who really deserves to burn!"

Reda spoke with fervour and his eyes shone bright with belief. What faith these young people had in themselves, thought Blake – they believed they could move mountains. Later, when the mountain proved intractable, they would learn it was easier to move round it...

"I'm sure your father would be proud of you."

The remark caused Reda to start – it had come out of the blue. Blake felt an explanation was required.

"It came to my attention," he said vaguely. "Let's just say I made some enquiries."

"I see…" Reda seemed slightly embarrassed. "My father (may he rest in peace) was a great man, Mr Blake. But this has nothing to do with him. He was an Islamist and I am not – the old choice between Mubarak and the Brotherhood is dead. This is a new Egypt. This is about the people, not their religion. They want their rights as human beings and that's something Mubarak has always denied them."

"And you think that's worth dying for?"

"I know it's not worth living without it. And if you're asking me whether I'd go back and do it again, well, yes, I would. I'd do it a hundred times if it meant that Egypt could be free. And there are thousands of my brothers and sisters who would do the same. The people are on our side Mr Blake – we have the numbers and they cannot stop us however hard they try. We will win – I promise you that – and in a few years' time you will see a different Egypt than you do today."

Blake shuffled uncomfortably on the edge of the bed. The concepts that lay behind revolution were interesting – but the effects were equally worrying. He'd grown to love Egypt the way it was – poor, oppressed, and yet proud – why should he want it to be different? For him, the country acquired its dignity from the way it coped with its adversities – not from how it would be once it had overcome them. That was partly what made it such a special place – that and its quirky, unpredictable nature. In pre-war Italy Mussolini had made the trains run on time – post-war Egypt had yet to manage it. Was all that lovable chaos to go in this new scheme of things? He sincerely hoped not. But then, he always did have a problem with change...

Reda's views were unsettling – and it was not just the content of them that disturbed Blake but the manner in which they were expressed. They did not admit of doubt and were held with a deep-seated passion of a kind he could never hope to emulate and it was a source of embarrassment and regret. There would be those who found such conviction appealing – Lee Yong amongst them, and she was drawn to the young Egyptian as a moth was attracted to a flame. The fire that fed it smouldered deep within him – she needed to be careful she did not get burnt.

Blake had no such beliefs with which to tempt her. His fire, if ever lit, had been doused some while ago. Reda was prepared to stand at the barricades to move old Egypt on – but Blake knew that he could not do the same to keep it. Deep in his heart an inner voice told him that, as usual, he would watch from the sidelines and decline to interfere. He stood up off the bed and allowed the young Egyptian to return to his television. For the moment he'd had enough of revolution.

In the hope of some solace he turned to Lee Yong. She broke off from her reading but he had nothing to offer her other than the balance of her money. The original envelope had been left with the fat policeman, and from amongst his papers Blake had found a replacement which he now placed quietly on the dressing table next to the recharging laptop.

He left soon after, but not before he'd persuaded her to come down to dinner that evening. He told her it would look odd if she did not, and by missing three meals in a row (she'd already skipped lunch in addition to breakfast) she would only attract unwanted comment. And besides, it would be cruel of her to deprive the others of her company purely on account of Reda. He wasn't the only fish in the sea.

Chapter Twenty-six

Lee Yong must have heeded his words as she did come down for her evening meal. Neither was she late, if anything too early, for when Blake and the others entered the dining room at seven, she was already in her place and looked as though she'd been there for some time. Nor had she 'dressed' for the occasion, although that was of no real consequence as neither had anyone else – it was not yet their last night together and therefore carried no special meaning.

Even so, it registered with Blake, because except for the three-quarter length jacket, she was wearing the same set of clothes as she had when he'd first seen her on that bitterly cold morning at Queen Hatshepsut's Temple – the Cuban heels, the jeans, the rock-band T-shirt. And yet in spite of this, her appearance had subtly altered. The long dangly earrings were gone and her hair was merely brushed instead of carefully styled. The faintest of lines had grown up around the corners of her eyes and with the moderation in her use of make-up, it had deprived her of that steely look which had so reduced him in the beginning. Then she'd looked stunning – now she seemed altogether softer and gentler, as though her aura of impregnable self-confidence had given way to a bout of melancholy. It was as if the events of the week had made her vulnerable – and in Blake's eyes she was all the more attractive for it. If he'd ever been in love with her (and it was still something he dared not think about), then it was never more so than now.

He understood her mood only too well – he'd suffered from the self-same kind of introspection himself. But what puzzled him was why it should still afflict her. Most of the cares that had been heaped on her were now in the past. Reda had been rescued and although hurt, was well on the road to recovery. They'd escaped the tyranny of Aswan and were on their way to the comparative safety of Luxor, where according to the latest reports, the airport was open and flights were running as normal. Once there, the door to the world was open and as she'd made clear to them on the night she'd introduced herself, she could go anywhere she chose. Money was no object – she still had the balance of her savings from the purser's safe, and when that was gone there was always the backing of her father's war chest. She'd used it to buy Reda's freedom and even if he'd repeated the same offence a hundred times over, as he'd told Blake he was prepared to do, she could still have set him free on each occasion. And yet she was learning it was not enough. She could buy all she wanted in the material world – but she could not, it seemed, buy happiness.

After the others had sat down and started chatting, the reason for her early arrival became apparent. She wanted to talk to Blake, and she waited patiently until the rest were all otherwise engaged before pulling at the sleeve of his linen jacket.

"Michael," she whispered. "I need to speak to you."

It was the use of his forename as much as the secretive nature of her approach that alerted him to the fact that something might be wrong. His initial thought was that Reda had suffered some kind of relapse.

"What, now?"

"No, after dinner will be fine."

"Is everything alright?"

"Yes..." Although something told him it was not. "I'll meet you in the foyer."

"Ok."

And so for the time being he was left to wonder.

He'd come to the table with the constant worry that Mrs Biltmore might begin another of her stories and inadvertently reveal their secret. The need to guard against the possibility remained at the forefront of his mind and with Lee Yong's request hovering at the back of it, it made for a tense and nervous meal-time.

He was fortunate that the bulk of the conversation touched neither on Reda nor the revolution. Ever since they'd left Aswan, the others had lost interest in political affairs and had become focused on how they were going to rescue the rest of their holiday and how they were going to get home. The idea that they were involved in an event that might change the world had not occurred to them. So when David announced he had news, it turned out to be of an entirely provincial nature.

"You'll be pleased to know that Keith and I have managed to get a trip to Karnak organised for tomorrow. We've persuaded the captain to lay on a couple of buses for eight-thirty in the morning so we'll get to spend a few hours there. There'll be a notice going up on the board fairly soon, if it's not there already."

"That's great." Blake seized on the issue. He was keen to keep the subject under discussion as it helped to keep attention away from Reda and Lee Yong. "I'm impressed – how did you manage that?"

"Pretty simple really. Keith told him that if he didn't, he'd report it to the tour company and ask for a refund. He jumped pretty smartish after that."

"That was a bit brutal."

"Not really. Karnak was on the original itinerary and we've missed enough already. We've paid for it, so I don't really see there's a problem."

"Evidently not. And what about tomorrow night? Wasn't there talk of a farewell function?"

"You mean the reception at Luxor Temple."

"Yes – is that still on the agenda?"

"Absolutely! I don't think they had any choice after I'd mentioned the Karnak business."

"Well good for you, that's a result. You must be feeling pretty pleased with yourself."

"Oh, trust me, he is," Joan cut in, a little sarcastically. She'd braved the drawback of her reddened appearance to join them. The areas of her face that had been exposed glowed like a lantern, but with the help of David's pair of dark glasses she'd succeeded in covering the white patches round her eyes. "In fact, he's been insufferable this afternoon. Although to be honest, I'm just glad of having something to do tomorrow. I don't know about the rest of you, but I've been bored silly just sitting around all day."

At this point Blake half expected Mrs Biltmore to chime in with some unwanted remark. He could imagine it would begin with the medical treatment of sunburn and would involve her experiences in Vietnam. This would lead on to a discussion about nursing and the fact that Joan would not have found the day half so boring had she known what was going on in Lee Yong's cabin. But to his great relief she did not and the moment passed without incident. Nor at any time during the conversation did she attempt to catch his eye (or Lee Yong's either as far as he could tell) to try and pass on a conspiratorial glance to confirm their collective involvement. Instead, she sat quietly restrained and restricted herself to a few whispered asides to Ira between courses.

After dinner, and for the second night running, he went to meet Lee Yong in the foyer. This time, rather than stand beneath the flashing images of the TV screen, they chose to sit in comfort on the sofa.

Blake had thought to bring his coffee up from the dining room and settled back, waiting for Lee Yong to begin. But she was unable to relax and the same anxieties that had driven her down to dinner early remained and brought her to the edge of her seat. Eventually, she took a deep breath and made a start.

"It's about Reda..." He'd imagined it would be. At the moment, it was all about Reda. "I've asked if he wants to come with me."

"What, on your tour of Europe?"

"No, to America."

"America? I thought..."

"Things have changed, Mr Blake." Obviously they had. "That business about travelling the world and visiting those faraway places – it seems a bit pointless now. It's all very well but you can't go on roaming around for ever – at some stage you have to make a decision about your future. You see, I've been talking to Mrs Biltmore."

"Yes, you told me – about her being a nurse in Vietnam."

"Yes, that was yesterday. This is something different."

"Go on."

"Well, when she was in my cabin this morning, she was telling me about Johns Hopkins." Blake recalled how she'd spoken about it at the start of the trip. "You see, Ira was Head of Department." So that was it – Blake had been wondering. "He retired a couple of years ago but he's still on the board and has quite a lot of influence. It's a tremendous university, Mr Blake, and they could get me a place, I'm sure of it – Mrs Biltmore said so. And they could get one for Reda, she said that too."

A few days ago he'd have been inclined to take Mrs Biltmore's pronouncements with a pinch of salt but in the new scheme of things, he was obliged to look on them with a degree of seriousness.

"And is that what you want?"

"Yes, I think it is now. It's what I was always going to do and to be honest, Mr Blake, the last few days have frightened me and I just want to get away somewhere safe. And I want Reda to get away, too. I heard what you said the other day – that it doesn't end here and that they'll always be looking for him. I've been thinking about it and you're right. There'll be no peace for him in Cairo – there'll be no peace for him in Egypt – and he'll always be looking over his shoulder. This is a chance for him to escape all that and find somewhere quiet to settle down. Oh, Mr Blake, after you've lived in a country where you're afraid to speak your mind or stand up for your rights, think what it must be like to wake up every day where you're free to say and do what you want. Isn't that a wonderful prospect?"

A light had returned to her eyes and it was as if the spark of childlike enthusiasm that had carried her to the head of the Valley of the Kings was re-ignited. Over the last few days she'd aged far more quickly than she'd have liked or expected but now it seemed there was a ray of hope, a light at the end of the tunnel, and it shone out in her like a beacon.

Blake sensed the change and felt an inner surge of shared emotion. If she'd come to a solution that meant she could be rescued from her dejected state, then there was hope for them all. There was even a chance that one day, he too might be saved.

These were grounds for optimism, but he still gave a guarded response. Even if Mrs Biltmore and Ira could do what they'd said, there were other practicalities to think of – not least of which was the position of the young Egyptian.

"Have you spoken to Reda about this?"

"I've tried."

"And how does he feel?"

"That's the point. It's difficult getting him to talk about it. He's so wrapped up in what's going on in Cairo that I can't get him to think about anything else. I know he's been hurt and needs to rest – but all he's done all day is sit in front of that television and watch the news. I don't think he realises the danger he's in. That's why I've come to you, Mr Blake. Can't you speak to him? I'm convinced he'd listen if you were to talk to him. Someone needs to make him see sense. Can't you tell him what it would mean?"

"Me? What makes you think I've got any more influence over him than you have?"

"He respects you."

"Really?"

Blake was genuinely surprised. He'd led such an independent

life that he wasn't used to the idea that he might have an effect on the emotions of others.

"Yes, he's told me that. He says you're the only one who's taken the trouble to hear what he has to say. You seem to know more about these things anyway."

Blake felt flattered for the second time in as many minutes. The comment sounded sincere, although something still didn't sit right.

"I'm not certain..."

...that I'm the one that you want.

His hesitation only caused Lee Yong to intensify her pleading.

"Do it for my sake, Mr Blake. You know how much I want to go – and now it's a chance for the both of us. This is a tremendous opportunity – and when opportunities are given to you, you have to take them. Don't you agree? Or do you think I'm being foolish?"

"No, I don't think you're foolish at all."

"You'll speak to him then? Please?"

She'd turned herself round on the edge of the sofa so she was almost confronting him. The tears of the last two days had all but dried up but there was still a suggestion of strain. Her voice had a begging quality and her face such an imploring look – how could he possibly deny her? Like a stray sheep herded into a pen, he felt he'd been manoeuvred into a position from which he could not escape. She'd cornered him and it left him no alternative – was that how she managed her father, in exactly the same way?

"Very well..."

"Thank you, Mr Blake. I knew I could rely on you. You'll do it soon though, won't you?"

"Yes, yes. As soon as I can. In the morning."

She might grant him one night's peace, at least.

Now she'd extracted his promise, Lee Yong sought to excuse herself. She had to look after Reda and there were doubtless things to do for the following day.

Blake watched as she made her way across the foyer toward the stairway, her shoulder bag swinging to the rhythm of her Cuban heels. Yesterday he'd agreed to contact the local chief of police and offer him a bribe on her behalf – and then he'd been down to the station with her to ensure the deal was met. Today she'd persuaded him to talk Reda into going to America with her – a task which in his view was likely to be just as onerous. How had he managed to get so involved? He wasn't the only one she'd drawn in – somehow she had beguiled them all, Mrs Biltmore, Ira, the others. If it hadn't been for her...

The hint of a mischievous smile crossed his lips as he suddenly saw the funny side. All in all, it was an unlikely situation they found themselves in. Halfway up the Nile an Englishman, a Malaysian and an American were all looking after an Egyptian – it sounded like the opening line of a particularly bad joke.

Chapter Twenty-seven

Blake rolled over, turned to face the net-curtained window then pulled the covers over his head and buried himself deep beneath his bedclothes. Not for the first time he found the darkness especially comforting. It was his first conscious act of the day and served a number of vital purposes.

Firstly, it relieved him of the need to stare vacantly at his tripod and telescope, both of which had lain unused against the wall by the doorway since his early morning excursion to watch Spoonbills the day before. With the exception of his boat trip in Aswan, they reminded him of how futile his birding trip had become. Secondly – and more importantly – it enabled him to shut out the rest of the world and in particular, his ill-considered promise of the night before to go and speak to Reda. Ever since he'd committed himself to doing it, he'd been consumed with regret and to put it bluntly, he was dreading it.

Lee Yong's request had placed him in an awkward position and he was unsure of what to do. On the one hand, he genuinely wanted to help her. He could feel his heart urging him forward on her behalf and he told himself that he must seek Reda out at the earliest opportunity and speak to him to put the case in her favour. Like the advice given to the pioneers in America, *Go west, young man!* he would tell him. *Go west, young man, and grow up with the country! For God's sake go! While you still have the chance…* It was what he'd failed to do himself and sometime in the early hours of the morning he'd come to the conclusion that Lee Yong was right – opportunities such as this were few and far between and when offered, they should be taken.

There was nothing that would give him greater pleasure at that moment than to see the two of them fly off together. Like migrating swallows bound for a distant land, after a long and perilous journey they might settle down and find a spot where they could build a nest. Later, they would return with young ones... It was a profoundly foolish thought, but somewhere deep within him an unrequited romantic was at work.

On the other hand, every logical consideration he could think of spoke against it. His abiding principle not to interfere with nature carried over into his human relationships – it was none of his business what other people did and he must not get involved. Reda and Lee Yong should be left to work things out for themselves and what would be, would be. He'd overstepped the mark at least twice before – firstly at the Egyptian Evening (although he'd somehow got away with it), and then his trip along the riverbank had been a terrible mistake and he rued the moment he'd ever thought of setting out on it. Far better to retreat now before he got drawn in too deep.

It was not just his principles that held him back – the mere idea of 'talking' to Reda at all made him distinctly uneasy. He was not in the habit of lecturing young men and telling them what to do and for him it was an altogether unnatural experience. He likened it to that dreaded moment when a father is obliged to take his son to one side and tell him about the birds and the bees. There would be an embarrassed clearing of the throat, then, *There's something we need to discuss...* Why couldn't they find these things out for themselves?

He began to formulate a compromise. Instead of tackling things head-on, what if he were to casually drop the subject into an existing conversation? If the opportunity presented itself, then it might not appear so deliberate. Curled up beneath the covers, he started to practise the words in his mind. *So, do you and Lee Yong have any plans? What are you going to do when this is all over?* It sounded an innocent enough question. If he could just find the right moment...

His train of thought was interrupted by a loud and yet naggingly familiar noise. From somewhere in the vicinity, the quiet peace of the morning was being shattered by the amplified voice of a loud-hailer. The shock of it caused him to sit bolt upright in the bed, and he immediately threw off the covers and went to the window where he drew back the net curtains and started to look for clues.

As he'd suspected, the gentle sensation of forward motion that had been present the previous day had stopped and the ship had come to a halt. They'd moored up some time during the night and instead of looking out across the river as he'd done at Aswan, his cabin now faced the town. On the other side of the Corniche, framed by the rising sun, was the familiar skyline of Luxor. The clock on his bedside table showed six-thirty-five. A little late for the call to morning prayers, and he could not recall hearing them when they'd been here some six days before. And besides, this was not the rallying cry of an Imam – it was the barked instruction of someone in command.

A horrible thought occurred and he hurriedly pulled on a pair of shorts and a T-shirt and stuck his feet into the first available pair of footwear he could find. Grabbing his fleece from its hook on the back of the door he ran down the corridor, up the stairs and out onto the sun-deck.

He was not the first to arrive – half the passenger list had already gathered on the port-side rail to investigate. A few had managed to get dressed but most were still in their nightclothes. The tall and craggy figure of Keith was easy to pick out and despite his pyjamas, dressing gown and slippers, he still gave off his usual air of authority.

"What's going on?" Blake called across.

"Damned if I know," said Keith. "But it looks as though the police are paying us a visit. Come and see for yourself."

He went over to join him.

They had indeed reached Luxor, but they were moored much closer to the town centre than they'd been before and the tour buses were now stationed in a row along the main road. Closer to hand, a line of three white cars was drawn up on the quayside.

Blake instantly recognised them. Behind them, a large blue truck was already disgorging a line of armed police out onto the tarmac. At the top of the steps leading down to the ship's gangplank, Mr Mohammed, the ship's captain, had adopted a pleading posture and was attempting to bar the way. More ominously, standing next to him was the unmistakable figure of Aswan's chief of police. Megaphone in hand, Hossein Rasheed was busily directing affairs.

Blake's hands tightened their grip on the ship's rail. The presence of the fat policeman meant only one thing – they were searching for Reda. A mixture of guilt and fear swirled around his stomach. After all the effort they'd made to secure the young Egyptian's safety, they were about to be undone. Why hadn't he seen this coming? Why hadn't he thought? And yet, of course he had. *I know these people – they'll come looking.* More to the point, why hadn't he done something about it? He'd told himself he needed a plan – and last night he'd meant to concoct one but Lee Yong's request had distracted him. He had to think quickly – although on board ship, sat out on the Nile, there were limited options available.

It was too late to debate the issue now – his first priority was to warn Lee Yong. With a quiet *You'll have to excuse me* and making every effort not to appear panicked, he quickly slipped away and went below.

As soon as he was out of sight he took the stairs two at a time and ran. The lower decks were crowded with people still making their way up. He tried his best to barge through but arrived too late and as he entered Lee Yong's corridor from one end, a group of blue-clothed police headed by Hossein Rasheed entered it from the other. Working their way towards him, they began knocking on doors.

Blake stood paralysed at the foot of the stairway, not knowing what to do. At any moment they would reach Lee Yong's cabin.

If he made a move to warn her they would only become suspicious – he dared not risk it. The alternative was to stand in their way and try to halt their progress while Reda made his escape. But he was hardly strong enough for that and it would only be a matter of time.

Outside Lee Yong's door, a young officer stood poised with a sledgehammer, ready to force an entry.

"Police! Open up!" he called out in Arabic.

She would not understand the words, but the meaning was abundantly clear.

The door cracked open and Lee Yong's face appeared. She looked as pale and as serious as she'd done at any time in the last few days. In the corridor outside, Rasheed recognised her at once and nodded vigorously, urging his men forward.

"Yes, yes. In here, this is the one we want, go on."

Pushing Lee Yong's slight frame to one side, they forced their way into the room.

Blake rushed in behind, followed by the fat policeman.

For a few hectic moments it was a confused and crowded scene. While one stood guard at the doorway, two other officers scoured the room from top to bottom – the en suite, the wardrobe, under the bed, anywhere a man might be concealed. Lee Yong had retreated before them and stood calmly by the window as she'd done the day before, her arms clasped about herself as if trying to ward off cold – or more likely, the lurking presence of Rasheed. With his hands held firmly behind his back, Aswan's chief of police thrust out his great belly and watched keenly from the far wall, waiting for results.

Blake caught Lee Yong's eye. He saw her give a tiny shake of her head, although whether this was supposed to mean *The game's up, we're lost* or *He's not here*, he wasn't sure. Either way, she chose to stay put by the window while presiding over the chair in which Reda had sat so recently that Blake was sure he could still make out the young man's impression. On the dressing table, the computer had gone along with the mobile phone and the wallet, although the envelope stuffed with cash he'd left the previous day remained hidden amongst the row of bottles. He thought to look at the bed and was horrified to see that although it had clearly been slept in and the covers hastily pulled up, there were still dents in each of the two pillows. But even if he'd noticed it, the policemen obviously had not and soon reported back.

"It's clear."

Over by the far wall, Rasheed scowled and waved them out of the room. He began to pace up and down in the space beside the bed, occasionally looking up at Blake and Lee Yong with an agitated frown.

"So! What have you done with him?" he demanded at last.

"What have we done with who?" said Blake. It was the obvious reply, but under the circumstances it sounded rather crass.

Rasheed stopped his pacing and turned to face them. His scowl had reappeared.

"Don't play games with me, Mr Blake. You know precisely who I mean."

"If you're talking about Reda Eldasouky," said Blake, "I can honestly tell you, I have no idea where he is. He's obviously not here," he waved his hand around the empty room, "and you're quite welcome to look in my cabin if you wish. I have nothing to hide."

"A fine gesture – but pointless," said Rasheed. "Your cabin is being searched even as we speak."

Blake shrugged – it made no difference.

The sound of heavy footsteps could be heard in the corridor as the three officers returned.

"Anything?" Rasheed called out, cocking his head to one side.

"No, Chief, nothing..."

Blake was tempted to smirk. It seemed that he'd worried for

no real reason.

"So what are you going to do now? You surely can't search the whole ship?"

"I wouldn't waste my time trying – there are far too many places for a man to hide. I have other, much more effective ways of finding what I want. Someone knows where he is – and before too long, someone will tell me."

"Oh really? So who do plan to torture next?"

Rasheed's failure had boosted Blake's confidence.

The policeman's piggy eyes narrowed.

"Just be thankful, Mr Blake, that you're not an Egyptian..." His scowl changed to a look of genuine annoyance. "I suppose you think you're both very clever. You've managed to hide him from me this time, but I will find him, make no mistake about that." His flabby jowls wobbled disconcertingly when he spoke. "It seems I should not have let him go. He's wanted urgently in Cairo and there's a price on his head. The big boss wants to talk to him, so don't imagine for one moment he'll escape us, because he won't – we're looking out for him everywhere. As for you British," he said, turning directly to Blake. "If you think you can come here and meddle in our affairs, you're mistaken. You can tell your friends at the British Embassy that when we catch this man the world will know it was you and your American allies who kept him hidden from us. You will regret this or my name is not Hossein Rasheed."

While he'd been talking, Blake had kept his eyes on Lee Yong. She'd remained rooted to the spot and seemed reluctant to move away from the window which he could see had been opened. The net curtains were drawn to one side and behind them, a small handrail protected the twenty-foot drop into the Nile. For an agile young man it would present little difficulty, but Reda was bulky and suffering from a sprained ankle. Even so, it was not impossible to think he'd gone over the side. The ancient river held many secrets – here perhaps was another.

Rasheed was quick to catch the subject of Blake's attention and immediately came to the same conclusion. He walked swiftly across to the window and shoving Lee Yong aside, looked out onto the Nile.

"Here!" He shouted to his troops and pointed. "This is where he's gone – look how the bitch covers up for him. Get back to the quayside and scour the riverbank. There's a reward for the man who finds him!"

There was a triumphal note in his voice. He gave a leer in their direction, then turned on his heel and stalked out into the corridor where his rasping voice could be heard echoing down the stairs.

"Move! Move! Come on you lazy dogs, there's work to do. Move!"

Suddenly the room was empty save for Blake and Lee Yong. In front of the net-curtained window, she drew her arms ever tighter about herself and shuddered.

"Ugh! That man... He gives me – what do you English call it? – the crepes?"

"I think you mean the creeps."

"Whatever..."

Blake studied her face. She seemed calm, and if what he had just witnessed was the worst of her reaction, then she'd clearly survived the ordeal quite well. He'd half expected her to burst into tears and collapse under the pressure.

"That must have been a close call. So where...?"

"Not now." She cut him off. "Let's wait until we're sure they've gone – you never know who might be listening. Anyway, I need to use the bathroom."

She disappeared into the en suite and left him to speculate.

There was one thing Blake could be certain of – Reda was no longer in the room. The police had been thorough and Lee Yong had shown no trace of anxiety. But neither had he gone out of the window...

Later, when Lee Yong told him where Reda really was, he found he couldn't help laughing. Rasheed had been right about their 'American allies' and there was yet more for which to thank Mrs Biltmore. Her cabin was a few doors down on the opposite side of the corridor and her quick-witted reaction on hearing the loud-hailer was to be commended. Reda's relocation had been timely, if a little awkward.

And as for his 'friends at the British Embassy', Carpenter would have been flattered.

Blake returned to his cabin to find it had indeed been broken into. The lock had been forced and it was this, rather than the intrusion itself, which annoyed him. Could they not have demanded a key from reception or a spare from the purser instead of causing unnecessary damage? If they'd asked him in person, he'd have been happy to let them in.

The room itself had hardly been touched. They'd been looking for the man and not evidence of his presence so there'd been no pulling out of drawers or rifling through belongings, and it was only that the bathroom and wardrobe doors had been left open that betrayed their search. That, and the opened window and net curtains left shivering in the breeze...

While he was arranging repair of the lock, Blake made a discovery – although his own things had not been disturbed, Reda's old room had been trashed.

According to the purser, nothing much had been spared. It seemed that if they couldn't find him, the alternative was to obliterate all trace.

At breakfast, the dining room was awash with speculation. Opinion ranged from the belief there was a jihadist on board with a bomb (this from the self-same lady who'd predicted they'd be murdered in their beds) to the idea that the police were hunting a gang of international diamond smugglers. Surprisingly little mention was made of Reda and as far as the others were concerned, he'd already been forgotten and had passed into history.

Blake found it hard to contain his amusement at these wild stories. So too did Mrs Biltmore. While Lee Yong and Ira remained expressionless and stared solemnly down at their plates, she allowed herself the widest of smiles and spent the whole meal grinning like a Cheshire cat.

Chapter Twenty-eight

Blake stared vacantly out of the tour bus window. Across the Corniche, a street vendor had set up a mobile stall and had been trying to attract the passers-by with an array of trinkets and fake jewellery. He'd been suffering a marked lack of success. Before long the police had arrived and after the usual heated debate and exchange of profanities, the vendor had moved off. He would no doubt return once the police had disappeared. It was an age-old game – and one that would continue to be played for many years to come, revolution or not. In this country, thought Blake, nothing ever really changed.

He'd sat there waiting a full ten minutes, the bus engine rumbling beneath his feet, the front entrance folded open ready to receive the last of the passengers to board. Other than watch the antics of the police and the street vendor, he'd attempted to pass the time by imagining how Mrs Biltmore and Lee Yong had succeeded in moving Reda from one room to another so quickly. Someone must have been alert. Could it all have been purely spontaneous? Or had they cooked up a plan in advance? In the rush to get ready there'd been little occasion to talk and he'd yet to hear the full story. All he'd been told was that Reda was fine and for the time being he was to stay in Mrs Biltmore's room – the risk of moving him again was too great.

Blake wondered how Reda's ankle was holding up. However hard he tried, the thought of the young Egyptian hobbling across the corridor with Lee Yong on one side and Mrs Biltmore on the other didn't seem to gel. But somehow they'd managed it and Blake was eternally grateful – their prompt action had got him off the hook. Not only had Reda been kept safe while he'd been on the sun-deck panicking, but his sudden disappearance had absolved Blake from the duty of 'speaking' to him. It was one less worry to start the day, although the problem of what to do with him still remained. Reda couldn't stay where he was indefinitely and at some point within the next twenty-four hours he would need to have gone.

A sharp puff of compressed air told him that the last of the passengers was now on board. David had been growing impatient. In conjunction with Keith he'd gone to some lengths to organise their outing and was sitting a couple of seats further forward.

"About time!" he called out.

A few days earlier, on the trip to Aglika and the Temple of Isis, it had been Blake who'd been late and had to apologise. When it came to the matter of punctuality, the British were an unforgiving lot. The bus gave a jolt and moved off into the morning light.

On the other side of the Corniche, the persistent vendor of trinkets had returned and set up his stall once more.

They were soon driving through the centre of Luxor. Known to the Greeks as the ancient city of Thebes, its modern name was derived from the Arabic, El-Uqsur, meaning 'the palaces'. And what palaces they were, great monuments to history that defined a whole civilisation.

In a sense they were coming home. This was the point they'd set out from some six days before. Then, their early morning trip had been to the west bank, the Temple of Queen Hatshepsut and the Valley of the Kings. Now they were staying on the east bank and were travelling to the religious complex at Karnak.

In one of her derisive moments, Joan had described Philae as 'just another pile of stones'. The same could hardly be said of Karnak – or at least, if it was, then they were some of the most famous stones in the world. Covering half a square kilometre in size and 1300 years in time (Blake had taken his guide book down to breakfast and had digested part of it along with his scrambled egg) it was the largest complex of its kind in existence. It could not be ignored and for many it would be the highlight of their trip. No wonder David was making such an effort.

But try as he might, Blake could not bring himself to share his enthusiasm. Perhaps he was tired after a long week, perhaps it was the effect of recent events (the problem of Reda was still hanging over their heads), but for whatever reason he couldn't generate the same level of interest. Karnak was important, and although it ranked amongst the most renowned, there were other sites of equal, if not greater, significance – the Monastery at Petra, the Blue Mosque in Istanbul, the city of Jerusalem itself – all these were places Blake had visited at one time or another during his service at the Embassy. He'd once thought them exciting but over the years their sense of mystery had faded and for the moment he could not convince himself that Karnak would be any different.

Outside the bus, the long façade of the Winter Palace Hotel slid by, dark against the rising sun. Soon it would grow unbearably hot, and he baulked at the thought of toiling through sprawling archaeological remains in the searing heat. He pushed his new pair of sunglasses tight to his face and patted the bottle of water in his pocket. At least he was well prepared – there was no chance of a headache today.

He arrived at the site determined to speak with Lee Yong at the first opportunity. As for the archaeology, he already knew the history and as much as he might denigrate Joan, for him it really was 'just another pile of stones'. After the disruption of the past few days, he was no longer in 'birding' mode either and although his binoculars were a permanent feature, he'd elected not to bring his telescope. It was hardly a habitat in which he could expect to see a great deal, but he'd no sooner descended from the bus than he became aware of a familiar outline perched on the railings next to the ticket office.

Little Green Bee-Eater.

His heart skipped a beat and he would dearly have loved to stop and admire the colours, but with the stand-in guide's introductory talk due to take place at any moment, he dared not linger. Lurking at the back of his mind was the thought of Lee Yong's admonition.

What are you doing, Mr Blake? You're for ever lagging behind...

Fortunately, the bird flew with them and alighted in a tree conveniently situated behind the tour guide's adopted position so rather than having to look round for it, it was always in view. And as luck would have it, Lee Yong was also in front of him so the thought that he might offend her as he'd done at Queen Hatshepsut's Temple did not arise. Knowing he could safely ignore the tour guide and watch the bird, a pleasant five minutes ensued. It was an auspicious start to the visit.

He need not have feared Lee Yong's intervention. She too was ignoring the tour guide and was engaged in earnest conversation with Mrs Biltmore. Decked out in her perennial attire of shapeless green top and white floppy hat, the American had sufficiently recovered from her previous exertions to risk another day out and had lathered herself with sun-cream. As the guide's speech ended, she and Lee Yong linked arms and sauntered off toward the entrance, sharing the shade of the young Malaysian's black parasol. Ira's position as permanent consort to his wife was currently redundant and he followed studiously behind. Blake fell in with him, primarily out of politeness rather than anything else – it wasn't as if Ira would want to talk.

As soon as they were out of sight of the main party, Blake sought to split the two women apart and tapped Lee Yong on the shoulder.

"We need to talk."

"We do?" She lowered her parasol to look at him, apparently surprised at the interruption.

"I think so."

"Alone?"

Blake glanced round at Mrs Biltmore whose face was still

wreathed in its Cheshire cat-like smile.

"Well, no, I suppose not. We're all in this together now."

"What do you suggest?"

"There's a café overlooking the Sacred Lake." If nothing else, the few moments he'd spent with his guidebook had at least taught him that. "Why don't we go and get a drink or something? We should be able to sit in comfort there."

"Very well."

It was less than a ten-minute walk to the café but by the time they arrived, Mrs Biltmore was already exhausted in the heat of the blazing sun and sank down onto a waiting bench beneath a large umbrella.

"Oh my!" she complained, removing her floppy hat and vigorously fanning her face. "I just don't think this country was designed for a body like mine!"

Blake ordered a round of mint tea and sat down to confer with his impromptu council of war.

His first question concerned Reda's state of health. As Mrs Biltmore had confidently predicted, the ankle which had so worried Blake was much improved to the point where the young Egyptian could walk unaided. So rather than the awkward scene Blake had imagined, Reda had managed to scuttle across the corridor under his own steam just in the nick of time, the door of Mrs Biltmore's cabin barely closing behind him before Rasheed's men had appeared at one end of the passageway and Blake at the other.

"And how is he in himself?" asked Blake.

"Why, he's just like a cat on a hot tin roof." Mrs Biltmore had cooled off in the shade of the large umbrella and was sufficiently refreshed to speak. "Pacing up and down the whole time – that boy just won't sit still! I told him he needs more rest but he won't have it. Goodness only knows what we're going to do with him."

"Exactly," said Blake. "What are we going to do with him? By this time tomorrow we'll all be at the airport and we can't just leave him."

"We were all rather hoping you'd come up with something, Mr Blake."

It was Lee Yong's first contribution to the conversation. Ira, of course, had so far said nothing and remained completely intractable.

"Hmm..." Blake felt flattered by her confidence in him but was worried that it might be misplaced. Keith was the one to look to in these situations... "Well I certainly wouldn't want to be doing anything in daylight. If we're to get him off safely, our best chance is under the cover of darkness. And if all else fails, we could always dress him up again and try smuggling him aboard the bus in the morning – although I for one wouldn't want to leave it that late."

"What about the police? What will happen if they show up again?"

"It's a risk we'll have to take." Blake's thoughts went back to the billowing net curtains and open window in Lee Yong's room. "And if push comes to shove, he'll just have to swim for it, I suppose..."

They talked around the options for another half an hour, weighing the pros and cons. Eventually, they resolved to meet in Mrs Biltmore's room at midnight and depending on the lie of the land, come to their final conclusion. In the absence of a viable alternative, it seemed the best they could do.

It was a temporary postponement, but the prospect of a definite course of action lifted whatever load had been pressing on Blake's shoulders and for the first time that day, he felt a sense of relief. Lee Yong too appeared less anxious and with the discussion about Reda at an end, the conversation turned to their surroundings. She expressed regret that in their hurry to get to the café, they'd bypassed the splendours of the Hypostyle Hall. It was one of the features she'd been hoping to see and after she'd finished her tea, she announced her intention of going back to study it in more detail. She looked to Mrs Biltmore but despite her extended rest, the American professed herself incapable of accompanying her.

"Why, honey, I don't think I could manage another step. Mr Blake's right here – I'm sure he'd be happy to take you."

With nothing else in view, Blake was pleased to volunteer and leaving Mrs Biltmore to bemoan her enfeebled condition to Ira, he and the young Malaysian set off back toward the Hall.

According to the guide book it was no more than halfway back to the entrance, although by now the crowds had grown to slow their progress. Temporarily deprived of her companion, Blake half expected Lee Yong to revert to the subdued state of melancholy she'd been in since Reda's arrest. But the hour or so at the café and its positive outcome appeared to have heartened her, there was a spring in her step and her old eagerness to explore seemed to have returned. It was as if she'd rediscovered herself after the traumas of the week and rather than dwell on the problems of the present, the prospect of a future had opened up before her. She still looked tired and it would take a while to recover the freshness, but for the moment there were no more tears and from time to time there was a smile to rejoice in.

Once inside the Hypostyle Hall, Lee Yong took photographs of anything and everything she could find. Nothing escaped her. Blake thought himself safe amongst the gigantic pillars, but even he found himself a target. He grinned willingly for her camera. For once there were no birds to observe, but in the company of Lee Yong he'd no need of them and the next hour was possibly his happiest of the week.

But it was soon over and with Lee Yong's appetite for photography sated, they returned to the café to rejoin Mrs Biltmore and Ira. It was approaching twelve-thirty and having had nothing more than the mint tea to sustain them since breakfast, they decided to take lunch. Another pleasant hour followed and with the aid of a glass or two of wine, Blake grew quite relaxed. The steady hum of conversation dulled his senses, a group of red-breasted Egyptian Swallows flitted obligingly above their heads and by the time they gathered in the Processional Way at half past two for the bus, he was in a mellow mood.

He must have dozed off on the return journey as he missed the Winter Palace Hotel and arrived back at the ship desperate for a nap. His intention was to escort Lee Yong and the Biltmores to their rooms and then go straight to his own, but a surprise was awaiting them which would jerk him out of his torpor – Reda had gone missing. He'd hardly deposited the Americans at their door when Mrs Biltmore rushed back out to report that he was no longer in her cabin. Rather than wait for their assistance, it seemed he'd taken matters into his own hands and had vanished without trace, taking whatever belongings he had with him. There was no sign of a break-in or the police and as to his where-abouts, no-one seemed to know. With all the plans they'd spent so much time debating confounded, Blake was stumped as to what to suggest.

"Now what do we do?"

Mrs Biltmore was of no help. Slowly shaking her head, her "Now isn't that the darnedest thing?" was as much as she could muster.

And with Ira his normal dumb and muted self, they all looked to Lee Yong for a reaction.

Strangely enough, she did not seem perturbed and maintained the same aura of untroubled calm she'd acquired earlier in the day as though this latest setback could not upset her.

"You don't seem worried," said Blake, noting her mood.

"I'm not, Mr Blake. Reda knows what he's doing. I'm sure he's found somewhere safe to hide. He still has his mobile phone remember and we've all got his number. Let me try and contact him. If it's at all possible to find him, I will, I can promise you that."

Her offer was delivered with conviction and it persuaded them to leave it in her hands. With no other option in prospect, there seemed little else they could do.

Chapter Twenty-nine

It was another quarter of an hour before Blake got back to his cabin. As he turned the corner and headed down the corridor, he noticed the edge of a white envelope protruding from beneath his door. While he'd been away, something had been delivered. It was an invitation, printed on white card with a gold border.

Worldwide Travel
Request the pleasure of your company
At a Grand Reception
To be held at Luxor Temple
8.30pm Friday 28th January

It was more of a reminder, since the event itself had been part of the tour from the outset. Although with the changes forced on them by the revolution, it could well have been cancelled had it not been for David's persistence over the Karnak visit. It was intended to be their farewell party before departing the following day, their opportunity to bid each other goodbye amidst the splendour of one of Egypt's finest monuments. Such events were normally discussed over breakfast, but the early morning visit by the police had taken precedence and forced it off the agenda. It had consequently slipped his mind.

He recalled that the subject had been raised at dinner the night before, but he'd been so preoccupied with Lee Yong's request to talk that he'd failed to pay much attention. As far as he could remember, the schedule David had outlined was to be much the same as for the Egyptian evening – they would take an early meal, allow half an hour to prepare themselves and be ready to leave at eight. The invitation implied a special form of attire and dreading what he might find, Blake reluctantly re-consulted the card. Luckily nothing formal was required – a fact for which he was extremely grateful. Black-tie affairs were part of the life he'd left behind and now that he no longer needed to attend those Embassy functions which had so bored him, he'd mothballed his dinner jacket. He'd suspected Keith of bringing one, but in an unguarded moment the man had confessed to leaving his at home. *Couldn't see the point – not just for the one event. I mean, it's not as if we're sitting at the captain's table every night, it's not that kind of a cruise.*

But if the men were happy to dispense with formality, the women were definitely not. It was their last chance to show themselves off and the potential grandeur of the occasion got the better of them. To match their surroundings, some made use of their Egyptian outfits for a second time, while others brought out something they'd kept hidden in their luggage. Lee Yong appeared in the gown that she'd worn on the night they'd passed through the lock at Esna. For Blake, it brought back memories. Mrs Biltmore was persuaded to dress up and pulled a lace cardigan on over her ubiquitous green top, although she professed this was as much to keep off the night chill as for the purpose of fashion. As for Ira – well, no-one noticed what he was wearing at all.

So later that evening, after another makeshift preparation by the chef, it was the full party of eight that clambered onto the bus for the trip downtown.

It was a different journey through the city at night. Landmarks which could be relied on in daylight vanished into the darkness, while areas that had lain unseen burst into life beneath a blaze of neon light – cafés, restaurants, late-night shops, it was hardly the same place. On the Corniche, the Winter Palace Hotel which had appeared dark and foreboding that morning, was reborn in the glow of a floodlit array. Across the road, the waters of the Nile slid by, dark and mysterious.

The temple itself was floodlit too, making its massive columns seem even taller as they were picked out against the night sky. As large as a cathedral, it dominated the waterfront – even the bulk of the Winter Palace Hotel appeared small by comparison. As its imposing structure came into view, a murmur of appreciation rippled around the bus.

"Oh my! Isn't this wonderful?" said Mrs Biltmore, marvelling at the sight.

The bus dropped them off at the ticket office where they were waved straight through and walked down toward the entrance gate. They'd arrived early (it was not yet twenty past eight) and took time to stroll along the Avenue of Sphinxes that led to Karnak, admiring the statues. Within the temple grounds, a welcoming committee had assembled to meet them although there were to be no introductory speeches that evening. The place spoke for itself – this was the home of the gods. Here lived the Theban Triad of Amun (the Unseen One), Mut (his Consort) and their son Khonsu (the Traveller). The signs of these all-powerful deities were everywhere – what else was there to say?

At 8.30 they crowded together at the gate. Inside, curving down through the darkness toward the front of the temple, the pathway was flanked on either side by a row of Nubian slaves, each wearing a white headdress and a gold breastplate and bearing a flaming torch. As the gate opened to let them in, from deep within the temple building the theme of the Grand March from *Aida* boomed out to greet them. At the rear of their party, Joan stiffened at the sound. In her lavish guise as Cleopatra, she was to have her entrance after all.

Keith had been waiting patiently at the front and whistled through his teeth.

"Well, they certainly know how to put on a show…"

He and Janet then led the way, followed in turn by Mrs Biltmore and Ira, then David and Joan.

Lee Yong seemed hesitant and stood alone in her silver dress, clutching a small evening bag and looking round, waiting for an escort. Blake offered his arm.

"Shall we?"

She took it gratefully and encouraged by the strains of the Grand March, they set off along the path.

On either side, the Nubian slaves paraded like ushers and for a moment, Blake imagined himself at a wedding. In her long dress, it was as if Lee Yong were the bride and he the father, guiding her down the aisle. Somewhere in the shadows beneath the temple wall, her husband to be would stand waiting. Would it be Reda? Blake wondered. Perhaps, tonight, under a starry sky and the influence of the moon, they would come to their conclusion.

The reception was held on a small mound situated at the rear of the ticket office – so once they'd descended the pathway, paraded in front of the temple and made their way up again, they'd succeeded in walking a circle. As they came up the slope, they were confronted by a table covered with a white cloth and laid out with drinks and assorted snacks. Close by, a row of smartly bow-tied waiters stood in attendance, proffering trays and prefilled glasses.

David had been at the rear of the party but he was the first to break ranks. The pressure he'd been under to make the arrangements seemed to have got to him and he was anxious to get started.

"Over here!" He beckoned to the others, then addressed one of the waiters. "This way, my good man. I'm ready if you are." He seized two glasses from a tray and thrust one in the direction of Joan before downing the other himself. "Ah! That's better!" He smacked his lips and winked. "Hair of the dog – can't beat it."

Keith eyed his glass with suspicion.

"What exactly is it?"

An orange-coloured liquid bubbled dangerously like a fomenting chemical.

"I haven't a clue," replied David. "I tell you what – why don't

I try another one and let you know." He grabbed a second glass from a passing waiter's tray and immediately made a start on it.

Joan, in line with her character of queen, sipped decorously at her own cocktail and looked on, appalled at her husband's behaviour.

Meanwhile, Keith had been conducting an investigation.

"It looks suspiciously like Bucks Fizz to me." He took a glass for Janet and one for himself. "Anyway, cheers everybody! And here's to us."

By now they'd all got something to drink and raised their glasses to join in the toast. *Here's to us...* This done, any formalities were at an end and the small talk could begin.

Janet took the bull by the horns and commenced the thankless task of conversing with Ira.

"So, home for you tomorrow is it?"

Her polite enquiry evinced the inevitable answer.

"Yup."

After which, she struggled to make further headway.

In contrast, Mrs Biltmore had buttonholed Keith and was regaling him with one of her stories.

Blake listened in to these snippets of conversation but didn't speak, restricting himself to the occasional courteous nod. He'd no desire to become engaged or attract attention. He hated small talk – it all seemed so pointless. It was a skill he'd never mastered, preferring instead to avoid it. After a while, he'd learnt he could shut himself off from the herd and isolate himself from the general conversation. He'd watch as a sea of mouths silently opened and closed – he presumed they emitted sounds but he'd become immune to them. With practice he could then project himself elsewhere – he'd imagine he was watching one of the beggars in the Sharia Salah Salem, or that he was birding on the Delta, telescope and tripod slung jauntily over his shoulder. The key was to retain sufficient presence of mind to know when you were being directly addressed and to trigger an appropriate response. Then he'd slip back into the real world and pick up the thread. *Of course,* he would say, *naturally...*

He'd perfected the technique through attendance at countless Embassy functions – the ambassador's residence, cocktails at seven, black tie and the dread of being trapped in a corner with some minor foreign diplomat or the colonel's wife and the unavoidable discussion about the situation in some far-off foreign country. *I don't know how those poor devils survive...* And if, by some awful miscalculation he was forced to make comment himself, he'd developed a 'get out of jail card' he could use – *You'll have to excuse me, I can see the consul's waiting* – after which he'd slip away into the crowd.

This was such a moment. All around, people were talking (Sam was taking his finals in the summer and it was a good year for plums). Blake heard the words, but his mind was disconnected. From his position on top of the mound he could look down at the temple. Down below in the glare of the arc lights, the row of pillars stretched into the night, while in front of the main pylon, a single obelisk rose up and pricked the darkness, pointing toward the heavens. Above it, a crescent moon gleamed, creamy white. From somewhere in the ether, the god Amun and his consort Mut looked down on them. If conditions allowed, they would surely come together. *Perhaps, tonight, under a starry sky and the influence of the moon...*

Suddenly, the sound of Keith's voice wrenched him out of his reverie.

"...easy for you, Michael. I mean, it can't be more than, what, an hour by plane, give or take, from here to Cairo? Provided everything's running of course (and the last time I looked it was fine) you'll be home by lunchtime tomorrow. As for us poor beggars, I don't suppose we'll see the inside of our front doors until gone midnight."

"Yes... I mean, no..." Blake struggled for a response. For once he'd been caught unawares – he was getting out of practice. Then he realised where he was and reverted to his pre-prepared script. "Of course, naturally… I'm sorry Keith, I was miles away. You were saying?"

Keith started over, but all Blake could discern was the mimed movement of his lips as the words floated by again unheard. He was indeed miles away and this time finding it difficult to return.

He was standing at the edge of the group, a glass of the orange concoction in each hand. In his capacity as Lee Yong's escort he'd gone to replenish their drinks, but now he was unable to find her. He'd hung around for a few minutes, catching snatches of the conversation as he peered over shoulders and behind his neighbours, looking for her, but to no effect. It was almost a quarter of an hour since he'd seen her and he was becoming concerned. She'd completely disappeared and ever since that thought about Mut and Amun he'd been consumed by a growing sense of foreboding. Was it Mut whose body had been cut into pieces and according to legend, distributed about the kingdom? Or was that some other god or goddess? In the heat of the moment he couldn't remember. And now Keith was on his case and wanting him to join in some discussion. He needed to get free and resorted to using his old get out of jail card.

"Look, you'll have to excuse me – there's something I've got to do."

I can see the consul's waiting…

He hailed a passing waiter and dumped the glasses.

Lee Yong was no longer at the reception, of that he was certain. Nor could she have gone out onto the Corniche – the exit gate by the ticket office had already been locked. She must have wandered off somewhere – but unlike at the souk where they'd been separated by the arrival of the police, this time her departure must have been deliberate. Looking around, there was only one place she could have gone and that was back from where they'd arrived. With every intention of finding her, Blake left the group and set off down the slope toward the temple.

He didn't stop to ask himself why. This was not a time for introspection and the answer to the question might prove unsettling. A week ago he'd been unaware of her existence and at first she'd been no more than a passing interest. But in the past few days he'd come to know her well and she'd become precious to him. Now, as at the souk, he could not rest until he knew she was safe. At last, it appeared he'd found something to care about other than birds.

The front of the temple was swathed in semi-darkness. The row of Nubian slaves lining their entry route had long since extinguished their torches and gone home for the night so there was no guard of honour to light his way. High above, the giant obelisk glowed beneath the thin sliver of the crescent moon, although in the shelter of the temple wall there was barely enough light to see by. Further to the left and still lit, the ghostly Avenue of Sphinxes stretched away toward Karnak. He scanned the surrounding area but it appeared deserted. So if she wasn't there, instinct told him she must have turned right and gone into the temple. He followed suit and with the seated colossi of Ramses II on either side, passed through the gateway.

Once inside, the passageway narrowed and a large structure to his left loomed incongruously above the stonework. This must be the Mosque of Abu el-Haggag. Perhaps Lee Yong had come down for midnight prayer – she was most likely Muslim, although they'd not discussed it and she'd never struck him as being devout. But all its lights were out and there was no sign of life. He dismissed it as unlikely and pressed on into the main courtyard.

Here, the moon shone bright on open ground and he was at last able to see where he was going. The place seemed empty, although there were plenty of dark corners where someone might easily hide. In front of him lay the huge colonnade whose massive pillars were visible from the Corniche. From outside they appeared gigantic, but viewed from within they were no more than vast shadows cast by the powerful lights. Guarding the way, another colossus, this time in black granite, dominated the entrance.

As he approached the statue he began to hear voices, faint at first, then growing in intensity as he moved forward. Deep within the shadows of the colonnade, two people were talking.

His immediate reaction was to hide behind the mound of stone. The temple was a natural amphitheatre, magnifying sound, and he leant out into the passageway in the hopes of catching what they were saying.

The first voice was unquestionably that of Lee Yong. It was high-pitched, vibrant and trilled like a soprano, echoing amongst the pillars. He'd found her – but more to the point, was she safe? And what was she doing here? The second voice was a man's – surely it had to be Reda. Much deeper, it was more baritone than tenor and lacked the resonant quality of its counterpart. So while her words rang out, his were dulled and to determine what was happening, Blake was forced to read between the lines.

At the Egyptian evening they'd billed and cooed like pigeons, but what Blake could hear now was the screech of squabbling starlings. Something had gone wrong and there was an argument in progress – was it just a tiff? Or something potentially more serious?

"No! I don't believe you!"

Blake had already experienced Lee Yong's reproving tone, but her outburst held more venom than that – now she was really angry.

Reda's baritone responded but Blake failed to make out the muted reply.

"How can you say that? You know how much it means to me..."

Lee Yong again – although this time more pleading than enraged.

The baritone cut in again, softer now but still sounding unmoved, intractable, although the words themselves were indecipherable.

"And is that your final decision?" Lee Yong was asking next.

The answer must have been 'yes' as it was followed by an anguished shriek. Then there was a heart-rending sob and the sound of slippered feet running across the flagstones.

Blake instinctively pressed himself against the black granite. For all that had happened in the last week, at heart he was still an observer and whatever his sympathies, he'd no desire to be discovered. He had assumed – and probably hoped – that she would run straight past, but she stopped on a patch of open ground directly opposite his position and turned to face him. Her expression bore no malice and she seemed not to object to his presence. It was as if she'd expected he'd be there, watching...

The neat black hair he'd once admired had become dishevelled and she looked distraught, but somehow still beautiful in the moonlight. They stared at each other for a moment and then she cried out.

"He won't go, Mr Blake. He won't go!"

He thought she'd continue to run off across the courtyard, instead of which she promptly burst into tears and came to him, flinging herself onto his chest. In what was now a cold and cheerless place, she would take whatever warmth and comfort he could provide.

Blake clasped her to him, feeling the hot sting of her tears through his linen shirt. He tried to soothe her as best he could but with every sob she uttered, he felt his heart beat faster. Why could she not have asked *him*? He would have followed her to the ends of the earth! If only he were younger...

More footsteps resounded on the flags and Reda appeared out of the darkness. Coincidence or not, he too stopped on the same patch of bare ground and stood in the moonlight to look at them. He'd lost his boyish looks and seemed chastened by his recent experience, although his face was calmer and much as Lee Yong must have seen it, implacable but saddened, as if to say *I didn't mean to hurt you.*

Blake raised a hand to signal that for the moment at least he should stay away while he took care of things.

"It's alright," he mouthed, "she'll be fine..."

But deep inside, he knew that she would not and that this would take time.

Reda gave a shake of his head and walked on across the courtyard and for a full five minutes after she continued to weep, her tiny body shaking in spasms. Eventually the convulsions ceased and she pulled away to compose herself, taking a tissue from her evening bag and dabbing at the trails of mascara that had run down her cheeks.

Blake waited patiently until she'd finished.

"We'd better go back..."

There seemed little else he could say.

He offered his arm yet again and they began to make their way slowly across the courtyard, entering the passage beneath the Mosque of Abu el-Haggag, dark and shuttered up against the night. So far she'd remained silent, but once outside the temple wall she stopped next to the obelisk and turned to speak to him.

"You won't say anything about this to the others, will you?"

"Of course not."

Why should he? It was the second time she'd asked him the same question. He'd pledged his silence once – why could he not be trusted now?

They returned to the reception to find they'd no need of concealment. While they'd been away, David had been up to his usual tricks. He'd succeeded in spilling a glass of the orange concoction down the front of Joan's Pharaonic gown and a serious mopping-up operation was in progress that involved the whole of their party. Her reported reaction had been anything but regal and in the hoo-hah that followed, their absence had gone completely unnoticed.

Later, on the journey back to the ship, they sat next to each other on the coach, her head resting against his shoulder. Further along the Corniche, the Winter Palace Hotel slipped by, a pale ghost behind the trees, and before long she'd fallen asleep, lolling awkwardly in her seat. Blake remained awake and sat rigidly to attention. If by any chance Lee Yong was wavering and needed his support, then he would be the rock against which she might secure herself.

They arrived back on the quayside to be greeted by a deputation from the management. Mr Mohammed, anxious to make amends after the partial desertion of his crew and the debacle of the last two days, had turned out to welcome them. Supported by his trusted lieutenants, the chef and the chief engineer, he'd brought a number of porters with him, each equipped with a torch to light the way across the gangplank onto the ship. Despite his recent setbacks, his face was locked in a rictus-like smile and he nodded continually as if to convince them all of their on-going satisfaction.

"Very good, very nice, much enjoyment..."

Given the chance, he'd have shaken every guest by the hand – he could not afford any more disasters – but settled for seeking out David.

Toward the back of the bus, Lee Yong had stirred awake and was looking out of the window. If she retained any doubts about what she must do, then they were dispelled by the sight of the waiting line. Sitting up straight, she calmly brushed her hair and checked the remains of her make-up, tidying up where she could. Then, when it was her turn to descend onto the tarmac, she walked resolutely by, staring straight ahead and going directly on board.

Blake escorted her as far as her room.

"Are you going to be alright?"

She was much recovered but he felt obliged to ask never-theless.

"Thank you, Mr Blake, but I'll be fine." She produced her key and turned it in the lock. Then, in her only reference to the evening's events, "I've learnt how to look after myself."

Blake wished her goodnight. She was not in the mood to talk and there was nothing to be gained by debating the point. He waited until she'd shut her door, then took himself off to bed.

Chapter Thirty

It was not often that Blake slept badly and he'd usually drop off within five minutes of his head touching the pillow. But that night he was still awake at twelve, and 2am found him sitting in the chair in front of the dressing table sipping a cup of herbal tea to try and soothe himself.

The scene at the temple had disturbed him and he couldn't shake it off. That Reda and Lee Yong should arrange to meet had not surprised him – he'd have been disappointed if they hadn't. Her calm demeanour following Reda's disappearance and the knowledge that she could always contact him had given him every confidence. After her persistence concerning the young Egyptian's imprisonment, it was unthinkable that she would simply walk away now – there would always be a reunion. *Under a starry sky and the influence of the moon, Mut and Amun in perfect conjunction...*

So it wasn't their meeting that had shocked him but rather the manner of their parting. Contrary to his normal disposition, Reda had seemed callous and uncaring. He'd made a sign to say he meant no harm – but whatever his intentions, the effect had been quite the opposite. Lee Yong had been upset, distraught even, to the point where Blake had barely been able to calm her.

But that alone was not enough to cause Blake a sleepless night. As much as he treasured her and couldn't bear to see her hurt, it might have been bearable had he not felt himself partly responsible. And it was this feeling of guilt that had kept him awake.

She'd asked him for help again and this time he'd failed to give it. The first time, it had been comparatively easy – a couple of phone calls, a visit to the police station, an interview with a high-ranking official. And yes, he'd baulked at it – but once he'd grasped the nettle, he'd found it wasn't as daunting as he'd feared. Then she'd asked him to intercede with Reda and that had been far more problematical. He'd struggled to address it and when Reda had gone missing, he'd felt relieved and had used his absence as an excuse to give up. His lack of moral courage disgusted him. Why hadn't he persevered? Whether it would have made any difference and whether the young Egyptian would have heeded his words, was open to question. Blake doubted it. His instincts told him that Reda had already made up his mind some while ago and that nothing would have persuaded him otherwise. But that wasn't the point – Lee Yong had needed his support. He'd failed her and it was that more than anything which had kept him awake.

Later, around three, once the calming effect of the tea had kicked in, he managed to doze off – only to be rudely re-awakened at six-thirty by the jangling call of his alarm. He desperately wanted to press the snooze button and go back to sleep, but with his packing to be done and a flight to catch there was no choice but get up. He had to fight to stay awake and his need was for the stimulus of coffee, so having gathered his things together as best he could, he went down to the dining room to find some.

Yet again, he was first to arrive at the breakfast table and sat there patiently with his drink. He was fervently hoping that Lee Yong would come down and join him, although experience spoke against it. He was anxious to see if she was alright, to speak to her and express his regret that things hadn't worked out and above all, to apologise. He thought of going to her cabin but decided against it – she'd made it clear she needed time alone and it didn't seem right. He poured himself another coffee and continued to wait as one by one the others drifted in.

Keith arrived in a buoyant mood. He'd already visited reception to confirm the day's arrangements and had found everything was in order. Suitcases were to be placed outside rooms by eight-thirty when they would be collected, duly locked and labelled, ready for departure at nine. The coach was parked on the

Corniche with the doors open and the driver in attendance (Keith had walked up there to check), and his latest call to the airport had confirmed that the flights were on time. Nothing, it seemed, stood in the way of their journey home. It all conspired to make him unbearably cheery.

"Well, I can't see any problems." He rubbed his hands together in anticipation. "And I'm sure I speak for us all when I say I'll be glad to get home. Ever since that do in Aswan I've been a bit on edge, I don't mind telling you. This is one holiday I won't forget in a hurry."

He turned to look at Janet who nodded and smiled back. Blake had the impression that had it been left up to her they might never have come in the first place.

David might well have shared her sentiment, although at the moment it was hard to tell. He was suffering from his second hangover of the week and with his head lowered to its customary position on these occasions i.e. below the level of the tablecloth, it was impossible to discern either his facial expressions or any of his disjointed mumblings.

"Looking forward to the flight home?"

Blake's question was loaded with mischievous intent. It was like poking a stick into a wasp's nest – something was sure to come buzzing out. Although in his current condition, all David could manage was a muted response.

"Go away..."

Joan was equally unresponsive. After the incident with the glass of Buck's Fizz and her new Egyptian dress, she was not on speaking terms with her husband and sat quietly smouldering with her mouth firmly shut, facing in the other direction. With her arms folded tight across her chest, her body language spoke volumes. She was deliberately holding it all in, but it only wanted the slightest provocation and it would all come bursting out.

In Lee Yong's absence Blake turned to Mrs Biltmore for inspiration. He wondered whether she knew what had happened and whether she and the young Malaysian had found time to talk. He raised an enquiring eyebrow in her direction but received nothing in return other than her disarming Cheshire cat-like smile. Sitting next to her and oblivious to everything else, Ira was intent on devouring his third piece of toast.

Blake gave a sigh of frustration. Soon, they would all congregate in the foyer for the last time. Herded together like sheep, they would pay their bills at reception and make their final arrangements. A series of prolonged goodbyes would follow and somewhere amongst the handshakes, hugs and kisses, contact details would be exchanged and promises made to visit, most of which would never be fulfilled.

It's been so nice meeting you. We must do this again sometime. You know where to find us. If you're ever in the area, do come and look us up...

It was this kind of scene Blake hoped to avoid and with the firm intention of avoiding it, he'd hide away in a corner until all the fuss had died down. Eventually, when the bags had been loaded on board, the bus would gather them up and whisk them off to the airport where they'd go their separate ways – he to Cairo, Mrs Biltmore and Ira to Baltimore, the others presumably back to Britain. Although as for Lee Yong, it seemed her destination had yet to be decided.

The airport was frantically busy, a Saturday morning rush of comings and goings. Their coach had been delayed (another problem with porters and the loading of luggage) and the party of Germans, booked on an early flight to Frankfurt, had begun to panic. They arrived no more than half an hour before their scheduled departure and insisted on being dealt with first, dismounting prematurely from the coach and pulling their cases out themselves before rushing off toward the terminal. Their agitated state was unsettling and soon infected everyone else. Before long, they were all caught up in a headlong dash to the airport building. And in the melee that followed, Blake completely lost track of Lee Yong.

He'd waited patiently for her in the foyer of the ship, watching the others make their way out onto the Corniche until finally, left alone, he checked his watch for the last time and felt obliged to join them. Clambering on board, he briefly saw her sitting at the back and realised she'd gone straight to the coach from her room. It was not until the Germans had left, escorted to their gate by a smartly dressed official with a 'priority' badge, and things had settled down that he was able to catch up with her again.

She was standing not far from the entrance, talking to Mrs Biltmore and Ira. It was a long and involved conversation at the end of which the large American folded her tiny figure up in a bear-like embrace before releasing her for a handshake with her thin stick of a husband. It did not take much for Blake to lip-read the parting words that dropped from Mrs Biltmore's mouth.

Now, honey, you look after yourself. Don't forget to call and maybe we'll see you soon...

Blake kept an eye on her at the check-in and after a tedious passage through security, they found themselves side by side under an information board confirming their departures. London, Paris, Rome – they were all inviting locations but where she was going next? Had she changed her plans or was she sticking to her original schedule? If so, it would be somewhere in the Middle East. Was it Israel she was headed for? Or Jordan? Blake couldn't remember. But whatever her destination, it was not in her nature to hang around. She might dally for a while with Mrs Biltmore but there would be no long goodbye for him.

"I see everything's on time," he began.

"Yes, I think so."

"Just remind me – where are you off to?"

"Petra."

"Ah yes, of course – the rock-cut city. You'll enjoy it – it's well worth the visit."

"I hope so…"

He turned toward her and looked at her face. It was the first time that morning he'd been close to her and he could see that she'd once more changed her appearance. The tiredness and worry that had accumulated during the week had been painted over and the girl that stood next to him now was the girl that had stood behind him at the Temple of Queen Hatshepsut – the same carefully styled hair, the long dangly earrings and beneath the make-up, the severest of expressions. It was as if after a week of close companionship she needed to re-assert her independence and accustom herself to the idea of being single once again. Whatever challenges lay ahead, she would have to contend with them alone – and what better time to start than now? In the hour that he'd been at breakfast, she'd spent her time in the company of her bottles and creams. She had fortified herself against the world and had literally put on a brave face. The result appeared unforgiving, but for Blake it was enough to break the hardest of hearts. He stumbled into his pre-prepared speech.

"Look – I'm sorry…"

"Whatever for?"

"I let you down. You asked me to talk to him and I didn't. I feel responsible and it's been playing on my mind."

"Don't be silly! You needn't be sorry – you have nothing to reproach yourself for. You did everything you could, Mr Blake. None of us knew he was going to go off like that."

"Really?"

Blake expressed his surprise. Ever since her unflustered reaction to Reda's disappearance, he'd harboured a suspicion it had all been planned in advance.

"No, really… And anyway, if it hadn't been for you, he'd still be cooped up in prison with that horrid policeman."

"Yes, I suppose you're right…"

That at least was true. He'd already saved Reda the once – this time the young Egyptian had been given the chance to save himself and had declined to take it. He could hardly be held responsible for that.

"Personally," continued Lee Yong, "I don't think it would have changed anything even if you had spoken to him. It seems to me that he never intended to go."

"D'you think so?"

"I'm sure of it."

There was a certainty in her voice that bordered on the cynical. For the first time in her life she'd placed her future in someone else's hands and had been brutally betrayed. Now they were going their separate ways and there was no chance of reconciliation.

Blake wanted reasons. If he could find them, perhaps there was a way he could try and salve her wound – but this was neither the time nor the place to pry and he decided it was best to move on.

"So what will you do now?"

"As I said to you, Mr Blake – Jordan, Petra, I've an itinerary planned."

"That's not quite what I meant."

He thought she might have deliberately misunderstood him and he was not prepared to let it pass. His comment seemed to catch her on the hop and she took a moment before giving a considered response.

"I must seem very naive to you, Mr Blake – but if there's one thing I've learnt about this world, it's that you mustn't look back. You have to move forward in life and that's exactly what I'm doing – it's the only way you make progress. I've no regrets, Mr Blake, if that's what you mean – none at all."

It was a bold statement, accompanied by a defiant upward tilt of the chin and a sense of bravado that went with the make-up.

It was a view she could afford to take. She was young and there were more opportunities in front of her than there were mistakes behind. For Blake it was different – he had a lifetime of regrets and nothing to look forward to. The envy he'd felt toward her when they first met re-surfaced.

"I see... Well that's good then."

Above their heads the information board refreshed in a cascade of blue, then a number started flashing red. She stiffened and came to attention.

"Look, my flight's been called. I'll have to go."

"Yes, of course..."

There was something on the tip of his tongue and he forced it out, knowing there would not be another possibility – although, when he eventually managed it, it sounded incredibly trite.

"Well, it's been lovely meeting you."

"And you."

"Perhaps we'll meet again sometime."

It was the same banal conversation he'd heard a dozen times in the foyer that morning – and a dozen more at the airport – but in his case the feelings were sincere. If there was the remotest chance...

Lee Yong didn't seem to think so.

"Perhaps..." She pulled up the handle of her cabin luggage and prepared herself to leave. "Well, goodbye, Mr Blake – and thank you."

He waited, wondering whether he might enjoy the close embrace she'd given Mrs Biltmore or the handshake accorded to Ira. In the event it was neither and suddenly she was gone, hoisting up her shoulder bag and trailing her little suitcase toward the exit, the clump of her Cuban heels drowned out by the buzz of an announcement from the PA system. She stopped briefly at the barrier and he thought she might turn and wave – but his hope turned to disappointment as it was only to show her papers. Without looking back she moved quickly on and then the tunnel had swallowed her up.

It would be over a year before he was to see her again.

Chapter Thirty-one

It was a very different Cairo that Blake returned to compared to the one he'd left some eight days before – although viewed from the air, there were no obvious signs of change. That muddy old river, the Nile, still flowed peacefully between its banks, the Pyramids at Giza continued to point skywards and the blanket of smog which had enveloped the city prior to his departure remained, turning the horizon to the west a delicate shade of pink in the early evening sun. In the half-light, even his trained eyes struggled to pick out the thin plumes of smoke rising from the smouldering ruins of burnt-out buildings.

As the plane approached the city centre, he tried to identify the glowing mass of Tahrir Square – but he couldn't locate it, hidden as it was beneath the smog. The tanks guarding the perimeter fence at the airport were easier to spot – in situations like this the manoeuvre would be standard practice. Buried deep in the basement at the Embassy, there'd be an entry in a Foreign Office manual – *In the event of a coup or civil unrest, be sure to secure certain strategic locations…*

He was prepared for changes, having spent the whole of his journey from Luxor devouring the contents of the newspaper. He'd fallen behind with the progress of the revolution but now he could catch up with events, and he needed something active to fill his in-flight hour rather than brood on his unsatisfactory parting from Lee Yong. The main headline of the Saturday edition of *Daily News Egypt* provided more than sufficient distraction. *CAIRO ERUPTS*, it proclaimed, which together with a series of lurid photographs depicting scenes of devastation and destruction gave the impression that the capital had been struck by a volcano instead of a potential coup. The city had indeed boiled over, but it had been mankind's rather than nature's doing.

In a staged uprising, it had begun following Friday Prayers. Opposition leader El Baradei had arrived and hundreds of thousands of protestors had come out onto the streets to demon-strate. There were reports of looting and some of the prisons in the city had been opened and then burned down – allegedly on the orders of the Minister of the Interior. This tactic had allowed the inmates to escape en-masse in an attempt to terrorise the protestors. And to make matters worse, the police had deliber-ately been withdrawn from the streets so there was no-one to enforce the law. Chaos had ensued and the military had been deployed to assist.

Coupled with this, after four days of continual protest Mubarak had made his first address to the nation and as a concession to their demands had pledged to form a new Government. His announcement had been met with scepticism and derision by the protestors. International fears of violence had grown, and later on the Friday night clashes had broken out in Tahrir Square between revolutionaries and pro-Mubarak thugs, leading to several injuries and the death of Karim Ragab. It was a confused and disorderly scene. Travelling around Cairo was never easy at the best of times, but getting back home, Blake realised, was not going to be straightforward.

His problems began with airport security. He'd checked onto the plane at Luxor without issue, but on arrival in Cairo he was stopped at least twice and asked to explain the purpose of his telescope and tripod. The thinking seemed to be that he was a mercenary hired by one side or the other and that his equipment was some sort of sophisticated weaponry, and it was only after he'd assembled it for inspection and shown them his bird guide that he was allowed to pass. With the personnel on guard excitable and a large number of guns on display, it was a worrying moment.

Then there was the question of transport. The shuttle bus he'd normally have used had been cancelled as there was no access to the city centre. He thought it might be safer underground and he considered taking the Metro, but in the light of Carpenter's comments about the closure of stations, there was no guarantee he could get off where he wanted.

He settled for the flexibility of a taxi and was faced with the inevitable touting. *You're a tourist?* And being of Western appearance and trailing luggage, it was not unreasonable to suppose that he looked like one – either that or a newspaper photographer come to take snaps, his telescope mistaken for a camera. *You're staying in Cairo? Your hotel will be closed. They're all closed. You come with me. I show you nice place that's open.* Blake's polite but insistent refusal was met with disappointment – it was a scam of course, and the driver would not now be earning his commission. To compensate he quoted double the usual fare, citing the hazardous nature of the journey. After a prolonged bout of haggling, Blake met him halfway and they eventually set off down Sharia Al-Druba. Some things in Cairo hadn't changed.

It was a long and convoluted journey. They couldn't take a direct route (that was understandable) so instead made a detour to the south – but even then there were alarms and excursions every step of the way. They'd barely started out in Heliopolis for instance when they were subjected to the unnerving crackle of gunfire.

The road the driver had chosen took them through old Cairo and a maze of narrow backstreets jammed with traffic. And what with this and the temporary roadblocks and informal security checks, what was nominally a one-hour trip turned out to be almost two. They arrived in Dokki in darkness – only to be confronted by a makeshift barricade erected across the entrance to the neighbourhood. Unable to make further progress by vehicle, Blake elected to pay the driver off and got out to walk the five-minute distance to his apartment.

It was these last few hundred yards that proved the most difficult. The barricade had been hastily constructed from a selection of wooden pallets, corrugated metal sheeting and anything that could be found lying about and was manned by a self-appointed militia. In the absence of the police, it seemed that the people were taking the law into their own hands. Partially obscured by the dark, the militia presented a motley and scary appearance. Brandishing a wide array of weapons (Blake saw sticks, golf clubs and at least one machete, but thankfully, no guns), they demanded to see his ID – although when he produced it they were still doubtful, saying he might have stolen it. There was no-one to vouch for him and it seemed he'd reached an impasse.

To break the deadlock he suggested they send for Abdu and after what seemed like an eternity, the old doorkeeper appeared. Wearing his usual toothless grin, he made a merciful sign of recognition and Blake was finally admitted. When at last he turned the key in the door of his apartment, he couldn't wait to get inside. He'd never felt so glad to be home.

The following day was a Sunday and after the excitement of the Friday and the Saturday, Cairo seemed relatively calm. Peace had descended out of a blue sky and the barricades were quiet. There was less traffic than usual and what there was of it worked at a slower pace. The frenetic bustle he'd left behind seemed to have gone out of the place and it was as though the city was enjoying a lie-in.

He'd been away for just over a week so there was little food in the flat. Early in the morning he went across to the corner shop for supplies. Mr Sayeed, the owner, was already out sweeping the pavement in front of his store. Blake was puzzled.

"What's this?" he asked. "I don't often see you out here."

It was an unusual occurrence – displays of civic pride were few and far between in Cairo.

"I'm cleaning up," said Mr Sayeed, proudly collecting years of accumulated rubbish into a plastic bag. "You see, Mr Blake, we are in charge now. We can look after ourselves. We don't need the police, we don't need the army, and above all, we don't need Mubarak! Thanks be to Allah, we have the shabab! They will protect us now!" (It was the shabab, or youth, who were manning the barricade). "I can tell you, Mr Blake, if the police so much as show their faces here they will get their noses broken!" Plastic bag in hand, he straightened his back to address his client. The tidying could wait – customers always came first. "You want bread? We have shamsi or baladi – which would you prefer?"

Seduced by the tantalising smell from inside, Blake took one of each and together with some cheese and a few vegetables he completed the rest of his shopping. As he walked back across the road he was pursued by the tang of disinfectant. Mr Sayeed had followed him out to resume his cleaning and was mopping down the steps. Little by little, Egyptians were reclaiming their country.

After breakfast he made a pot of coffee and took it to his desk where he sat with his bird guide and notebook. Behind him, the muted sounds of a subdued city drifted in through the open window. After previous trips away it had been his practice to reorganise his bird list and compile a report of his visit. But this time he could not, for as soon as he started he realised that the list was still incomplete. At Karnak there'd been Red-breasted Swallows and a Bee Eater – but he could not for the life of him remember whether it had been Blue-cheeked or Little Green. Compared to everything else, it didn't seem to matter anymore. Try as he might, he could not focus on birds and his head was full of the same subject he'd successfully pushed to one side on the aeroplane with the judicious use of the newspaper.

Why had he let Lee Yong go in the way that he did? It went against the grain but could he not at the very least have taken some form of contact? Somewhere he thought he might have written down a mobile phone number – but was it hers or was it Reda's? A forwarding address would have been better – or anything that would have allowed him to stay in touch. After what they'd been through together, it didn't seem a lot to ask. At the airport, he'd had to push himself to use the words he professed to despise so much – *Perhaps we'll meet again sometime* – but he'd lacked the courage to follow it through. Such trivia came so easily to others, why couldn't he do the same? In the end he'd done nothing and he was left with the thought that he'd let an opportunity slip through his fingers. Reda had rejected her – and so, in his own way, had he.

He poured another coffee and tried to concentrate, but he couldn't shake off his feeling of self-reproach. After an hour of inconclusive contemplation he grew exasperated with himself, and in a fit of pique finished off the list the only way he knew how, adding *Reda* and *Spoonbills* after *Lee Yong* and *Hossein Rasheed*. Thinking it would put an end to his torture, he meant to rip the page out, throw it into the bin and start over. But when the time came he could not bring himself to do it. What he'd written down was the truth – it told a story, although it wasn't the one he'd intended.

Eventually he got up from the desk and began wandering round the flat, searching for some form of distraction. In the kitchen he looked through the cupboards to see if he'd forgotten anything at the store. In the sitting room he checked his answer-phone for messages, but there were none – a fact which only added to his depression. Then, as if to prove he still had a friend, he rang Carpenter on the off-chance. Rather predictably, there was no reply. Finally, when he'd exhausted all the possibilities, he decided to abandon the project for the day and settled for an early lunch.

That afternoon he took a stroll down to the barricade. He'd been boxed up in the flat for almost twenty-four hours and needed to stretch his legs. It was also an opportunity to make his face known to the shabab – he didn't want to have to call on Abdu every time he needed to go in or out of the neighbourhood.

At close quarters and in daylight the shabab were nowhere near as frightening as they'd appeared in the dark. They were mostly fresh-faced lads from the locality and their purpose, they told him, was to prevent infiltration by strangers. There'd been reports of pro-Mubarak thugs and plainclothes police entering the suburbs and creating unrest through looting and violence. The shabab had sworn against this and were determined to defend their families, their friends and their neighbourhoods against all-comers. They would rather die, they said, than fail.

With the intention of clearing them from the streets, the Government had imposed a curfew for sixteen out of the twenty-four hours of the day. The shabab had vowed they'd ignore it – and to show proof of their defiance, when the appointed hour arrived and a flight of jet fighters flew low overhead with a deafening roar, instead of going home as they were supposed to they shook their fists and gestured rudely. *You don't scare us like that!* Neither they, nor the tenants of Tahrir Square, were going to be easily evicted.

And so the protests continued.

Monday was another quiet day. But that wasn't to say things had returned to normal. Quite the reverse – things were far from normal and if anything, it was much too quiet. During the hours of curfew the buses and the trains stopped running, and apart from those who relied on their own efforts for a living, no-one was going to work. Across the road from Blake's flat, Mr Sayeed continued to sweep the pavement with newly acquired pride, but there was little in the way of passing trade to disturb him. Like an engine that lacked oil, deprived of its commerce the city had ground to a halt.

As for Blake himself, he was unsure as to what normality was any more. After a lifetime accustomed to work, he'd returned from holiday on Saturday and had spent Sunday supposedly tidying his affairs. Now it was Monday and normality meant he'd have gone into the office. But even if the political situation had been otherwise, he couldn't go in now, and it was the fact that this comfort was denied him that induced a feeling of restlessness. He called the Embassy twice, but the switchboard was closed. He tried Carpenter again but there was still no reply. This lack of response and the unnerving quietness of the place began to make him feel uneasy. It was as if he were being lulled into a false sense of security.

In the meanwhile, the city slumbered on – but there was an underlying sense that sooner or later something was bound to happen.

It began on the Tuesday morning – quietly at first, starting as a low murmur of voices in the street outside. Then, as the day wore on, it grew to a fully-fledged crescendo. Singing and chanting, like a floodtide coming unstoppably into shore, a sea of faces was passing by his window, heading for Tahrir Square. It was difficult to tell, but it looked as if all of Dokki had turned out. Slowly but surely, and in ever-increasing numbers, the people of Cairo were on the march.

The sound drew Blake out onto his tiny balcony. In the road below a throng of protestors was moving steadily towards Sharia Tahrir and the Gala'a Bridge. He'd seen gatherings like this before – and had been in them in fact. It reminded him of trips he'd taken to football and rugby matches with his father when he was a youth – the long walk through backstreets, alone to begin with and then in company as others joined from side roads, until finally they'd arrive at the ground surrounded by the excitement of a massive crowd. United by the support of their team, they cheered for them, just as the protestors cheered now. But what united these supporters was not that they were of one faction or another, but the idea that they were Egyptians. It was not just the shabab who were marching, but citizens of every age and class – the rich and the poor, men and women, covered and uncovered,

Muslims and Christians. Whole families, even children, were involved.

Some carried banners and placards they'd created especially for the day. The slogans ranged from the obvious such as *MUBARAK OUT!* and *DIGNITY, JUSTICE AND FREEDOM* to the more satirical eg. *THE LAUGHING COW WILL SOON BE IN TEARS.* (La Vache Qui Rit was not just a popular cheese in Egypt, it was also a nickname for the reviled president). Many were humorous in content and there was much laughter. It was an altogether good-natured gathering.

At around midday, Mr Sayeed emerged out of the corner shop and stood on his freshly-swept pavement, watching the crowds passing by. Here was the potential for trade – and masses of it – but none of it was coming his way. After a while he went back inside and ten minutes later he reappeared with his wife. Taking his keys from his pocket he locked the door, and arm in arm they joined the throng.

Blake was left alone and retreated back into his apartment. He switched on the television and tuned to Al Jazeera where images appeared of Tahrir Square packed to capacity with peaceful demonstrators. Here and there, music was playing and there was singing. In the background, buzzing gently overhead, police helicopters circled the scene, powerless to act. Gradually, and without ado, the centre of Cairo had become flooded with people. And now that the army had pledged not to intervene, there was nothing the regime could do about it.

Later that night, Mubarak appeared on state-run television for the second time. In response to the overwhelming display of public opposition he announced certain concessions, namely that he would not seek another term of office and that he would stand down after the elections scheduled for September. It marked a significant change in his position and for the moment, it looked as though the crowd had beaten him.

When the speech was over, Blake switched the television off and slumped into his wicker chair. He was still troubled and the events of the day had done nothing to relieve him of his feeling of restlessness. The people of Cairo had spoken and the revolution had moved on, but he had remained silent and if anything, he felt as if he'd gone backwards. In fact, he was more unsettled now than he'd been the day before.

He got up and went over to the window. The heat of the day had passed, the night was turning cold and there was a moon now too, high and white above the city. He drew back the shutters and stepped out onto the tiny balcony. Across the street a light was on in the room above the corner shop and he arrived just in time to see it turned off. Having watched their president admit defeat, Mr and Mrs Sayeed were on their way to bed. They could count themselves happy with their day's work as along with a million others, they had marched and they had won.

Blake felt a surge of resentment and brought his fist down hard on the iron rail. What on earth was he thinking of? Why should he feel envious? The Sayeeds were no more than simple shopkeepers – but he would give anything to be in their shoes right now. They'd helped to salvage their country from the grip of a dictator, while he had done nothing. Why had he not marched with them? It would have been easy enough – all he'd needed to do was step outside the downstairs door and he'd have been swept along with the tide. Instead of which, he'd chosen to stay put on his balcony and adopt his usual stance of observer.

It pained him to admit it, but the reason in his eyes was simple. However much he liked to think otherwise, he was not, and never could be, an Egyptian. He loved the country and he loved its people – but he was not one of them. He'd failed to understand their need for revolution and when Reda had outlined the reasons, he'd shied away from it. They were desperate for change, but he wanted things to stay as they were, the way he had always known them, the way the country he called 'his' had always been. And yet it was no more 'his' country than it was Mubarak's. What right did he have to dictate?

When he'd been in the company of the others, he'd prided himself on how 'Egyptian' he was and he'd despised them for their British ways. How shallow he had been! The fact was, they had more genuine 'roots' than he did. He'd chosen to abandon his – and the country he'd adopted had not adopted him. High up in the sky, the moon closed its face to him and disappeared behind a straggling cloud. His life was full of regrets, and for one intensely bitter moment he wished he'd never come to the place. He'd failed in his career as a diplomat and he'd chosen instead to write meaningless notes that would never be read in a dingy back office. He once might have thought himself in love, but had not had the courage to disclose his feelings. And now the country he professed to belong to had cried out for help and he'd been unable to give it.

Filled with remorse he took himself to bed, haunted by the fear that whatever else may have happened on his trip up the Nile, he remained as he'd always been, an outsider to the truth.

Chapter Thirty-two

The following day brought a distinct change in sentiment. Mubarak's concessions had split public opinion and there were those amongst the demonstrators who believed that with his agreement to step down, albeit later in the year, they should pack up and go home. They'd done enough, they said, to claim victory. But the hardliners were still sceptical. They didn't trust the president's words – they'd heard these kinds of promises before and saw them as a ploy to maintain the regime in power. Not only that but they'd sworn an oath to stay in Tahrir Square until he'd gone – and unless he did, they weren't going to budge.

To reinforce his position, pro-Mubarak demonstrations were held in the morning. But when it became clear that the protestors weren't going to give up their ground, plainclothes police and paid thugs were sent in to clear the square. By mid-afternoon things had turned ugly. The army had already announced that they'd stand aside and with this pledge not to intervene, violence broke out on a scale as yet unwitnessed. State-run television declined to show pictures but with every other network anxious to focus on the action, horrific scenes began to be relayed around the world. Mubarak had tried to suppress it but for anyone who cared to look, the evidence was there for all to see.

Blake watched avidly along with the rest. Just as Reda had been on his day of convalescence, he found himself addicted to the situation. He was not going to work, he'd lost interest in his bird report and he was affected by an overall feeling of pointlessness. With nothing else to distract him, it was easy to collapse into his wicker chair, switch on the TV, and let the images wash over him. Isolated and alone in his own front room, there was no obligation for him to respond.

The sudden introduction of the horses and the camels shocked him, but did not alter his underlying mood. Charging at speed like cavalry, the distraught animals reared and plunged repeatedly while their riders whipped at the crowd. A surge of pro-Mubarak supporters pressed towards the square from Sharia Talaat Harb. The defenders retreated beneath a bombardment of stones, but later they regrouped. Sheltering beneath makeshift shields of corrugated iron and bits torn from wrecked cars, they pushed their assailants back.

The president's men now sought to outflank the protestors and looked for a different point of attack. Moving westwards they turned their attention to the street outside the museum where a running battle began. There were soon reports of heavy casualties, looting and the destruction of antiquities. In a brief moment of madness, the country was turning in on itself.

This potential loss of history saddened Blake more than anything else. The Egyptians could find a new president, the streets could be swept clean and the concrete broken up for missiles repaired – but the past could not be replaced and all that made the country proud was being destroyed. It was this development, allied with the continual and sickening violence that persuaded him to turn the coverage off. Surely he could find better ways of spending his time than watching his beloved Egypt tear itself apart.

Outside the museum, gangs of shabab were pelting each other with stones. An ambulance was on the scene, doors open, loading a stretcher. The doors slammed shut and it roared off, lights flashing and siren blaring. Another casualty, another victim. He got up and approached the set with the firm intention of switching it off, but as he came closer his eye was drawn to a form in the background. The camera obligingly homed in and a familiar shape became apparent. There, in the thick of the battle was the unmistakable figure of Reda, directing and supporting those around him as they sought to protect their heritage.

In yet one more of his guises, he'd forsaken his suit and his peasant's garb for the clothes of a streetwise youth. His appearance was distinctly dishevelled. Bobbing and weaving to dodge the continuous stream of missiles with a skill that belied his portly frame, he cut a wild and romantic figure. What would Lee Yong think of him now? Blake wondered. Was this why he'd spurned her, so he could give himself to his country in this way?

And for that matter, what would she think of Blake, ensconced in the comfort of his apartment and content to merely observe, while those who dared decided the fate of a nation? It could only be contempt. The same cold pang of guilt ran through him that he'd felt before. Whatever else, he did not think of himself as a coward, and whether it was this, or the need to put an end to the overwhelming feeling of restlessness, or perhaps a combination of the two, but he knew the watching had to stop. If ever there was a time to act, this was surely it.

It did not take him as long to reach the museum as he'd thought. Normally he'd have walked it in half an hour but under the circumstances he thought it best to allow double. He envisaged the journey as though it were some vast reality computer game during the course of which he'd have to pass tests and gain certain objectives. At the same time he'd be subjected to attack from stones and missiles – or possibly bombs and bullets – and they would all take time to negotiate. As it turned out, there were definitely 'events' along the way, but they were not of the type he'd imagined.

He considered taking a weapon. It was ostensibly with the idea of defending himself (he'd no thought of committing violence) and spent five minutes searching the apartment for something suitable. He didn't possess a golf club (unlike Carpenter who kept a full set hidden behind one of the filing cabinets in the office), nor did he have a hockey stick. The best he could come up with was a long-handled broom from the kitchen – too long as it happened, as it proved awkward to carry and looked rather foolish. There were knives in the drawer, but they had a steely edge and purpose about them that turned his stomach and he didn't fancy them at all. In the end he left it and decided that if necessary he'd pick up something en route.

The first obstacle he thought he'd have to surmount was the barricade at the end of the street. But when he got there he found it unmanned (the shabab had all gone to the square) and he was able to walk straight past it and out onto the Gala'a Bridge. Once beyond the safety of his neighbourhood, he felt as if he'd entered a no-man's land where anything might happen, although Gezira was quiet and he was able to pass through unimpeded. It was at Tahrir Bridge where he imagined there might be trouble.

There were only so many bridges across the Nile and entry to the square from the west would depend on who controlled them. Later on, he discovered that immediately to the north, the 6th October Bridge had been held by pro-Mubarak thugs, one of whom had gone berserk with a rifle. Four people had died and thirteen seriously injured. But Blake was lucky and there were no such disturbances on Tahrir. Part-way across, a group of a dozen or so lads passed by in the other direction, shouting and jeering. Whether they were pro-Mubarak or pro-change, he couldn't tell – this was a war where none of the combatants wore uniforms. On the service road below, a burnt out CSF truck lay shattered in the dust, its twisted and blackened frame still smouldering.

At the entrance to the square he was halted by an army check-point. A group of soldiers were sitting on top of a tank, laughing and smoking. Some of them had taken off their forage caps and were persuading the local girls to try them on. As he approached, their corporal jumped down and insisted on stopping and searching him. He knew then that even if he'd found a weapon to bring, it would have been confiscated.

They let him pass and he entered Tahrir at what must have been a lull in proceedings. He'd expected to be joining a battle-field where he'd have to fight to get through, but what he found was merely the aftermath of one. Unlike the day before when the square had been packed to capacity by a friendly crowd, large parts of it stood empty save for the random detritus of violence which lay scattered on the ground. Here were the same objects he'd seen in Aswan – rubble, bottles, discarded clothing – even down to the same forgotten shoe.

Any action taking place was now on the perimeter and from over to his left a section of the crowd began chanting – *Mubarak! Mubarak!* – inviting another section to respond – *Traitor! Traitor!* – all to the accompaniment of the thunderous clamour of sticks beaten onto pieces of corrugated sheeting. It ended with a great cheer, as if of victory, but was followed by an eerie silence broken only by the wail of an ambulance siren.

A small group of protestors suddenly rushed quickly by in front of him. Three young men were carrying a fourth who appeared to be unconscious with blood streaming down the side of his face. They hurried on, calling out as they went – *Make way! Make way!* – and headed towards the tented camp in the centre of the square. Momentarily disoriented and for want of a better direction, Blake fell in behind and followed them.

Yesterday the protestor's camp had been decked out with banners. Today they'd all been taken down and the place had been transformed into a makeshift field hospital. In Aswan he'd seen just the one person wounded, propped up against a shop front in a side street. Here, they numbered a hundred or more. Scattered amongst the tents with no particular sense of order, some were lying down, some were standing up, some were being attended while some were still waiting for treatment. They were mostly bruised and cut but they all needed help.

He picked his way slowly through the confusion but found his route blocked. Immediately in front of him, a man sat cross-legged on the ground as a young girl in sunglasses and a leather jacket finished winding a bandage round his head. Caught in a moment of childlike fascination, Blake stopped to watch. The girl looked round at him.

"Are you injured?"

He shook his head.

"Then make yourself useful and take this."

She held out the roll of bandages. Blake backed away and raised his hands to apologise.

"I'm sorry, I can't. I'm looking for someone."

He'd willingly have helped her but he had other, more pressing, things to do – a man was waiting to be rescued and there was a soul to save. He moved on, anxious to reach the museum, and began to search round for Reda.

Blake had no idea of what he might say when they met. Since leaving the apartment he'd purposely not thought about it. Something at the back of his mind told him that if he started asking questions, doubts would creep in and his determination would falter. *I'm not sure what I'm doing* he'd told Carpenter when they'd been discussing Reda's release. *But I'm going to do it anyway.* It was probably best to keep it that way now.

As to the cause he was fighting for, he hadn't thought much about that either. Whatever it was, it didn't matter whether it was 'right' or 'wrong' – it was precisely these pros and cons that he wanted to avoid. What mattered was that there *was* a cause and that he'd committed himself to it. When he'd rescued Reda before, it had been for the sake of Lee Yong. Now it was not so much about saving the young Egyptian, but more about saving himself.

It was beginning to grow dark and the street lights in Mirit Barha had already come on. In the distance the facade of the museum shone dusky pink, while in front of it there were signs that the street fight was still raging. A crowd was milling round the entrance, there were shouts and cries and something went off with a *Bang!* He sensed that a line had been broken and a gang of people were running back down the street towards him. The sight of this sudden retreat made his stomach churn, although it wasn't fear that gripped him but rather the thought that he'd left it too late.

He reached the museum in time to see the crowd had melted away. Outside the entrance to his left, half hidden between the ornamental fishponds, were the remains of one of the barricades. Lying with his back to the shelter, hunched over his mobile phone as he tried to tap out a text, Reda was seeking refuge beneath a piece of corrugated sheeting.

When Blake had seen him on television he'd appeared inordinately active, but now he looked exhausted. His flabby cheeks were drawn, his face and clothes were streaked with dirt and a florid bruise was swelling up on his forearm. He looked up and saw Blake, then continued with his messaging. There was a flicker of recognition, but no expression of surprise – it was as though he'd been expecting him.

"You'd better get down, Mr Blake. There'll be another shower of rocks any minute."

Blake crouched beside him and instinctively covered his head as a volley of stones clattered against the sheeting. Reda hardly seemed to flinch.

"Damn it! No signal." The young Egyptian shut down his mobile phone and shoved it into his pocket. "It's been on and off all day."

Further down the barricade, one of the young shabab lay in a similar position. The side of his face had been badly burnt. Reda glanced across and saw Blake looking.

"Oh yes, that's their latest trick – Molotov cocktails. Sons of bitches! It's Mubarak's men – them and the plainclothes police. They're pigs. We've been holding them off for almost eight hours. It's been a long day, we're tired and some of us are injured. They've got us bottled up I'm afraid, but we're not going back. We can't afford to lose this, Mr Blake. If we do, they'll take the square – then our revolution will be over and you can come and collect the body bags from the morgue in the morning."

Blake shuddered. It was not an outcome he wanted to contemplate.

Head back down, Reda had resumed tapping at his phone.

"Lee Yong sent you, I take it?" he said almost casually, without looking up.

"No!" Blake refuted the idea. It was one that hadn't occurred to him – although he could see why the young Egyptian should think it. "No, as a matter of fact, she didn't. To tell you the truth, she doesn't know anything about this."

"Really? Then why have you come, Mr Blake?"

This was the question he'd deliberately avoided asking himself. In the face of the challenge, he cleared his throat exactly as the First Secretary would have done and mumbled an apologetic reply.

"I don't know. I suppose I just wanted to help..."

"Hah!" Reda was sceptical. "That's all very well, but I'm not sure as an ex British diplomat it would be wise to get involved. Although you could always lend us a couple of your tanks, of course."

Blake chose to ignore the joke.

"I simply want to make myself useful."

"I didn't think you were all that keen about our revolution." Reda must have been thinking of their conversation in Lee Yong's cabin. "Had a change of heart, have you?"

"Sort of..."

"Well, well..." Reda pocketed his mobile phone and addressed Blake directly. "Your 'enquiries' will have told you that my father (may he rest in peace) was a devout Muslim. He tried to teach me the faith but I resisted him and now I believe what I want. He was also a great educationalist and had many teachings, one of which was this. Allah works in mysterious ways, Mr Blake. Sometimes you have to put your trust in Him and let Him lead you, even though you don't always know where He's taking you. My father would have said that Allah has brought me here although I prefer to think I came of my own free will. Perhaps your God has brought you, who knows. Well, God or no God, you are welcome to join us and I can't deny that we could use all the help we can get."

It was a convenient theory – but it lacked the practicality Blake desired.

"So what can I do?" he asked.

He was desperate for a task, anything – although prior to Reda's remark about body bags, it hadn't occurred to him that he might have to be prepared to die. Despite his St Paul-like conversion he was not seeking martyrdom and he was hoping there was something more meaningful for him to undertake other than a reckless charge beyond the barricade.

"Well, if I were you," said Reda. "I wouldn't stay here. And to be honest, I don't want to see you get hurt." His comment came as a relief. "But if you're serious, then there's something you could do for me. Go back to the camp. Find Tarek. They all know him there. I've been trying to contact him for the last half an hour but I can't get through. Tell him how things are here. Tell him you have witnessed it with your own eyes." He gestured towards the crumbling barricade. "Tell him that Reda says to send more of the shabab, else we are lost. I'd go myself, Mr Blake, but you can see how it is."

He jerked his head in the direction of the street on the other side of the makeshift shelter. Some fifty yards away a group of thugs had gathered beneath a street lamp, plotting their next move.

"And is that it?"

"Yes, that's it."

Blake hesitated. He'd expected something rather more grandiose than being used as a messenger boy.

Reda saw his doubt and frowned.

"Well? Are you with us or not, Mr Blake? If so, what are you waiting for? Go! Go now, for goodness sake, before it's too late! We don't have much time to waste."

Blake sighed. It wasn't that long ago since he'd thought about saying the same thing to Reda about America.

He stood up to take a last look at the young Egyptian. He was dishevelled and caked in mud – but he'd managed to retain his boyish charm and there was something in his face that was quite irresistible. Despite his situation, the inner glow that had so captivated Lee Yong still shone through.

"You're a good man, Mr Blake," said Reda. "And as my father would say – may Allah go with you."

And with you...

Blake turned – and began to run.

Chapter Thirty-three

He arrived back at the camp feeling hot and out of breath. It wasn't far, a quarter of a mile at most, but it had been years since he'd run like that – years since he'd run at all. He liked to think of himself as fit, but clearly there were limits. He headed straight for the only person he knew then stood, hands on knees, panting out his words between each deep inhalation.

"Excuse me...Tarek...Where...?"

The girl with the sunglasses and leather jacket was hard at work applying more bandages. Another stained and bloodied head lolled beneath her nimble fingers. She didn't look up, preferring to shrug instead.

"Tarek? Who is Tarek? I don't know Tarek. You'd better ask someone else. Can't you see I'm busy?"

After his earlier refusal to help, Blake couldn't expect much more. He heaved himself upright and moved on.

Another tent, another girl, another invalid. And no, she didn't know Tarek either – but this time the invalid did. With one arm strapped across his chest (it jutted awkwardly as if it had been broken above the elbow) he pointed with the other. Some twenty yards off, gathered round the base of some stone steps, sat a group of eight or so shabab. Most were smoking and busy checking their mobile phones. Unsure if they were 'on duty' or not, Blake tentatively approached.

Sure, they knew Tarek. But he wasn't there. There was trouble at the 6th October Bridge – someone was throwing concrete blocks onto the protestors below and he'd gone off with another group to sort it out. If Blake wanted, they could show him the way.

Blake shook his head. It was too far off – further even than Reda's position. He'd come from the museum, he told them. There was trouble there too.

They nodded. Yes, they'd already heard. There was trouble

everywhere.

Blake tried another tack. Did they know Reda?

There was a pause while they looked round at each other. Then one of them, a tall youth with fancy sideburns, randomly stubbed out his cigarette so he could speak.

"Reda? Reda who?"

"Reda Eldasouky."

Another pause, then a voice from the back.

"Reda Eldasouky? Yes, he's a friend of my cousin's..."

And one by one they slowly hauled themselves to their feet.

The tall youth with the sideburns introduced himself as Khaled.

"These are my brothers," he said, jerking his thumb at the rest of his gang. Blake assumed he meant comrades – there were too many to be family. "We're from Mohandiseen. And you?"

"I'm Michael," said Blake. "From Dokki."

There was a grudging nod of respect.

"The same side of the river then..." Khaled extended a hand and they shook as if there were a pact between them. "So, do you want to show us where we're going?"

"Follow me," said Blake.

The running was easier on the way back. His breath came more readily – although whether this was because of the practice he'd had or the adrenalin flowing through him, he didn't stop to think. He'd set off almost at once and the group fell in behind but he used a slower pace to ensure they kept together. They'd hardly gone a few yards when Khaled touched him on the shoulder and whispered in his ear.

"Here, Michael. Why don't you take this?"

He'd been carrying a flag slanted jauntily over his shoulder and he thrust it into Blake's hands. It felt awkward and at first it held Blake back – but once he'd got used to the heft of it and raised it aloft, the red white and black bands streamed out easily behind him. It was a symbol, an icon, and drew others in like a magnet.

At the exit from the square they passed another group of shabab, lounging around one of the wrecked cars.

"Hey! Khaled!" they shouted. "Where are you going?"

"The museum!" Khaled called back. "We're going to save the museum! Why don't you come with us?"

He waved his hand, pointing forward and inviting them to follow him.

"We're with you!" they chorused and got up to tag along.

Soon, another group joined them, then another, and in a matter of minutes they were twenty, thirty strong. Now it was Blake who took up the cry.

"The museum!" he shouted. "We're going to save the museum!"

They left the square and headed up Mirit Barha. In the distance, the dusky pink facade of the museum still shone out like a beacon, drawing them on. They were all shouting now, surging up the street in a mass. Blake took the lead, a tidal wave of voices rising behind him and pushing him forwards. He raised the flag higher and began to run that bit faster. His blood ran faster too and he was filled with an intense feeling of exhilaration. It seemed to lift him up so that all he had to do was raise his feet from the ground and he would fly. He'd never felt quite so alive.

"The museum!" he cried. "The museum! We're going to save the museum!"

We are all Egyptians now...

Then, suddenly, he *was* flying as his feet momentarily left the ground. Suspended in mid-air, he flailed like a long-jumper and the flag he'd so proudly been carrying was ripped from his grasp. He stretched out to save it but it was too late, the red, white and black bands streaming into the distance. He crashed to the ground, his left shoulder crumbling beneath him. Sprawling forwards, he fell face down, his cheek tight to the tarmac.

For a moment he lay motionless, half dazed by the collision. While he'd been racing forward, a large and heavy object had careered into him unseen from the right and sent him tumbling. He struggled for air, the breath he'd done so well to conserve knocked clean out of his body. He gulped in, then, as the panting ceased, the stabbing pain in his shoulder shot through him and forced him fully into consciousness.

Everything was now in confusion. Odd pairs of feet, some in boots, some not, ran back and forth before his eyes. Behind him, the chanting had stopped, replaced by the violent yells of a street fight as thugs and protestors engaged. He could hear sticks clashing, batons being rapped on shields and the intermittent crackle of what he thought must be gunfire. Shortly, there was another huge *Bang!* and somewhere off to his left, someone let out a scream. And everywhere the air was filled with the acrid smell of smoke and burning cordite and the high-pitched cries of frightened horses.

He raised his head to look up from the tarmac. He was facing toward Sharia Champollion. Out of the side street, a group of Mubarak supporters had mounted a cavalry charge and the area in front of him was a melee of men and animals. The particular horse and rider he'd so spectacularly failed to see was still towering over him, its flanks dark and heavy as he lay prostrate beneath it. Its eyes wide and white with fear, the massive beast reared up and pawed the air in front of him, neighing loudly.

Then, all sound was turned off, muted, save for a tinny clatter audible even above the tumult. And as if from out of nowhere, a little metal canister rolled slowly toward him from beneath the belly of the horse. No bigger than a coke can, it came to an ominous halt and settled in front of his face, so close that he could read the signage. The message it carried – *Danger! Made in the USA* – stared back at him. Hissing like a venomous snake, it began to emit a thick grey smoke and for one brief but transparent moment he knew that he should move.

But he could not and suddenly the world exploded with a terrifying clap of thunder, there was a flash like lightning and his eyes were seared with a fearful pain. He tried to open them again but everything had gone black.

Chapter Thirty-four

During the course of the months to follow, Blake learnt as much about himself as he did about his medical condition. His state of physical health was actually easier to deal with as his medical problems were readily diagnosed. He'd dislocated his shoulder and he'd been blinded. The one was repairable, the other was not – it was as simple as that, there were no grey areas. It was the mental effects of his blindness and the problems it gave rise to which were more difficult to handle.

"How will I cope?" he'd asked Dr Aziz.

The doctor was peculiarly philosophical.

"You'll find that blindness is both a curse and a blessing," he said. "Before it came to you, all you did was look out. Now you will look in, and you will discover far more of yourself than you did when you could see. Learn to embrace it, Mr Blake, and it will be of enormous benefit to you."

The statement puzzled him, but in time he was to find it was true and as his strange new world opened up to him, he began to understand much more, not just about himself but also about the rest of mankind. At last he started to realise why he'd stayed in Egypt, why he hated the Diplomatic Service, why he'd never married – and why he so loved birds.

It had begun immediately after what he called 'the accident'. As the battle raged around him he'd lain for a while, semi-conscious, and his first recollection was of being moved onto a stretcher, the stabbing pain in his shoulder jerking him rudely awake. Later, as he forced himself to focus in on it to try and bring back the moment, he recalled the dry dusty smell of canvas and, at his side, the cool touch of polished wood.

They must have taken him back to the camp because rather than load him straight into an ambulance, he was physically carried some distance. He remembered that well enough, the bouncing ride performed at the trot, his unhinged shoulder flapping from side to side in agony. When they mercifully came to a halt, he was raised up and taken to a chair where he imagined himself seated as if in a barber's shop. Someone was talking behind him, then a woman approached (he could tell by her scent) and she began to apply first aid. As his head was being bandaged, just as he'd seen done before, he reached out for her arm and felt her sleeve between his fingers. And yes, it was a leather jacket she was wearing.

"Are you...?" he asked.

Although as soon as she replied, "Am I what?" her voice told him it was not the same girl he'd met earlier.

And all the time he kept telling himself *I will get through this. Don't panic and it will be alright.*

The hospital was packed – he was not the only person injured in Cairo that day – and the entrance lobby was full of the whine of sirens and gabbling voices. He'd imagined he'd be met by the pine-fresh scent of disinfectant, but it was the warm and overbearing smell of his fellow human beings that greeted him. He lay on a trolley and there was a sense of being hemmed in (he thought he might be queued in a corridor) but he was happy to wait, quietly stretched out, breathing deeply. His instincts told him he was badly hurt and he was ready to submit himself to whatever might be needed.

Later on, after his initial treatment, as he lay motionless on his ward bed with his head neatly swathed and his re-set arm strapped to his chest, he was asked for a point of contact. Was there family, a next of kin, someone they should inform? No, he said, there was not – but then he thought how sad that sounded and told them he'd be grateful if they'd tell the British Embassy.

But as soon as he'd let the words slip out, he regretted it. An image had formed in his mind of Carpenter turning up with fruit and flowers in his typically puppy-dog fashion. He was the closest thing he had to a friend but at the moment it would be more than he could bear. Instead of which, it was the First Secretary who arrived out of the blue two days later. He bore no such gifts or blandishments and other than a brief statement of condolence, he was brutally matter-of-fact.

"We found your name on the hospital list yesterday and I thought there can't be more than one Michael Blake in Cairo for this to be a coincidence, so I came as soon as I could."

Bandaged up and blinded as he was, Blake could tell there was an air of contrition about his visit. Guilt was a powerful motivating force – as he knew only too well. If only they'd read his memo, he thought, if only they'd acted sooner. It was too late now of course, and all that was left for the First Secretary to do was come and commiserate.

"Are you still planning to leave?" Blake asked. The last he'd heard from Carpenter they were on the verge of departing.

"No," the First Secretary replied. "The evacuation procedure was purely precautionary. For the time being we're staying put – although we're obviously ready to go at a moment's notice. Between you and me," he lowered his voice to a conspiratorial whisper, "HMG is still unsure as to who to support. Mubarak's position is getting weaker by the day but there's no clearly defined opposition. I mean, who are we supposed to talk to? The Brotherhood are still persona non grata, so that's out of the question – publicly, at least, although I believe that privately..." The First Secretary faltered, conscious that in his desire to appease, he was giving too much away. He abruptly changed tack and returned to his original intent. "Well, I'm sorry to see you this way, Blake. If there's anything we can do... Is there anyone back home, in England?"

Blake shook his head – but the First Secretary had known it was a futile question.

"Hmm... Well the good news is I've been able to arrange a private room for you. We like to look after our own in the

Diplomatic Service, you know. You don't really want to stay here..." Blake imagined him looking scathingly round the ward. "We'll get you somewhere nice, somewhere away from all this."

Blake's heart sank. The First Secretary didn't understand. He didn't want to be on his own – at this time of crisis he was happy to be in the company of his fellow Egyptians.

It was another week before his bandages could be removed. Time was required for his injuries to heal and for things to settle down before he could be looked at. He was not in any hurry. He was not going anywhere (the keys to his flat were in the drawer next to his bed) and he'd come to think of his coverings as a comfort rather than an inconvenience. It was as if they were a barrier that shielded him from reality and the cruelty and injustice of the world. As long as they stayed on, he felt safe.

They came off on the day Mubarak resigned. While he'd been in hospital he'd kept up to date with affairs by means of a portable radio. There was no TV on the ward and hence no access to news so he'd asked the nursing staff to go out and buy him something (there was plenty of money in his wallet and he told them to take what they needed). They'd returned with a small wooden box fitted with a row of knobs and switches and he'd set himself the mental task of discovering how it worked. Soon, he'd taught himself to turn it on and tune it to the BBC so he could profitably occupy his time.

On the day in question, after it had become clear as to what was happening, he'd switched it off to listen to the reaction of his fellow patients. There'd been cheering and applause and in this newfound spirit of joy and conciliation, the nursing staff visited him and made their proposition.

"Ah, Mr Blake. Let's get these bandages off so we can have a look at you."

Up until then he'd have resisted the idea, but now he was happy to let go and allow them to do their work. It was as though he'd waited for that specific moment when he could open his eyes on a different world and see the new Egypt in all its glory.

But his eyes could not open, they remained intractably shut and instead of being bathed in the light of the country's new dawn, his new world was a dark and impenetrable place. The longer he'd been swathed up, the more he'd begun to feel he might recover and that he would see again. With his bandages on, there had been hope – once they were off, there was none. It was a shock and for the first time in his life he understood the meaning of the words 'blind panic'.

It was as well this coincided with him meeting Dr Aziz. The consultant who'd been assigned to treat him was a renowned eye surgeon but he also liked to think of himself as a practitioner of mental health and occupational therapy.

"I'm here to help you see," he said, "with or without your eyesight. Vision is only one way of interpreting the world – there are many others. Here, let me show you what I mean." He thrust his hand into Blake's. "Now, tell me, what do you see?"

Blake thought it a pretty foolish question.

"Nothing," he replied, dejectedly.

"What? Nothing at all? You cannot mean to tell me there is not some image or another formed in your mind – what is it?"

"Well, yes, obviously – a hand, I suppose," he grudgingly admitted.

"Good! That's a start. And what kind of a hand is it that you can see?"

Blake felt the long smooth fingers and there was a warmth about the palm. He desperately wanted to believe it was the hand of a skilled surgeon and a kind and caring man. He passed on his hoped-for description.

"Excellent! Well done! I can tell that you and I are going to get on famously together. Work with me, Mr Blake, and we will achieve miracles."

It was the first of a number of sessions that Dr Aziz was to have with him on the art of seeing without sight. In the beginning he thought them puerile and gimmicky, but after a while they started to have an effect and he began to feel more confident about himself and his surroundings. The experience taught him a valuable lesson. Perhaps his life had not come to an end. Perhaps there was a point after all.

His first task was to familiarise himself with his hospital bed and to learn how to get in and out of it unaided. Then he set about conquering the ward and was soon able to walk smartly from one end to the other without clattering into some obstacle. With practice, the combination of these techniques allowed him to visit the toilet without help, a feat that some of his fellow patients couldn't perform even though they were sighted.

For a blind man these were great triumphs – but they bred an unwarranted sense of faith in his own abilities. On the day he was discharged, he was escorted back to his flat. He'd been given a thin white cane to tap about but once left alone, he thought himself familiar enough with the place to dispense with it and tried to move around with the same confidence he'd had on the ward. He immediately tripped over some forgotten object and fell heavily, cracking open his shin. He cried out, in shock as much as in pain, and as he lay face downwards, blood seeping from his wound, he found himself gripping the cracks in his wooden floor with his fingertips. Moving his hands from side to side, he discovered that the boards were tightened down with square-headed nails. It was a feature he'd never noticed before.

It was his first setback and he was determined to overcome it. It convinced him that he needed to do more and after he'd cleaned himself up, he went on a detailed voyage of exploration of his own apartment, delving into every nook and cranny. Soon, he knew every inch of it and he could see it all in his mind's eye as clear as day. Before long he fell into a set routine and started closing his shutters at night, just as he'd done in the past. But to be on the safe side, he still kept hold of the thin white cane.

Within a month he was ready to receive visitors. That meant Carpenter and one Friday afternoon he came lumbering noisily up the stairs with a bottle of his best malt tucked beneath his arm.

"Thought we might have a couple of snifters," he said. "Cheer things up a bit."

He'd already sent a get-well card. It had a joke on it ridiculing Mubarak which Carpenter had found particularly funny, although how Blake was supposed to read it was a mystery.

"Hmm... Sorry about that." Carpenter was quick to apologise. "Silly of me, I didn't think."

Blake wondered why he hadn't come to the hospital.

"To tell the truth, old boy, I can't stand places like that. The thought of all that blood and guts turns my stomach. Besides, you can't get a decent drink in there for love nor money. Dry as the Gobi desert. Thought I'd wait until you got home and we could celebrate in style."

Blake had guessed as much and had prepared things in advance. That morning he'd spent an hour or two reminding himself of the exact whereabouts of his spirit glasses, ensuring that the soda siphon was fully charged and practising the use of it. So when his guest arrived, the drinks tray was laid out ready and the wicker chairs arranged neatly in position.

He'd wanted to ensure that despite his disability, everything would appear normal. His shoulder had ceased to bother him and the scarring round his eyes had virtually healed – but no-one wanted to look at the blank and vacant gaze of a blind man so he'd taken to wearing the pair of dark glasses he'd bought on his trip up the Nile. His idea then had been to cut down the light – now there was none, but he still needed them as disguise. To complete the deception, having first tidied the flat so there was no chance of another accident, he'd dispensed with the cane for the afternoon. The effort proved worthwhile.

"Are you sure you can't see anything?" Carpenter had

remarked. "Damned if I'd known you were blind if you hadn't told me."

On the strength of his comment, Blake poured him another Scotch.

It was this and the general success of the meeting that encouraged him to venture further afield. He'd already been out and with the help of Abdu, across the road to Mr Sayeed's where he was able to order and collect supplies. The next step was to negotiate the bus ride into Cairo where he could visit the eye clinic. He asked to be taught Braille and lessons were duly arranged. Books in the language were hard to come by in Cairo – so he found a specialist supplier in London and ordered them direct. Inspired by Dr Aziz he began to learn the fundamentals of philosophy so he could explore the furthest reaches of his mind. And when he grew tired of reading, he could always listen to his radio.

It took a while but he adapted. He was engaged, his mind and body were active and he could look after himself. Inside the flat he was totally independent – outside it he could manage (Abdu was a boon and delighted to help). There was not much else he could want for – but somehow things didn't quite feel right. Despite his interests and his ability to fill his time, there was still something missing. He could read, he could write, he could hear and he could all but see – but he'd not yet found a way to replace his precious birds.

Chapter Thirty-five

Blake shifted in his seat and its reassuring creak reminded him of his whereabouts – mid-morning, his flat, Cairo. He'd been away on a nostalgic mental journey through the backstreets of his memory but now he'd returned to his old familiar surroundings – the wicker chairs, the table, the solid presence, somewhere close by, of bed and bookcase.

The light, that vague shadow he could sense but could not see, and which had begun the day as no more than a glimmer behind the minarets in the eastern sky, would now be a bright white shaft searing into the room through the open shutters. For the past hour he'd felt the warmth of it, stealing across his sandaled feet then hot through the thin fabric of his linen trousers until at last it had reached the hands he clasped together on his lap. He'd opened his palms to greet it, as if he'd been waiting for the moment when he could gather up the weight of sunshine and bathe his face in it. Sometimes, it was all he needed to survive...

Outside in the street, the early morning cries of the vendors had abated while in the background, the roar of occasional traffic had turned to a steady drone. Somewhere in the distance, masked by the cooing of the Palm Doves and the chirruping of sparrows, he thought he could hear a bulbul calling. Before long there would be the click of a nearby door as Mrs Ibrahim left her flat to go out to Mr Sayeed's for groceries.

He'd habitually track her progress, marking the clump of her feet as she went down the stairs then exchanged greetings with Abdu. Across the road, Mr Sayeed would doubtless be sweeping his pavement and keeping the new Egypt clean. He'd listen to them talking.

"Good day to you, Mrs Ibrahim."

"And good day to you, Mr Sayeed."

"May Allah keep you well."

"And you, Mr Sayeed..."

It would not be long before his visitor arrived. But today there would be no ritual arrangement of spirit glasses and the soda siphon – it wasn't Carpenter he was expecting. His calls had become less frequent and although still regular, they were confined to a Friday afternoon, usually at the end of the month. Today was Tuesday – and that meant someone else.

Well, goodbye Mr Blake – and thank you.

Were those really the last words she'd said to him? How he'd clung to them! There'd barely been a day gone by in the last twelve months when he hadn't thought of them. It was as if by bringing them to mind he could somehow bring her back too.

Well, goodbye Mr Blake – and thank you.

Thank you? What on earth for? He'd done nothing, he'd failed, he'd let her down and yet she'd insisted on showing her gratitude. Did she realise that by doing so her remarks had given him hope? Or was he reading too much into it?

But still he'd done nothing about it. Despite his failure to take her details at the airport, she'd still have been easy to find. Somewhere there was a passenger list and even if that hadn't proved fruitful, he could always have found Mrs Biltmore and he was sure she'd have provided a contact. The Biltmores of Baltimore – they'd made a boast of it, there surely couldn't be too many of them, they would have been easy to trace. And then, all he'd have needed to do was ask.

Instead of which, it had been her who had contacted him. It had been over a year and he'd still not plucked up the courage, when one day he'd heard the telephone ringing. He'd been in the kitchen preparing a simple lunch and had hurried to pick up. He didn't get many phone calls these days.

"Is that Michael Blake?"

"Yes..." he'd answered tentatively.

"The Michael Blake that used to work at the British Embassy?"

"Why, yes. Who is it calling?"

"I don't know whether you remember me but we met on the Nile cruise last January. It's Lee Yong." His grip on the receiver had instantly tightened. How could he forget? And yet he hadn't recognised her voice – somehow she sounded different on the phone. "I was wondering if I could come and see you."

She didn't know it at the time, but there was nothing in the world he'd have liked more.

"Why yes, of course..."

And so it had all begun.

At first he didn't understood why. She'd travelled halfway round the world to be there and he was not so vain as to think it was purely for his sake – there must be some other reason. When it had dawned on him, when it had become obvious as to the purpose of her visits, he'd not tried to resist it or push it away, but had sought to help her as much as he could as if there were still time to make amends. Although now it was no longer guilt that moved him – the fact that she'd returned was forgiveness enough – and he did what he did out of friendship rather than contrition. What made it doubly rewarding was that what he gave out was as readily given back as when, like today, she'd come and make her report. Although given his involvement he could hardly describe himself as a disinterested party...

The scuff of familiar footsteps ascending the wooden stairs alerted him, then came the knock he'd been waiting for. He'd no need to ask the identity of his caller – the tramp of her feet was sufficient.

"Come..."

There was the scrape of the latch lifting (he'd shown her how to open the door without the need of a key) and he could tell that she'd entered the room.

When she'd first visited him, he'd expected the click of her Cuban heels but he'd been disappointed. It seemed that they'd gone, replaced by the tread of soft-soled shoes. The jeans must have gone too as there was often the swish of a dress. It was as if her clothing had mellowed along with her mood. She'd left the airport dressed severely, hardened against the world. But the last twelve months had chastened her and she'd become thoughtful and subdued as if the anger she'd felt had gradually burnt itself out. He sensed there was a sadness about her now and he imagined it was reflected in her appearance. As she approached, it was the faint smell of scented soap rather than the sharp tang of perfume that accompanied her.

"Good morning, Michael."

"Good morning…"

It had become their regular greeting. It had taken a while, but at last she'd dropped the formality of addressing him as 'Mr Blake'. How things had changed since they'd first met!

"I passed your neighbour on the stairs."

"Mrs Ibrahim?"

Shrouded deep in thought, he must have missed her leaving.

"Is that her name?"

"I think so… Funnily enough, we've never met." Prior to his 'accident', he'd always been at work and there'd been no contact – and yet he knew more about her now than any introduction could provide. Later on, around 3pm, the car carrying her 'escort' would arrive, the low rumble of its engine filling the street. "I've often wondered what she looks like – do tell me."

"Ooh, let me see… Middle-aged, dark hair, short – a little on the stout side perhaps…"

Just as he'd always thought.

"So, any news?"

"No, I'm afraid not…"

"You've checked the hospitals again, I take it?"

He'd given her a list and suggested she visit them all in person – it was no use trying to telephone.

"Yes, I've been to every one. They've no record of any admission."

Blake was not surprised. In the aftermath of the battles of Bloody Wednesday, with the corridors full and the staff overrun, who was going to stop to fill in paperwork? You were lucky to get treatment, never mind documentation.

"I've asked around the nurses as well but they've no recollection of the name."

That was more of a disappointment. But it was equally understandable – the casualties must have been in their hundreds. All the same, it was frustrating. A month gone by and still no trace.

The closest they'd come had been via the tour company, Worldwide Travel. Yes, Reda Eldasouky had been one of their guides, but after his imprisonment in Aswan they'd heard nothing further from him and he'd been taken off their list. However, they'd retained a last known address for the purpose of correspondence, a flat in the district of Masr Al-Qadima. Lee Yong had immediately gone there but had found the place empty. She'd enquired amongst the neighbours and had been told that a Mrs Eldasouky, an elderly lady, had lived there but that she'd passed away. They assumed it must have been his mother – but of the son there was no sign.

How could someone disappear so easily? Even in Egypt where records were at best spasmodic and at worst false, there should have been some form of evidence of Reda's whereabouts. But there was none. Was it deliberate on his part? Or was it something more sinister? Perhaps Hossein Rasheed had finally caught up with him. In the cheerless cells of Al-Fayoum, hundreds lay rotting – was Reda somewhere amongst them?

In an attempt to find out and put an end to the speculation, he'd once more called on Carpenter. He'd honoured his debt by means of a case of six Glenfiddich he'd ordered through Mr Sayeed, and was now, he reckoned, two bottles to the good. But this particular line of credit was running out and the longer he was away from the Embassy, the less effective it had become. The cuts which had seen off Blake had gone even deeper and

Carpenter had become protective of his position and not so amenable to favours. Not only that, but their source of information had dried up as the police closed ranks under the pressure of public acrimony and nothing was forthcoming. The 'missing' were, by definition, 'missing' and that was how it would remain. And with that avenue closed to them, they'd exhausted almost every possibility. All that was left was the morgue – and Blake had decided not to go there.

"So what will you do now?"

For the moment he'd run out of suggestions.

"I don't know – keep looking I suppose. I can always try again tomorrow. Maybe I should go back to some of the private clinics."

They'd been down that road before but it had yielded no positive results.

"Hmm... It's a possibility – but I don't think you'll have much success."

"Perhaps not..."

He sensed that she'd wandered off across the room and in his mind's eye he could see her standing at the bookcase. The bird guide must have been in its usual spot (in fact he'd made sure of it an hour or so before her arrival) as she immediately selected a volume and took up her seat in the wicker chair next to his. Then he could hear her, riffling through the pages.

"Now, where were we?"

She found her place and was about to begin reading when he stretched out a hand and placed it unerringly on hers.

"Wait."

He was not quite ready – there was a question he'd been meaning to ask for a while but had not yet dared put. Now seemed a suitable time.

"You were in love with him, weren't you?"

And as soon as he managed to get it out he realised how accusatory it sounded, as though he were a barrister in a court of law.

"Who?"

"Reda."

Who else did she think that he meant?

"No!" Her first form of defence was a vehement denial. Then, like a witness who had relented under questioning, "Yes... I suppose I must have been..."

The sudden introduction of the subject had confused her and he felt the muscles in her hand tighten. Had she blushed? Even if he could see, it might have been hard to tell.

"And now?"

"Yes, still, even more perhaps..."

With the matter out in the open, her confession was all the easier.

"But what if he's not here?"

"What do you mean?"

"What if he's gone to England, to study? You know his father always wanted him to go to Oxford. What if he's gone there? Would you follow him?"

There was a pause as she weighed out her answer. Then, when it came, her reply was delivered slowly.

"Yes, Mr Blake, I believe I would..."

In the heat of the moment he noticed that she'd reverted to her old form of address. It was as if the work of weeks had been undone at a single stroke.

She withdrew her hand, rose from her wicker chair and went over to stand by the window. And if ever there was a time when Blake wanted to recover his sight – and over the past year there had been many – it would have been now above all. To have seen her as she must have been at that moment, leaning against the open shutters and looking down onto the street he knew so well, would have meant everything.

"But I don't think he has." He sensed that she was shaking her head. "I don't think Reda would ever leave the country – if he wouldn't come with me to America, why would he go to England? It doesn't make sense. No, I'm sure he's still here, hiding out somewhere."

"And if you can't find him? What will you do then? Go back to America?"

"To be honest, no, I'm not sure that I will." There was another thoughtful pause. "You see, Reda was right."

"In what way?"

"We talked about it a lot before I left. He said I was deluding myself. He said America was a fool's paradise – it promised much but would deliver little. And anyway, we were supposed to be in love and with what we had, we didn't need to go to America. Why take the risk? But I come from what is essentially a poor country. I wanted a New World but the truth was there to be found in the Old, if I'd only looked for it. And Reda already knew that – more than anyone in fact."

"So are you saying it wasn't what you expected?"

"Yes and no. America is a land of opportunity, it's true, and the American Dream is still very much alive. There's fame and fortune to be had for those who want it – and are lucky enough to find it. But that wasn't really for me. I already had money – that wasn't why I went there. I was looking for something else and I didn't find it. Oh, don't get me wrong. I was made very welcome in America. Baltimore is a wonderful city and Mrs Biltmore is a wonderful person – and Ira too, once you get to know him. But the thing is, you get the feeling everyone's trying to make a fast buck and as soon as you pull aside that materialistic curtain, there's nothing behind it. America has no soul, Mr Blake, that's the problem."

Soul? What was soul? For many years Blake had wondered whether such a thing existed, and it was only since he'd been blind that he'd truly found out. For Lee Yong to expect it so early in life was unreasonable.

"That's all very well, but look what it could give you. The

qualifications you could get would be worth something alone. Surely you can see that?"

Lee Yong was forced to agree.

"Yes, that's true – and I'm grateful for it. Although I could get my qualifications anywhere – I've even thought of staying in Cairo to finish my studies. You see, I have no need to work, Mr Blake – I could live on the money my father sends me. But I wanted to do something useful with my life. Of course my parents would think I was wonderful, their little girl gone out into the world and come back successful. Every time I go home they could roll out the red carpet. 'Make way for the Great Professor' my mother would say. I don't think they've any idea of the truth – the fact is that despite all this achievement, my life is actually rather empty."

It was a feeling with which Blake could sympathise.

"And you think that finding Reda will help you fill it? That's a bit selfish, isn't it?"

"Yes, I suppose it is – I must admit I hadn't thought of it that way. But they do say love is a selfish thing, don't they, Mr Blake?"

This time he was unable to comment. What did he know about love? It was not a subject on which he felt competent to speak. All he knew was that as soon as she'd mentioned staying in Cairo, his heart had skipped a beat and that now she'd come to him, although it was only a few hours a day, he valued her visits above anything and would be reluctant to see her go.

She fell silent for a moment. Outside the apartment, the bustle of busy life filled the street as Cairo went about its business. Across the road, Mr Sayeed would be doing duty with his broom and before long the Mullahs would begin calling from the minarets, urging the people to midday prayer.

After what seemed like an age, she eased herself away from the shutters and returned to her wicker chair.

"Well, that's more than enough about me for one day. Time's getting on and we haven't started our reading yet."

"Hmm…"

Blake was torn. He would have liked to hear more, but perhaps Lee Yong was right and there was not much else they could say.

"Now, where had we got to?"

She retrieved the bird guide from the table where she'd abandoned it earlier.

"Purple Gallinule…"

"Ah yes, the big bird that lives in a marsh. What did you call it? A swamp hen?"

"That's right." He was genuinely impressed. "You've done well to remember."

"You'll find I pick things up quite quickly, Mr Blake."

"I'm sure you do – except you're supposed to be calling me Michael."

"I'm sorry – Michael."

Had she blushed again? If so, he would not make much of it. It had occurred to him that he might not have her for too much longer and he felt anxious to move on.

"So, what's next?"

She thumbed quickly through the pages.

"Ah, here we are. See if you can guess this one. 'A rather featureless bird, similar in size to Skylark. The bill is fairly heavy, with an orange-yellow base. Plumage varies depending on the local rock type, but is usually grey-buff with slight streaking on the breast and with an orange-brown tail …"

Desert Lark

And suddenly he was back to where they'd first met, standing on the approach to Queen Hatshepsut's Temple, shivering in the cold of a January early morning. In front of him, a young Egyptian was lecturing on the wonders of his country, while a few feet behind, a beautiful Malaysian girl stared at him with a look of disapproval. As to the bird, he never had decided whether it was really Desert Lark – her intervention had put paid to that. How strange that she should choose it now – it was as if she were trying to remind him.

Soon they would get back on the bus and begin the ascent into the Valley of the Kings. There he might find Trumpeter Finch or African Rock Martin and in the burial chambers of the dead, pictures of geese and egrets and herons. Deep in the darkness of the tombs, they had lain undiscovered for over 3000 years.

Meanwhile, it was almost midday and the bright white light of Cairo was flooding into his room, searing across his face. Sitting next to him, barely an arm's length away, Lee Yong continued her reading. Did he imagine it or had some shadowy form passed in front of him? Perhaps, if he focused exceptionally hard...

Acknowledgements

Firstly I would like to thank David Cottridge and Richard Porter for allowing me to quote from their book 'A Photographic Guide to Birds of Egypt and the Middle East' (published by New Holland Publishers (UK) Ltd). This was the guide I used myself when I visited Egypt.

I must also mention 'Tweets from Tahrir', edited by Nadia Idle and Alex Nunns (published by OR Books) which provides a first-hand account of the day-by-day action of the Egyptian Revolution as it unfolded. Besides giving me the historical background, I found it a compelling and moving narrative in its own right.

Lastly, I used 'The Rough Guide to Egypt', written and researched by Dan Richardson and Daniel Jacobs (published by Rough Guides), in an attempt to keep the names and descriptions of places as accurate as possible.

Author's Note

The characters in this book are entirely fictional and are not intended to be a representation of any real person, alive or dead.

Biography

N.E.David is the pen name of York writer Nick David. Nick began writing at the age of 21 but like so many things in life, it did not work out first time round. Following this disappointment he was obliged to work for a living, firstly in industry and more recently in personal finance. 30 years later, with a lifetime of normal experiences behind him, he is able to approach things from a different perspective.

After the death of his father in 2005, Nick started writing again and has been successful in having a series of short novellas published. He maintains he has no personal or political message to convey but that his objective is merely to entertain the reader and he hopes this is reflected in his writing.

Birds of the Nile is his debut novel.

Other Works

Carol's Christmas
Feria
A Day at the Races

For more information visit the author's website at www.nedavid.com.

You can also follow N.E.David on Twitter @NEDavidAuthor.

At Roundfire we publish great stories. We lean towards the spiritual and thought-provoking. But whether it's literary or popular, a gentle tale or a pulsating thriller, the connecting theme in all Roundfire fiction titles is that once you pick them up you won't want to put them down.